Mia Sheridan is a *New York Times*, *USA Today*, and *Wall Street Journal* bestselling author. Her passion is weaving true love stories about people destined to be together. Mia lives in Cincinnati, Ohio, with her husband. They have four children here on earth and one in heaven.

Learn more at:
MiaSheridan.com
Twitter: @MSheridanAuthor
Instagram: @MiaSheridanAuthor
Facebook.com/MiaSheridanAuthor

Also by Mia Sheridan

GRAYSON'S VOW

MIA SHERIDAN

PIATKUS

This book is dedicated to my grammy, who always had a word of wise advice, a listening ear, and a heart filled with love. I miss you every day.

PIATKUS

Originally self-published in 2015 by Mia Sheridan
This updated version published in the US in 2023 by Bloom Books,
An imprint of Sourcebooks
Published in Great Britain in 2023 by Piatkus

1 3 5 7 9 10 8 6 4 2

A CIP catalogue record for this book
is available from the British Library.

ISBN 978-0-349-44119-1

Printed and bound in Great Britain by Clays Ltd, Elcograf S.p.A.

Papers used by Piatkus are from well-managed forests
and other responsible sources.

Piatkus
An imprint of
Little, Brown Book Group
Carmelite House
50 Victoria Embankment
London EC4Y 0DZ

An Hachette UK Company
www.hachette.co.uk

www.littlebrown.co.uk

LIBRA

"Even a happy life cannot be without a measure of darkness, and the word happy would lose its meaning if it were not balanced by sadness."

—Carl Jung

CHAPTER ONE
Kira

"Never fret, my love, the universe always balances the scales. Her ways may be mysterious, but they are always just."

—Isabelle Dallaire, "Gram"

In a long history of bad days, this one was at the top of the list. And it was only nine a.m. I stepped from my car and took a deep breath of the balmy, late-summer air before walking toward Napa Valley Savings Bank. The sultry morning shimmered around me, the sweet scent of jasmine teasing my nose. The peaceful beauty seemed wrong somehow, the bleakness of my mood in direct contrast to the warm, sunshiny day. An arrogant idea, I supposed. As if the weather should express itself according to my mood. I sighed as I pulled open the glass front door of the bank.

"May I help you?" a cheery brunette asked as I approached her teller window.

"Yes," I said, withdrawing my ID and an old savings

book from my purse. "I want to close this account." I slid both toward the teller. A corner of the savings book was folded back, revealing numbers my gram had entered when showing me how to keep track of our deposits. The memory tore at my heart, but I forced what I hoped was a cheerful-looking smile as the girl took the book, opened it, and began entering the account number.

I thought back to the day we'd opened the account. I'd been ten, and my gram had walked me here and I'd proudly deposited the fifty dollars she'd given me for helping with yard work throughout the summer. We'd made trips to this bank over the years when I'd stayed at her house in Napa. She'd taught me the true value of money—it was meant to be shared, used to help others, but it also represented a type of freedom. The fact that I currently had little money, few options, and every material possession I owned was stuffed in the trunk of my car was proof of how right she'd been. I was anything but free.

"Two thousand forty-seven dollars and sixteen cents," the teller stated, glancing up at me.

I nodded. It was even a little more than I had hoped. Good. That was good. I needed every cent. I joined my hands together on the counter and exhaled slowly as I waited for her to count out the cash.

Once the money was safely tucked into my purse and the account closed, I wished the teller a good day and then headed toward the door. When I spotted a drinking fountain, I turned to make a brief stop. I'd only been using the air conditioning in my car sparingly so as to save on gas and had been consistently hot and thirsty.

As the cold water hit my lips, I heard faintly from the office around the corner, "Grayson Hawthorn, nice to meet you."

I froze, then stood slowly, using my thumb to distractedly wipe the water off my bottom lip. Grayson Hawthorn...*Grayson Hawthorn?* I knew that name, remembered the strong sound of it, the way I had repeated it to myself on a whisper to hear it on my lips that day in my father's office. I thought back to the quick glance at the file my dad had slid closed as I'd placed a tray of coffee on his desk. Could it be the *same* Grayson Hawthorn?

I took a few steps and peeked around the corner, but saw nothing more than a closed office door, the shade on the window pulled down. My curiosity still piqued, I walked to the restroom on the other side of the corridor from the office Grayson Hawthorn occupied. *Snoopy much, Kira?*

Once inside the restroom, I locked the door and leaned against the wall. I hadn't even known Grayson Hawthorn lived in Napa. His trial had taken place in San Francisco, so that must have been where the crime was committed—not that I knew what that crime might have been, only that my father had taken a brief interest in it. I bit my lip, moving to the sink and staring at myself in the mirror above it as I washed and dried my hands.

As I was leaving the restroom, a man in a suit, most likely a bank executive, entered the office across the hall. He closed the door behind him, but it didn't click into place and stood very, very slightly ajar, allowing me to hear a few words of introductions. I paused, pulling the restroom door most of the way closed and then standing there trying to listen.

Really, Kira? This is shamefully nosy. An invasion of privacy. And worse, somewhat pointless. *Seriously, what is wrong with you?* Ignoring my own reprimand, I leaned closer to the crack in the door.

I'd leave this less-than-stellar moment out of my memoirs. No one needed to know about it but me.

A few words drifted my way. "Sorry…felon…can't give…this bank…unfortunately…" Felon? Yes then, it *had* to be the Grayson Hawthorn I thought it was. What a strange, random coincidence. I barely knew anything about him. All I really knew was his name, the fact that he'd been convicted of a crime, and that my father had participated in using him as a pawn. Grayson Hawthorn and I had that in common. Not that it was likely my father remembered the name of one man when he ruined lives so regularly and with so little afterthought. In any case, why was I eavesdropping from inside a bathroom, trying to listen in on his private conversation? I wasn't sure. However, an abundance of curiosity was one of my confirmed faults. *Okay, enough lurking.* I took a deep breath and started to exit when I heard the scraping of chair legs and paused yet again. The words from across the hall were clearer now that they had probably moved closer to the door. "I'm sorry I can't approve a loan for you, Mr. Hawthorn." The male voice that spoke sounded regretful. "If you were worth more—"

"I understand. Thank you for your time, Mr. Gellar" came another male voice, Grayson's I assumed.

I caught a brief glimpse of a tall, male figure with dark hair in a heather-gray suit leaving the office and leaned back inside the restroom, clicking the door closed again. I washed my hands once more to stall, and then left the small room. I glanced at the office Grayson Hawthorn had been in as I passed and saw a man sitting behind the desk in a suit and tie, his attention focused on something he was writing.

Outside, the day had grown brighter and warmer, and I let myself into my car, which I had parked up the street. I sat there for a minute, staring out the front window at the quaint downtown area: crisp, clean awnings adorned the fronts of the businesses, and large containers of brightly colored flowers decorated the sidewalk. I loved Napa, from downtown to the riverfront, to the outlying vineyards, fruit ripe in the summer and colorful with the vivid-yellow, wild mustard flowers in the winter. It had been where my gram retired to after my grandfather passed, where I'd spent summers at her cottage-style house with the covered front porch. Everywhere I looked I saw her, heard her voice, felt her warm, vibrant spirit. My gram had been fond of saying *Today may be a very bad day, but tomorrow may be the best day of your life. You just have to hang on until you get there.*

I drew in a deep inhale, doing my best to shake off the loneliness. *Oh, Gram, if only you were here. You would take me into your arms and tell me everything was going to be okay. And because it was you saying it, I would believe it to be true.*

I leaned back against the headrest and closed my eyes. "Help me, Gram," I whispered. "I'm lost. I need you. Give me a sign. Tell me what to do. Please." The tears I'd been holding at bay for so long burned behind my lids, threatening to fall.

I sighed as I opened my eyes, movement in the passenger side mirror immediately catching my attention. As I turned my head, I spotted a tall, well-built man in that same heather-gray suit I'd seen inside the bank...Grayson Hawthorn. My breath faltered. He was standing against the building next to my car, to the right of my bumper, the perfect location for me to see him clearly in my mirror without moving. I slunk down in my seat just a bit, leaned back, and turned my head to watch him.

He had his head leaned back against the building behind him, and his eyes were closed, his expression pained. And my God, he was...breathtaking. He had the beautifully carved features of a knight in shining armor, with almost-black hair a tad too long, making it curl over his collar. It was his lips that were truly devastating though—full and sensual in a way that made my eyes want to wander to them again and again. I squinted, trying to take in every detail of his face, before my gaze traveled down his tall form. His body matched his beautifully dark masculinity—muscular and graceful, his shoulders broad and his waist narrow.

Oh, Kira. You hardly have time to be ogling beautiful felons on the sidewalk. Your concerns are slightly more pressing. You're homeless and well, frankly, desperate. If you want to focus on something, focus on that. Okay, except…I was unable to drag my eyes away. What had his crime been, anyway? I tried to look away, but something about him pulled at me. And it wasn't just his striking good looks that made my eyes linger on him. Something about the expression on his face felt *familiar*, speaking to what I was feeling right that very minute.

If you were worth more…

"Are you desperate too, Grayson Hawthorn?" I murmured.

As I watched him, he brought his head straight and massaged his temple, looking around. A woman walked by and turned as she passed him, her head moving up and down to take in his body. He didn't seem to notice her, and fortunately for her, she turned, looking ahead just in time to narrowly miss colliding with a light pole. I breathed out a laugh. Grayson stood staring off into the distance again. As I watched him, an obviously homeless man moved toward where he stood, holding his hat out to people walking by. They all moved quickly past him, looking away uncomfortably.

When the man began to approach Grayson, I pressed

my lips together. *Sorry, old man. It seems to me the person you're asking for help is in pretty dire straits himself.* But to my surprise, Grayson reached into his pocket, hesitated only briefly, and then grabbed the bills inside. I couldn't be sure from where I sat, but when the dark interior of his wallet flashed my way, it looked like he'd emptied it for the old man. He nodded his head once at the man in rags, who was thanking him profusely, and then stood for a moment watching the homeless man walk away. Then Grayson strode in the other direction, turning the corner out of sight.

Watch what people do when they think no one's watching, love. That's how you'll know who they really are.

Gram's words floated through my mind as if she had spoken from somewhere just outside my car. The shrill ringing of my phone startled me, and I let out a small gasp, grabbing my purse from the passenger seat to rifle inside for my phone.

Kimberly.

"Hey," I whispered.

A beat of silence. "Kira? Why are you whispering?" She was whispering too.

I cleared my throat and leaned back. "Sorry, the phone just startled me. I'm sitting in my car in Napa."

"Were you able to close the account?"

"Yeah. It had a couple thousand dollars in it."

"Hey, well, that's great. That's something at least, right?"

I sighed. "Yeah. It'll help me get by for a little bit."

I heard Kimberly's boys laughing in the background, and she shushed them, holding her hand over the phone and speaking to them in Spanish before coming back to me and saying, "My couch is always yours if you want it."

"I know. Thank you, Kimmy." I couldn't do that to

my best friend though. She and her husband, Andy, were squeezed into a tiny apartment in San Francisco with their four-year-old sons. Kimberly had gotten pregnant when she was eighteen and then learned the shocking news she was carrying twins. She and Andy had beaten the odds so far, but they hadn't had an easy time of it. The last thing they needed was their down-and-out friend sleeping on their couch and putting a strain on their family. *Down-and-out? Homeless. You're homeless.*

I took a deep breath. "I'm going to come up with a plan though," I said, a feeling of determination replacing the hopelessness I'd felt all morning. Grayson Hawthorn's face flashed quickly in my mind's eye. "Kimmy, do you ever feel like…a path is laid out in front of you? Like, clear as day?"

Kimberly paused for a beat. "Oh no. No. I know that tone in your voice. It means you're scheming something I'm going to try—probably unsuccessfully—to talk you out of. You're not considering that plan to advertise for a husband online are you because—"

"No." I cleared my throat. "Not exactly anyway."

Kimberly groaned. "You've gotten another one of your spur-of-the-moment Very Bad Ideas, haven't you? Something completely ludicrous and most likely dangerous."

I smiled despite myself. "Oh, stop. Those ideas you always call 'Very Bad' are rarely ludicrous and seldom dangerous."

"The time you were going to market your own all-natural face mask from the herbs in your garden?"

I smiled, knowing her game. "Oh, that? My formula was almost there. Right within reach, actually. If my test subject hadn't been—"

"You turned my face green. It didn't go away for a week. *Picture day* week."

I laughed softly. "Okay, so fine, that one didn't work out very well, but we were ten."

"Sneaking out to Carter Scott's party when we were sixteen—"

"Totally would have worked if—"

"The fire department had to come get me off your roof."

"You always were such a wuss," I said, grinning.

"The time you were home from college on summer break and hosted that Japanese-themed dinner party where we all had to wear kimonos, and then you almost killed everyone there."

"An ingredient error. How was I to know you needed to be licensed to cook that particular fish? Anyway, that was forever ago."

"That was two years ago." She tried to deadpan, but I could hear the smile in her voice.

I was laughing now. "Okay, you've made your point, smartass. And despite all that, you love me anyway."

"I do." She sighed. "I can't help it. You're completely lovable."

"Well, that's debatable, I guess."

"No," she said firmly, "it's not. Your father's an ass, but you already know how I feel on that subject. And, honey, you need to talk about what happened. It's been a year. I know you just got back, but you need—"

"Not yet," I said softly, shaking my head even though she couldn't see the movement from the other end of the phone. "And thank you for making me laugh for a minute there. But seriously, Kim, I'm in a very bad predicament right now. Maybe a Very Bad Idea is what I need." I couldn't help the small hitch in my voice at the end of my sentence. Kimberly never failed to lift my spirits, but truly, I was scared.

"I know, Kira," Kimberly said, understanding in her voice. "And unfortunately, if you're determined not to use any of your father's business contacts, you might have to get a waitressing job until you figure out what you're going to do."

I sighed. "Maybe, but would you really want me anywhere near food preparation?"

"You do make a valid point." I heard another smile in her voice. "Whatever you decide, it'll always be the Kira and Kimmy Kats, okay? Forever. We're a team," she said, referring to the band name I'd come up with when we were twelve, and I'd devised the plan to sing on the street corner for cash. I'd seen a commercial on TV about kids who didn't have enough to eat in Somalia, and my dad wouldn't give me the money to sponsor one of them. In the end, we'd been caught sneaking out of the house in the very inappropriate "costumes" I'd made from construction paper and tape. My dad grounded me for a month. Kimberly's mom, who worked as the live-in head of our housekeeping staff, gave me the twenty-two dollars I'd needed to help feed and educate Khotso that month—and then every month I couldn't come up with the money on my own after that.

"Always," I said. "I love you, Kimmy Kat."

"I love you Kira Kat. And I gotta go, these boys are getting out of control." I heard Levi's and Micah's squeals of laughter and shouts ringing in the background over the sound of small running feet. "Stop running, boys! And stop *yelling*!" Kimberly yelled, holding the phone away from her mouth for a second. "You gonna be okay tonight?"

"Yeah, I'm fine. I think I might even splurge and rent a cheap hotel room here in Napa and then walk along the riverfront. It makes me feel close to Gram." I didn't mention that earlier that morning, I'd hurriedly packed my stuff and climbed down the fire escape of the apartment my dad had paid for as he'd yelled and banged on the front door. And that now, said *stuff* was jammed into my car's trunk. Kimberly would just worry, and for now, I had some cash and a partial but arguably Very Bad Idea roaming around in my head.

And in my illustrious history of Very Bad Ideas, this one might just take the cake.

Of course, I'd be thorough in my research before making a final decision. And I'd make a list of pros and cons—it always helped me see things in a clearer light. This one required some due diligence.

Kimberly sighed. "God rest her soul. Your gram was an amazing lady."

"Yes, she was," I agreed. "Kiss the boys for me. I'll call you tomorrow."

"Okay. Talk to you then. And Kira, I'm so glad you're back. I've missed you so much."

"I've missed you too. Bye, Kimmy."

I hung up and sat in my car a few minutes longer. Then I picked my phone back up to do a little internet sleuthing and to find a hotel room I could afford.

CHAPTER TWO
Grayson

"The pump can't be fixed, sir. It's gonna have to be replaced."

I swore under my breath and placed my wrench back in my toolbox. José was right. I used my arm to wipe the sweat off my forehead and nodded, leaning against the useless piece of equipment, just another thing that needed to be fixed or replaced.

José gave me a sympathetic look. "I got the destemmer working though. Good as new, I think."

"Well, that's some good news," I said, picking up the toolbox I'd brought with me. One piece of good news to add to the long list of bad. Still, I'd take what I could get right now. "Thanks, José. I'm gonna go clean up."

José nodded. "Any news from the bank, sir?"

I stopped but didn't turn around. "They said no to a loan." When José didn't respond, I kept walking. I could practically feel his disappointed gaze burning into my back. I had vowed to keep my family winery running, and nothing on earth was more important to me, but José had a family to feed, the newest member only weeks old. If I failed, I wouldn't be the only one out of a job.

If you were worth more…

I clenched my jaw against the way those words had stabbed, implying more to me than just my financial value. Reminding me I'd never been worth much.

If you were worth more…

If indeed.

With that mighty *if* and four quarters, I could buy myself something off the dollar menu at McDonald's. Did McDonald's still *have* a dollar menu? Maybe not. I'd even come up short in the world of fast food.

I'd gone over the what-ifs of my life more times than I could count. It was a painful, useless waste of time.

And I hardly needed another reason to despise myself.

I shut those thoughts down though. I was slipping dangerously close to self-pity, and I knew from personal experience that was a deep hole to climb out of once you'd let yourself descend. Instead, I made a concerted effort to wrap myself in the coldness that kept the desperation at bay. And allowed me to continue to do the work that needed to get done.

In the end, I reminded myself, my *father* had found me worthy. And I'd made a vow not to let him down—not this time.

The late-afternoon sun was high in the sky when I stepped outside, the smell of the roses my stepmother had planted so long ago filling the air, the lazy drone of a buzzing bee somewhere nearby. I stopped to survey the rows and rows of grapes ripening on their vines, pride swelling in my chest. It was going to be a good harvest. I felt it in my bones. It *had* to be a good harvest. And that was what would keep me going today, despite the fact that I'd have no way to use the fruit if my equipment wasn't ready by fall. I'd already sold almost everything of any value in my family home to raise the money to plant those grapes, so broken equipment was very bad news and one more hurdle I had to figure out how to overcome.

A few minutes later, I was stepping inside the house, a grand stone estate built by my father, designed with plenty of vintage, old-world character. It had been a showplace in its day, but it needed as many fixes as the winemaking equipment. Fixes I had no way to finance.

"The pump's unfixable."

I gritted my teeth as Walter, the family butler turned jack-of-all-trades around the place, greeted me. "So it seems."

"I've made a spreadsheet of all the equipment needing to be fixed, what requires replacement, and color-coded it according to priority."

Great. Just what I needed—a visual aid of the hopelessness of my situation. I paused in my rifling through the mail on the foyer console. "You're my secretary now too, Walter?"

"Someone needs to be. Running this place is too big a job for one person, sir."

"Let me ask you this, Walter."

"Yes, sir."

"Did you come up with a list of ways I might *pay* for those color-coded items that need to be fixed or replaced?"

"No, sir, I don't have any ideas that you haven't already thought of. But I hope the list in and of itself is helpful."

"Not even a little bit, Walter," I said as I headed for the main staircase. I had a constant running tally of all the things I needed to repair if I was going to pull off a harvest. "And I've told you a million times to stop calling me sir. You've known me since I was a baby." Not to mention that I hardly deserved the respectful title. Walter was worth three of me, and he surely knew it. Nevertheless, I also knew he would never let go of the professionalism. Walter Popplewell was from Wandsworth—a proper English gentleman in all respects—and had been with our family for more than thirty years.

Walter cleared his throat. "And there's someone waiting to see you, sir."

I turned. "Who is it?"

"Someone"—Walter cleared his throat again—"looking for a job, sir."

I rolled my eyes to the ceiling. *Jesus.* "Fine, let me get rid of him. What kind of fool is trying to get a job here anyway?"

Walter swept his hand toward the kitchen, where I heard his wife, my housekeeper, Charlotte, laughing with someone.

When I entered the kitchen, I saw a man sitting at the large, wooden table, a plate of cookies in front of him. When he saw me, he stood quickly, knocking the plate to the floor, where it crashed onto the tile and splintered into a thousand pieces.

"Oh dear!" Charlotte exclaimed and rushed from where she was pouring a glass of milk at the counter. "Don't worry about that, Virgil. You just talk to Mr. Hawthorn and I'll clean that up. Not to worry a bit."

The man before me was large—at least six six—wearing khakis, a red-and-blue-striped shirt, and a Giants baseball cap. His round face was full of fear as he glanced between the shattered dish and me.

I walked toward him and held my hand out. "Grayson Hawthorn."

His eyes darted to my hand. He reached out hesitantly and shook it, and when his glance finally met mine, I could see in his guileless eyes he was mentally delayed.

Good God.

"My name is Virgil Potter, sir, Hawthorn, Grayson, sir." He let go of my hand and looked down shyly, glanced over at Charlotte sweeping up the plate and cookies, winced, and then looked back at me. "Like the wizard, sir, only I don't got a scar on my forehead. I do got a scar on my backside though, where I got too close to our electric heater once when I was—"

"What can I do for you, Mr. Potter?"

"Oh, you don't got to call me mister, sir. Just Virgil."

"Okay, Virgil."

Charlotte gave me a sharp look from where she was kneeling on the floor. I looked back to Virgil, ignoring her.

Virgil hesitated, shifting from one foot to the other, glancing again at Charlotte, who looked up at him, smiled, and nodded. He took the baseball cap off his head quickly, as if he'd suddenly remembered he was wearing it, and held it clutched in his big hands. "I was hoping, sir…that is…I need a job, sir…and I thought I might do something for you. I heard some people talking in town and saying you was going to have a heap of trouble keeping this winery running, and I thought I could help. And I would come for cheap, seeing as that I've never had a job before. But I'm a real hard worker. My mama told me so. And I could work for you."

I sighed. This was just exactly what I needed. I was barely scraping by with the staff I had now—far fewer than needed, but all I could afford and the only ones who'd stayed. I could hardly take on one more. Much less one I'd have to supervise around the clock, no doubt. "Virgil," I started, to let him down, but he interrupted me.

"See, sir, my mama, she can't clean houses no more on account of that her back is so bad. And if I don't work, we won't have enough money to get by. And I know I can do a good job. If someone would just give me a chance."

Good Lord. When Charlotte caught my eye as she stood to empty the dustpan, I gave her my most icy glare. *She* was behind this. What was she thinking? When this place failed, both she and Walter would be out of jobs. I closed my eyes for a second and then opened them. "Virgil, I'm sorry, but I—"

"I know you probably think I'm not worth much, just looking at me, but I am. I know I am, sir. I could work for you." His expression was filled with wary hope.

If you were worth more...

The broken pieces of the plate clattered into the garbage can loudly, and I glanced again at Charlotte, who still had her eyes trained on me despite her busy hands. I pressed my lips together.

If you were worth more...

"Fine, Virgil. You're hired," I said, keeping my glare trained on Charlotte, whose lips curved ever so slightly in a tiny smile. When I finally looked back to Virgil, his eyes were wide with joy. I raised my hand as if I could hold back the intensity of his happiness with my gesture. "But I can't pay you much, and we're going to do this on a trial basis, okay? Sometimes we work past dark, and I didn't notice a car outside. I have a set of bunks down at the winemaking facility. You can stay there if you ever need to. One month and we'll see how you do." *If this vineyard is even still running in a month.*

Virgil nodded exuberantly, wringing the poor cap in his hands so vigorously it would probably be unwearable now.

"You won't regret this, sir. No, I won't let you down. I'm a hard worker."

"Okay, good, Virgil. Come back tomorrow morning to fill out the paperwork, and bring your ID. Nine a.m., okay?"

Virgil still hadn't stopped nodding. "I'll be here, sir, even earlier. I'll be here at seven."

"Nine is fine, Virgil, and you can call me Grayson."

"Yes, sir, Grayson, sir. Nine a.m. Okay."

Virgil turned his large, clumsy body, grinned and waved at Charlotte, then darted out of the kitchen, presumably before I could change my mind. I stood, silently watching out the window as Virgil left the house and started a lumbering run up my driveway, toward the decorative steel gates at the beginning of the property. I swore under my breath for the hundredth time that day and gave Charlotte another icy glare. "If I didn't know better, I'd say you were trying to sabotage me from the inside out."

"Ah, but you do know better, my boy. I only ever root for your success."

Of course I knew it. I snorted anyway, for effect.

Charlotte grinned and started humming as she worked at the sink.

I turned without another word and headed for the shower. I didn't do it often, but tonight, I was going to drink myself into a stupor.

———

Morning sunshine streamed through the windows, bathing the foyer in golden light as I descended the stairs, way too early seeing as I'd only returned home a couple hours before. I flinched, shielding my eyes against the too-bright glare. My head was pounding. No less than I deserved. But the alcohol had drowned out my problems for a night and so it'd been worth it. I'd been working from sunup until sundown most days, and it still wasn't enough. And after yesterday at the bank... Well, I'd deserved a night of drunken oblivion. A man could only take so much.

"Gray, dear, there's someone here to see you. Good morning." Charlotte smiled at me as I reached the bottom of the stairs. "Oh." She frowned. "You look just like something the cat dragged in, don't you?"

I ignored her last remark. "Who is it now?" First thing in the morning? What exactly couldn't wait until a decent hour? It was barely past sunrise. And I felt like hell. "I suppose it's someone else wanting a job? Someone with no limbs perhaps?"

Charlotte only smiled. "I don't think she wants a job, but I didn't ask what her business was about. And she has all the appropriate limbs. She's waiting in your office."

"She?"

"Yes, a young woman. She said her name is Kira. Very pretty." Charlotte winked. Okay, well, maybe this wasn't the worst way to start the day. Unless it was someone I'd slept with...and likely wouldn't remember.

I downed a couple Tylenol, grabbed a cup of coffee from the kitchen, and walked to the large office at the front of the house that had once belonged to my father.

A young woman in a loose, cream-colored dress, in some sort of silky material, belted at the waist, stood with her back to me, perusing the large bookshelf against the wall opposite the doorway. I cleared my throat and she whirled around, the book in her hands falling to the floor as she brought her hands to her chest. Her eyes widened, and then she stooped to pick up the book, laughing tightly. "Sorry, you startled

19

me." She stood, moving suddenly toward me. "Sorry, um, sorry. Grayson Hawthorn, right?" She placed the book on the edge of my desk and held her hand out. She was barely average height, slender, with hair a deep, rich auburn pulled back severely into some sort of knot at the nape of her neck.

Not my type, but Charlotte was right: she was pretty. I tended toward tall, elegant blonds. One tall, elegant blond in particular, actually. But I shut that painful thought down immediately. No use going there. It was only when the girl named Kira got close that I really noticed her eyes—large and framed with thick lashes, brows the same rich shade as her hair arching delicately above them. But it was the *color* of her eyes that stunned me. The greenest I'd ever seen. They were luminous, like twin emeralds. I got the sudden feeling those eyes saw things other eyes didn't. Bewitching. Magnetic. I felt like I couldn't take a deep breath.

I stepped back slightly and narrowed my gaze but took her hand in mine. It was warm and small in my own. The warmth seemed to travel up my arm and through my ribcage. I frowned and removed my hand from hers. "And you are?" I hadn't intended on the hostility in my tone.

"Kira," she said simply, as if that explained anything at all. *Okay*. Kira closed those stunning eyes of hers, and I felt a momentary twinge of disappointment. She shook her head slightly before she looked back at me. "I'm sorry, do you mind if we sit down?" What did this girl want? She didn't look familiar.

I inclined my head toward the chair in front of the massive mahogany desk. I rounded the piece of furniture, set my coffee cup down, and took a seat in the leather chair facing her. "Would you like a cup of coffee?" I asked. "I could call Charlotte."

"No, thank you." She shook her head. "She already offered." A lock slipped out of her pulled-back hair, and she made a small, annoyed frown as she attempted to smooth it back again.

I waited. My head pounded, and I massaged my temple absently. Her gaze followed my hand, and I wanted to squint against it.

She took a deep breath, straightening her spine and then crossing her legs. As her chair was positioned away from my desk, my eyes could easily wander down her shapely calves to her slim ankles that ended in a pair of blue, heeled sandals. The purse, which had been on her shoulder and now rested in her lap, had beads on it in the same shade as her shoes. I didn't know fashion, but I knew expensive when I saw it. My coldhearted stepmother had been the epitome of coiffed decadence.

"I don't mean to rush you, but I have a lot to get done today."

Her eyes widened. "Right. Of course. I'm sorry to hesitate. Well, I guess I'll just get right to it. I have a business arrangement to offer you."

I lifted one brow. "A business arrangement?"

She nodded, twisted the long, gold necklace she was wearing. "Yes, well, in actuality, Mr. Hawthorn, I'm here to propose marriage."

I laughed, almost spewing the sip of coffee I'd just taken all over my desk. "Excuse me?"

Those magnificent eyes lit with something I couldn't define. "If you'll just hear me out, I think perhaps this is something that could benefit both of us."

"And how exactly do you know anything about what might benefit me, Ms....what is your last name? You didn't say."

She raised her little chin. "Dallaire. My last name is Dallaire." She eyed me with some sort of expectation.

"Dallaire?" I paused, frowning. I knew that name. "As in the ex-mayor of San Francisco Dallaire?"

"Yes." She raised her chin higher. Ah, *haughty*, that's what that gesture was. She was political royalty. An heiress. I didn't know a whole lot about Frank Dallaire, except that he'd been the mayor for two terms and was extraordinarily wealthy—a result of not only his political career, but I thought…real estate dealings? Something along those lines. He was consistently on the list of the country's wealthiest men. So why in the hell was his daughter here making a ridiculous offer?

"So I guess a better question, Ms. Dallaire, is how on God's green earth would a marriage to me benefit you?" This ought to be good. I reclined back in my chair.

She sighed, looking only slightly less haughty. "I'm in a bit of a situation, Mr. Hawthorn. My father and I are"—she chewed on her lip for a second, seeming to be searching for the right word—"estranged. To put it bluntly, I need money to live, to survive."

I studied her for a second and then chuckled softly. "I can assure you, Ms. Dallaire, marriage to me would not benefit your financial portfolio. Very much the opposite actually. Someone's misinformed you."

She shook her head, leaning forward. "Which leads me to the part that would benefit *both* of us."

"By all means, please educate me," I said, not trying to hide the boredom in my voice. I massaged my temple again. I hardly had time for this.

"Well, it's come to my attention that your vineyard is, uh, well, it's failing, to be honest. You need cash."

Anger swept through me at the way this little rich girl summed up my situation. I jerked my hand from my temple and gave her my chilliest look. "And you know this…how?"

She raised her chin again. "I researched you."

"Ah."

"And, well, I was at the bank yesterday. I accidentally overheard part of your meeting. You were turned down for a loan."

I froze as a slow stain of color rose in her cheeks. Well, at least she had the grace to be embarrassed. "Accidentally" overheard, my ass. But then that little chin went up again.

Anger—and a small measure of shame about what she'd heard—speared down my spine, causing me to sit up straight. "You rudely eavesdropped on my appointment at the bank, googled me, and now you think you understand my situation?" *What the fuck?*

Her expression gentled and her pink tongue darted out to moisten her bottom lip. My body reacted to that small movement, and I tamped it down with violence. I was not attracted to the arrogant, little rich girl playing games with me. Plus, I'd had a woman last night as a matter of fact—a blond named Jade who smelled like watermelon…or had it been pineapple? She'd been highly energetic. And yet, even so, the whole escapade had left me vaguely dissatisfied… and reeking of fruit salad. I focused my attention back on the redhead sitting in front of me. Or was she a brunette? Almost the perfect mixture of both… As if her hair was responding to my thoughts, another lock slipped out of her updo. Kira tucked it behind her ear.

"I'm sure I don't know all the particulars of your situation. But I know that you need cash, and you have few options left, especially considering your…record." That blush rose in her cheeks again before she continued, "I need cash as well. I'm desperate too, actually."

I let out a sigh. "I'm sure if you went to Daddy, all this could be resolved. Things are rarely as desperate as they seem." Except in my situation they actually were.

Her eyes spit fire at me, but her expression remained neutral. "No," she said. "Things will not be resolved with my *daddy*. We had a falling out over a year ago."

"Uh-huh. And how have you been getting by since then?"

She paused as if she was considering her answer. "I've been overseas."

Shopping, most likely. Or sunning herself. I ran my eyes down her legs again—lightly tanned legs. And now her personal funds had run out and Daddy wasn't going to supply her with more. How tragic.

"Do you have something against getting a job? Do you have an education?"

"My college career was...cut short. And no, of course I'm not against getting a job if need be. But"—she sat up even straighter—"suffice it to say, I came here today believing this was the better course of action for all involved."

My head throbbed again. What did I care about her exact situation anyway? "Okay, can we cut to the chase here? Like you so succinctly pointed out, my vineyard is failing. I've got a lot of work to do today."

"Right. Well, yes. Mr. Hawthorn, you see, my grandmother, my father's mother, lived modestly, but thanks to some fortuitous investments my grandfather made, she died with quite a bit of money. She left it to her two grandchildren, me being one, the other a cousin I don't know well. However, she stipulated in the trust that we only get the money either when we turn thirty or get married, whichever comes first."

I sat back again, steepling my fingers.

"And so," she went on quickly, "what I propose is this: we marry, split the money, and in a year's time, file for divorce."

I raised an eyebrow. "Split the money? How much money are we talking exactly?"

"Almost a million dollars."

My heart started beating faster. *Five hundred thousand dollars.* It was even more than the loan I'd hoped the bank would approve. It would be more than enough to make all the equipment *and* house repairs. Enough to bottle the wine sitting in barrels right now. Enough to add at least a couple employees too. And if the newest harvest was as good as I predicted, this winery would be successful again in less than a year. *I could fulfill the vow I'd made in my father's name.*

I remained silent, not only going over what she'd just said but also to make her squirm. She didn't. Finally, I said, "Interesting. There's no clause about how long we'd have to remain married?"

She released a breath and shook her head, no doubt assuming my question meant I was actually considering this insane idea. Was I? Was this even legit? Surely there was some catch. It was too preposterous to be true. My head was reeling just a bit and not only from the hangover anymore. "No, but my father would be…displeased if he knew I had married to get the money my grandmother left only to split it with you…that is, with anyone." Something raced across her expression, but I couldn't read it. "If he had any indication this was a fake marriage, he might very well try to contest the payout of the trust. It would be in both our best interests to make the marriage look as legitimate as possible.

25

However, like I said, my father and I are estranged. I imagine our effort would only need to be minimal but convincing."

I raised my eyebrows, allowing myself another moment to go over what she'd said. It was outrageous, unbelievable. "Wait, you're not"—I leaned forward—"one of those crazy women who used to write to me in prison offering marriage, are you?"

Her eyes went wide. "What?"

I reclined back again. "Yeah, there were lots of them. Apparently, some women find a sick thrill in that sort of thing."

"For what…why?" She shook her head slightly as if she wasn't sure how the conversation had veered off track. Her confusion seemed genuine.

"Apparently, some women like a bad boy."

She looked at me blankly for a moment. "I can assure you, I'm not one of those women."

I nodded slowly, regarding her. "Well, good, because I can assure *you* that you're not my type anyway."

She bristled, sitting up straighter. "Even better, then. What I'm proposing is strictly business, nothing more." She looked away, and I couldn't see those witchy eyes, but when she looked back, her cheeks were rosy again. "However, it would look suspicious if I didn't live here, and frankly, Mr. Hawthorn, I *need* somewhere to live. And so I was thinking that in exchange for the housing, I could do accounting work for you. I assume you no longer have much of a staff."

I leaned forward. "I'm impressed by your research, Ms. Dallaire. No, I had to let my bookkeeper go. And my secretary. And most of the rest of the staff as well." Not that any of them had lived on the grounds.

She nodded. "I'm good with numbers. I worked as an

intern for my father's accounting team. I'm well acquainted with accounting programs. I could work for you in exchange for room and board, and obviously for appearance's sake. I don't propose I'd have to live here for a year—maybe just a couple months or so, or until I know my father has accepted the marriage and resumed ignoring me. I could discreetly move away, and we would never have to see one another again—except, of course, in divorce court. It really would be very straightforward. And very temporary. And of course, we'd put it all in writing. And please, just Kira."

I studied her for several long moments, noting the way she'd just rambled. She looked to be polished and sure, but was she actually nervous sitting here in front of me? I held eye contact for just a beat too long, but she didn't look away and didn't flinch. "And what will you do with your half of the money, Kira? If I may be so bold as to ask."

She cleared her throat. "Well, other than live, I'm involved in several charities in San Francisco. One of the centers is in dire straits and will have to close if they can't come up with the funding."

I smiled a tight smile. Ah. *Just* like my stepmother. An heiress with an empty life. I could just see her pulling up in her Bentley to save the lowly peasants from starvation so she could refer to herself as a philanthropist before dashing off to the Louis Vuitton store to add to her luggage collection. "I see." What did it matter to me what she did with her money? Or what her purpose was? I needed only to be concerned with my own situation. "It's a highly unusual proposition. I'll think about it and get back to you." I started to stand.

"Well, see, I kind of need your answer quickly." Her voice came out fast and breathy. My body, or at least the parts between my legs, twitched again. Dammit. Something about my body's reaction to her made me angry. Although the parts reacting had never been very discerning.

I sat back down.

"I wish I could give you more time to consider, Mr. Hawthorn, but unfortunately, circumstances dictate that I——"

I put my hand up to stop her. "I'll get back to you by the end of today. How can I get a hold of you?"

She paused. "I'm staying at the Motel 6 tonight. I can give you my cell number, and you can call me."

Motel 6? My, how far the princess had fallen. Yes, her situation was quite desperate. I watched as she grabbed a sticky pad and a pen at the edge of my desk and carefully wrote out her phone number. I took it and tossed it casually onto the pile of messy papers.

She looked at where I'd thrown it and then back to me, her lips pressed together. "I can assure you my proposition is legitimate."

"It very well could be. Of course, I'd want to meet with the executor of this trust anyway. But it's still something I need to consider. I do have to think about other ways this might affect my life. A felon is one thing, but a felon and a divorcé? How will I fend off the ladies then?"

She narrowed those startling eyes. "Yes, well, if there were any other options, I wouldn't be considering this either. Trust me." This princess wouldn't know a real problem if it smacked her in the face. But as we stared each other down, something flashed in her eyes. Under her cool demeanor and formal business language, she was just barely holding back a temper. She was a princess, but oh yes, just as I'd thought, she had a little witch in her too. We were both silent as she leaned forward slightly as if waiting for…something. Did she expect me to thank her?

"Have a good day." I didn't stand. She could show herself out. She stood slowly, holding her hand out so I could shake it. I reached forward and took her hand in mine for the second time. That same heat spiked through me, and I quickly pulled away. Kira Dallaire turned on her heel, her chin in the air, and left my office without looking back.

I stood and went to the window, lifting the shade. I watched as she walked toward a white Jetta. It surprised me she was driving such a non-flashy car. When she got to the door and began to climb in, she paused and looked around at the vineyard. There was something in her expression that made me unconsciously take a step toward her, my face almost hitting the glass. What had that been? Appreciation, I thought. *For this run-down place?* But with something else too…understanding? Before I could consider it any longer, she ducked inside her car, slamming the door behind her, and a minute later, was driving through the gate and out of sight.

Maybe I was judging her unfairly. If anyone knew what that felt like, it was me. Maybe I was just hungover, and she had reminded me of the type of woman my stepmother was. And of course, there was the fact that she had just strode in here and blatantly offered me a marriage for money… But perhaps Kira Dallaire wasn't exactly what she seemed to be.

I sat back down at my desk and turned on my computer to google her. One good turn deserved another. As soon as I typed in her name, a whole slew of images appeared: Kira Dallaire in an evening gown, exiting a limo; Kira Dallaire at the premiere of a movie at some theatre or another; Kira Dallaire standing beside the man I recognized as Frank Dallaire at a black-tie benefit. Always with the same small, distant smile. In several photos, she was standing beside a good-looking blond man who appeared to be at least five to ten years older than her. I clicked on one of the photos and read the byline, identifying the couple as Cooper Stratton and his fiancée, Kira Dallaire. *Fiancée?* I looked at the date—a little over a year ago. Had that been what had "cut short" her college career? Had she dropped out to become a society wife?

I clicked through several articles, my disdain growing as I pieced together Kira Dallaire's actual situation. None of the news stories came right out and said it, but it was easy enough to read between the lines. Kira had been engaged to Cooper Stratton, a young assistant district attorney running for superior court judge in San Francisco, when she was involved in some sort of embarrassing scandal—drugs were heavily hinted at—that took place in a penthouse suite in a luxury downtown hotel. Her father, in an effort to protect her and get the help she needed, shipped her off to some rehab center, more likely a glorified spa in London or Paris. And her fiancé had broken off their engagement. Who could blame him? But now she was back and her father…he what? Wouldn't fund the partying lifestyle she was accustomed to? Refused to give her any cash until she could prove she was willing to improve her life? Of course, on that I was only guessing. Either way, Kira Dallaire had decided to take matters into her own hands.

I'd been right in my judgment of her: she *was* just like my stepmother. A woman who'd been given everything in life and thought it was because she was entitled to it. A *selfish* woman who expected life to bend to her will. And when it didn't, she'd go to extreme lengths to bend it back, regardless of whom it hurt.

I leaned back for a minute, thinking things through. Never in a million years had I expected to wake up to this.

We were both desperate in our own ways. The question was: Was I desperate enough to hand over my name—even temporarily—for the cash I needed to save this vineyard and fulfill my vow?

Something on the computer screen caught my eye, a small picture at the bottom of the article I'd been reading, and I clicked on it, making it as large as possible. It was another picture of Kira Dallaire and Cooper Stratton. He had his hand resting possessively on the small of her back and was smiling proudly as she grinned up at him. My eyes homed in on her right cheek. She had a dimple. The little witch had a *dimple*. And what it was about that small feature that made my pulse quicken, I couldn't have explained if my life depended upon it.

CHAPTER THREE
Kira

He looked like a prince, but if I were going to cast him in a fairy tale now, I'd cast him as the dragon. A beastly, judgmental, fire-breathing dragon.

Of course, it wasn't surprising, really. My skill in judging character was sadly...not skillful. That had been proven once. Quite painfully.

Still, I hadn't been prepared for his mocking contempt. And yeah, okay, so my offer probably sounded outrageous to him initially. But I was the one doing him a favor here. I was offering him free money. Or practically free. There *was* a price—I admitted that. I was asking him to marry for money. I couldn't help cringing at the blunt truth. But I'd made a list, and there were far more pros than cons for both of us, I thought. Although, arguably, the cons were very weighty and could tip any scale, regardless of what you titled it. Despite having tried to present the offer in a very businesslike manner, he'd looked at me with such disdain, as if I were yesterday's trash. The fact that I *felt* like yesterday's trash only made it that much worse.

The more condescension he'd shown me, that faint derision never leaving his expression, the more nervous and ruffled and unsure I'd become. I hated that feeling. I'd known it my whole life. Being scorned felt heartachingly familiar.

And then he'd told me I wasn't his type. As if it mattered. It didn't matter. Not at all. Not one bit. I only needed my *money* to be his type.

So why had it hurt?

I let out a sigh. He'd said he would call me, but based on his rude dismissal, I wouldn't hold my breath. Well. I'd tried. Another one of my Very Bad Ideas and Grayson Hawthorn had let me know that's exactly what he'd thought of it. In that slightly bored, pleasantly masculine voice of his, no less. I frowned. So the question was, what was I going to do now? Going back to my father was out of the question. I'd sooner sleep on a street corner. Or at the drop-in center. My heart sank when I thought of the center. What were *they* going to do now? So much was riding on getting my hands on the money Gram left. I supposed I could pull my car over and choose any number of people off the street to make the same offer I'd made to Grayson Hawthorn. Or place an ad on the internet, like I'd joked about with Kimberly. I could sell my car. It was in my name, one of the few things I'd bought with my own money. But then I wouldn't even have a place to sleep if and when my cash ran out.

I'd just thought…well, seeing Grayson Hawthorn at the bank, it seemed like *fate*. The more I'd thought about it yesterday in my small, lonely hotel room, the more my heart had felt like there was something very right about sharing my gram's money with *that* man in particular, considering the connection I knew existed between him and my father. Not that I could share that with him, and not that it would do him any good to know anyway. But I *could* share the money with him—money he desperately needed—and maybe set something right, balance the score in some small measure.

I had to admit his looks had swayed me too. He looked like every hero in every fairy tale I'd ever dreamed come to life. And God, I wanted to believe in heroes again.

But sometimes, I supposed, a girl just had to be her own hero.

Especially when the "hero" in question turned out to be a dragon.

I knew Grayson Hawthorn had done wrong in his life, but after examining his case particulars, it seemed more like a terrible accident. And regardless, it was a mistake he'd paid for. More than paid for. And now he was still paying in people's perceptions of him. No one would give him a chance—or at least the loan he so desperately needed.

So I'd gone with my gut, decided at the very least to reserve judgment until I'd met him in person, and rushed to his home the next morning before I could completely lose my nerve.

Well. The Dragon would have to figure out his life for himself. Just as I would. I alone controlled my destiny. I hardly had time to indulge in despair. I parked my car in the motel lot and made my way to my room.

I stripped out of the dress and sandals I'd worn to meet with Grayson Hawthorn—an outfit from my old life I hadn't even realized I'd packed as I'd hurriedly thrown items into my suitcase willy-nilly. As I'd dressed this morning, I'd been happy for the mistake though. I'd wanted to appear professional, and the jeans or frayed shorts I normally wore didn't exactly say "take me seriously." I paused. But maybe they did say "I'm desperate! Marry me!" Perhaps I should have worn those after all.

After changing, I left the motel and spent the day walking around downtown Napa, doing some window-shopping, browsing through several shops including a bookstore, and stopping for a leisurely lunch at a small café Gram had liked. Despite being hopeless and without a plan, I made a conscious effort to clear my mind and enjoy the day as much as possible. If I had to get a waitressing job like Kimberly had suggested, then that's what I'd do. I wasn't afraid of hard work. I had hoped for a plan offering more options, but that wasn't to be. I straightened my spine and channeled my inner Scarlett O'Hara. I'd take today and then I'd come up with a *new* plan once the disaster that was this morning had rolled off my shoulders.

It was late afternoon when I returned to my motel, the sky a clear, calm blue. I let myself into my room and lay down on my bed for a minute, fatigue overwhelming me. I had tossed and turned the night before in anticipation of my morning call on Grayson Hawthorn. I was exhausted and fell asleep almost immediately.

I came awake blearily, confused for a minute about my surroundings, still in that gap between sleep and wakefulness, knowing something was wrong but not yet recalling exactly what. Reality flowed back in slowly, the pieces coming together to sit heavily on my chest. Wincing slightly, I rolled over and looked at the bedside clock. It was after four, so I'd only slept for a little over an hour. I sighed and sat up.

A warm shower soothed my muscles if not my heart, and when I got out, I felt a little more alive. I partially dried my hair and then stuck it up in a topknot that was sure to fall out. My grandmother had always said my hair was as fiery and unmanageable as I was. But she'd said it with so much love in her voice, I couldn't help but hear it as a compliment. God, how I missed her, even after all the years she'd been gone. The absence of her unconditional love was still a painful wound.

Just as I was pulling clean clothes out of my suitcase, my cell phone rang. Kimberly, I was sure. But when I looked at the screen, it was a local number I didn't recognize. My heartbeat stalled and then sped up in my chest as I ran my finger across the screen.

"Hello," I answered breathlessly.

A deep voice returned my greeting, no warmth in it at all. "It's Grayson."

"Oh." I feigned nonchalance as I collapsed on the bed in my towel. "How can I help you?"

"What room are you in?"

"Room?"

"Motel room. Motel 6, right? Solano Avenue?"

"Uh, yes. But—"

"What room?" he repeated.

"Two eleven. What time will you... Hello?" *Did he just hang up on me? What the—*

Three swift knocks sounded at my door, and I let out a startled squeak, dropping my phone on the bed and jumping to my feet. "Hold on!" I demanded, rushing to my suitcase and hurriedly pulling on a bra and underwear. The knocking resumed.

"Hold *on!*" I yelled again. Of all the rude...*dragons.*

I pulled the dress I'd worn this morning over my head and buckled the belt before I pulled the door open. Grayson Hawthorn filled the doorway, wearing the same thing he'd been wearing earlier—a pair of jeans and a blue T-shirt that stretched nicely over his lean but obviously well-muscled chest. His masculinity hit me in the gut. He smelled like he

36

had that morning too—some sort of fresh, manly smelling soap. But now there was the slight addition of a salty tinge of sweat. I leaned forward, drawn to the masculine scent of him, but then suddenly realized what I was doing. Crossing my arms, I stepped back. "This is highly unprofessional. You should have given me some warning you were on your way."

Grayson stepped into the room, taking his time looking around. His eyes stopped for a second on my Louis Vuitton luggage before he finally made eye contact. "I wasn't sure I was coming until about fifteen minutes ago."

"I see. Well, would you like to go downstairs? We could get coffee—"

"This is fine. I won't stay long. I've gotta get back to work."

I glanced around my room at the unmade bed, the clothes strewn about. I dragged the chair from the desk forward and then sat down on the upholstered bench at the end of the bed as Grayson took the chair. "I've been considering your offer. Before we go any further, I'd like to meet with the executor of the trust to make sure the money will be paid out as you said it will, upon our marriage or shortly afterward."

I nodded, my heart rate accelerating. "Of course. I understand."

Grayson gave one succinct nod. "And if everything looks fine there, we'll need to have a prenuptial agreement drawn up, stating the financial terms of our marriage."

"Obviously."

"No matter what happens financially in the next year when we're married, no finances or property will be split in any way, shape, or form."

"No, of course."

His expression remained enigmatic. "Once I meet with your executor, I'm going to have to trust that upon the payout, you'll actually give me half of it."

"That would be our deal." A piece of hair fell out of my knot and I tried to tuck it back up. Grayson's eyes followed my hand and then lingered there as the lock slipped loose again.

"Yes, but, Kira," he said almost distractedly before looking back to my eyes. He leaned forward, his gaze steady and alert now. "I don't know you. For all I know, we get married, then you get the check and take off for Brazil. Trusting you in any respect would be an act of faith on my part."

I bristled. "I would never do that."

"So you say. I've found that people say what suits them in the moment. That doesn't always mean it can be counted on."

Yes, I knew what he meant. I took a deep breath and nodded. "I…realize that. But I intend on keeping my word."

He regarded me for one heartbeat…two, before he looked away. "I'll agree to you living at Hawthorn Vineyard for two months. That should be enough time to notify your father of our marriage and for you to find a place of your own with your share of the money. If there's an issue with your father, we can renegotiate the timeframe. There's an old gardener's cottage on my property that you can live in. It's small and doesn't offer many luxuries, but it has a bed and running water." He eyed me in some way I couldn't read.

"Sounds quaint."

"Quaint would be a generous description." Was that challenge I read in those black dragon eyes, perhaps a small quirk of his lip?

"Fine." I lifted my chin. I'd never backed down from my father, and I wouldn't back down from this man.

"You *are* desperate."

"So are you."

"True enough." He paused. "If you don't mind me asking, why'd you pick me? I mean, other than my desperation?" His lip did quirk up slightly then, but there was no amusement in his eyes. "You could have picked some homeless guy off the street and shared half your inheritance with *him*. There are lots of desperate people in this world, Kira, if you're looking to give money away."

"My father would never believe I had fallen in love and married a homeless man, *Grayson*. It would be too easy for him to contest the payout of the trust. My father is well connected, as you can probably imagine, and I have to be careful. I had to pick the right person. A convincing person."

He tilted his head. "Your father contesting the payout of the trust…is that something I need to worry about?"

I shook my head. He would more likely expend effort toward covering it up or putting a spin on it that worked in his favor, should a marriage to Grayson Hawthorn actually occur. Still… "I don't think so, no, but I've learned that where my father's concerned, it's wise to be diligent." Despite my optimistic words, a chill went down my spine.

"I see. So you intend to convince your father you saw me on the street, fell madly in love, and we married in a week?"

I sighed. "He won't find it such a stretch. He sees me as…impulsive…flighty…irrational."

His dark eyes regarded me speculatively. "And are you? Are you those things?"

I bit my lip. "Impulsive, yes, I admit I can be. Flighty, no, I don't think so. Irrational…aren't we all sometimes?"

He seemed to consider my answer for a second. "So that will be our story? We bumped into each other here in

Napa, fell in love, and impulsively married because we were irrational—but not flighty—with new love?"

I gave him a small smile. "Basically. I guess we can discuss the details so we're in sync." My heart had started racing again. "So you agree? We have a deal?"

"If all pans out once I meet with the executor, yes, we have a deal."

I nodded and let out a breath. "You won't regret this, Grayson."

"Oh, I'm sure I will in some way or another, Kira. But… desperate times—"

"Call for desperate measures. And this is about as desperate as measures get."

He smiled, flashing me a set of straight, white teeth, but the same disdain he'd shown me earlier was back in his expression. He didn't see me as someone giving him a gift but as someone driving him to do something he didn't want to do. As if I hadn't given him a choice. Well, that was fine. I didn't need his gratitude. I needed his name. I couldn't deny the disappointment I felt though. When I'd seen him on the street the day before, he'd seemed…lost, broken, but still compassionate. However, the man sitting in front of me now was completely different—stiff and cold. Had I really misjudged him that much?

As if he had read my thoughts, the smile disappeared from his face as quickly as it had appeared. "There are just a few more things I think we should discuss briefly."

"Okay." I crossed my legs and his eyes followed my movement.

He clenched his jaw and looked away before speaking. "Since you're going to be living on my property, I think we should be up front about the nature of our relationship."

"Relationship? I thought that was clear. We're marrying for money. We have no relationship." The awkward, stilted nature of this meeting highlighted that fact perfectly.

"We'll be business associates. Nothing more."

"Agreed. As long as you're discreet, conduct your personal life as you see fit."

"I intend to."

"Fine."

"Good. I don't want you to get any…fanciful ideas about this arrangement."

I raised a brow. "Fanciful?"

"Romantic. Inaccurate."

I gritted my teeth. "Yes, you've made it clear I'm not your type. And I'll try my *very* best not to fall for your irresistible charms and make things"—I narrowed my eyes—"unbearably awkward."

"Good."

I wanted to kick him. Regardless of what else he was, he was obviously a man used to being pursued by the opposite sex. And apparently he either assumed I was some sort of nun, or he had zero concern with how I conducted my own personal life. Most likely the latter. "What else?" I asked coldly.

Grayson—henceforth referred to as the Dragon—studied me. I didn't try to figure out what he was thinking. Probably trying to ascertain whether or not I was *actually* going to be able to keep myself from falling in love with him. He was getting uglier by the second. *Arrogant* reptile. "You mentioned my record. I'm assuming you know about my crime?"

That immediately cooled the anger I'd been feeling. I felt heat creep up my neck. "I hope you don't find it too intrusive, but I thought it best that I research you before making my offer."

He shrugged. "A good business decision. Do you have any questions about what you read before we move forward? I'll answer your questions now, but I don't intend to discuss it later."

I couldn't hide the surprise that came over me. "I...well, from what I understand, you got in a fight with a man outside a bar in San Francisco, and you hit him...ah, repeatedly. He fell and hit his head and died. It was an accident. You didn't intend to kill him. Is that the truth?" I felt embarrassed to sum up what was certainly an extremely upsetting situation, even now. He'd gone to prison for five years for his crime.

He was silent for so long, I wondered if he'd answer me. Finally, he said simply, "That's accurate enough." I regarded him for a moment, but his face was unreadable.

"Prison must have been...very hard for you."

Something passed over his expression, but he schooled it with passivity before I could attempt to name it. "You have no idea."

There was an awkward silence.

"And now, you're a felon."

He leaned forward, his steady, dark gaze fixed on me. "Yes, Kira. I'm a felon. I can't get a loan—as you well know. My employment options are limited to say the least. Many doors are now closed to me. You're going to be married to a felon. Frank Dallaire's daughter is going to be married to a felon."

All the more reason for him to extend our estrangement, perhaps make it permanent. Which suits me just fine. But I didn't say that. Instead, I answered, "It'd be difficult for me to disappoint my father more than I already have."

He studied me again with his dragon eyes, the ones that seemed to see right through me. "I'll take your word for that." He suddenly stood, startling me slightly. I jumped up, and we almost collided when we both went to step forward. He steadied me by putting his hands on my upper arms. I raised my eyes to his, and when he looked down at me, he seemed startled too. "I have to go," he said, turning and beginning to walk toward the door.

"Oh, okay," I said, following him. "Just one more question, um, regarding the timing of this arrangement." I looked around the motel room, calculating quickly how many days I could stay here. Of course I'd also need to hire a lawyer to draw up a prenuptial agreement with the Dragon, someone who had no connections to my father. "I know you probably want to…well, the thing is…"

"You don't have the money to stay here."

I let out a breath. "I do, but not for long. Especially if I'm going to need to pay lawyer fees."

He stood in front of the door, rubbing the back of his neck. Finally he said, "Pack your suitcase. You can come with me now. We'll arrange a lawyer tomorrow. But, Kira." He turned, looking me in the eyes. "If this doesn't pan out in a way we're both satisfied with, I'm going to ask you to leave immediately."

"You wouldn't have to ask."

He jerked his head in a quick nod. "I'll give you five minutes to pack."

Yes, sir, Dragon, sir I was tempted to respond sarcastically. But I zipped my lips and hurriedly began packing my things.

———————

Thirty minutes later, I had checked out of the motel and was following Grayson's black truck through the gates of Hawthorn vineyard.

I had been taken aback by the vineyard's beauty the first time I'd arrived here, and I was just as taken now. Massive oak trees bordered the long driveway, the canopy of leaves shading our vehicles as we drove beneath them. The Hawthorn home, which stood just behind a courtyard with a courtly, round fountain in the center, was a vision of grace and elegance, and yet it managed to look warm and inviting at the same time. Ivy climbed one side of the large structure, and elegantly curved wrought-iron balconies flanked every window on the upper floor. The acres and acres of vineyards created a breathtaking background to the house and gardens, and I could see a small grove of fruit trees off to the left of the house—peaches, perhaps, or maybe apricots.

At first glance, it looked like a lush paradise just waiting to be explored. It was only as you drew closer that you noticed the fountain wasn't running, the ivy needed tending, and the lawn and surrounding gardens were overgrown. The gardener had been dismissed, no doubt. It was beautiful nonetheless. In its glory, this place must have been magnificent. My eyes lingered on the rolling hills of vines in the distance, as I wondered at the state of grapes they'd produce. I looked forward to seeing it restored, not just for Grayson's sake but for the sake of beauty itself. A place like this shouldn't be allowed to crumble to ruin. I thought Gram would agree. But I pushed the thought of my gram aside for the moment. No, she wouldn't want to see this beautiful vineyard in the place she'd loved so much crumble to ruin, but she'd also roll over in her grave to know I was marrying for money. *I am a woman who will marry a complete stranger for money. That is me.* Despair filled my chest momentarily. I knew that about myself now, and it brought another small measure of self-loathing.

Grayson pulled the truck over before we'd driven around the fountain, and I parked behind him, just noticing a small house on the right, partially hidden behind a very large oak and overgrown foliage. He had called it the gardener's cottage, but most likely, any gardeners who had worked here recently hadn't lived on the property and had used this "house" strictly for equipment storage. Still, there *was* something quaint about it, half-hidden as it was, and draped in overgrown wisteria. I got out of my car and Grayson did the same, walking toward me. There was a glint of devilish challenge in his expression. Did he expect me to balk at the accommodations? Probably. Surely he saw me just as everyone else did: a spoiled princess, a daddy's girl who lived a frivolous, useless existence. And now he was going to have some fun with me. Well, let him try. What did I care what he thought? In a few months' time, I'd never see him again. Our lawyers could handle the extremely straightforward divorce proceedings and I wouldn't think of him again. And vice versa, I was sure.

I followed Grayson to the door of the cottage, where he moved the large, showy blooms of purple wisteria aside and opened it without a key. Inhaling a big breath of the vining flowers, I stepped inside. Well. Rusty, obviously unused gardening equipment filled the front room. It was dusty, dirty, and smelled of mustiness and motor oil. I fought my way through the cobwebs and walked into the second room, what had once been a bedroom but now only held a small metal bed with rusted springs.

"I'll have Charlotte bring you some blankets and a pillow, of course," Grayson said from behind me. I whirled around and eyed him. Was that amusement in his eyes? Why yes, it was. His lip trembled as if he was trying to control a smile

45

that wanted to burst forth. *Think this is funny, do you?* Well, what he didn't know was that the accommodations I'd been keeping for the past year had featured a dirt floor. To the people I'd been living with, this would be a castle.

"I'll bathe in the fountain, I suppose?" I asked, smiling sweetly at him.

"The fountain doesn't work. There's running water here. Only cold, though, no hot. That won't be a problem, will it?"

"Noooo," I drawled out. "A nice cold shower invigorates a person, I've found. I prefer cold showers actually."

The scaly dragon appeared to consider that. "I'll bet you do," he finally said, leaning one narrow hip on the doorframe as he watched me. How nice for him that he was having so much fun. I'd never back down now. I'd sleep on the floor in this dusty shack if it meant getting the best of Grayson Hawthorn.

"Is there a kitchen? A place I might eat the crusts of bread you'll throw me?" I asked. "*After* I give you your portion of my inheritance, of course."

"No, you'll have to eat up at the main house. I'll tell Charlotte to expect you for dinner," he said, ignoring the second part of my question. I remembered Charlotte from that morning—a plump, sweet-looking, gray-haired woman.

"Will you be there?"

"No. I'll be going out." Silence. *Okaaaaay.*

"Who will you tell Charlotte I am exactly?"

"I'll tell Charlotte and her husband, Walter, the truth. They've known me my whole life. They're the epitome of discreet." My heartbeat sped up at the thought of his housekeeping staff knowing our marriage was fake, but I decided to trust his *epitome of discreet* description. Plus, there would be no way to pretend we'd fallen in love when, yesterday, I hadn't existed in Grayson's life at all and they'd very well know it.

I wished this were something I could do on my own, but it wasn't. I needed him.

"I see. Okay." I looked around the cottage again, distracting myself with an assessment of the space. "Well, there are some definite cons, but there are pros too."

His brow dipped, but he nodded once and then turned to leave. "Dinner's at seven thirty." That was in less than an hour. I guess I'd get started cleaning this place up as much as possible.

Grayson came back inside a few minutes later, set my suitcase down, and then turned to leave. Suddenly he stopped, and I thought he was going to tell me he'd just been kidding about this place. Instead, he said coldly, "By the way, I absolutely prohibit the use of drugs on my property. If I find that you've brought them here, our deal's off."

My mouth dropped open as I tried to think of a retort, but before I could come up with anything, he turned and walked out, closing the door behind him. A second later, I heard his truck roar to life and drive away. Clearly he'd looked me up and read about the "situation" I'd been in a year ago.

Too late, I picked up an empty soda can off the floor and hurled it at the closed door. *Vile serpent!* I should call this whole sham off immediately. How dare he treat me like this after I'd made him the most generous offer of his scaly life? His arrogance knew no bounds. And he'd judged me to be a spoiled brat. A spoiled, *druggie* brat. But beneath my anger, there was an undeniable feeling of shame and sadness. *Was this worth it?* God, I had to believe it would be. Someday.

CHAPTER FOUR
Grayson

She'd remained as if she was really going to live in that small, dirty hovel. I smirked to myself, wondering how long it would take her to come running to the main house, telling me there was no way in hell she'd stay there. Fifteen minutes? At dinner, tops. I had to give her a small measure of respect though. She'd played along with the joke. I'd expected outrage, foot stomping, breath holding perhaps. The little witch had a tad more grit to her than I'd originally thought. And I hadn't had so much fun in…in a really long time. I'd even wanted to laugh for a minute there. I hadn't realized how foreign that feeling had become until the amusement rose in my throat.

I took a quick shower, changed into clean clothes, and then went downstairs to let Charlotte know there'd be a guest for dinner. When I walked into the kitchen, light was streaming through the windows and the room was fragrant with the smell of her beef stroganoff.

"Beautiful evening, isn't it?" Charlotte asked, smiling brightly at me.

I grabbed a beer from the refrigerator, opened it, and downed half the bottle before grunting an affirmative response. "I have something to talk to you about."

She stopped stirring and eyed me. "That sounds ominous."

I shook my head, taking another swig of the cold beer. "For me, yes, but not for you."

"You know anything that affects you negatively affects me too, Gray," she said softly. A small corner of my heart, the part that still lived, throbbed with regret at the mess I'd made of things.

"I know, Charlotte."

"So what is it? Just get it out there."

"I'm getting married. Probably."

The spoon clattered to the stovetop, and Charlotte brought her hands to her mouth. "You got someone with child. Oh, Gray!"

I choked on the sip of beer I'd just taken. "No, God no." I was always careful about that. Always.

"What then? Why? Who?" Charlotte sputtered.

I gave Charlotte the bare facts of what Kira had presented to me in my office that morning. Even after having a whole day to think on the topic, it still sounded crazy. Insane. "The facts haven't been confirmed yet. But she'll be here for dinner, so I wanted to let you know. Actually, she's staying at the vineyard for the time being."

Charlotte's face was a study in disapproval. She clearly hated this idea. "Marrying for money, Gray? No, I don't want this for you. And does this girl have no ethics? You deserve more. You deserve—"

"It's temporary, okay? If it turns out to be as Kira said, it will be a good thing for this vineyard. And frankly, it's my

49

last hope." I set my jaw, unwilling to argue about this with Charlotte. "You know my situation."

"Yes, but…temporary? Marriage isn't temporary. Marriage isn't a business deal—a matter of contracts and negotiations. Marriage is *sacred*, a sacred vow to love forever."

I snorted. Charlotte knew I had little to no respect for the sanctity of marriage after witnessing the frigid nature of my own father and stepmother's "wedded bliss." "Most people aren't like you and Walter, Charlotte. Just look at Jessica and Ford Hawthorn."

Tenderness filled Charlotte's expression as she stepped closer to me. She took a moment, seeming to collect her words. "Gray, I know since you've come home, things have changed so much and everything has been very hard for you. I know you blame yourself…for all of it. And you've changed. You don't smile—you just work. You've shut down. But this is not the answer to your problems. It can't be. I can't let you do this."

I set the empty beer bottle down, the glass clanking loudly on the marble countertop, anger and helplessness filling my chest. I hardly needed Charlotte's summation of who I'd become. Who I'd been forced to become. I lived with myself every second of every bleak day. "You're my housekeeper, Charlotte, not my mother. I won't discuss this further. Set another plate."

Hurt flashed in Charlotte's eyes, but she pressed her lips together, turning back to the stove, muttering something I couldn't hear and didn't care to. Charlotte was as soft as her husband was rigid. "You'll be staying for dinner, of course," Charlotte said without turning, as I started to leave the kitchen, "to introduce us to your future *wife*."

I halted, the word "wife" making me jolt slightly. I much

preferred "business partner" when it came to Kira. Of course, Charlotte was purposely trying to rattle me, trying to make clear what I was considering. I hadn't planned on eating dinner at home, but I said, "Of course." I'd give Charlotte that much at least.

I closed myself in my office and opened up the website for the Napa county clerk's office. There was no waiting period for getting married. We'd simply need to make an appointment and show up with a witness, or use one provided by them. Hopefully Kira wouldn't have a problem quickly making an appointment with the executor of her trust. The sooner we got this fake marriage started, the sooner we could get this fake marriage ended and could both get on with our lives.

I rifled through my mail, setting the bills aside. For the first time in months, I didn't cringe at the very large pile. *If this worked*...if this worked, I could pay them all. I wouldn't let myself think about specifics, though, until everything had been confirmed. I halted when I saw a personal letter addressed to me in feminine handwriting I recognized immediately. My chest squeezed momentarily before I had a chance to steel myself. Curiosity pricked at my mind, but I tossed the letter aside. There was nothing she could say that would ever change anything. I didn't need to hear her pitiful words of explanation or apology.

"God damn you, Vanessa," I whispered, leaning my elbows on my desk and taking my head in my hands for a few moments.

Now I really wanted to get out of here and blow off some steam. Instead, I had to dine with a stranger who might very well be my wife in a short time. Charlotte was right. This was a terrible idea. Ridiculous. No matter in *what* capacity I let them in, somehow women always had a way of ruining my life. And the truth of the matter was, Kira Dallaire would end up being the worst of all. She would be a constant, shameful reminder of just how far I'd fallen. A constant reminder of what I'd been reduced to—marrying a stranger for money. If I could find any humor in it at all, I'd laugh at my own pitiful predicament. I'd laugh at the fact that I was even considering this ridiculousness.

A few minutes later, I heard the front doorbell. I finished up what I was doing, knowing Walter would answer it in his formally cold, no-nonsense demeanor. Of course, if anyone was used to dealing with servants, it was undoubtedly Kira Dallaire. She was probably used to a whole swarm doing her bidding and meeting her every whim.

When I finally made my way to the kitchen, Kira was seated at the large, well-worn, farmhouse dinner table, a glass of wine in front of her. She was wearing jeans and a deep-green blousy-type shirt. Her hair was pulled back as severely as it had been that morning. Had that been only hours ago? It seemed more like a decade.

Charlotte was moving around the kitchen, ignoring her. She addressed me without looking my way, "I didn't clean the dining room today, as I was unaware there'd be a guest." She shot a disdainful look at Kira. "I hope eating in the kitchen meets with your approval, *sir*." She put the emphasis on *sir*, obviously trying to make me feel guilty about referring to her as nothing more than a housekeeper earlier.

"You know I don't like to eat in the dining room anyway, Charlotte. This is fine." I sat down at the table, nodding once to Kira and taking a sip of my water.

"You don't drink wine?" she asked.

"Only sometimes."

"Isn't that unusual for someone who runs a winery?"

"I suppose." She kept looking at me, but when I didn't continue, she glanced away, taking in the kitchen.

"This kitchen is really beautiful," she said softly.

Before I could answer, Charlotte placed a plate in front of Kira, a little harder than necessary, I noted, causing a small dollop of sauce to splash onto the table. She delivered my plate in the same fashion, turning up her nose as she walked away. Without acknowledging her, I began to eat. Charlotte started clanking around in the kitchen, ignoring us both. Other than the noise of dishes being handled, an awkward silence ensued.

And continued...and then continued some more.

The clock on the kitchen wall ticked loudly, the only other sounds Charlotte's angry dish-washing and our forks hitting the plates now and then. I noticed Kira shifting in her seat and looked up to see a red flush in her cheeks. She caught my eye.

"Have you ever been to Africa?" she suddenly asked.

Africa? I opened my mouth to answer, but she spoke first. Apparently the question had been rhetorical. "Kenya, specifically. They have a wonderful welcome custom there. The warriors of the tribe, wearing their most vibrant costumes, do what's called a jumping dance. They all form a circle and compete to jump the highest, demonstrating to their guests the strength and bravery of their tribe. It's magnificent! The heights some of them can jump, it's unreal." A lock fell loose from her pulled-back hair, but she ignored it, taking a big bite of stroganoff, not bothering to swallow before continuing. "I was just thinking what a run for their money you could give them with the Hawthorn welcoming custom though. It's heartwarming. I can't tell you how

53

comfortable you've made me feel. Of course, in Kenya, you can also expect a mixed cocktail of cow's milk and blood to be part of your greeting, so that does knock off a few points for them. Still—"

"Are you done?" I asked, setting my fork down.

Sparks seemed to flash in her eyes as she met my gaze. "No, as a matter of fact." A jolt traveled through me at those sparks making her large green eyes bright with indignation. But then she took a casual sip of wine and returned to her meal.

I looked at Charlotte and swore I saw one side of her lip quirk up before she turned away.

I clenched my jaw at Kira's sarcastic response but had to concede that she was right about our welcome, or lack of one. We'd been rude to her. I was in a shitty mood. But she hadn't really done anything wrong. I didn't like her...or rather, I didn't like her *type*, and her existence in my home was a blatant reminder of the many ways I'd failed. But that didn't mean I couldn't be civil. She was also presenting a way out. I wouldn't act like she was doing me a huge favor, despite the money, though. And I wouldn't pretend I liked this situation—or that we weren't *partners* in this distasteful business deal. We were both making a sacrifice here. She was handing over what amounted to a lot of money, but she was going to be disrupting my life for the next few months, the next year, maybe longer when it came to taxes, seeing her name on forms for the rest of my life... But we'd be civil business associates. She'd been all right so far. I'd even had a little fun earlier with the whole gardener's cottage thing. Which, come to remember, she hadn't brought up yet.

"We should discuss—"

"The fact that you're the offspring of a fire-breathing lizard? That's already become clear."

Charlotte snorted from the kitchen but covered it up with the bang of a pot.

"Listen, Kira—"

"No, *you* listen, Grayson." More hair fell to frame her face as she banged her little fist down on the table and glared at me, her witchy eyes flashing again, heating my blood, much to my own dismay. "I'm making you a very generous offer here. If this is going to work, I refuse to let you treat me as you've done so far. I can assure you that, with your credentials, you won't get a better offer than mine. Keep treating me like you of all people have the right to look down on me, and I'll leave and take my inheritance with me."

Anger raced through my blood, and I banged my own fist on the table. I had the satisfaction of seeing Kira jump slightly. "If this is going to work, I won't be treated like you're taking *pity* on me and I'm not making as much of a sacrifice as you are," I gritted out. "Do you think I have any desire *whatsoever* to marry you or anyone else?"

"No, I'd imagine you're about as capable of monogamy as a junkyard dog. Not that that has anything at all to do with me."

As if from a great distance, I heard Charlotte cough again.

I narrowed my eyes to slits. "Exactly. Do you think I'd be doing this if I weren't utterly desperate and if you weren't my Very. Last. Option? So, throw the money in my face if you will, but don't act like you don't need me too. Don't act like you're not just as desperate as I am. And don't act like I'm not your best and only prospect. You said it yourself. For someone who came here begging, it'd be in your best interest to treat me with some respect."

Her cheeks flared with even more color. "*Begging?*" she

hissed. "Begging?" Heavy cascades of dark fire fell around her face as her hair came completely loose from whatever she'd been using to hold it back. I almost sucked in a breath. I hadn't realized she had so *much* of it. It surrounded her face and swung around her shoulders, looking as if it went halfway down her back.

She stood up slowly, and I did too, until we were both glaring at each other across the expanse of the kitchen table. The space between us crackled with…something, the heat in the air practically shimmering. And strangely, that tingling heat was now dancing through my blood in a full-blown performance much like the Kenyan welcome dance Kira had described, making me feel vitally…*alive.*

"I was out of my mind to come here. This"—she waved between us—"is crazy. It'll never work. We should call it off. I could find someone else to marry. I can't imagine why I chose you. I find you…*exceedingly* difficult to like."

"I agree. It's ridiculous. And vice versa."

"Good. It's off," she hissed.

"Good," I growled. We stared each other down, her eyes dancing with angry fire. And why the hell did I like that so much? After several tense, heated moments, I made a conscious effort to control my breathing, raising an eyebrow at her. "And by the way, next time you offer to marry someone, you should try to be a little more meek. A man likes some obedience in a wife." I'd said it purely to anger her and was rewarded by heat flashing in her narrowed stare. Another undeniable thrill shot from head to toe.

"Charlotte," she suddenly said very sweetly. "Do you have a pen and paper I could borrow?"

"Oh, yes," Charlotte said, grabbing a pen and pad of

paper out of the junk drawer and practically running it over to Kira, as if she were suddenly at her beck and call.

I watched Kira closely, waiting to see what she would do next.

Kira smiled politely at Charlotte and then uncapped the pen carefully, putting it on the end with deliberate slowness, and then holding the pad of paper up, the pen poised before it. "What was that now? I want to make sure I get every single word of wise advice," she said, stretching out the word *every*. "Meek, was it? Does that have double *e* or is it *ea*? I can never remember."

I regarded her through lowered lashes, resisting the urge to laugh at her overdone display of sarcasm. "I wouldn't worry so much about the spelling of the word meek as how to embrace the concept."

"Hmm," she hummed. "Noted. And obedient, you said?"

"Yes."

"Obedient—*yes*." She made a big checkmark on the paper. "And?"

"Your sarcasm—that will be a turnoff to future husbands."

She pretended to write that down. "Sarcasm—*no*." She marked a big X on the paper. "What else?"

We stared at each other for a few more strained seconds, her expression a phony look of intense interest and mine a mild smirk. The truth was, I didn't even know if the legal aspects of the fake marriage she'd proposed were legitimate. But talking about calling it off before even knowing caused disappointment to descend. I hated the idea, hated the little spiky-tongued witch standing in front of me, hated that in reality, she *did* have more power in this situation than I did… but at the same time, it was the first thing in a long while that had given me some hope. And I didn't even realize until that moment how sweet that hope tasted.

I looked away first, breaking the intensity flowing between us, but she was the first who spoke as she set the pen and paper on the table. "Listen, this situation is... unusual to say the least." She paused again and I looked back to her. The spark had gone out of her eyes as if the idea of calling it off wasn't exactly what she wanted either. "I called the executor of my trust before I walked over here. He can see us late in the day tomorrow. Maybe we could find a way to coexist at least until we've determined that everything is as I've said. And then we can make a final decision from there."

"I can agree to that."

She took a deep breath. "Okay, good." She held out her hand. "Truce?" She arched an eyebrow. I looked at her hand and held out my own from across the table.

"Truce. Come here so we can shake."

"You come here," she challenged.

I smiled slowly. "Meet in the middle."

She narrowed her eyes but nodded, stepping away from her chair. We met next to the center of the large table and I took her warm hand in mine and shook it as we regarded each other warily. With a concise nod, she returned to her seat and so did I. When Charlotte came over to refill Kira's wine, she regarded her not with disdain but with a guarded curiosity. Interesting that somehow our fighting had ingratiated Kira to Charlotte. Women were all a mystery to me.

"Would you like to see the rest of the house?" I asked, trying to make a small peace offering.

Kira looked surprised but nodded yes. We got up from the table, and Kira thanked Charlotte for the delicious dinner. Charlotte smiled a smile that seemed genuine but didn't offer me one.

I brought Kira back to the main foyer and we started from there. "My father had this place designed to mimic a French chateau."

Kira nodded as we entered the formal living room. "It really does. It reminds me of a smaller-scale fairy-tale castle. There's something…enchanting about it." She gasped when she spotted the large window overlooking the back of the house. The pool was directly below, down a set of steps and off a natural stone patio. However, her head was lifted and I knew she was staring at the hedge maze just beyond that. She whirled toward. "It's a maze!" she gasped. "And it's massive."

I clenched my jaw just as I did each time I looked at that hateful thing. "It's completely overgrown. If I had the extra money, I'd have had it mown down when I moved back."

"Oh, why?" she gasped. "It's incredible! Can I go inside sometime?"

"No. Absolutely not." I gentled my tone, though when I said, "It isn't safe." She didn't know why I hated it and she never would, but I had spoken the truth—it was too overgrown to be safe.

She was studying me with those bright, penetrating eyes. I could feel them boring into the side of my face. When I made eye contact, she raised one delicate brow. "The heart of your lair, I suppose?" She smiled prettily. "Where you were…hatched?"

I attempted a scathing look, but I knew she was joking and I couldn't resist the smile that made its way to my lips. "Perhaps." I raised my own brow. "But in all seriousness, just stay away from it."

After a short pause, Kira looked away and shrugged. "Well, okay, it's your house."

I took her through the rooms one by one and watched her reaction. This house had been a showpiece at one time, but signs of neglect were everywhere. Despite the now-sparse furnishings, Charlotte, being only one person, could hardly keep the whole thing spotless as it had once been. When I said as much, Kira looked at me and stated, "You grew up in a life of privilege." I knew what she wasn't saying: I had acted as if she was the only one who'd known luxury.

"Privilege isn't only defined by material wealth, Kira. I grew up in a beautiful home with hired help, but I can assure you, I never lived a life of privilege. For all intents and purposes, I never had any parents at all."

She tilted her head, confusion filling her expression. "What does that mean, Grayson?"

I shook my head. "The specifics of my family dynamics don't matter. What does matter is that I'm used to hard work, and I won't let a dollar of the money you're so generously offering me go to waste. In fact, I'm considering the money you're giving me a loan. Once the vineyard is bringing in a profit, I'll pay you back."

She was quiet for a moment. Finally, she simply nodded. "We don't need to put that in the paperwork, but should you choose..." She waved her hand in the air as if I could do as I pleased on that front. *Interesting.* I wasn't sure what to think of her response.

When we walked through the upstairs corridor, Kira stopped at the picture of my father and stepmother. "They've both passed?" she asked softly, glancing back at me.

"Only my father. My stepmother lives in San Francisco."

She turned slowly toward me. "Does she have no interest

in helping with the vineyard her husband loved? Or does she not have the financial means…?"

"She has plenty of money. My father left this vineyard to me. I won't ask my stepmother for a dime of the money my father left her. We have no relationship and we never have." *I should have to tolerate you when your own mother couldn't even be bothered?* she'd asked me when I was twelve. I could still hear the cold words echoing through my head. "I'd rather… well, I'd rather marry a stranger for money before going to her for a loan." I gave her a wry smile, but she didn't smile back. "Anyway, the vow I've made is to my father. It's for me to fulfill."

She looked at me, tilting her head. "I understand vows, Grayson. I've made them too. I've vowed never again to depend upon my father." She turned back to the photo and looked at it for another long minute.

"You must favor your mother," she said, obviously noticing my father's very light coloring.

"Yes, to everyone's dismay," I said. *A constant reminder that I was an outsider and a burden.* She glanced at me but didn't question that cryptic remark. I wasn't sure why I'd made it. I hardly wanted her questioning anything about my life.

She looked back to the wall of pictures, leaning closer to a photo. I studied her profile, the straight slope of her small nose, the gentle curve of her jaw, the feathery curl of her lashes, that long, silken hair falling around her face and down her back. "You have a brother," she said, looking at the picture of Shane and me.

"Yes."

"Does he live nearby?"

"No, he lives in San Diego."

"Are you close?"

"I haven't spoken to my brother in over five years."

She turned to me again. "Oh, I'm so sorry."

"Don't be," I said, my voice clipped as I led her away before she could ask any more intrusive questions. I was already feeling very uncomfortable with this tour. And I couldn't blame *her*—it had been my own idea.

"Well, I'll leave you with Charlotte. She'll get you settled into a room. I'm going out," I said dismissively once we'd descended the stairs.

She looked confused for a second. "Yes, okay, well, thanks. Have a good night."

I nodded curtly and started to walk away, narrowing my eyes when I heard her humming. I turned back and walked toward her. "Are you humming 'Puff the Magic Dragon'?"

Her eyes blinked, looking big and innocent. A clear act. "Is *that* what that song is? I never knew the name or *who* exactly lived in Honahlee, just the tune mostly."

I glared down at her for several long moments. She held eye contact with me, that little chin tipped up. The air buzzed, pinpricks of awareness hitting my skin. Finally, finished with her little game, I turned away again, leaving her standing alone in my front foyer.

CHAPTER FIVE
Kira

God, that dragon ran hot and cold. As reptiles tended to do, I supposed. I almost preferred the fire he shot at me to the icy act he put on when he was finished with a certain topic of conversation, or when he looked at me with frigid disdain. I wasn't precisely sure how I knew the iciness was an act, but I did. Deep down, he was all dragon—barely contained heat…and probably passion too. I shivered. I would *not* think of Grayson Hawthorn in those terms. I would only get burned. He had spelled it out for me himself. I was not his "type," whatever that might be.

I took a deep breath, my eyes lingering on the words carved ornately into the stone above the doorway: In Vino Veritas. I'd have to look that up. I went back to the kitchen, where I found Charlotte still wiping down the counters. She looked up and offered me a smile—a much warmer greeting than she'd given me earlier tonight.

"Would you like some coffee?"

"Oh, sure." I smiled. "But only if you'll join me?"

Charlotte hesitated but then nodded. I sat down on a barstool at the counter while she poured two cups and then placed one in front of me with cream and sugar, put a pie dish and two plates with utensils next to her, and sat down with her own mug.

"Grayson went out," I said, taking a sip of coffee.

Her lips came together in a straight line. "Yes, so I heard. Salted caramel pie?" she asked, cutting a huge piece and plopping it on a plate.

"Oh, um, okay." I hesitated as she slid the plate in front of me, the delicious smells of caramel and sweet cream wafting to my nose. "I know this situation probably seems…" I shook my head, at a loss for a word other than *ridiculous*, *inadvisable*, *disastrous*.

Immoral.

"Unusual" was the word I finally uttered to Charlotte.

"Yes, it does," she said, cutting her own slice of pie. Despite her agreement, she smiled. "I had hoped for more for Gray. No offense to you. You seem like a spirited girl. I just…I hoped he'd marry for love, of course."

"Of course." I couldn't help blushing. I hoped to marry for love someday too. "You care for him very much." I took a bite of pie, the sweet and salty flavors bursting across my tongue. I tried not to let my eyes roll to the back of my head. *God that's good.*

"Very much. I've been working here since Gray was first dropped off—" She seemed to catch herself. "That is, since Gray came to live here."

I wanted to pry, to ask her what she'd meant by "dropped off," but I didn't. This was the first time I was having a conversation with the woman. I didn't want to seem like a busybody.

"But of course," she continued, "I understand why your

offer seems appealing to Grayson. He"—she shook her head again, looking very sad—"will stop at nothing to bring this vineyard back to what it once was."

"It's his family legacy," I said. "I can't blame him."

She nodded, her eyes meeting mine again, her thoughts seeming to return from somewhere far away. "And what about you? Are there no other options than this?"

"This seems like my best option at the moment," I said quietly, for some reason feeling shameful in front of this sweet-faced, older woman with the lilting English accent and the kind eyes. "Did Gray explain my situation?"

"He gave me the CliffsNotes." She looked at me for a moment, her stare assessing. "All I can say is this situation may have more ramifications than you're considering. I implore you to think this through before you do something you can't undo."

"I do understand what you're saying, Charlotte, and I appreciate the advice, but—"

"You've made up your mind."

"Yes, I've made up my mind. I hope you can try to understand."

"Well," she said, "then that's that." I looked down at the piece of mostly eaten pie on my plate, not knowing why it mattered to me that I was disappointing this woman. She continued before I could say anything. "And perhaps you'll be good for him. I admit I haven't seen any fire in his eyes for…well, for far too long."

"Hmm…" I hummed, taking another sip of coffee, not knowing if that was a good or bad thing. It probably indicated we brought out the worst in each other already— and I'd only known him for a few hours. I finished off the last couple bites of my pie.

"Oh, hey, Charlotte, can I bother you for some linens? I need some blankets and a pillow to take to the gardener's shed where I'm staying."

Charlotte looked at me blankly. "The gardener's shed? That's only been used for storage for decades. You can't *stay* in it. Surely Gray was only joking when he put you there."

"Maybe." I took the last sip of my coffee. "But I like it. And it's a space of my own. I won't bother anyone that way."

"I can't abide by that," Charlotte said, shaking her head. "I don't like this idea of you and Gray getting married, but I won't see you living in a dirty, spider-infested shack."

I laughed. "Remember when I mentioned Kenya? I lived there for a year. I just got back less than a week ago, actually. The spiders here would be shamed by the insects there. I can handle a daddy longlegs or two. And with a bed and some clean linens, it's a step above the floor mat I've become accustomed to sleeping on."

"And why were you in Kenya?"

Hiding. Escaping. Being banished. "To help a friend build a hospital." I smiled, the first one that felt genuine since I'd arrived back in San Francisco. "It will help so many women and children. I'll tell you all about it sometime."

Charlotte patted my hand, that wary look in her eye seeming to have turned down several notches. "I would like that."

An hour later I had swept the bedroom of the cottage with the broom Charlotte had given me, thoroughly cleaned the metal bedframe, and made it up with the mattress Walter had carried over. When Charlotte brought the blankets, she looked around in horror, asked me again to come back with her, and then when I declined, left as quickly as possible.

I'd tackle the bathroom in the morning. I used the frigid water from the tap to wash my face and brush my teeth. I peeked behind the musty curtain over the shower and cringed when I saw the rusty fixtures, dirt-caked floor, and the thick cobwebs covering the ceiling. *Blech*.

Being late summer, the evenings were getting just a bit chillier, but I opened the windows wide anyway. The cool breeze wafted inside, carrying the very faint scent of roses and the wisteria covering the cottage, dispelling the smell of dust and oil.

Although it wasn't much to look at, the bed was comfortable, and I climbed under the covers with my phone, sending a quick text to Kimberly. I hadn't filled her in completely on what was going on, but I wanted to wait until after we'd met with Mr. Hartmann, the executor of the trust Gram had left me. I'd spring this on her once everything was official, and no sooner. She'd try to talk me out of it and Kimberly was persuasive. Likely she'd have me doubting everything I'd already come to terms with. And I couldn't afford that. Literally.

I had four messages. I took a deep breath and hit play on the first one from my father.

Kira. I know you were inside when I was banging on your door, and I know you heard me. I sent James to your apartment with a key, and he said it looked like you had moved out. Call me immediately and tell me what you think you're up to. We need to sit down with Cooper and make sure we're all on the same page. Dammit, Kira, you knew enough not to disappear. I need you at my disposal. Has nothing changed since you left the country? Just call me.

Click.

Hot tears filled my eyes. *I need you at my disposal.* Of course you do, Daddy. Because that's what I am to you—disposable. The next two messages were from my father's number too. I deleted them without listening. Thankfully I'd thought to turn off the tracking on my phone so my father couldn't find my location—it was how he had to have known I was at my apartment packing my suitcases…unless he had spies in the building reporting in to him, which was just as likely.

The final message was from Cooper. I hit play tentatively, biting my lip until I tasted blood. I forced my body to relax.

Hey, Kira <pause> Damn, I hoped I'd come up with something to say once I heard the beep. <deep sigh> Your father told me you were back. Kira, we need to talk. We need to… Listen, I had hoped you'd answer my call. You never answered any of my letters, but please call me. I missed you so much.

Click.

You missed me? You *bastard*. Tears poured down my cheeks and I turned my face into my pillow, thinking back to that terrible day, the soul-stealing betrayal, the shock, the humiliation, and finally, only pain.

I eventually fell into a restless sleep, only waking once when I heard a vehicle on the gravel driveway outside the open window of my cottage. I turned over groggily and opened my eyes, but there was too much foliage outside the window to see the driveway beyond. I heard footsteps as the person I assumed to be Grayson, got out of his truck and walked directly to his house. My heavy lids fell closed, and I was back to sleep in moments.

Morning sun shone through the open window, scattering lemony light and causing my dreams to fade like mist. I sat up and stretched. After washing up quickly and knotting my hair on top of my head, I pulled on a pair of jean shorts and a navy-blue tank top. I'd tackle the shower today and get myself together before our appointment this afternoon.

The gravel crunched underfoot as I trekked to the main house and knocked at the door. Walter answered with the same remote look on his face he seemed to favor. "Mr. Hawthorn is in the kitchen eating breakfast," he said formally.

"Thanks, Walter." I smiled and headed toward the kitchen.

Grayson was sitting at the same spot he'd sat at dinner, a wine magazine of some sort in front of him. I took the seat I'd occupied the night before as well—at the other end.

"Good morning!" Charlotte singsonged.

"Morning," I said to both she and Grayson.

There were plates of eggs, bacon, toast, and hash browns, so I loaded the plate in front of me. After several bites, I looked up to see Grayson watching me eat. When I caught his eye, he seemed momentarily surprised and looked away. "I have a lot of work to do today. What are your plans?" he asked.

I finished chewing the bite of toast I'd just taken. "I'm going to do some more cleaning at the cottage first and then I thought I might take a walk around your property if you don't have any objections."

He froze. "The cottage? You can't mean to actually stay there. That was a joke, Kira. I thought you knew that."

I shrugged. "I don't mind. It's a place of my own, away from you…out of your hair, I should say. It'll be like I'm not even here." I offered him a big smile, which he didn't return.

Grayson eyed me for a second, but then casually picked up the magazine. "Suit yourself."

A few minutes later, Grayson excused himself—seeming just a tad less frosty—and went off to work, stating he'd meet me in front of the house at three o'clock. I finished my breakfast and offered to help Charlotte clean up, but when she refused, I asked if I could borrow some cleaning supplies and then returned to my cottage fully armed.

I spent the next four hours cleaning decades of dirt and grime from the small bathroom—most likely a relic from the seventies—scrubbing windows, floors, and even the walls in the bedroom. There was nothing much I could do about the front room, given it was filled with gardening equipment, so I simply created a path through the mess and cleared out the worst of the cobwebs. I could close the door to that space and simply live in the two cleaned rooms.

I only took a break to walk to the house and eat a quick lunch, which Charlotte had said would be waiting for me.

When I was finished with the cottage, every muscle in my body ached, but I felt accomplished as I stared around the new spic-and-span rooms. My home for the next couple months. It was far from elegant, although luxury had never brought me true happiness anyway. No, I liked this place because it was my own little space. And it was where I had landed…where the path I'd chosen to take had led me.

It had been a warm day, but the cottage was completely shaded by trees, and the temperature had dropped now that it was late afternoon. I squealed when I stepped under the cold water of the shower and danced in place with discomfort as I speed-washed my hair and body with the toiletries I'd brought with me. I had forgotten to ask Charlotte for towels—maybe I'd go buy a few to have my own—so I dried off with a T-shirt and pulled on clean clothes. Thankfully, the blow-dryer warmed me as I used it to dry my hair which I left hanging down my back.

Outside, I stood admiring the rolling hills of grapevines again, set before a clear blue sky. I didn't know much about the winemaking process, but I hoped to learn. Not that I'd be here very long, but it was interesting to me in general—an age-old practice holding so much tradition. I strolled behind the house, just meaning to get an up-close look at the maze. When I was standing in front of the huge natural structure, I saw that the entrance wasn't closed off in any way, so I ventured inside, walking cautiously, only intending on turning a corner or two. It was terribly overgrown, the pathways far more narrow than they should have been, the ground patchy with weeds and grass, but it was magnificent. And it was at least fifteen degrees cooler in here. If I could be assured I could find my way out, I'd stroll through it endlessly. I wondered if there was anything in the center. Why in the world would Grayson want to tear something so special down? It was a travesty. I hoped he would change his mind once he had the funds to maintain it.

Turning around before I became hopelessly lost, I began walking down the small hill toward a large stone structure I assumed was where the wine was made and stored. There were several tractors and trucks parked in front of it, and I could hear equipment operating inside.

As I got closer, I noticed a couple men standing next to a tractor close to the building, a pair of muscular thighs on the ground under it. One of the men called a greeting, and I waved back. The man underneath the tractor scooted out and stood. Grayson. My heart stalled. He was shirtless. He came to his full height and waited for me to walk the short distance to them. I had already noticed he was beautifully built, but the sight of his wide shoulders, rippling chest muscles, and flat, ridged stomach made my breath catch and my cheeks flush. He was broad but lean, his smooth, tanned skin glistening under the sun. He was a study in masculinity, and I couldn't help the way my body instinctively responded to him, the muscles in my stomach flipping and clenching. Too bad his perfection was only skin deep. Damn dragon.

Grayson took off the baseball cap he was wearing, smoothed his hair back, and then replaced it that way men do. I made an effort to shake off his effect and smiled brightly. He introduced the two men with him, a man with a small mustache who wasn't much taller than me named José and a giant of a man with a shy smile named Virgil. I greeted them both and nodded to Grayson. "Tractor broken?" I asked.

"No," Grayson answered. "But it's one of the only things that isn't. I was just giving it a tune-up, ensuring it's ready for the harvest."

"Well, you do it all, don't you?" I smiled. "No wonder you work from sunup to sundown."

"Have to. As you can see, my staff is pretty limited." He nodded to José and Virgil.

The man named Virgil stepped forward. "I'm real happy to meet you, ma'am. Mr. Grayson says he might be marrying you, and I think that's real fine. He says he can't figure whether you're a spoiled princess or a little witch, but I think if you are a witch, it's the good kind 'cuz you sure are pretty." He blushed and looked down, grinding his toe into the dirt.

I smiled tightly at Grayson, who had the grace to look just a tad embarrassed.

José coughed slightly, obviously trying to hold back a laugh.

"Is that so? What else does Mr. Grayson say, Virgil?"

Grayson gave a short laugh. "Well, I think that's enough chatter," he said. "We should be—"

"He says the reason he likes you is 'cuz you have a whole bunch of money," Virgil continued innocently. "I'm gonna have a whole bunch of money someday so people like me too." His brow wrinkled up in thought. "Course, my mama says it's not what a person has, but how he treats others, so I don't know." He scratched the back of his neck, looking confused.

José rocked back on his heels, a quiet smile of amusement on his face. He was enjoying this.

"Well, Virgil, if I were you, I'd listen more to your mama than to Mr. Grayson." I shot Grayson a dirty look. What was he thinking, flapping his jaw in front of this sweet man? Plus, he'd let more people in on our business arrangement. Hadn't he heard a word I'd said about my father?

My consternation had nothing to do with what he'd said about me. None at all. It was information I knew already anyway. He didn't have to like me. And he could think I was a witch if he liked. What did I care about the regard of a dragon?

Grayson took the T-shirt that must have been hanging from his back pocket, removed his cap, and pulled the shirt over his head. I let out a silent sigh of relief. Naked reptiles disturbed me. "Gentlemen," Grayson said, nodding to José and Virgil. "See you in the morning."

He took me by my elbow and led me away as I smiled and waved to the two men watching us. Then I looked disinterestedly up at Grayson. I would not let on that I cared in the least about his assessment of my character. I needed him for one thing and one thing only.

Grayson sighed. "Come on, I'll drive you back to the house. Then we'll go find out if we're getting hitched or not."

CHAPTER SIX
Grayson

I looked at the woman sitting next to me. The woman who was going to be my wife in a matter of days. *My wife.* I shook my head subtly, hardly able to believe the course of events that had transpired in the last twenty-four hours. The marriage was nothing more than a business venture, but still, the fact remained, fake or not, I was going to have a wife. When I was younger, I had always assumed I'd get married someday—hell, I'd even thought I'd known exactly who that woman would be. I'd had a deep desire to create a family of my own—the type of home life I'd always longed for but never had. And then Vanessa...and well...life was full of surprises. And not all good ones either.

She shifted in her seat. "Do you think it's a good idea to tell your workers that our marriage is anything other than legitimate?" she huffed out. "I told you about my father, and the fewer people that know, the—"

"I trust José like a brother," I interrupted, pulling into a parking space and shutting off the ignition. I couldn't help the unhumorous chuckle that rose in my throat at my own words. Not all brothers were trustworthy—who knew that better than I did? "José can be trusted," I amended. "As for Virgil, I doubt if anyone is going to listen very carefully to his account of anything."

Kira shot me a look that was a cross between disdain and nervousness as she opened the door. "Well, that would be a mistake because he's honest. And also, he seems to be a very wise judge of character," she said when we met on the sidewalk.

"Kira, I wouldn't worry about what either of them knows. They're both my employees, and employees don't know everything they might think they do." Someone was approaching on the sidewalk. I got in her space and walked her backward until she was pressed up against my truck, a look of utter panic on her face. I grinned as I leaned my body into hers.

"What are you doing?" she hissed.

"Convincing the general public our relationship is very legitimate," I said close to her ear. God, she smelled good. Not just good—*incredible.* Her scent was faint, like distant flowers on a breeze. I hadn't known what she smelled like until my nose was right up against her. I nuzzled my face into the side of her neck, inhaling deeply and feeling the warmth of her skin against my own. She felt as stiff as a tree branch. I pulled away. Jesus, despite the fact that it'd only been a couple days since I'd been with fruit-flavored Jade, I was turned on. "You're going to have to do a better job than that if you hope to persuade anyone I'm marrying you and not molesting you." I turned and started walking. After a second, she caught up to me. When I glanced in her direction, I chuckled at the stiff set of her shoulders and the way that little chin was thrust in the air. *Why do I enjoy needling her so much?*

During the meeting with Mr. Hartmann, the executor of Kira's grandmother's trust, he went over the terms with both of us. It was straightforward, he said. The payout would occur immediately once we brought him a copy of our officially filed marriage license.

Kira and I had sat next to each other, holding hands like a pair of lovebirds, the heat of her skin searing into mine, the recent memory of how she'd felt pressed against me clear in my mind.

Mr. Hartmann seemed delighted as he looked between the two of us. "Your grandmother was a fine woman, Kira. She would be so pleased to see you in love."

The wince was slight and Kira covered it immediately with a smile. "Thank you. She would have loved Grayson. I just know it."

"I don't doubt it. And of course, she'd be so pleased you were planning to make your life here. She did love this town."

"Yes, she did," Kira said, smiling a gentle smile. Clearly she'd loved her grandmother very much. Guilt coiled in my gut, but I ignored it as best as I could. This was Kira's choice. I hadn't even known her grandmother. I had no loyalty to her—or her money.

"You know," Mr. Hartmann continued, "your grandmother believed that if age and maturity didn't make a person more aware of the needs of others, or at least *one* other, marriage certainly would. It's why she put the conditions on the trust money. She wanted it to be used well and ideally in partnership with someone you chose to share a life with." He winked at Kira. "I'm so glad that's the case with you."

Kira looked vaguely ill as she smiled and nodded at him.

"I haven't seen your father in quite some time. How's he doing?" Mr. Hartmann asked.

Kira visibly swallowed. "He's fine, Mr. Hartmann." She paused. "I haven't told him about Grayson yet." She gave me a tight smile. "If you wouldn't mind not mentioning this until I've had a chance to tell him myself…"

Mr. Hartmann furrowed his brow but answered, "Of course."

Once the appointment was concluded, we sat in my truck and I called the lawyer in town that had handled my father's affairs for years. I thought he might see me quickly and I was right. We were able to make an appointment for the following day. My head started spinning. This was happening very fast. But that's what I had wanted. Again, the quicker this marriage got started, the quicker Kira would leave.

"If Mr. Kohler can have the agreement drawn up within a week, we could get married next Friday," I said, glancing at Kira as I drove back to the vineyard.

She nodded. "I'm agreeable to that," she said quietly.

"I'll make the appointment, then. We'll need one for the license and then for the actual ceremony. I looked at the website."

"Oh. Okay." She pulled her skirt down modestly and my eyes slid down her bare legs. She had great legs. Sleek and slim. The kind of legs a man wanted wrapped around him as he—

I clenched my jaw, shutting those thoughts down immediately. When I noted her silence, I said, "Not getting cold feet, are you?"

"No! No. This is all good. Quick but good."

"The sooner we get this done, the sooner we can get it

over with too," I said, voicing the thought I'd had more than once.

"Yes. True." She gave me a small smile, not showing any teeth. I still hadn't seen that dimple in person. Maybe I'd imagined it on my computer screen.

I glanced over at her as she took her long hair in her hands and used a rubber band from her purse to put it up in a knot. Tendrils slipped down around her face where they always seemed to be when her hair was up, apparently too silky to stay put for long. I wondered what that hair would feel like wrapped around my fist.

Damn it! Shut those thoughts down.

She was a conundrum. A pretty princess with the temper of a fiery, little witch. I liked to make those crystal-green eyes flash with heat. I wondered what she'd be like in bed. A hot, little temptress who... *Goddamn.* I gritted my teeth, frustrated with my thoughts as the gardener's cottage came into view. She'd surprised me by making the choice to stay in that dirt-caked space that only had cold water. Surely she wouldn't have used the shower? Yet somehow she looked fresh and clean. I cringed at the thought of the dank rooms. It really wasn't even livable. Why she wanted to spend five minutes there, much less inhabit it, was beyond me. I'd lived in a small concrete cell for five years and even I wouldn't have any desire to live there. Of course, maybe that was precisely why. I couldn't abide small spaces for long. Many nights I'd woken up in a cold sweat from nightmares about my time inside. I'd never spoken to anyone about my experience, and I doubted I ever would.

For a very brief moment, the feelings of loneliness and grief, my constant companions during those five years, assaulted me, and I felt heavy with the weight of my own failures. I squeezed my eyes shut and pushed the memories away, turning my thoughts back to Kira Dallaire and the fact that she was living in my gardener's shed. Apparently, I'd misjudged her at least in some small measure. I wondered what other secrets I'd discover about her if I cared to look hard enough.

Which I didn't. Not in the least.

When I came to a stop in front of the cottage, she hopped out of my truck and stood in the open doorway for a moment. "I'll be ready for our appointment in the morning and then I'm going to drive to San Francisco tomorrow to take care of a few things. I'll be gone through the weekend."

I nodded. That suited me just fine. And I figured she needed to shower at some point. The less I had to see of her before our wedding, the better. The less I'd have to think about the reality of it. "Okay, meet me out front at eleven."

She nodded and closed the door, turning and walking through the foliage. I sat there for a minute, warring with myself. It really wasn't right to let her stay there. *Christ, screw it.* It'd been her choice. Maybe a dose of hard living would be good for the princess. Or was it that witches preferred small houses in the woods? I couldn't help chuckling to myself as I pulled away.

————

The appointment with Mr. Kohler went smoothly and quickly. We weren't agreeing to a settlement "should" there be a divorce, but rather stating we would both leave the marriage with only that with which we'd arrived. The contract was extremely straightforward, and we made an appointment for Thursday to come in and sign the paperwork. And with that, we were finished with the red tape involved in our union. I made an appointment at the clerk's office for the following Friday morning at ten a.m. The only thing left to do was to show up. My stomach felt slightly queasy. If Kira's green-tinged complexion was any indication, she did as well.

I dropped Kira off at her cottage and told her I'd see her on Monday. She didn't look back as she walked away. As quiet as she'd been after our appointment, I half wondered whether she'd return at all. Maybe it'd be best if she didn't. But I didn't believe that. For the first time in a year, I felt an eager anticipation for the future. That morning I'd opened the list Walter had made of equipment needing repair or replacement and felt a flutter in my gut. Soon, I would be able to go down it and check the items off one by one. Tension had released in my shoulders and I'd finally allowed full-blown hope to surge through my system. The power of it had left my heart beating wildly. When was the last time I'd felt that sensation? I couldn't remember. "I won't let you down," I vowed for the hundredth time, addressing my father. "I'll make you proud of me, I swear it." I *had* to believe that, somehow, he'd know. It was what kept me going.

I spent the weekend working with renewed vigor. There was going to be a lot of work to get done despite the incoming funds. And I still had a meager staff. I'd have to hire a couple more people once I had the actual check in my hands, or at least knew it was coming very shortly.

When I arrived back at the house Sunday night, I remembered the bottle of Vosne-Romanée I'd asked Walter to bring up to the main wine cellar. Pangs of guilt and despair had crippled me when I'd considered selling my father's pride and joy—his rare wine collection—to bring some much-needed income into the vineyard. The thought alone had felt like a betrayal. *I'm trying. I'm trying so hard to salvage all that was precious to you.* Relief at not having to go through with selling it was overwhelming. *Success*—another thing I hadn't felt in years settled in my heart.

When I saw Walter, I instructed him to put the bottle back in the lower wine cellar where it'd originally been kept.

"Yes, sir. I'll do it this week."

"Thank you."

"And may I offer my most heartfelt congratulations on your…marriage, sir?" The word *marriage* was offered with the coldest disdain I'd ever heard from Walter. And that was saying something.

"No, Walter, you may not."

Walter's lip quirked. "Very well, sir. I do wish you the best, however. My mother used to say that marriage is much like wine. They both mature slowly and grow deeper and more complex with time."

I turned to Walter. "Walter, I think you know as well as I do that my marriage will not be allowed to mature. It's temporary—for business purposes only."

"As you say, sir."

I halted, frowning at him.

"I do say."

"Very well, sir."

I scowled at him and started for the stairs before I got overly annoyed with the man. He had a way of making me feel like I was twelve again. And he had a way of making me question myself with his insolent, "yes, sirs" and "no, sirs." I'd fire him for real one of these days. Without severance.

I ate dinner alone, wondering when Kira would return.

I hadn't asked her anything about her trip. I didn't want to set a precedent that we would ask about each other's where-abouts or actions. I certainly didn't want her thinking she could do that with me, and I had no desire to do it with her. Still…if she'd changed her mind, I'd rather know now than have to wait for her to call me at some point this week after not showing up.

Reluctantly, I picked up my phone and used the cell number I'd only used the one time before, when I'd visited her at her motel room. I debated what to say in my text. I didn't want to leave her with the impression I was checking in with her.

Me: Should I have Charlotte keep a plate warmed for you?

A few minutes later, my phone beeped.

Kira: That's thoughtful, but no, thank you.

I scowled. Was she dense?

Me: I'll have Charlotte set a place at breakfast for you then.
Kira: No, that won't be necessary either. Thank you.

I growled at the phone, punching at the small letters on the keyboard.

Me: Goddamn it, Kira, are you coming back or not?

Several minutes ticked by, a strange panic rising in my throat.

Kira: Yes, I'll be back tomorrow afternoon. Miss me?

I exhaled.

Me: No. Good night.

Little witch.

CHAPTER SEVEN
Kira

Hawthorn Vineyard was suffused with dappled, late-afternoon sun when I drove through the gates a little after four o'clock. I'd spent the weekend with Kimberly, filling her in on everything that had taken place with Grayson Hawthorn since I'd last spoken to her. At first she refused to speak to me, and then she ranted and raved for fifteen minutes—breaking into frequent bouts of Spanish—while I sat before her on the couch with my arms crossed like a child being disciplined. She'd brought up at least twenty examples of Very Bad Ideas that had ended terribly. When she'd finally calmed down enough to discuss the matter with me though and when she realized I wasn't going to back down, she'd taken me in her arms and offered me her support. That was generally the way of things with Kimberly. I knew enough to wait her out. And she knew enough to know that once I'd committed to a Very Bad Idea, it was unlikely I'd change my mind. Still, I knew that ranting at me made her feel like she'd done her duty, so I took it in stride. At its core, it was filled with love. I had missed her so much while I was away. She had always been a balm to my soul, the one who kept me sane.

I'd also made a quick visit to the drop-in center, where I'd spent so many hours. I assured them I had a large donation coming their way, one that would allow them to make it through the next six months until one of their larger grants kicked in.

I had wished I could stay a little longer, visiting with the people there I'd grown to love and hadn't seen in so long, but I assured them (and myself) I'd be back very soon.

Being away from the Dragon for a couple days had enabled me to put things in perspective. I was driving back with a renewed sense of surety. This plan was going to work. Everything had fallen into place and I tended to think that when that happened, you were on the right path. In a matter of days, we'd be married, have my gram's money, and I'd be on my way to being self-sufficient. I could decide what I wanted to do with the rest of my life. I wouldn't be under anyone's thumb. I would finally be *free*.

Surprisingly, I'd missed my little cottage. After opening the windows and putting my suitcase down at the end of the bed, I fell onto the mattress and smiled up at the stained, peeling ceiling, twirling a piece of my hair and humming loudly the song that had been on the radio in my car a few minutes ago. Outside the window, I heard the distant sound of a vehicle, most likely a tractor, and the shrill chatter of the birds that filled the trees. I'd find a little place similar to this somewhere in Napa Valley when I moved out. Somewhere simple. Somewhere I could be myself. Somewhere I might find happiness. Sighing, I sat up, slipped out of my clothes, and unpacked the new, fluffy towels I'd purchased in San

Francisco. After rooting around in my luggage for my toiletries, I turned toward the shower.

A man was standing in the doorway.

I startled so abruptly that my toiletries went flying out of my hands and I screamed, a piercing, horror-stricken sound.

"Whoa, whoa," Grayson said, moving toward me, his hands up in an *I surrender* pose, meant to calm me, I supposed. His eyes were wide with surprise, and I couldn't help notice that they swept down my body.

"Oh my GOD!" I shrieked, realizing I was as naked as a jaybird. I looked around wildly for something to hide my nakedness, grabbing the shirt at the top of my open suitcase and attempting to cover as much of myself as possible. At practically the same moment, Grayson whirled around and went stalking out the door.

I sagged against the end of the bed, my face hot, my legs shaking. "Don't you *knock*?" I yelled.

"You don't have anything I haven't seen before," I heard said loudly outside my open window as he walked away from my cottage.

I might have growled.

Thoroughly humiliated, I got in the shower, still grumbling angrily about rude, disrespectful stalkers. *Nothing he hadn't seen before.* Ugh!

After scrubbing myself just a bit too harshly—if my stinging skin was any indication—I pulled on clothes, put my hair up in a wet bun, and went marching up to the main house.

Charlotte greeted me kindly when I met her in the kitchen. "Is Grayson around?" I asked, trying to keep the brittleness out of my voice.

"He—"

"I'm right here" came his voice from behind me.

I whirled around, shooting daggers at him. "May I speak with you privately?" I said with fake sweetness.

He narrowed his eyes and didn't move, apparently ignoring my request or just not caring if Charlotte overheard us. What did it matter? She'd heard us fight before. I crossed my arms. "You can't just flounce into someone's personal habitation without knocking!" I said, my words tumbling out in exasperated anger.

"I did knock," he said, his tone bored, causing me to seethe even more. "And I've never flounced in my life." He turned toward Charlotte. "Charlotte, have you ever seen me flounce?"

"No, it's true," she said, wrinkling her brow. "You're not a man inclined to flounce."

I sputtered in frustration. "Flounce, prance, *intrude*!"

"*Prance?*" Grayson asked incredulously. "I've *definitely* never pranced. Ever. Charlotte?"

Charlotte shook her head. "No, no prancing." She put one finger up, turning her attention to me. "I did see him skip once. But he was still just a wee lad…"

I threw my arms up in the air in irritation, trying my best to ignore Grayson's mocking—and Charlotte's *support* of his mocking—and stick to the subject at hand. "You didn't knock! Or if you did, I didn't grant you permission to enter. I wouldn't have, seeing as I was *naked*!" Was that a faint pink color tingeing his cheekbones?

Charlotte coughed. "Oh *my*" I heard her breathe.

"Yes, well, it all happened very fast. I barely saw anything. I've already wiped the vision from my mind. Cross my heart." He said it as if it'd been a particularly distasteful vision.

"*If* you have a heart, which is debatable." I gritted my teeth.

"It was an accident, Kira. I apologize. I have no interest in seeing you naked, I promise. It won't happen again." He rubbed a finger beneath his eye as if smoothing away a twitch, his tone bored once again.

I stood up straight, raising my chin. Why was I bothered by his attitude at having seen me naked? What did I want, for Grayson to have stood with his tongue lolling out of his mouth at my mouthwatering sexiness? I knew I was far from mouthwateringly sexy. Cooper had taught me that lesson. I crossed my arms across my chest, hugging myself, feeling the fire burn out of my anger. I took a deep breath. "Well, fine, what did you need anyway?"

Grayson paused a moment, studying me. "I saw your car pull in. I was just coming to tell you that our prenuptial agreement will be ready on Wednesday. I moved our appointment to get married to Thursday." He paused. "As long as that's okay with you."

"Oh, um, yes. That's fine." My heart started beating faster. "Okay."

He kept watching me but didn't say anything.

"Well then, it's a plan," I mumbled. "I'm going to drive into town for dinner tonight. I'll see you tomorrow." He kept looking at me suspiciously, not saying a word. I turned and walked quickly out of the house, practically running back to my cottage once I closed the front door behind me.

———

Grayson and I avoided each other for the next two days. Or at least I thought it was mutual. I saw him a few times in passing, but other than that, I spent the time mostly alone. I took long walks around Napa, including the Hawthorn property, read, helped Charlotte with a few meals—meals

Grayson didn't show up for. But I loved chatting with Charlotte. She was so very easy to get along with and had the same kind, open spirit that my gram had had. Even though I barely knew her, it was as if she filled the void created when Gram passed away—a grandmotherly figure that I'd missed so much in my life.

My father's number had appeared on my phone a couple times, but I didn't answer. Finally, though, I sent him a text telling him I was taking some time for myself and I'd call him soon. I didn't receive a reply.

At eleven on Wednesday, Grayson and I met outside the main house, then drove into town to the appointment with the lawyer he'd hired. We'd waived having separate lawyers to save both time and money. Neither of us spoke on the way there. Ever since the naked incident, there'd been a strange tension between us. I couldn't figure out if it was anger or awkwardness—perhaps a little bit of both? For my part, I definitely felt angry and awkward. Why *he* should feel angry, I had no idea, but he seemed to. Perhaps I just didn't know him well enough to read him. And, I reminded myself, I never would.

We parked and when we realized we'd arrived a little early, I asked if he'd mind if I went inside a small wine shop on the same street. I wanted to buy a little something for Charlotte, who had so kindly gone out of her way to include me in Grayson's home—far beyond her role as a housekeeper merely doing her job. I wanted to let her know I appreciated it, especially under the circumstances.

Once inside, Grayson started looking over the wine selections at the front, and I headed toward the back of the store, where wine openers and other kitchen items were kept. As I perused some pretty cheese trays in one of the aisles, I overheard a woman say in a loud whisper, "Did you see Grayson Hawthorn at the front of the store? God, I used to have the biggest crush on him."

I stiffened slightly as another woman giggled. "Who didn't? Go talk to him. I mean, you couldn't take him home to Mama now, but for a one-night fling, hot damn, I'd *pay* to experience that."

"Maybe I will. He's so hot. Have you gotten a good look at his ass?" The other woman giggled and when I heard them walking toward me, my pulse skyrocketed, and I hightailed it in the other direction, grabbing Grayson's arm as I walked quickly toward the door.

"Whoa," he said, keeping pace with me.

"They didn't have what I was looking for," I explained, not even understanding exactly why I felt so flustered other than I had no interest in hearing about the opinions on Grayson's ass.

"What were you looking for?"

"Uh, a cheese tray or a cake stand or something, I don't know," I hedged.

"They had all that back there."

"Look," I said, adjusting the strap of my purse and slowing to a normal paced walk. "I heard some women discussing you, and I felt like I was eavesdropping." I paused. "It's just... just that it was weird and uncomfortable."

Grayson looked at me, and when I turned my head, he raised one brow. "Discussing me?"

I huffed out a breath. "I'm sure you're aware that women find you...appealing for some unknown reason."

"Appealing?"

"Hot, panty-melting," I elaborated. "They think your ass is..." I waved my hand around, forcing myself to stop babbling.

Grayson stopped, and I did as well, turning to face him. The look on his face was filled with amusement. "No, please continue. I'm enjoying this discussion."

I snorted and walked away. He caught up, turning around so that he was walking backward in front of me, his expression disgustingly smug. "Wait, were you uncomfortable because…*you* find me…appealing, little witch?"

You don't have anything I haven't seen before.

"No," I said, possibly a bit more sharply than intended. "Not in the least. Here we are." I moved around him and walked through the door of the lawyer's office, Grayson's annoying chuckle following me inside.

Scaly, winged creature.

The paperwork was straightforward and easy enough to understand. I ignored Grayson entirely while we signed it, although I still felt vaguely annoyed by his teasing outside. Mostly because it was true: I found him physically appealing, while he'd made it very clear I *wasn't his type.* We both perused the paperwork carefully though, and signed our names, taking a copy with us. And it was done. The only thing left to do was to get married. *Married*. To a dragon. A completely annoying dragon. For money. I groaned internally. This was, by far, the craziest scheme I'd ever concocted.

Cons: Crazy, ridiculous, probably shameful…*definitely* shameful. Disrespectful to the sanctity of marriage. Disrespectful to my grandmother. Those were a lot of cons. But…but it was going to work. I'd be free of my father. *Focus, Kira. Focus on that.* It was an incredibly weighty pro.

I'd made a list about the Dragon the night before, after he'd come into the kitchen to eat dinner, had seen me sitting at the table, and had promptly informed Charlotte he'd be eating in town. I had been avoiding him too, so why that had stung, I wasn't sure. The list had been made out of hurt pride, but it had helped, and the one I'd just made about our sham of a marriage helped too. At least a little.

"Our appointment is for two thirty tomorrow afternoon. Appointments, that is. We have one to get the license and one directly afterward to tie the knot."

I nodded vigorously, as if this was all just fine and dandy. *Married!* Tomorrow. Two thirty. *Tying the knot!* That made it sound so casual. No big deal. Just tying the knot—if you tie it loosely enough, a knot can be untied just as easily. I had the sudden desire to laugh crazily, perhaps until I cried. Grayson's mood seemed different too—more subdued.

"Are you going to tell your father before or after?" he asked.

"After. Once we've cashed the trust check." My skin prickled at the mere thought of confronting my father.

I saw Grayson nod from my peripheral vision but didn't look over at him. He seemed to be studying me. "If you... want to back out, I—"

I shook my head. We'd come too far. "No. I don't." I met his eyes. "Do you?"

"No."

He drove us straight back to the house, and I followed him inside, planning on getting something to eat. In the dimness of the foyer, I removed my sunglasses and stuffed them in my overfilled purse, pushing them toward the bottom, where they were less likely to fall out.

"I'll meet you here at two o'clock tomorrow then," Grayson said, obviously intending on getting to work for the day, doing whatever it was he did down at the stone building.

"Okay," I agreed, trying to sound nonchalant.

"Oh, here. You dropped this." Grayson bent and picked up a piece of paper and began handing it to me.

I frowned at it. "I don't think that's—" And then I realized what it was by the color of the paper. It was the list I'd made about Grayson. The one I'd also scrawled "Kira Hawthorn" on several times in the margins, testing out my new signature. It must have fallen out of my purse. I felt heat rising in my face, and I grabbed for it. Grayson, eyeing me suspiciously, pulled the paper back. "Don't you dare," I breathed.

He looked down at the paper in his hand and back at me, obviously more interested now that I was making such a big deal over it. *Stupid, Kira!* It had just happened so quickly, and I hadn't had time to mask my reaction.

"What do we have here?" Grayson asked.

"It's personal," I said. "Give it back."

"Personal? We're about to be married. We shouldn't have any secrets between us," he said, his tone dripping with sarcasm.

"Very funny. Let me have it."

He unfolded half of it as I lunged. He sideswiped me gracefully, grinning as I let out a squeak and almost fell on the ground. He turned and walked briskly to the large living room to the right of the foyer. "I think I'll pull up a reading chair and see what this is all about."

"Give it back!" I yelled, sounding like a petulant child. He unfolded it the rest of the way as I ran behind him.

"The Dragon, AKA Grayson Hawthorn: Pros and Cons," he read aloud. He looked back over his shoulder at me, raising one dark eyebrow, and then stepped behind the large, leather sectional and turned to face me. I tripped over the matching ottoman, almost falling again.

"Don't," I warned, trying to put all my much-deserved wrath into that one word.

He tilted his head, obviously reading my scrawled signature. "I'd really prefer it if you kept your maiden name," he said. *Ouch.*

"Yes, well, of course." My face was throbbing with heat. "Give it to me." He didn't.

"Pro: He's an ass, but his actual ass is easy on the eyes." He lowered the paper and looked at me over it. "So you do like my ass, little witch. You should have told me. I warned you not to develop feelings for me. But I suppose it's okay to admire my ass, if you *do* in fact find me...*appealing.*" He smirked. "You're only human after all," he said, scratching his chin as if in thought. "Are witches human? Hmm..." He looked back to the paper.

"You..." I halted, unable to think of how to finish that sentence, flailing my arms in utter helplessness, seething with rage. He seemed to *enjoy* deliberately arousing my anger. I wanted to wipe the arrogant look off his stupid, handsome features.

"Con: He's a pompous dragon," Grayson read calmly.

"Proven fact," I growled.

"Pro: He needs me." Grayson's eyes darted to mine, darkening. "Correction, I need your *money.*"

Well, he wouldn't get it now! He had crossed the line. I'd never give this dragon a damned thing. I looked around the room wildly for something to wound him with, spotting a bottle of wine sitting far back on a buffet next to a door that presumably led to a cellar. I ran over to it, grabbed it, and went to throw it at him.

"No!" he yelled, a note of panic in his voice that stopped me in my tracks. "Kira." He dropped the list and put his hands up in a pose of surrender. "That bottle of wine is irreplaceable." He bent slowly to pick up my list and rose just as slowly, holding it out to me. "Trade," he said, moving cautiously in my direction as if I were an untamed animal.

I looked down at the bottle in my hands. Something French. When I looked back up at Grayson, his face was white. "This one?" I asked innocently, switching it to my other hand with a little toss. A choked sound came from his throat. "This one right here? Irreplaceable?" Surely he was exaggerating. Otherwise, why would it be sitting out on a buffet in the living room? Still, it obviously meant a lot to him. He went to move toward me again.

"Stop where you are," I commanded. He did. I raised my chin. "Apologize to me for your extreme rudeness and…" I waved the bottle of wine around, trying to come up with the words for what he'd done to me and my pride.

That same choked sound came out of Grayson's throat, his eyes tracking the bottle. "Yes, yes, I apologize. I was just having some fun with you. I didn't mean any harm. I swear it. Come here and give me the bottle of wine, Kira."

I tilted my chin. "No."

He blinked. "No?"

"I won't come to you. You come to me."

Something flashed in his eyes, but he carefully checked his expression as his gaze landed on the bottle in my hands again. "Meet me in the middle."

I thought about challenging that. After all, I was the one clearly in control now, but I decided the middle was adequate. "Okay. Quick swap."

He nodded once and I went to move toward him but stopped. *Hmm.* I'd enjoy seeing that look of helpless panic in his eyes and hearing that odd choking sound come from his throat one last time. Intending on passing the bottle from my left hand to my right, I swung my left arm out in a wide arc and reached forward with my right to grab it, keeping eye contact with the Dragon, a small smirk on my lips. The sound of shattering glass rang out loudly in the silent room and I froze, sucking in a breath, time seeming to slow as I looked to my left where I had forgotten stood a large stone pillar. I'd raised my arm and smashed it right into the unforgiving rock. I swallowed thickly, watching what looked like blood drip down the stone into a growing puddle on the floor.

A gasping sound came from the doorway and I whipped my head in the direction of the small noise. Walter stood there, his mouth hung open, his complexion a ghastly white. "I had just gone to get the key to the wine cellar," he said, his voice a choked whisper. "I'm sorry, sir."

Oh God. I looked down to the broken neck of the bottle in my hand and then slowly, very slowly up at Grayson. He was seething with what looked to be barely controlled fury. "It wasn't your fault, Walter. You may go," he said, his voice full of deadly calm.

There was a pause. "Yes, sir," I heard Walter say before he quickly walked away.

I blinked, my hand letting go of the broken bottleneck as it, too, shattered on the floor. I stood glued to the spot as Grayson slowly made his way to me. I could practically feel the fiery rage emanating from him. When he got to me, he moved in close, taking his fingers and tilting my chin up to him. A muscle twitched in his jaw. I stood straighter, meeting his eyes. "That bottle of wine," Grayson gritted out, "was my father's pride and joy. He spent years trying to obtain it. When he finally did, he wept. He *wept*, Kira. Tears of joy over that bottle you just smashed out of spite."

I shook my head, trying desperately not to flinch. "It was an accident. It was just…sitting there…" I hated the catch in my voice as my words faded away.

He let go of my chin, his midnight eyes still staring down at me intently. "Two o'clock," he said finally. "Meet me here tomorrow at two o'clock."

Two o'clock? What was two o'clock? I couldn't remember. Oh God, we were getting married. I almost told him it was off. I opened my mouth to say the words, but they didn't come out. Clearly he was going through with it now to punish me—or at the very least to recoup the cost of that "irreplaceable" bottle of wine.

Grayson went striding out of the living room. I stood there for a few minutes, finally walking on wobbly legs over to where he'd dropped my childish list. I picked it up and walked to the kitchen where Charlotte was wiping down the counter, the sweet smell of cinnamon and apples filling the air. She glanced at me with a clearly nervous look. "He's not a bad man, Kira."

I swallowed. "I…" I shook my head, beginning again. "I'm sure he's not always, but I have a way of…bringing out the very worst in men."

"I'm sure that's not true."

I shrugged. It really was. It really, really was. Bile rose in my throat. I thought I might be sick, but I managed to swallow it down.

"And perhaps it's more them than you, my dear. Perhaps it will take a very special man to, um…"

"Handle me?" I laughed, a small sound that held little amusement.

"Love you," she corrected. I wasn't sure I should take that as a compliment, except for the fact that Charlotte was smiling warmly at me.

Love. Fierce longing rose in my chest. For just once to be cherished. I sighed. "In any case, my arrangement with Grayson has nothing to do with love. And it doesn't matter anyway. I won't follow through. It was a terrible idea from the very beginning." I turned to Charlotte who was watching her hand move the dishcloth over the counters, a thoughtful look on her face. "That wine, Charlotte, was it really irreplaceable? Did his father really search for it for years?" I fought the urge to cry.

Charlotte was quiet for a moment before she put the dishcloth over the edge of the sink and came around the counter to sit next to me. She took my hands in hers, a look of sympathy in her eyes. "He'll likely never tell you himself and so I'm going to let you in on something about Grayson and his father, Kira. I don't like to gossip, but maybe knowing some of Grayson's background will help you understand why he's so hell-bent on bringing this bloody winery back." She pursed her lips for a second but then her expression cleared. *Bloody winery?* This was her home too. Didn't she love it here?

"Grayson and his father, Ford Hawthorn, did not have a good relationship." She shook her head sadly. "The reasons were many and perhaps Grayson will share those with you someday, but suffice it to say he was never made to feel like he belonged in this home—either by his father or his stepmother. They...misguidedly blamed him for things a child should never be blamed for. They treated him wretchedly—excluded him, each trying to convince the other they hated him more." A look of raw sadness filled her expression. "Grayson tried so hard. All his life, he… Well, it didn't matter. Nothing he did was deemed good enough." She shook her head. "Later, after he got arrested…" She grabbed a tissue off the counter and dabbed at her nose. "His father never visited him, not even once. Ford was diagnosed with cancer while Grayson was away, and he perished quickly. Or at least it seemed that way. When Grayson returned home, he found out his father had left this vineyard to him, a business that had begun failing as soon as Ford found out he was ill. He left the money to his wife and Grayson's brother, Shane, but he bequeathed the vineyard to Grayson." Something went skittering across her features, but it was gone before I could try to read it. "Grayson vowed that day he would bring the vineyard back, not for himself, but for the father who had shunned him his whole life and, in the end, given him this property as a final peace offering. Grayson felt Ford had entrusted him with his most beloved possession because he'd finally believed him worthy. Worthy of reviving it, worthy of running it. And Grayson will do practically anything to prove his father wasn't mistaken in that belief."

I sagged back on the barstool. That was a lot. "Even though his father treated him so terribly before that?"

Charlotte nodded. "I believe *because* his father treated him so terribly before that. To Grayson, redeeming this vineyard means redeeming his own value."

I nodded slowly, biting my lip, thinking about how much Grayson Hawthorn and I had in common. Both raised by fathers who never thought we were enough.

"Thank you, Charlotte. I understand him a little better now. And I can relate." I pressed my lips together in thought. "I'd even think maybe we could be friends except that…he

100

thinks I'm a witch, and I'm still pretty sure he's a dragon. At least when it comes to me."

She laughed merrily, apparently finding that amusing.

"Why did you tell me all that, Charlotte?" I asked, tilting my head in question.

"I think you can see people in a different light when you understand their motivations. And perhaps you think you bring out the worst in Grayson, but since you came into his life, even though it's been such a short time, he's been more alive than in the entire year he's been home…even if that's translated into lots of fire breathing. I believe that's a *good* thing. Grayson can be arrogant—due to his looks largely. But inside, his hurt runs very deep." She looked sad for a moment but then smiled at me. I couldn't help smiling back. There was something so wonderfully comforting about Charlotte. "Here, let me cut you a big slice of cinnamon apple cake straight from the oven," she said as she stood.

"And by the way, my dear," Charlotte said, resting her hand on mine on the counter, a glint in her eyes, "forget the prince and princess. I always imagined the most interesting story was between the witch and the dragon." Her musical laughter rang through the kitchen.

CHAPTER EIGHT
Kira

I hadn't envisioned my wedding day quite like this. I'd awoken alone, taken an icy shower, and then quickly left the Hawthorn property for downtown Napa to buy something to wear. But once I'd started browsing in a few shops, I'd realized how ridiculous it was. Why did I need a new outfit? And what *did* one wear to say false wedding vows to the man they were marrying for money? The man who most likely hated me after what had happened the day before.

I pulled in a deep breath. Still, I was going to go through with it. I'd made up my mind as I lay in bed the night before, thinking about my own reasons for needing the money Gram had left me and thinking about Grayson's reasons as well. After what Charlotte had shared, I couldn't help feeling like we had even more in common than either of us understood. And perhaps we'd never know the full extent, but somewhere deep down, I felt an inexplicable peace about sharing the money with him, dragon or not.

I finally picked out a semicasual, white lace sundress and

a pair of silvery-blue strappy sandals. It wasn't fancy, but at least it would appear that I'd put some effort into looking like a bride to the people at the clerk's office. *It's all about the show*, I thought sadly.

As I drove back to Hawthorn Vineyard, a memory suddenly came into my mind. When I was seven or eight, I'd found my gram's collection of catalogues and old magazines. One of them had bridal gowns in it so I'd cut out all my choices for an entire wedding party and glued them to a piece of cardboard. I'd spent hours going through each book, picking out flowers and cakes and whatever else I could find that added to my vision. When I'd proudly shown my gram, she had gushed over it, of course, as my gram tended to do, but then she'd asked me why there was no father of the bride. "Oh," I'd said, "he was working. He couldn't make it." My gram had looked at me so sadly and then hugged me tightly. "You are going to be the most beautiful bride, my love," she'd said, "and your groom is going to love you to pieces."

I felt a lump form in my chest. "Oh, Gram, I'm so sorry about this," I whispered into the silence of my car, feeling like even though she was gone, I was somehow disappointing her.

Just as I was finishing getting dressed, I heard a soft knock on my cottage door and startled slightly, wondering if Grayson had come to get me rather than meeting at the house where we'd planned. Or maybe he was coming to call it off? My heart took up an erratic beat as I called, "Come in."

A moment later I heard Charlotte's singsong greeting and I relaxed my shoulders. She smiled as she entered my room. "Oh my, you look lovely, dear."

I gave her a small smile, fidgeting slightly. I hardly wanted her to make this seem as if it were in any way a *real* wedding day. It would only add to my shame.

"I brought you a little something for good luck," she said, holding open her palm to show a small silver and crystal pin in the shape of a rose.

"Oh, no, Charlotte. I couldn't. This marriage doesn't require any luck. We already set it up to fail," I said, my cheeks heating.

"Well, then, it's good luck for *you*," she said. "Please, let me. My mother gave this to me on my wedding day and I don't have a daughter to give it to, nor will I have any granddaughters. It would mean the world to me if you would accept it."

"I really couldn't," I squeaked, trying not to tear up.

"How about just for today?" She smiled hopefully. "You can give it back if you want." She clapped her hands. "Oh, that works too. Something borrowed."

I let out a breath. "Okay. Only if you'll let me return it."

"Here," she said, leaning in and pinning it to the bodice of my dress. She leaned away and smiled gently. "Lovely."

Not able to help it, I threw my arms around Charlotte, inhaling the calming scent of talcum powder. She laughed softly and hugged me back. "Now then," she said gently.

At two o'clock I walked up to the main house where Grayson was leaning casually against the stone front. He was wearing a pair of khakis and a blue button-down shirt. I tried not to note how strikingly handsome he was—it served no good purpose. When he heard me approaching, he looked up and I caught a brief flicker of surprise in his eyes, and then it was gone.

"Ready?" he said simply, making no comment about how I looked.

Neither of us spoke for the first five minutes of the ride in his truck. I finally turned to him and his gaze was on my bare legs. I crossed them and his eyes flew to mine. He clenched his jaw. Did he disapprove of my outfit for some reason?

"Grayson, I'm...I'm sorry about your father's bottle of wine."

His shoulders seemed to release just a bit as he stared out the front windshield. "It wasn't entirely your fault. You couldn't have known that such a valuable bottle of wine would be sitting in the living room. And I did push you to that point, I admit. I'm not innocent for teasing you about your...list. I'm sorry too."

I exhaled even as I felt my cheeks flush at the mention of my list. "We're even, then?"

He gave me a slight smile. "Even. Especially considering you're paying me back for it today." He turned his face to me and gave me a devilish smile that made my heart stutter in my chest. But then it gentled and I saw he was making a joke. "Ready to pledge forever? Or at least twelve months?" he asked, eyeing me sideways.

I gave a nervous laugh. "As ready as I'll ever be, I figure. This isn't exactly how I pictured my wedding day."

"No? Pictured the big white dress and all the crème de la crème of society in attendance?" His eyes lingered on me for a second.

It was true. When I'd been engaged to Cooper, that had been what I'd envisioned for my wedding, mostly because that was what my father and Cooper had planned. But that had never been *my* dream. I had just been trying so hard to please them both.

I smiled, but it felt sad on my own lips. "I suppose."

I wasn't going to go into all that with Grayson, especially not right now. His eyes searched my face for a few quick moments, but then he focused back on the road.

The mood between us was still slightly tense after that and neither of us spoke, each preoccupied with our own thoughts. Although Grayson had said I was forgiven about the wine, he still seemed a little tense, if the tick in his jaw each time he looked at me was any indication. Ah well, after today, we'd avoid each other. I'd offered my apologies and he'd accepted. If he still harbored a general hostility, it made no difference to me whatsoever. I bit down on my lip until it hurt, trying to distract myself from any thought at all. I didn't want to consider what I was really doing.

When we arrived at the Napa County Clerk's Office a few minutes later, the sky suddenly opened up and started pouring rain. Grayson chuckled. "The fates are against us."

I gave a small laugh too. "Apparently. Although I've heard that rain is good luck on a wedding day."

"Only people who get rain on their wedding day say that to make themselves feel lucky. We're going to have to make a run for it."

"Okay. On the count of three," I said, cracking the truck door. We both jumped out, me squealing as we ran for the building. He grabbed my hand halfway between the car and the office, and his deep laughter rose above the pounding sound of the downpour. For a blink of time, we were just a boy and a girl, running and laughing in the rain on our wedding day. The moment was sudden, dreamlike, but when we burst into the lobby, we both blinked at each other and I knew he'd felt it too. The spell ended abruptly as we looked around at people now watching us. There were two other couples obviously there to get married, both holding hands, both looking serene, *both* looking like it was the happiest day of their lives. It made me intensely aware of what we were about to do. By the look on Grayson's face, he was thinking the same thing.

"Ready?" he asked.

No, no, no. "Yes."

I walked through the next hour as if I existed outside my own body. I tried not to consider the reality of the situation. I pictured the faces of the people at the drop-in center, the small house I'd get settled in once I left Hawthorn Vineyard, anything to keep my focus on what this day was ultimately about. We obtained the marriage license and waited in line to say our vows. Grayson's expression was distant and slightly cold. I didn't ask what he was thinking though. My own emotions were difficult enough to manage, so I really didn't need to add his to the mix. He'd be no support to me—he wasn't even trying to make this easier. Although, really, what did I expect him to do? The lightness of the moment when we had been running in the rain was long gone, replaced now by silence and discomfort.

Finally, a court employee stood in as our witness, and I recited my vows and promised to love, honor, and cherish Grayson Hawthorn all the days of my life. I felt a snake of fear slither down my spine as I committed the sacrilege of pledging love and devotion to a man I had no intention of loving or devoting myself to. It was a lie, a farce of something sacred. I'd never been a particularly religious person, but I had to wonder if we'd both be punished somehow for this mockery.

He recited his vows to me, his voice steady, his manner removed. I watched him, my chest aching at the serious expression on his handsome face. When the marriage commissioner asked if we had rings to exchange, Grayson reached into his pocket and brought out a beautiful gold ring with an opal in the center surrounded by diamonds. I gasped as he slid it on my finger. I tried to catch his eye, but he looked at it for several seconds on my hand and then raised his eyes to the man performing our ceremony. I stared down at the beautiful, antique-looking piece of jewelry, a lump forming in my throat for his thoughtfulness at remembering to bring a ring. I hadn't even thought of it myself.

"You may kiss your bride."

Grayson leaned forward and gave me a quick peck on my mouth. At the feel of his lips brushing across mine, the hysteria I'd kept at bay since I'd woken that morning suddenly bubbled up my chest, and I snorted out a barely contained laugh. I pretended a small cough, my eyes widening at my body's betrayal. His kiss reminded me of one my old, crotchety uncle Colburn would give. Uncle Colburn smelled like mothballs. Hilarity and insanity warred inside for control. I let out another small snort and again tried to cover it with a cough.

Grayson's brows shot up and then his eyes narrowed, growing almost lazy as he stared me down, something tense and challenging in his expression as if he thought I had laughed solely to mock him and his dry, stuffy kiss. I swallowed, very suddenly serious. *What had come over me?* The stress of this had clearly cracked my brain right in half. He *should* kiss me like a dried-up, old uncle. This was a business deal.

Grayson stepped right into my space and took my face in his hands as I chirped out what sounded like a surprised little cheep. He pressed his lips to mine, sweeping his tongue over the seam of my mouth. I had no time to think and my body responded to him instinctually, as I parted my lips eagerly to take his tongue, melting against him. The kiss showed no mercy, his tongue plundering my mouth and making my knees weak as I clung to his shoulders. Just as suddenly as he'd initiated it, he pulled away, our mouths coming apart with a wet pop as I stumbled forward, catching myself before I fell into him.

The marriage commissioner grinned. "Well now!"

Well now, indeed.

I tried to regain my composure, using my thumb to wipe the saliva from below my bottom lip, as the final words were said. "By the authority vested in me, I now pronounce you husband and wife."

And it was done. We were officially Mr. and Mrs. Grayson Hawthorn. Forever and ever. Amen.

Or at least for the next year or so. Which probably didn't deserve an amen.

I walked with Grayson back to his truck on legs that felt strangely numb, still reeling slightly from his kiss, feeling a measure of humiliation. Still, he *had* done something thoughtful. "Thank you for remembering a ring," I said softly. "I didn't even think to get one for you. Where did you get this on such short notice?"

"It was still in the house. I just hadn't gotten around to selling it." I looked down at it, figuring he had the tight look on his face because it had been a piece of his stepmother's jewelry. Well, it would serve to make our union look legitimate to the outside world, so what did I care where it'd come from? "I'll give it back when, um—"

"Okay" was his terse reply.

"Okay," I said, deciding not to mention the kiss at all, or the fact that I'd laughed at his first one. Now that my mind was clearer, I realized he'd likely done it for no other reason than to make our ceremony look convincing. After a moment of silence, I asked, "So, do you want to, um, go to a late lunch or something?" I had no idea of the protocol for this day.

This is my wedding day. Oh God...

Only, not really. I wouldn't consider this my wedding day. Someday I'd have a real one and it would be the polar opposite of this one. "Can't. I have to get back to work," Grayson said, not looking at me.

All right, then. "Dinner tonight maybe? We should at least celebrate the windfall we're about to get." I gave him a smile that felt less cheerful than intended.

"Kira..." He sighed, running one hand through his hair as if my conversation and then asking him to go to dinner was a grave annoyance. Did he think this meant I suddenly expected a relationship with him now that I was his wife, had received an obligatory kiss, and wore a bauble he'd found lying around some dusty corner of his house? Anger, and a hurt I didn't really want to look at, burned within me.

"Never mind," I said. "I just remembered I have plans anyway."

He looked at me as if he knew very well I was lying. "Maybe another time, okay? I'm having an issue with a piece of equipment. Taking these few hours today has already put me behind."

I had just thrown the sanctity of marriage off a cliff, and he could barely manage to be cordial? I didn't expect his thanks, but I also didn't expect to feel like I was an inconvenience to his day. I swallowed back my disappointment because it was obviously wasted on the arrogant dragon. "Of course. I understand," I lied.

When we pulled up to his home, I hopped out, calling, "I should have the check within a week or so. I'll drop by with your share." I wouldn't look back.

I looked back. Grayson was standing at the side of his truck with his hands in his pockets watching me walk away. As I began walking through the brush to my cottage, I raised my chin and flipped my hair. And then felt a sharp branch as it jabbed my thigh, tearing a large rip in my dress. I let out a small yelp. *Damn.* I raised my chin higher and kept walking. I heard his low chuckle from far behind me and resisted the urge to turn around, run back, and claw his reptilian eyes out. Instead, I slammed the door to my cottage when I got inside, but the old door didn't fit exactly right on the hinges and gave a very unsatisfying click as it weakly met the doorframe.

This was the most pitiful wedding day that had ever existed. *What did you expect? You did this.*

I removed the opal ring, which was really nothing more than a prop, and set it on the windowsill. I also removed the pin Charlotte had given me so I wouldn't forget to return it. Then I sat down on my bed, toying absently with the torn piece of material on my dress, finally giving in to the tears I'd felt burning behind my eyes all morning.

Exhausted and emotionally drained after the events of the day, and because I hadn't slept well the previous night as I'd tossed and turned and reevaluated my decision, I took a long nap. My dreams were filled first with a vast landscape of ice. I wandered aimlessly, crying out with the cold, shivering violently as I tried in vain to warm myself. Suddenly, I was in the midst of cascading fire, caught in a waterfall of lava, my body liquid, my skin raging with a heat that felt deliciously erotic. Flames consumed me, and yet somehow, I wasn't being burned. I woke up moaning, my breasts tingling, and wet and throbbing between my legs. I collapsed back on my pillows. I'd never had a sexual dream quite that intense before. I guess it went to show how long it'd been. My hands went to my aching breasts as I heard a car purr to a stop and then a door slam outside. *That definitely isn't Grayson's rattly truck.* I sat up quickly, running to the window. *Then who is it?* Not my father—there was no way for him to have found out about my marriage. *Right?* Or did he have minions in every court system in the country? I would hardly doubt it if he did. No, no, I reassured myself. Despite his intrusion in my life, he had bigger fish to fry than me. Still, adrenaline flooded my system and my heart leapt with panic, cooling my heated blood at least a few degrees. I smoothed my hands over my torn and wrinkled dress, taking a deep, calming breath. He couldn't do anything to me anyway. I'd tell him I was married—that was that and to leave me alone.

I walked the few strides through the brush, and when I came out on the driveway, I saw a blond woman talking to Grayson in front of a small red sports car. They both turned, obviously having heard me, and so I didn't turn back as I had first intended upon spotting them. Instead, I walked to where they stood. As she watched me approach, the woman had a look on her face as if she'd just tasted something sour.

I held out my hand when I got to them. "Hi, I'm Kira."

The woman looked down at my hand as if I were offering her a dead fish but finally grasped the tips of my fingers and shook it weakly. *Okay.* "I'm Jade. I stopped by to see if I could cook dinner for Grayson tonight at my place." She looked sweetly at him, batting her false eyelashes. A heavy aroma of artificial peaches hung on her, but I couldn't deny she was pretty. If you liked that type. Which Grayson obviously did.

I glanced at him and found him looking me over with an expression that seemed intense and…angry? *What did I do now?* His mood swings would eventually give me whiplash.

I shifted on my feet, realizing how terrible I must look. I could feel that my face was still flushed from my dream and knew my hair must be in wild disarray as it always was after I'd slept. My dress was ripped and wrinkled and disheveled and…I was the exact opposite of this coiffed beauty standing in front of me. I ran my tongue along my bottom lip nervously, feeling insecure and hating it.

I waited for him to tell this woman I was his wife.

Grayson looked back to Jade. "Sure, that sounds good."

I felt my eyes widen and I let out a tiny gasp. He was going to take *Jade* up on her offer to cook him dinner after he'd turned *me* down for dinner on our wedding day? What if someone saw them? What if Jade had a big mouth and spread the word that she was dating Grayson? My heart pounded and my skin felt suddenly itchy.

My husband was going on a date on our wedding day. *My husband was going on a date on our wedding day.* I had the sudden, intense desire to double over with laughter.

Only you, Kira. Only you would be in a situation like this.

"Just give me two minutes to clean up," Grayson said to Jade.

"Sure thing, babe." She smiled sweetly at him. *Babe.* This woman had just called my fake husband *babe.* "You can shower at my place if you want." Her lips turned up in the form of a smile, but her eyes shot daggers at me.

Grayson walked into the house, and Jade and I stood

staring at each other. "So who are you exactly, Kira?" Jade asked.

Why, I'm his wife, peaches. I hope you have a lovely evening on your date. It took everything in me not to say that. I had agreed we should carry on as usual as long as we were discreet, although I hardly thought this qualified. Still, it was up to Grayson to handle this situation with Jade. I hadn't actually done any secretarial or accounting work for Grayson yet, but I suddenly remembered I had offered to. "I'm, um, his new secretary slash accountant slash…well." I'd let that *well* sum up the other stuff. Little did she know, it was a mighty big *well*.

She narrowed her eyes at me, glancing down at my bare feet and then behind me from the direction I'd walked. "Do you…live here?"

We both looked up to see Grayson trotting back down the stairs. He barely had enough time to wash his hands and splash some cold water on his face. Apparently he either didn't care that Jade would enjoy him in all his sweaty glory or he planned on taking her up on her offer to shower at her place. A flash of her in the kitchen cooking him dinner as he came up behind her in a small towel to kiss the back of her neck suddenly came to mind. And why oh *why* did that vision bother me so much?

Idiot, Kira!

"Ready?" Grayson asked Jade.

"Mmhmm," she said. "Kira here was just telling me she's your new secretary slash accountant slash…" We both stared at her, waiting for her to continue, and she stared at us, evidently waiting for one of us to say something too. She'd obviously picked up on the weightiness of that *well* and it'd bothered her.

Grayson cleared his throat. I coughed. Jade narrowed her eyes farther and stepped closer to Grayson, clearly staking her claim. "And you live here now?" she asked again.

"Yes. I'm staying over there." I waved my hand in the direction of the gardener's cottage. As if it were completely normal for secretaries to live in on-site, grimy tool storage sheds.

Jade wrinkled up her cute, little nose. "Eww! That ugly shack buried in the woods that you can barely see from the driveway? There must be rats in there." She appeared satisfied by the news, as though the knowledge of where I'd been placed spoke of Grayson's feelings for me. Which wasn't entirely untrue and was perhaps why it'd stung. I resisted gritting my teeth. And anyway, who said that about someone's...*home*? Temporary home, but still!

I widened my eyes and began speaking breathily. "Oh *yes*! There are. Snakes and spiders too," I said excitedly. "They're very shy though. The rats are the friendliest. In just a short time, I've grown close to a husband and wife named Ogilthorpe and Ortensia," I said, shooting a look at Grayson. He stared back at me blankly. I returned my gaze to Jade and carried on. "*And* I'm pretty sure Ortensia is pregnant!" I put one finger on my chin in thought. "I'll have to come up with some O names before the little rat babies arrive. If you have any good suggestions, let me know." I gave her a fake grin, resisting the urge to cross my eyes.

Her features screwed up in an expression of disgust, and Grayson turned slightly and coughed into his hand, but I swore I saw his lip twitch slightly before he covered his mouth.

"Let's go," Jade said to Grayson, ignoring me.

"I assume you'll find a way to entertain yourself tonight?" Grayson asked, raising his eyebrows.

"Oh, no doubt I will," I said, giving him a small, phony smile.

His eyes lingered on my face for the space of several heartbeats and then he turned away with Jade. When they reached her car, she turned to him and said loudly enough for me to hear, "I don't like her. She's weird."

If Grayson commented, he said it softly enough that I couldn't hear.

I watched as the car turned, drove down the driveway, and disappeared out of sight.

It was only a matter of time before my father knew this marriage was a total ruse. Not even one day had gone by and Grayson was going to ruin everything by going on a date. As I turned and marched back toward my *shack*, I made a concerted effort to control my rapid breathing.

If there were ever a day that had called for wine, and lots of it, this one did. And how lucky for me, I lived at a winery!

CHAPTER NINE
Grayson

"Thanks," I said, stepping out of Jade's car. She gave me a tight smile and waved, no doubt disappointed about where the night had gone, or *not gone* as the case was. I didn't generally go back for seconds, but I had had every intention of working off some steam in Jade's bed. However, once we'd eaten some dinner at her apartment and she'd pushed me down on her couch and started pawing at me, all I could think about was the fact that it was my wedding day. Which was so fucking annoying because it wasn't like my wedding day meant anything at all. But in the end, it just seemed in bad taste to sleep with one woman on the day I'd given my name—temporarily or not—to another. I wouldn't call it honor because, clearly, I didn't have a lot of that, but it just felt…distasteful, wrong. And so before she'd even kissed me, I'd asked her to drive me home.

My thoughts turned back to Kira for the hundredth time that night. Kira and those stupid O-named rats. It *was* weird, so why had it made me want to kiss her again? Kiss her *right*.

Kiss her long and hard as I wrapped that fiery hair around my fist? Something had clearly come between me and my good sense.

I watched Jade's car drive out of sight and stood in the driveway for another minute, considering my witchy, spirited, little wife. I had fully expected she wouldn't show up that morning, that she'd call off this fake marriage idea and move out after what had happened the day before with the list and the wine. And I couldn't decide if I wanted that or not. Clearly, we did not complement each other in any arrangement, business or otherwise. I had still been stewing about the wine, but if I really considered it, things had gone awry for me when I'd seen her naked. If I could erase the vision from my brain, I would because I hadn't been able to stop thinking about her since. Totally unwelcome…and yet utterly undeniable. When I'd walked into her cottage and seen her standing there completely nude, lust had gripped me so tightly, I'd almost grabbed the doorframe for support. For a moment, I'd been overcome by something strong enough to make me feel weak in the knees, my mind going suddenly and briefly blank. I'd never experienced anything quite like it before. I had to believe it was partly the shock of the situation that had stolen my breath right from my body, making me almost savage with want. I was picturing her now, my mind's eye conjuring up her smooth, supple skin; full, delectable breasts with rose-hued nipples; gently flaring hips; and legs that were long and shapely despite her smaller stature. She was slim, but her clothing hid just how luscious she was. But I knew now. And I wished I didn't. This did not bode well for the business relationship we had arranged. This did not bode well for my peace of mind. I had no desire to have lustful thoughts for my wife. Like the ones I'd had when she'd shown up in the driveway this afternoon, looking like she'd spent the day in bed having sex, her cheeks and lips flushed, her eyes bright, her nipples hard, and her hair tousled wildly. For a brief instant, I'd wondered if she *had* been having sex with someone in her cottage, and something that felt suspiciously like jealousy had made my stomach cramp. Then I'd wondered if she'd just been alone in that small bed, her hands on her own body... I knew the look of an aroused woman. It had made me crazy and frustrated enough to accept Jade's offer.

My body throbbed at the memory of naked Kira, and I swore under my breath at my own unwanted reaction to her. No, thinking about my wife that way made me decidedly grumpy and hostile. Today would have to be the only day off-limits as far as sleeping with other women, because there was *no* way I'd survive thinking about Kira the way I was. I'd need to distract myself with other willing bodies. And, I admitted, with more mindfulness than I'd almost shown tonight. Spending time with women who knew my name and where I lived wasn't exactly following the agreement Kira and I had made regarding conducting our personal lives with discretion. And now there was even more reason to get this part of our marriage over with so she would be out of my hair sooner rather than later.

Kira. Who was now my wife.

No, not for real. Shut up. Stop repeating that to yourself.

She'd been a little spitfire yesterday. This morning, she'd been quiet and subdued, *except* for the way she'd laughed at the chaste kiss I'd given her, heating my blood in front of God and our court-appointed witness, and challenging me—knowingly or not—to kiss her again in a way that was anything but platonic.

119

She had grown up in the very lap of luxury and yet she'd spent half a day (Charlotte had told me) scrubbing out what must have been a disgusting bathroom in that little cottage and was now living there. She was an enigma. I couldn't figure her out, and I didn't have the time or the inclination to try. And yet, for some reason, I had trouble resisting the allure of meeting the challenges she dished out, trouble resisting the desire to make that fire flash in her eyes. I already craved it. The way she looked when she flew into a rage—her cheeks flushed, her eyes smoldering and filled with indignation... She kept me constantly off balance, and for the life of me, I couldn't figure out why I liked it so much. That's why I'd teased her with that stupid list of hers, and things had gone downhill from there.

And now we were married. Till divorce do us part.

I turned to go back into the house when I heard what sounded like voices coming from...above me? I frowned, turning and squinting up at the dark sky. No, they were coming from farther over—right at the edge of Kira's cottage. I walked slowly in that direction, confused. "Hello?" I called. The voices stopped, although I thought I heard a small, muffled laugh.

"Who's there?" I called again, louder this time. No answer.

"Ouch!" I said as something small and hard hit my head and more muffled laughter came from above. I craned my neck. Someone, or a few someones, were up in the trees. Another acorn made contact with my skull and I grunted. *What the hell?* "Who's up there?" I repeated angrily. "Come down now before I call the police." There was a silent moment and then I heard what sounded like someone climbing down. A pair of beefy, jean-clad legs appeared first and then Virgil's head came into sight. He hopped down, his head bent as he looked at me nervously.

"What are you doing up in my trees?" I asked incredulously.

"I, um, well, sir, we wanted to see if we could catch a few wishing stars, see… Kira and me, we thought…"

"Kira?" I asked, just as another pair of legs appeared, these slim and shapely. Kira landed on her feet in front of me, leaves stuck to her clothing and that damn silky hair falling in disarray around her face. Just like earlier that evening, her cheeks were flushed and she was breathing hard. But this time, she smelled like alcohol. My new wife was climbing trees…*drunk*. I clenched my jaw. "So…you're insane," I declared.

"Well, hello, Husband," she slurred slightly. "How was your date?"

"My date… Kira, do you realize you could have broken your neck and Virgil's neck too for that matter? I suppose this was your idea."

Kira glanced at Virgil, who looked like he was a little boy who had just been sent to the principal's office.

"It was all my idea actually," Kira admitted, standing up straight and crossing her arms under her breasts. "Did you know that if you sit in a tree all day, you can watch people to your heart's content? No one *ever* looks up. It's the most interesting thing."

"Hmm. You have a lot of tree-climbing experience then?"

She tilted, and I righted her. "Quite a bit."

"And of course, there's the wishing-star thing."

"Well, yes, that. Might as well try, right? No one ever got anywhere by sitting in their cottage in the woods, drinking alone on their wedding night." She frowned, as if trying to recall something, perhaps whether the person she was describing was herself.

"In the future, will you please leave my employees out of stunts like this one? I would hate to have to call Virgil's mother and tell her that her son tumbled out of a tree."

"Oh, there wasn't any danger. I mean, very little. Haven't you ever climbed these trees? They're the *perfect* climbing trees. The"—she let out a little hiccup—"branches are so huge and strong and wide. You could sleep on one."

"You're drunk, Kira. If you had tried to sleep on a tree branch, I'd be scraping you off the ground tomorrow."

She laughed as if that was funny. "Seriously, though, surely you've climbed one of these trees?"

"No."

"No?" she whispered. "Why?" She looked at me so seriously, her expression as confounded as if I'd just admitted I'd never tried breathing air before.

Without answering, I turned to Virgil who was shifting back and forth on his feet. "You should go on back to your bunk, Virgil."

"Yes, sir," he muttered. He turned to Kira, his face lighting up as if she were the sun and he had just been looking into the darkness—me being the darkness in this particular circumstance. He gave her the most openly enamored smile I'd ever seen on a grown man and said shyly, "Good night, Miss Kira."

Kira shot him a grin and I startled slightly. There it was. That dimple I'd seen in the online photograph. *Virgil* got the dimple. I'd never gotten the dimple—not even once. And I probably never would, especially after tonight.

"*Mrs.* Kira," she corrected, winking.

Virgil gave me a look that I swore was suspicious even though I was the one who'd given him a damn job, and then nodded at Kira, smiling again as he turned and walked away. I faced the little witch. We stared at each other for a few moments. "My father never would have allowed it," I said. "Climbing trees."

She furrowed her brow as if trying to remember what we'd been talking about. Her eyes met mine, and although she was clearly inebriated, her expression gentled. "My father didn't allow it either."

"I take it you didn't listen?" I raised a brow.

She laughed softly and shook her head, looking suddenly sad in a way that made me want to reach out to her. But then she smiled and raised her gaze to the tree above. "I've never been very good at obedience. Or meekness. Or curbing my sharp tongue for that matter. I'd make a terrible wife." She swayed again very slightly and took a step toward me on a small laugh.

I couldn't help smiling back at her joke as I caught her by her upper arms.

Something suddenly seemed to occur to her. "Speaking of my father, I told you to be discreet about your personal life. *Discreet.*" She dragged out the word, leaning toward me. "It's very important."

I cleared my throat. "I thought you said you weren't overly worried about your father."

Her shoulders dropped. "I'm always worried about my father," she whispered, looking somewhere off in the distance. Her eyes focused on me again and she stood up straighter. "I just don't want to invite trouble."

"Noted" was all I gave her as she swayed again. "Okay, little witch, let's get you back to your cottage in the woods." I almost offered one of the guest rooms in the house again, but she had turned me down before, and frankly, I thought it better that there was distance between us—for a whole slew of reasons I didn't much want to contemplate any more than I already had.

When we made it to the door of her cottage, she turned to me, her eyes bleary, her cheeks flushed. She tilted her head, and as the leaves of the trees overhead blew in the wind, a shaft of moonbeam hit her face, lighting it just enough that her green eyes shone like emeralds. Her hair, perhaps put up in a twist earlier tonight, had slipped almost completely loose and as usual, silky tendrils framed her face. Her lips curved up just the slightest bit, and I felt momentarily stunned silent. Had I thought this girl was merely pretty? I was the stupidest man alive.

A blind fool.

A complete moron.

She was beautiful.

Irrationally, I felt duped, as if the little witch had put some kind of spell on me. Maybe it wasn't so irrational—she probably had.

I turned on my heel. "Good night," I called over my shoulder, not even bothering to wait until she'd slipped through the door of her cottage. I went back to my house and took a *very* cold shower.

I avoided Kira for the next couple days. I was busy, but more than that, she unsettled me, and I didn't need the distraction. The only female companionship I had the time or desire for right now was very temporary and, admittedly, very shallow. Getting involved with my wife would be a bad idea on almost every level.

The only contact we'd had was her text advising me she'd requested a certified copy of our marriage license, but that it would be several weeks before it would be processed and posted. More waiting—but we were one step closer. A couple weeks and we'd have the check we both desperately needed. The end.

I had no idea what she was doing, nor did I much care. Or at least that's what I kept telling myself. In any case, she seemed to be happy enough to avoid me as well. She didn't show up at any of the normal mealtimes, and I refused to ask Charlotte whether she ate at the vineyard or not. Although I did catch sight of her scampering around here and there, and I thought she might have brought the men I worked with lunch a couple times. I always ate up at the house, so I couldn't be sure, and I didn't ask them.

A week after we'd gotten married, I was walking back down the hill to the vineyards where José, Virgil, and the two new part-time guys I'd hired the day before were working, when I stopped short, squinting my eyes to make sure I was really seeing what I thought I was seeing. Kira was standing on one leg, her other stretched out behind her on the back of one of the tractors as it moved around the perimeter of the grapevines. She had a long ribbon of some sort in one hand and was waving it through the air. As I watched, she changed legs, bringing her arms out in front of her in some sort of pose. The men cheered and clapped, holding up their fingers as if scoring her for her performance. She turned toward them, the tractor still moving, José at the wheel, and did a deep curtsy, her long, loose hair falling forward, and then stood and spun around, bringing her leg up again in a ballerina-type pose. My heart leapt with panic and my breath stuttered at the dangerous stunt, which got my legs moving again. I half walked—half jogged toward her. When I was close, José looked to where I was, the smile on his face disappearing as he slowed the tractor, finally stopping completely. Immobile, I glared at them, at a complete loss for words. Finally, I managed to grit out, "What in the hell are you doing?"

José scratched his neck and wisely looked away, while Kira stood straighter, staring down at me defiantly. "I brought lunch down," she said, gesturing to the In-N-Out Burger wrappers strewn on a blanket at the base of a tree to the right of the tractor's path. "I was simply showing them the routine I planned to use to join the circus. I was going to be the girl who dances on the back of an elephant. I perfected it years ago while my best friend, Kimberly, drove my father's golf cart. We all got talking about childhood dreams and…" She trailed off, smiling around at the men.

"Oh, well, clearly," I said, my voice laced with sarcasm.

She had the grace and wisdom to look momentarily embarrassed. But then that little chin came up again and fire danced in her eyes. "We were just having a little fun—not on your time either. It was their lunch break." She put her hands on her hips.

"It's my equipment, Kira. If you had gotten hurt, I'd be responsible." Before she could answer, I looked at José. "And you? What do you have to say for yourself?"

José shrugged his shoulders, but I could see amusement in his expression, despite trying to hide it. "When the missus wants to dance on the back of a tractor, who am I to tell her no? She owns half of this vineyard."

I stared at him, gritting my teeth. I wasn't going to go over the exact terms of the prenuptial agreement Kira and I had signed, but in any case, I could see José was thoroughly enjoying himself, so it wouldn't matter anyway. *Traitor.* I looked around at the men who were staring at Kira as if she'd hung the moon.

"Get down," I demanded, recalling that this was the second time in a week I'd had to order my bride off something high and dangerous. "You will no longer climb trees nor dance on tractors at my vineyard."

She squinted her eyes at me, defiance clear in her expression. She crossed her arms. "And if I do?" she challenged.

"If you do, I'll show you just how much of a dragon I can really be," I said with cold calm.

She jumped down in one smooth, elegant maneuver, landing perfectly on her feet and executing another small curtsy. "Maybe," she said, standing straight and lashing her ribbon through the air, "I should have practiced being a dragon tamer!" Her long, auburn hair swirled around her as she moved, tendrils of heavy silk brushing her cheeks that were flushed a deep pink. I moved in, but she whipped her ribbon back and forth in front of me.

"Drop your weapon, witch," I growled, hot blood swirling through my veins.

"Or what?" she demanded.

"Or I'll disarm you myself." And then I was going to take her over my knee and use that makeshift whip to teach her a lesson.

She lifted her chin and jumped toward me and then away quickly again, taunting me, all agility and elegance. "Oh, I dare you," she said, something fiery and thrilling flaring in her eyes. "*Show* me that dragonish side. Do your worst."

I stepped in immediately to the challenge. "Dragonish? Oh, you haven't even *glimpsed* dragonish yet." I moved in just as she whipped her ribbon toward me, and I felt the hot sting of slicing pain across my jaw. I froze.

She'd whipped me!

The little witch had literally whipped me and...drawn blood! I was momentarily stunned, my hand moving slowly to my jaw, where it came away with a bright red smear. Hot fire ignited in my body as my eyes met Kira's. She was clearly as stunned as I was. Her wide eyes moved to the thick ribbon in her hand and then back up to my cheek as if she couldn't compute what had just happened. Her mouth opened, but then she closed it again.

"Run, Mrs. Kira!" I heard Virgil's voice suddenly call out. I looked back at him and he was wringing his hands, a look of dread on his face as he stared at us.

Kira let out a small squeal, dropping her ribbon/whip, and doing just as Virgil had suggested. I took a moment to glare at each of my men. *Kira's men* was probably more accurate.

"It wasn't really her fault, sir," José said. "We dared her. It seems neither one of you can resist a good dare." He was holding back laughter and doing a very poor job of it.

I gave him my very best scathing look. "In the future," I said, turning in the direction Kira had run, "please abstain from daring my wife to pull dangerous stunts on moving equipment."

"Yes, sir," I heard muttered behind me. I picked up my pace, jogging after the insufferable brat.

I saw her pause ahead of me, as if deciding whether to head toward her cottage or the main house. She chose the main house, most likely thinking she'd have some support in Walter and Charlotte. We both knew there was no lock on her cottage.

I had thought she might try to escape out one of the many back doors, but when I entered the house, she was standing in the foyer, looking around as if trying to decide where to go.

The door clicked softly behind me and I used the hem of my T-shirt to wipe at the blood I could feel dripping down my jaw. When I lowered it, I saw that her eyes had been on my bare stomach. I felt myself harden and swell, my blood pumping swiftly. Damn her.

"It was an accident," she said, glancing up the stairs as if contemplating trying to escape in that direction.

"Why is it you seem more accident prone than most? And, Kira"—I gestured my head behind her—"if I have a mind to catch you, you won't even make it halfway up that staircase."

Her eyes widened and determination filled her expression. She faked a right toward the kitchen and then made a sudden lunge left toward the living room instead. I went after her, chasing her exciting all my senses and causing arousal to surge through my body.

Kira ran toward the couch, and I was right behind her as she tried to climb over it. I pulled her down as she shrieked and fought me. "Charlotte!" Kira screamed. "Walter!"

I managed to get her under me and pin her arms, and when I did, gazing in her face triumphantly, she flinched and turned her head as if expecting a blow. I froze, immediately letting go of her.

"Did you think I was going to hit you?" I asked.

She blinked up at me with those gorgeous eyes, suddenly looking uncertain and very young.

Tenderness filled my chest, replacing any anger I'd felt. "I'd never hit you."

Her eyes darted around. "I...I know," she said, but the tone of her voice told me she wasn't completely sure.

"Gray? Kira?" I heard Charlotte from behind me, but I didn't move and didn't look up, and Kira didn't turn her head.

"We're fine, Charlotte," I said emphatically.

"I heard—"

"We're fine, Charlotte," I repeated. "Give us a minute, please."

She hesitated for a moment, and then I heard her footsteps moving away.

Kira was still watching me with large, wary eyes. Did she think because I'd been arrested for hitting someone, that I'd strike her? No, she had only ever acted fearlessly with me, never backing down until we were in *this* particular position.

"Someone hit you before," I guessed.

Her gaze held contact with mine. "Yes," she whispered.

I closed my eyes, exhaling a long breath. When I opened my eyes, she was still looking at me, her stare fixed on the cut on my jaw, the one I'd completely forgotten about. In truth, it was barely a flesh wound. That dumb ribbon must have hit me just right—what were the odds of being sliced by a ribbon?

"I hurt you," she said, her voice full of regret. My body was pressed into hers, her light flowery scent surrounding me, her lips parted just slightly. Her eyes were full of tender concern and so beautiful my heart raced.

I couldn't stop myself. I lowered my lips to hers. She startled slightly, and after a tense moment where we stared into each other's open eyes, she relaxed back into the couch and brought her arms up and around my neck, her lids fluttering closed.

I groaned and used my tongue to trace the full contours of her lips before slipping inside the warm recesses of her mouth. She tasted like sweetness and fire, her tongue reaching out to tangle with mine as I brought my hand under her body and stroked the curve of her spine. She arched up into me. The kiss took on a feverish intensity as our tongues played. Lust, as sharp and sudden as lightning, arced between us. She felt so *right* under me. I felt my control slipping, and the shock of that feeling was as surprising as it was worrisome. I broke my lips from hers and stared into her face—her cheeks flushed, her lips wet and red from my kiss, her eyes half-lidded. *Stunning.* I picked up a lock of her mahogany silk hair and felt it in my fingers. "This hair..." I murmured gently.

She blinked, her expression taking on a cautious confusion. She wriggled and I hissed in a gasp of air as she moved against my hard, aching groin. She slipped out from under me and I sat up abruptly. I reached out to her, but she backed up instead, looking at me almost accusingly. I opened my mouth to say something—I had no idea what—but before I could, she turned, and again, she ran.

CHAPTER TEN
Kira

What the heck had happened? I thought he was going to kill me one minute, and the next minute he was kissing me! I raised my fingers to my lips, pressing gently to feel the tenderness from his mouth on mine as if I might have dreamed the moment.

Even worse than the fact that he'd kissed me was how deplorably I'd responded to him. *Again.* My mind had been crowded with all the reasons I should pull away. But I hadn't been able to force myself to move, instead letting him know *exactly* how much I'd liked it. *How humiliating.*

Especially after what he'd pulled on our wedding night with peachy *Jade.* I was surprised he didn't still taste like her.

I flopped down on my bed, the rusty bedsprings creaking loudly and mixing with my groan of distress. I had been avoiding him, and vice versa, since the day he'd gone on a date with another woman and presumably slept with her. I grimaced as I remembered that day but did my best to shrug it off, as I'd been doing since it happened. Mostly successfully. And, when necessary, with the help of the few bottles of wine I now kept in my cottage. Thus far, being married to Grayson Hawthorn had turned me into a heavy drinker who lived in a dirty gardener's shack. The plan to improve my circumstances was going splendidly so far!

I groaned again, rolling onto my back. I didn't understand the kiss because he'd made it so perfectly clear I wasn't his type, and I shouldn't get any ideas. And then he'd done that? It had to have been out of anger; there was no other explanation. Surely it was similar to the first time he'd kissed me: an attempt to gain the upper hand. It was confusing and left me feeling glum. But I'd been partially to blame both times. We could move past this. We just needed to go back to ignoring each other.

And I had to control my impulsive escapades for once in my life because they obviously triggered Grayson. He clearly hadn't enjoyed the tree climbing and had appreciated the tractor dancing even less. But truthfully? I was bored. And my father said too much excess time on my hands always brought out the worst in me. He was probably right on that score at least. But life was full of so many possibilities—why should you spend even one day of it being *bored*? I'd always had a problem accepting inactivity.

I stared up at the ceiling. What I needed to do was drive to San Francisco and spend a couple weeks working at the various charities I supported. I longed to be busy in a way that made a difference to others. However, I hadn't gone because I wanted to take some funds with me. I also wouldn't be able to afford even a temporary place to stay until I got our official marriage license and the trust money came through.

My disjointed thoughts were interrupted by a loud knock on my door. I stood up quickly. "Who's there?"

"It's me." *Grayson*.

"I'm busy," I called. I wasn't ready to face him. "Go away."

"Kira." His voice held the vague hint of annoyance. "This cottage doesn't have a lock. I'll come in whether you grant me permission or not. I'd rather have permission."

I fisted my hands. "Fine, come in," I gritted.

I stood still as I listened to him enter and make his way through the front room. And then he was standing in the doorway to my room. I looked away because I didn't want to think about how handsome he was and how good his soft, full lips had felt on mine when he actually put some effort into a kiss. I didn't want to think about how I could still taste him on my tongue.

"We should talk about what happened just now," he said.

"What?" I asked flippantly, turning my body toward the window.

"You don't remember?" he asked, and I heard the note of humor in his tone. "If my kiss was that forgettable, maybe I should try again. I thought I'd improved my efforts compared to the first time, but maybe we need even more practice."

"No," I said, whirling back toward him. I took a breath. "No, that won't be necessary. We were both…heated. That sort of thing happens sometimes when emotions are high. It's no big deal." I waved my hand around. "You can rest assured I won't get any ideas from it. No *fanciful* notions."

He gave me a boyish half smile filled with the irresistible charm I was sure resulted in women throwing themselves at him every hour on the hour. Women like Jade. The woman he'd slept with on our wedding night. Not that I was thinking about that again because I wasn't. He moved a step closer. "Maybe I'm the one who's getting a few fanciful notions."

"Oh." My breath had suddenly grown thin, and I took in a lungful of air. "Well, that's not a good idea either. It would only complicate things. Plus, I'm not your type, remember?"

He moved even closer. "I think I might have been wrong about that, Kira."

Wrong how? "You wanted to kill me," I reminded him. But I couldn't deny that my heart had picked up speed.

"Yes, well, you do need to curb your antics. Climbing trees and dancing on tractors…I can't have you getting hurt. Also, you taunted me in front of my men and then whipped me and drew blood."

Well, when he put it that way…

"By accident," I defended, regarding the whipping part. My eyes moved to the small cut on his jaw, and I couldn't help feeling a twinge of guilt.

He took a strand of my hair and my eyes watched his fingers at the side of my face as he tucked it behind my ear. His closeness was making me feel all jumbled and confused, his blatant maleness turning my limbs to jelly. I could feel the heat of his body against my own, picture the taut muscles beneath his clothes. My eyes moved to his beautifully carved mouth, and I couldn't help recalling the feel of it on mine. I licked my lips and his gaze tracked my tongue.

"I know it was an accident," he said distractedly. My mind scrambled to remember what we'd been talking about. "For some reason, with you I'm especially…" He paused, seeming to be searching for the right word.

"Reptilian?" I offered, standing up straight and trying to shake off his effect on me.

"Temperamental," he corrected, giving me a lopsided grin meant to disarm me, I was sure. It didn't work. Mostly.

His eyes moved over my face for a few moments. "You

mentioned some accounting experience and wanting to work. If you meant it—"

"I did. I worked at my father's office. Secretarial work, accounting…"

He gave a succinct nod. "Okay. The office up at the house is yours now. I'm sorry to say I haven't had much time to organize anything recently. You'll have your work cut out for you."

"I'm not afraid of hard work."

His face became pensive as he regarded me, his eyes dark and fathomless, hooded by those impossibly long lashes. He looked around at the room we were standing in, his eyes landing on the vases of flowers I'd put out that morning and then roaming to the open doorway of the now-immaculate bathroom. "Yes, I can see that."

Pride filled my chest. I'd had precious few compliments about my character or work ethic from men in my lifetime. I was almost embarrassed by how much those four words meant to me. I wanted to turn them over in my head and savor them for a few minutes, and to linger in the impressed look in his eyes, but Grayson spoke again. "Maybe we were rash in defining our relationship," he said. "We're married. There's obviously an attraction between us. Is there any reason we shouldn't…explore that?"

My breath caught in my throat. He was attracted to me after all? He…wanted me? *Why?* Because he was horny and I was convenient? I felt a thud inside as I pictured the first time I'd been with a man. I stepped back and looked down, unable to hold eye contact with those dark eyes—eyes I now saw from up close were the rich color of coffee beans. Not black at all but the deepest, darkest brown. "You have Jade to explore," I reminded him. *Not bitter—not at all.*

"I didn't sleep with Jade, Kira. I didn't even kiss her. You were right. It wouldn't have been discreet, and it wouldn't have been right. Not to mention, I didn't want to. I'm sorry I didn't make that clear to you sooner than now."

I scoffed, but relief was a cool balm spreading through me—not only hadn't he slept with Jade, but he'd realized his actions could have caused our relationship to look far less than legitimate. "I'm glad you realized you weren't acting discreetly, but I hardly care *what* you did with Jade for any reason other than that," I insisted, lifting my chin.

He just smiled. "So what do you say? About…us?"

Fear trickled slowly through me. No. No, I had no interest in going there with the Dragon. He'd likely been with countless women who knew exactly what to do in his bed. I wouldn't be compared to them. But on the heels of the fear, came resentment. Now that he'd deemed me attractive after all, I was supposed to fall at his feet? *Nope.* I shook my head. "It's not a good idea and I'm not interested anyway. I don't like you much and I find you…unattractive. Hideous actually. Sorry if that's blunt, but it's the truth."

He chuckled as if I hadn't just insulted and rejected him. God, he knew no woman in her right mind would ever find him unattractive. Also, there was the small matter of the way I'd responded to his kiss less than fifteen minutes ago…

"Also," I went on for further emphasis, "you have the manners of a dyspeptic reptile."

The corner of his lip trembled. "I can be civilized if I put my mind to it," he said.

"I doubt it," I muttered under my breath.

"I'll prove it to you. Be ready at six o'clock. I'll pick you up. We never did have that wedding dinner."

Wait, what? No. "I'm busy," I shouted as he turned away.

"Six o'clock," he shouted back.

I gritted my teeth, considering standing him up. But the truth was, I was pitifully lonely and had been bored for a week. A dinner out was hard to resist—even if it had to be with my husband.

I sighed, shifting from one foot to the other. And also? Maybe it would be good to talk, try to get to know each other a little, and start over on a better foot. A one-time dinner date. And then, I'd be less inclined to come up with Very Bad Ideas once I was involved in doing his books. Not to mention, he'd be extremely busy soon too, when the trust money came through. Things would smooth out, and before I knew it, I'd be able to leave here and wipe Grayson Hawthorn from my memory forever.

I stepped toward my suitcase. But first…what did I have to wear to my overdue wedding dinner?

———

Grayson's truck pulled up in front of my cottage at precisely six o'clock. I took a deep, fortifying breath and walked slowly through the brush. He was standing at the passenger side door, holding it open. "My, *my*," I said, "you *do* have manners when you care to use them. Who would have guessed?" His smile was that of a very satisfied, decidedly non-dyspeptic reptile—sweet, with a devilish twinkle. I took his hand and stepped up into the cab. He was freshly shaven and his still semi-wet hair glinted in the sunlight, the almost-black strands glossy and tousled. I looked away, making a vow to harden my heart against him. If there was one thing I knew, men like him were adept at getting what they wanted by using charm, and I wouldn't fall for it.

Once he was seated in the cab and we were pulling through his front gate, I asked, "So where are you taking me?"

"A local place I think you'll like." He said it casually, but a worried expression settled on his features for a brief moment before it flitted away.

I twisted the necklace I was wearing as I watched his profile, wondering what he was thinking. He looked over at me and his eyes moved to my hand, where I had one finger wrapped around the chain at my chest, and then lowered to my cleavage, his gaze lingering for several beats before he looked back to the road. I had settled on an empire-waisted yellow sundress and a pair of navy wedge heels. But at the moment, with the way Grayson's eyes had lingered on my exposed skin and with the feel of the low simmer of sexual tension in the cab of the truck, I was simultaneously wishing I'd chosen something less revealing and feeling a surge of satisfaction.

"So, Kira, you said you were in Africa up until recently. What was it you were doing there?" Grayson asked conversationally. Ah, now that he suddenly wanted to *explore things*, he'd decided to take an interest in me. How typical. Still, if we were going to get to know each other, we'd need to talk.

"A friend of mine was building a hospital. I decided to help with the effort," I told him.

He glanced at me. "A friend?"

"Well, actually, a boy I had sponsored through a charity program. Anyway, Khotso had become a good friend over the years—through letters of course. His mother had suffered with something called an obstetric fistula after his birth when she was only thirteen, and it fueled his lifelong dream to become a doctor." Pride filled my chest as I considered Khotso's determination.

"A fistula?" he asked.

"It's a childbirth injury. It's practically unheard of here in America, but it's a big problem in some parts of Africa due to the very early age many girls marry and become pregnant. Their young bodies simply aren't ready to bear children and they have a wretched time—often in labor for days and frequently losing their baby too—and then they live in a terrible state due to the fistula they develop. Anyway, Khotso opened a hospital to provide medical care for those women, some of whom have lived with the condition for years. It's an amazing accomplishment for someone so young." I suddenly stopped talking, realizing I'd gotten caught up in the passion of the project. "Sorry, I…"

"You're obviously passionate about it," he said. "And it sounds like a very worthy endeavor. You helped one person, who in turn helps so many now." He looked over at me with a look I thought might be sincere respect. My heart warmed despite my vow to keep it cold and removed. "So you stayed to see the hospital completed and you came home?" he asked.

I let out an uncomfortable laugh. "Well, almost. I would have stayed until the ribbon-cutting ceremony, but there was an, um, an incident."

Grayson raised a brow. "An incident?"

"I, uh, challenged a tribal leader to a foot race."

"Of course you did."

I noted his sarcasm, but as I glanced over at him, I saw amusement in his eyes that looked almost affectionate. "Apparently, tribal leaders don't appreciate being bested publicly. In any case, I thought it best for Khotso and his project that I distance myself, literally. So I flew home a bit earlier than I originally intended." *And before I'd had a chance to come up with a better plan than marrying you, Grayson Dragon Hawthorn.*

We pulled into a parking spot in downtown Napa and walked to an Italian restaurant I'd seen before but never dined in. It was in a stately old bank building with large stone columns flanking the front. "I thought it was apropos," Grayson said, opening the front door for me, "that our first date be inside a bank. After all, a bank is where it all started."

I raised my eyebrows. "True. Although, this isn't a first date. It's merely our friendly wedding dinner. Practically a business function, actually."

Before he could answer, a hostess greeted us. "Grayson Hawthorn," he said. "I have a reservation for six thirty."

The girl gave him an admiring look, smoothed her hair back in an obvious preening gesture, and turned to lead us to our table.

I couldn't help but notice the glances our way as we walked through the restaurant to a table near the back of the main dining room. Some of the looks were merely female admiration for Grayson, but many of the glances seemed decidedly disapproving. I couldn't help but hear whispers of his name, and it didn't sound like the talk was of a positive nature. I frowned, noticing the rigid way Grayson was holding himself as we followed the hostess.

I recalled overhearing the two girls in the store: *you couldn't take him home to Mama now...*

Once we were seated and had each been served a glass of wine, Grayson started to relax slightly. I looked around, people glancing away from us rather than making eye contact. We were obviously being discussed. I remembered what a small town Napa was. All these people were gossiping about Grayson, judging him. Perhaps for his crime, perhaps for the reasons he was back...perhaps for the fact that his family business was in ruin, perhaps for the "fact" that you *couldn't take him home to Mama now*. My heart went out to him. I knew just what it felt like to be judged...and to be found severely lacking.

He appeared almost immune to the whispers around him, but the stiff set of his shoulders told me he wasn't. I looked at him, sitting ramrod straight and studying his menu just a tad too intensely, and the vow I'd made to stay detached crumbled. "Sometimes," I said softly, moving my hand slowly across the table, "the very best thing you can do is smile." When my hand made contact with his, he jolted slightly, his eyes meeting mine. The look there was so intensely vulnerable, my heart stuttered for a few beats. *There he is, the man I first saw outside the bank. The prince.* "Try it," I encouraged gently, tilting my head and giving him a big, bright smile, the one I brought forth when I wanted to convince others that I had not a care in the world even if, inside, I was dying.

He returned a small, tightlipped grimace.

"I realize you're more of a cold indifference kind of guy, but surely you can do better than that. You look like a demented hyena." I pretended to shudder.

He looked shocked for a second, but then he laughed, and the resulting smile was big and bright and very, very beautiful.

I grinned back. And suddenly, the tension waned. I withdrew my hand, yet my skin still felt warm from where we'd touched. We eased into mostly casual conversation after that, talking about mundane things through our meal. I didn't want to break the spell of easygoing friendship we'd unexpectedly seemed to find.

As our dessert was served, an older woman came up to our table, a young woman lingering behind her nervously. "I thought that was you, Gray Hawthorn," the older woman said. "I wasn't sure, though. You've neither shown hide nor hair of yourself in public since you...ah, returned."

Her gaze flickered over me and she held out her hand. "I'm Diane Fernsby. You must be one of Gray's girls," she said, contempt practically dripping from her surgically plumped lips.

"Actually, Diane," Grayson cut in, "this is my wife, Kira Hawthorn." My eyes flew to his and I swallowed, shock rendering me silent. I hadn't been prepared to hear those words.

Diane's eyes widened. "Your wife? Why, Gray, your mother's oldest friend and I didn't get an invite to the wedding?"

"Stepmother," Grayson corrected. "And we had an intimate ceremony." He took my hand and smiled into my eyes. "We couldn't wait."

"I...see," she said, her eyes moving over me, landing on my hand that was on the table, widening when she saw the ring on my left hand. "Well, this is certainly a—"

"Mom, we should go. Hi, Gray," the younger woman standing just behind her mother said.

"Hi, Suzie," Gray said, more warmth in his tone. Suzie blushed, looking away. *Ex-girlfriend?*

"Yes, you're right, dear. We should go." Diane Fernsby turned back to us. "Well, my congratulations," she said, sounding anything but congratulatory. "After what happened with Vanessa...I was worried you wouldn't be able to move on." She shook her head. "Breaking your engagement and then, while you were in prison, marrying—"

143

"We weren't engaged," Grayson said, his voice steady and cold. My heart gave a kick. *Vanessa? Who is Vanessa?*

Diane waved her hand in the air. "Oh, well, we all knew you would be soon enough. Your mother told me you'd even bought a ring. And then—"

"*Mom*," Suzie said harshly from behind her. She smiled apologetically at both of us, pulling on her mom's hand. "Have a nice evening," she said. "And congratulations. Gray, good to see you."

"Ah, well, good evening," Diane Fernsby said, allowing her daughter to lead her away. When they had only moved a few steps from our table, Diane leaned toward her daughter and whispered none too quietly, "You dodged a bullet with that one, dear. I hear the vineyard is barely scraping by…and now an ex-con… After all the heartache he put his parents—" Her words faded as she moved farther away, but the sound of her tsk-tsking carried through the restaurant.

I waited until they had disappeared from sight, giving Grayson a worried glance before speaking. "Every small town has a graceless gossip," I said. "I see Napa's goes by the name Diane Fernsby."

My remark elicited a small chuckle and a flash of that demented hyena. "That's for sure," he said.

I tilted my head. "I didn't expect you to refer to me as your wife. You could have warned me." But I made sure to infuse some lightness in my tone. It didn't bother me. We were trying to make this marriage publicly convincing, after all. I was just glad I hadn't taken a drink of water before he said it.

Grayson made a visible effort to relax, leaning back in his chair and regarding me. "You said we should make our marriage look real for the sake of preventing your father's suspicion. I just figured if word gets around town that I'm married, it couldn't hurt in that effort. Diane Fernsby will definitely help with that now."

"True…" She'd probably already spread the news to several people and might only be down the block.

Grayson took the credit card receipt from the waiter and began signing the slip. I wanted to believe he was putting some effort into making our marriage appear legitimate in public, but I suspected he hadn't mentioned I was his wife for my sake or because of my father. I had a feeling he'd mentioned I was his wife as a way to shut Diane Fernsby up and for that reason alone.

The disappointing thing was, I had known he ran hot and cold, but we had been getting along so well before Diane Fernsby showed up and mentioned his ex. What was that all about anyway? It sounded like some woman named Vanessa had jilted Grayson. Where was she now? I wondered if she lived in Napa and if one of the people Diane Fernsby would spread the news of our marriage to was her.

Ah well, I couldn't concern myself with my husband's personal life. No matter how physically tempting he could be, trying to read him was frankly exhausting.

Grayson led me out of the restaurant to his truck. The comfortable mood we'd managed during dinner was slightly stilted now. But when we were both seated in the cab of his truck, he turned to me. "I'm sorry about that, Kira. I've lived in this town my whole life, and a lot has happened with my family in the last six years. People are curious, I suppose. I'm sorry I exposed you to it. I'm sorry if that was uncomfortable."

People are curious. Sure. I was too sometimes. But… "Curiosity is different than blatant rudeness," I murmured, staring out the front window.

"I probably deserve their rudeness," Grayson said. "As far as Napa is concerned, I'm a murderer and an ex-con. And I murdered a neighboring town's golden boy."

I studied his profile as he stared out the window. I remembered what I'd read about his crime online. The boy who had died had lived in the nearby county of Sonoma.

I bit my lip, not knowing exactly what to say. "You didn't murder him, Grayson. It was an accident. You told me so yourself."

"And yet he's still just as dead."

"Do you want to talk about it? I'm a good—"

"No."

We sat in uncomfortable silence for a moment before he glanced at me. I thought I saw regret in his dark eyes. Was I beginning to read him better? "I know how to show a girl a good time, huh?"

I breathed out a laugh. "According to Diane, there are quite a few of them." I shot him an ironic smile.

Grayson made a face. "Sorry about that. Despite the fact that my stepmother was never very fond of me, Diane wanted her daughter and me together. Suzie just—"

"Wasn't your type?"

Grayson chuckled. "Was always just a friend."

I nodded, glad the awkwardness of a few moments before was gone. But speaking of curious… "Grayson, who's Vanessa?"

Grayson didn't answer immediately, but I saw his shoulders tense. "Vanessa is my brother's wife."

"Oh." His brother had married his girlfriend—the woman he'd been planning to marry—while he was in prison? *Ouch.* I barely suppressed a wince, imagining what that must have been like for him. No wonder he didn't speak

146

to his brother anymore. No wonder he was so damn moody. Not that I wanted to make excuses for him, but he carried the weight of betrayal. And that was a heavy load to bear. "I'm sorry, Grayson," I said.

He nodded once, acknowledging my words, and then started the truck and pulled out of our parking spot. The ride home was mostly quiet, the radio playing softly in the background. When we pulled around the fountain and stopped in front of his house, Grayson turned to me. "Do you want a drink? I happen to own a bottle of wine that I have on expert authority is richly layered and exuberant." His mock snooty smile went serious. "One drink to make up for being ambushed at dinner?"

I smiled. What could one drink hurt? "Richly layered, you say? Exuberant too? How can I resist?"

He laughed softly. Grayson came around the truck and offered me his hand and then I followed my husband inside his house.

CHAPTER ELEVEN
Grayson

We were sitting on semi-rusted lounge chairs on the patio, a glass of wine in each of our hands, sipping in comfortable silence as we looked out over the covered pool—most likely murky and sludge filled beneath. It wasn't the most romantic location and I'd had every intention of trying to seduce her tonight. But after what happened at the restaurant, I wasn't exactly feeling very enthusiastic about wooing her. Mostly, I felt humiliated. "You know what we should do?" Kira suddenly asked, leaning forward abruptly and taking me by surprise.

"I have a feeling nothing good ever follows those words when they're coming from your mouth," I said.

"Funny. No, really. It's a good idea."

"Okay, what?"

"We should throw a party!"

I leaned my head back on the chair as I watched her. "A party? Why in the world would we do that?"

"Well," she said, sitting up completely and swinging her legs to the side so she was facing me, "it seems to me the town is...leery of you right now. It certainly couldn't hurt the Hawthorn Winery's image to obtain a better social standing in your own community. Am I right?"

"Probably." She *was* right. If I was going to have a fighting chance of bringing my family business back to life, being the black sheep of wine country wasn't going to help. Still... "How would a party help exactly?"

"It would just be a start," she said, looking thoughtful. "But word spreads, you know. If we invited some of the more influential people in the community and they felt welcomed by you, they'd be more likely to extend the same courtesy your way. Gossip has a way of making people forget that there's a human being behind the story. Inviting people here would remind them of that. I think, innately, people want to understand and forgive."

"You give people too much credit."

She appeared to consider that, a small wrinkle appearing between her eyes. "Maybe. But I really do believe it. I think it's true more often than it's not."

After taking a sip of wine, I said, "You must be familiar with gossip."

She let out an agreeable chuff that ended in a small sigh. "Most of my life has been spent in the public eye." Her eyes slid away, and she appeared troubled. I had the sudden instinct to reach out to her. *Strange. Unfamiliar.* I looked away, taking another sip of the buttery white wine, savoring the hints of butterscotch and pear.

"Anyway," I said, changing the subject, "how will people be reminded I'm a human being? I thought you considered me more dragon than human."

"True." She smiled. "You'd have to curb your reptilian tendencies for one night. Do you think you could manage it?"

"Maybe." I chuckled, studying the shadows and highlights of her features in the dim light of the moon and the few house lights still on behind us. "Seriously though, Kira, it's a decent idea, but I don't have time to plan a party."

She shook her head. "No, of course not. I'd do it. It will keep me out of trouble. We could do a theme. Maybe a tropical luau or a masquerade ball. I'll think of something perfect." She grinned, and I got a flash of that witchy, little dimple.

My heartbeat stuttered, but I couldn't help the small chuckle that found its way up my throat at her clear excitement. "You're supposed to be helping me organize my books to stay out of trouble."

"I can do both."

I sighed. "Fine. Just wait until we get the check, please, to start spending money neither of us has yet."

"I will. Well, except for invitations. I'll pay for those. Do I have your permission to pick a date?"

"Go ahead. I can assure you I don't have any social plans on the calendar."

A few moments of silence settled between us. The mild night air was fragrant with nearby roses, the flavor of the wine crisp on my tongue, the rustle of the trees whispered all around, and the iridescent mist floated in the grapevines beyond. I closed my eyes, relishing the assorted sensations, wondering when I'd lived in the moment just as I was now. *Have you ever?*

"Do you plan on restoring this pool when you have the money?" Kira asked quietly, nodding her head toward it.

"Probably not. I'd like to tear it out."

"Why? Don't you like to swim?"

I shrugged. "It's not that. I don't have very good

memories of this particular pool. My father decided he'd teach me how to swim by throwing my puppy in to the deep end."

Kira drew in a breath. "Your puppy? Why would he do that?"

Jesus. I hadn't thought about that in so long. Why was I remembering it now? I supposed because the pool was right in front of me and my mind had been wandering uninhibited... *God, he was a mean bastard.*

Yes, he had been a mean bastard. But in the end...in the end he'd held regret for the things he'd done. Him leaving me the vineyard was proof of that. And one of the reasons these memories hurt less than they otherwise would have.

"I was six and I was afraid of the deep end. No matter how my father threatened me, I wouldn't get in. He would stand on the side of the pool in his damn business suit and rail at me as I cried." Twenty-two years later and I could still feel the humiliation. "I had found this stray puppy wandering just outside our gates and begged my parents to let me keep it. They'd agreed as long as it was an outside dog and I solely took care of it." I allowed myself to picture that little dog I'd named Sport, a brown-and-white mutt with these big, trusting eyes. I hadn't brought him to mind in so long, and suddenly, it felt like a terrible travesty that I'd allowed him to go unremembered. "Anyway, we were out here for a lesson and I again refused to get in, so my father picked up the puppy, who was sitting right there on the patio"—I pointed at the exact spot—"and he threw him in. Told me either I jumped in after him, or he'd drown."

"Oh God, Grayson," Kira breathed, her eyes wide.

"It was a long time ago," I told her. So why did my chest still ache as I recalled it? Why did regret sit heavy in my gut?

"I stood on the side of the pool crying and screaming as that puppy drowned," I admitted to her. "My father eventually scooped him out, but it was too late." And the guilt of that still tore at my soul. I'd been a coward. "I just wish I had it to do over again… I'd save him this time. I'd drown myself if I had to. But I'd save him."

"Of course you would," she said, her voice filled with conviction. "You were a scared child then. You're a man now, with the courage of an adult," she said, moving over to sit on my lounge chair. "I'm so sorry, he did that to you, Grayson. How did you ever learn to swim after that?"

I ran my hand through my hair, holding a handful of it as I recalled. "Walter. My father went away a couple weeks later, and Walter spent the weekend teaching me how to swim. He wore this weird black suit that went from his knees to his neck." I chuckled softly recalling how Walter had had me practice over and over in the shallow water until I felt confident enough to go in the deep end, and then he'd come with me and let me hang on his shoulders until I told him I was ready to let go. "Later that year, I taught my brother to swim anytime my father was away so when he eventually tossed *him* in the deep end, he swam like a little fish. My father was so proud," I said, trying to sound ironic, but the statement came out with the true pride I felt. I *had* been proud of my brother and proud I'd secretly helped him avoid the terror and guilt I'd faced. And maybe I'd been looking for some small amount of redemption for Sport, though I hadn't found it.

"It wasn't your fault," she said softly, seeming to know what I was thinking. "What your father did to you was an evil, awful thing to do to a little boy. I'm so sorry you experienced that." She leaned forward and put her hand on my cheek, her expression gentle and filled with compassion. She'd done something similar at the restaurant—reached for me to provide comfort when she noticed me being shunned. Our gazes met and held. I'd been wrong about this little witch. Completely, utterly wrong. As I looked into her forgiving eyes, something inside me felt as if it unclenched and began to drift away.

I had surprised myself by telling her that story. Why had I when I rarely shared painful memories with anyone? Was it because, tonight at the restaurant, under the judgmental stares of all those eyes, she had made me feel like someone was on my side? Was it because she had come up with the idea of planning a party in an effort to help me elevate my social standing in people's eyes for no reason other than she cared and thought she could do something to help? Or was it because I suddenly felt this unexpected friendship and understanding from my unpredictable wife?

Or was there some kind of spell floating on the mist tonight that would eventually dissipate?

"Sweet, beautiful witch," I murmured, pulling her down to me so I could kiss her. I wrapped my hands in her thick, silken hair as our lips met. She tensed very slightly but didn't pull away, and I traced her lips with my tongue slowly until she opened for me. I pulled her closer and delved inside, exploring the wet, silken contours of her mouth, heat coiling through my body. When she finally began participating in earnest, I wanted to groan with satisfaction, but I didn't dare do anything to break the spell I was willingly under and have her pull away.

I brought my hands down to run up and down her back, and after a few moments, I felt her muscles relax. Our first kiss had been harsh and challenging, our second ravenous yet tender, but this one was slow, sensual, as if our mouths were making love. I'd never experienced a kiss exactly like this one. It confused me almost as much as it aroused me. I hadn't known there were new types of kisses to experience.

What else can you teach me?

Something about that thought…scared me, and I pushed it aside and then shifted her—quickly but fluidly—so she was under me and I was hovering above her, my weight on my hip to the side of her body on the lounge chair. She blinked up at me as if uncertain about what had just happened. I wanted to pull her fully against me so she could feel the full extent of my arousal, but I instinctively knew that would be the wrong move right now. And I was all too willing to do whatever it would take to warm Kira slowly to passion. The quick spark earlier in the day had scared her off for some reason—a reason I'd find out, but not tonight.

I took a moment to drink her in. Her hair was splayed around her, her lips shining with the wetness of my kisses, and her eyes regarded me with hazy passion and just a touch of wariness. I leaned in and kissed her again, my body tensed with the effort to hold back. I wanted to strip off her clothes and plunge into her soft, tight heat right here. My body was pulsing with need. I started to pull the straps of her sundress down and she made a small squeak of protest, so I halted but leaned in and kissed her neck, dragging my lips down her soft, fragrant skin, darting my tongue out to taste her. She leaned her head back and arched up into me, and I took the opportunity to pull her dress down so her breasts popped free. I wasn't able to repress the deep animal groan that rose from my throat at the sight of her beautiful, full breasts. "You have the prettiest nipples I've ever seen," I murmured. "I haven't been able to stop thinking about them." I leaned in and kissed one and Kira let out a small feminine gasp. At the sound, my cock hardened to painful proportions. "I've wanted to taste them and suck on them since I walked in on you the other day," I admitted, my lips against her skin as I kissed the other breast. "I've wondered if they taste as sweet as they look." The memory of her breasts had been distracting me for days now. And I hadn't even been remembering how beautiful they really were.

"Grayson," she groaned, tangling her fingers in my hair. I lowered my mouth to one stiff peak and licked at it, swirling my tongue around and around.

"God, you do," I moaned, "taste as sweet as you look."

"I said we shouldn't… This isn't…" Her words left off in a breathy sigh. A few seconds later, those breaths turned to pants. At her response, I wrapped my lips fully around her nipple and suckled, pulling it into my mouth and then using my tongue to soothe it gently. She cried out, pulling at my hair. "Oh God, Gray," she groaned. "You, we have to—"

"Shh, little witch," I soothed, taking the other nipple in my mouth and sucking gently before pulling back. "Let yourself enjoy this." There was no reason we shouldn't. No reason in the world.

I eased her thighs apart, putting one of my knees between them. She gazed up at me with eyes unfocused and drugged with arousal. My gut clenched at that look. *I put that there.* This woman was so filled with passion…for everything. For life. To have it focused in my direction felt like a bright ray of light. Warm but blinding. I pressed my erection against her belly as I leaned in to kiss her again. Her body suddenly went rigid and she turned her head. "No," she said, her voice soft and still scratchy with desire.

"Yes," I said, leaning back in. She pushed at my shoulders.

"No," she said more firmly. I groaned, rolling to the side. She stood quickly, pulling her dress up over her breasts. It appeared as if she was having trouble making her legs cooperate. "This isn't a good idea… Just… Bad things will come from this."

Bad things will come from stopping. My body pulsed painfully with unspent lust. God, I wanted her.

She exhaled and smoothed her dress down, pulling herself together while at the same time attempting to look unaffected. Her flushed skin and the hardened points of her nipples poking through her dress gave her away. It also made me smile. "I should get to bed."

She turned to go and my arm shot out and I grabbed her hand before she could run. "I understand if you have to think about this, about us, but, Kira, there's no reason we have to sleep alone. It wouldn't have to change anything. You obviously feel what we have between us as much as I do." I attempted a smile but it felt pained and tight, like my body.

She looked away and pulled her hand free of mine, her expression distressed. It worked to cool my blood. I didn't want to upset her. It was the last thing I wanted right now. "Did you tell me that story so this"—she moved her hand back and forth between the two of us—"would happen?"

Confusion made me pause. "What story?"

"About the puppy."

"The puppy? What? No." Did she think I had told her about that to manipulate her into kissing me? A splinter of hurt stabbed at my insides.

She studied me for a moment and then let out a sharp breath. "I told you, Grayson, I'm not interested in that… in this." She gestured between her and me once again. "It would only complicate an already complicated situation. This wasn't our deal."

"Deals change all the time," I murmured as I sat up and brought my leg over the chair and stood up to face her. I took a lock of her hair between my fingers, testing its silky texture, wishing the moon brought out its fiery highlights the way the sun did. But in this light, its fire was shadowed. My body throbbed again, still hard. I wanted her...for hours and hours. Or, hell, even just once... Was she worried I was going to try to control her in some way if she slept with me? Try to...lay claim? "It can be temporary, Kira. Just like our marriage," I reassured her.

She blinked and then brought her hands to her cheeks as if they were warm. I couldn't tell in this light whether that was the case though, or not. I had an inkling I was saying all the wrong things, but I had no clue what she wanted from me. "It wouldn't work. Just trust me." She turned toward the stone staircase up to the house. I called her name, but she didn't look back.

I sat back down on the lounge chair, letting out a long, sexually frustrated sigh, trying to figure out what had just happened. I had no idea how to handle my own wife. Women had always come easily to me. *Keeping* them...well, Vanessa had proven that might be a different matter. But Kira and I had already established our relationship would be temporary, so with her, that wasn't an issue. I'd never experienced being turned down for sex, though, especially when I focused my charm. I wasn't being arrogant—it was just the truth. I rubbed at my head. Did I actually know how to seduce an unwilling woman? Maybe not. How ironic that the first woman I'd have to *work for* was my very own wife.

"See you on Monday, Charlotte," I said, leaning forward and kissing her soft cheek. It was Friday morning, and she and Walter were taking a weekend trip to San Francisco to visit friends.

"There are several casseroles in the freezer, with instructions written right on top," she said. "Oh, and I baked a batch of those citrus butter cookies you like. They're in tin foil in—"

"Charlotte." I chuckled. "I'm a grown man. I can take care of myself for the weekend."

She smiled, shaking her head and pinching my cheek affectionately. "I like taking care of you. Just let me dote. Oh! And please tell Kira I baked her the brown sugar oatmeal cookies she likes. Where is she anyway? I thought she'd come up to the house to say goodbye."

"We were out late last night. She's probably sleeping in," I said, picturing her tangled in her sheets in her little cottage, that glorious hair splayed all—

I set those visions aside.

Charlotte eyed me as if she could read my thoughts. "How are things going with you two now that you're actually married?" She'd wanted to come with us to the ceremony, but I'd told her absolutely no. At the time, I hadn't wanted anything that would make the ceremony more awkward than it already was. Charlotte's presence there would have only served to make us feel more uncomfortable…and make me feel guilty.

I sighed. "I don't know. It's hard to say with her. I barely know what she's going to do from moment to moment, much less what she's thinking." *Except that she's resisting me.* Was that why I wanted her so badly? The thought was oddly comforting.

"Hmm," she hummed, looking thoughtful. "Yes, not many match that one for spirit, that's the truth. Except maybe you." She winked at me. "I'm glad you two went to dinner last night. It's a good start." She smiled, and before I could address that comment or tell her not to get any grand ideas, she continued, "Tell her to have a nice weekend. Oh! And tell her I got her list about the party. What a splendid idea! I'm not sure what the big rush is, or why she was emailing me at two in the morning, but Walter and I will stop in town this morning and order the invitations—I know a place that will print them right away. I still have Jessica's address label list of who's who in Napa and can email that to the printer once I've had a few minutes to go through it." *Kira had been up in the middle of the night? Why? Had she, too, been unable to sleep after what we'd done on the patio? Had she been tossing and turning, remembering the feel of—*

"Tell Kira they'll go out in the mail Monday," Charlotte continued, interrupting my thoughts. Thankfully.

"And here, drink your orange juice," she said, handing me my half-full glass. "There's a terrible flu going around." I did as she said, draining the glass just to stop her party talk and incessant nagging. She watched me carefully as I drank it, something almost nervous in her expression. Was she that worried about a flu? When I was done, she took my glass and rinsed it in the sink before I shooed her out of the kitchen, calling goodbye to Walter who was waiting in the foyer with their small suitcase sitting on the floor at his feet.

"Goodbye, sir," he said, giving his wife a small, affec-tionate smile as she came toward him, fussing about all the things that were left undone, as if we might perish without her caretaking for the weekend.

I worked until late afternoon that day and then made

a trip into town for supplies, returning about five. After a quick shower, I went down to the kitchen to put one of the casseroles in the oven for dinner. I texted Kira to let her know dinner would be ready at six, but an hour later, when she still hadn't texted me back, I started to get restless. Was she ignoring me? I hadn't seen her once all day. Was she holed up in that little cottage of hers, avoiding me? Come to think of it, wasn't she planning on getting started in my office? I went to see if there was any sign she'd been there, but there wasn't. I puttered around for a little while, but when my frustration levels had risen too much for me to focus on any one thing, I pushed away from my desk and went to grab my phone. I texted Kira again and then waited five minutes, drumming my fingers on the kitchen counter. Nothing. *What the hell?*

I was striding past the fountain before I even realized I'd left the house. What if she'd taken off for Brazil like I'd mentioned that day in the motel room where she'd been staying? Had she *left* me? Had what we'd done last night spooked her that much? My blood was pulsing through my veins with something I couldn't identify—either panic or anger, or perhaps a mixture of both.

Would her suitcase be gone? Had she made a complete fool of me? Leaving me with nothing but shattered pride and a very real leg shackle, but no wife or the inheritance we'd agreed to split? I didn't even bother knocking, striding through the cluttered front room and bursting into her bedroom, my heartbeat pounding in my chest at what I'd find. *Don't be gone. Please—*

I expelled a giant breath when I saw her suitcase open on the floor, her clothes falling out the same way they'd been the day before. My gaze swung around the room, resting on the lump under the bedcovers. She was *sleeping*? At six at night? "Kira?" No answer. I moved to the bed and ripped the covers back. A small groan emerged and Kira pulled her legs up to her chest, rolling into an even smaller ball. "Kira?" I asked again, this time with the sudden worry that had swept through me lacing my voice.

Her face was covered with all that beautiful hair of hers, so I moved it back and put my hand to her forehead. Her skin was hot to the touch and she was sweat slicked but shivering. "Oh no, Kira, you're burning up, sweetheart." She only groaned again, moving her face in my direction but keeping her eyes closed. She mumbled something unintelligible and then shivered violently. *Fuck me.* This was *my* fault. I'd let her stay in this drafty, dusty place, caused her to take frigid showers for days on end. What was wrong with me? Guilt hit me in the gut and I put my arms under her, lifting her gently along with the quilt. "You're coming up to the main house and that's final. I'm laying down the law. I know somewhere in there you're arguing with me, but I'm not taking no for an answer. You have no choice but to obey me. How do you like that, Wife?" I asked, trying to get some kind of reaction from her. She gave none other than pressing herself closer to me and shivering again.

I walked her carefully through the dirty, equipment-filled front room and kicked the door closed behind me, moving quickly through the unseasonably chilly, mist-filled evening. As I climbed the stairs with Kira in my arms, my head suddenly grew dizzy and I stopped, leaning against the banister for a moment. Well, that was strange. God, I hoped I wasn't getting sick too. It would not be good timing. After a moment, the feeling passed, leaving only a strange buzzing in my blood. I brought Kira to the bedroom that had once belonged to my stepmother and laid her gently on the bed. I pulled the blankets back on the other side and then moved her over onto the sheets and covered her.

After smoothing her hair back and laying a cool washcloth on her forehead, I went to get some Tylenol. When I'd returned with the tablets, I shook Kira gently. "Kira, you need to tell me if you've already taken something. Kira?" She stirred, her eyes blinking up at me, the green even more vivid with the fever. "Kira, did you take anything? Any medicine?"

She shook her head and winced. "Didn't have anything," she croaked.

"Okay, then I need you to take these," I said, holding the pills close to her mouth. She swallowed them and took several long drinks of the water I'd brought up, collapsing back on the pillows and closing her eyes once again. I took a moment to study her face. Her skin was flushed with the fever, her eyelashes long and dark on her cheeks, her lips dry and slightly parted.

"Beautiful little brat," I whispered, smoothing her hair back. I became aware of the strange buzzing in my veins again and frowned. The buzzing seemed to flow down to my groin and I grimaced as I hardened. This was hardly the time for lust and yet my body seemed to have ideas of its own. I felt mildly ashamed. The woman in front of me was sick for God's sake.

Over the course of the next day and a half, I worked to keep Kira comfortable as her body fought to break the fever, and I struggled to keep my own body under control. Need raged through my blood in some sort of fiery swirl of uncontrolled lust. I found myself doubled over repeatedly from the pulsing intensity of an erection that seemed to come out of nowhere and last for hours. It wasn't normal. Something was drastically wrong.

I called José and told him I was too sick to work for the first time in the year since I'd been back. I wouldn't have worked that day anyway, as I wouldn't have left Kira alone—but the truth was, I was in no shape to leave the house. I was like an out-of-control animal. I wanted to fuck like a Viking—pillage and tear clothes and sate my throbbing desire over and over and over until the pulsating pain left me limp and finally satisfied. The thought itself seemed ridiculously dramatic, and yet I couldn't think of any other way to explain it, even to myself.

I looked away as I wiped cool cloths on Kira's neck and upper chest, shaking to control the urge to roll on top of her and take her, unconscious with fever or not. I had to relieve myself four times alone in the bathroom just to function enough to care for the little witch. No, this was not normal. Had she put some kind of evil spell on me? I felt possessed by a sexually aggressive demon straight from the depths of Hades.

I was on the verge of calling a doctor—or perhaps a priest to perform an exorcism on me—when the symptoms finally began to abate late Sunday afternoon. Mentally exhausted and physically drained—quite literally—I lay down on the bed next to Kira for just a moment. She felt markedly cooler, her breathing smooth and even. The dusky beginnings of twilight filtered in through the edges of the heavy drapes, and the low whir of the ceiling fan lulled me to sleep almost instantly.

CHAPTER TWELVE
Kira

I came awake slowly, feeling as if I was emerging from somewhere deep and dark, the light far, far above. I blinked, trying to understand where I was, the feel of something warm and solid at my back. Turning groggily, I looked into the staggeringly beautiful face of a sleeping dragon. *What? How?* I tried to piece together what had brought me here and could only remember climbing into bed, practically unable to stand, feeling first like a boulder had fallen on my body and then as if I were being boiled alive. Even now, I felt groggy, my limbs heavy.

Visions of Grayson feeding me broth, putting cool cloths on my head, and smoothing my hair back came to me in scattered memory. He had cared for me while I was sick and feverish. Tenderness slipped around me as I gazed at him. My mind not fully awake, uninhibited by neither fear nor rationale, I brought my hand up to his face and moved my thumb down his rough jaw, shadowed with black stubble. *This is what it would be like to wake to him. This is what it would be like if he were really mine.* He hadn't shaved in a couple days. Had I been here, in this room, for that long?

Grayson's eyes blinked open and he stared at me for several moments, comprehension coming into his sleepy expression. "Hi," he murmured, bringing his hand to my forehead. He sighed as he brought his hand away. "Fever's gone," he said.

"Yes. You took care of me," I whispered. "Thank you." *He's kind.* The thought came sudden and sure.

Our gazes held. Yes, he had kindness and caring within him, but most of the time, he covered that kindness in ice and fire. And I now understood the reason. Charlotte had mentioned how he hadn't had a good relationship with his father and stepmother. But she hadn't told me how cruel Grayson's father was. He sounded like a horrible man. The puppy story had broken my heart. What a wretched thing to do to a child. It had softened me toward Grayson too, which had led to me giving in to the physical temptation. Those kisses…the feeling of his mouth on my skin felt like part of a fever dream now. Maybe it was…

We lay like that, the moment seeming to be caught between sleep and wakefulness, both of us still tangled in the foggy web of dreams. His eyes were so beautiful—as dark as the night sky and just as easy to get lost in. He brought his hand to my cheek and brushed his thumb over my cheekbone. I sighed, leaning into his touch. Suddenly, he blinked, his eyes opening fully as if something had just occurred to him.

And *pop*, the spell was broken.

He rolled onto his back, looking almost guilty as he brought his hand to his hair and ran his fingers through it, gripping it at the top of his head. "It was—"

The doorbell rang, echoing through the house. He sat up. "Walter and Charlotte are still gone. I'll get that." He stood, his jeans and T-shirt wrinkled, his hair in disarray, the dark shadow of stubble making him look even more handsome somehow. His gaze ran over my body, and again, he looked away almost guiltily.

I came up on one elbow. "You didn't...take advantage of my feverish state, did you, dragon?"

He clenched his jaw, his eyes growing impossibly darker, and said tersely, "No." Then he turned and headed for the door. "Take a hot shower. I brought your suitcase up," he said. I looked to where he inclined his head before he exited the room, and indeed, my suitcase and toiletry bag were sitting beneath the window.

I did as Grayson said, taking a long, hot, luxurious shower, savoring the feel of the heat raining down on my sore muscles, lathering and washing my skin with my shower gel again and again. It felt heavenly. When I finally emerged, clean and scrubbed, I felt fully awake and human again. After drying my hair and dressing, I went downstairs to find Grayson and get some food. I was ravenous.

Voices from the living room caught my attention and I turned in that direction, coming to a halt when I saw Kimberly sitting on the couch, Grayson across from her. They were both laughing about something but stopped when I entered the room. Kimberly let out a small shriek and stood up, running to me and swooping me up in a giant hug.

"What are you doing here?" I asked breathlessly, taking her in, my heart squeezing with happiness.

"You haven't answered my calls in two days! I was worried. I came to make sure you weren't shackled in a wine cellar being tortured mercilessly." She smiled back at Grayson as if it was a joke they'd already shared. They seemed mighty chummy already. I wasn't sure how I felt about that.

Grayson stood. "I'll leave you two to talk," he said, his gaze fixed on me as he approached us. I couldn't help but notice that despite having recently woken up, he still looked tired, as if he hadn't slept much. "I need a shower anyway. Nice to meet you, Kimberly."

I looked away, biting my lip at the sudden picture of Grayson Hawthorn naked under a hot spray of water. Soap cascading—

"Kira? Hello, Kira?" Kimberly said. "Do you want to sit?" She was obviously repeating the question I'd just missed.

"Oh, yes. See ya," I said to Grayson who was already walking past us. "Um, thank you again." His head turned slightly, but he didn't say a word.

"Get *over* here," Kimberly said, pulling my hand. "What is going on? I haven't gotten a decent update from you since you two got married, and then you didn't answer even one of my calls or texts this weekend—"

"I was sick. Like, really sick." We plopped down on the couch and I brought a pillow into my lap, hugging it to me. "Grayson took care of me." I was still confused about that and hadn't had the chance to ask him anything about it. Why had he done it? How had he found me? And God, had it really been only a couple days since he'd kissed me and touched me with such passion, causing me to lie awake, tossing and turning with frustrated confusion? I'd finally gotten out of bed and made a list of details for the party and emailed it to Charlotte. Putting my mind to work on something besides *him* had helped, and I'd eventually been able to sleep when I'd returned to bed.

Kimberly raised an eyebrow. "I'm glad you're better and we'll talk about that in a minute. But I have a bone to pick with you. You purposely left out that he's a Greek god."

I scoffed. "*Greek god?* I have no idea what you're talking about. He's one of the ugliest men I've ever seen. I can barely look at him."

Kimmy grinned. "Liar." Her expression became contemplative. "It does worry me though. It's going to be easier to fall in love if you're already attracted to him. Since the plan is to walk away from him in a couple months, find a way not to let that happen, that's all I'm saying. And whatever you do, do not let him kiss you."

I sighed and leaned my head back on the couch. "Okay."

Her mouth fell open. "Oh my God. You let him kiss you!"

I couldn't help laughing. It felt so good to be known. I updated Kimberly on everything that had taken place since our wedding day. She listened, her expression moving between anger, mild horror, surprise, and finally pensiveness. "I'm not surprised about the kissing." She sighed. "The way his eyes tracked you when you came into the room... Well, now what are you going to do?" *His eyes tracked me?* He was probably trying to make sure I could walk given how sick I'd been.

"Nothing. He just wants to turn me into a convenient plaything and then watch as I walk away. That would never, well...you know me, Kimberly. I don't operate that way. It would be an utter disaster. For me."

Kimberly opened her mouth to respond when we heard Grayson yelling from the kitchen. I jumped up and Kimberly followed as I hurried to the other side of the house. Grayson was just exiting the kitchen. Charlotte, who must have returned while I was upstairs showering, was on his heels. "It was meant to be helpful," she called after him. He turned around, the lines of his body tense, his eyes shooting fire at Charlotte.

"I almost molested her. When she was feverish and unconscious," he ground out.

"Oh dear," Charlotte said. She looked up, placing one finger on her chin. "Was it meant to be halved not doubled?" She took her finger down. "Yes, that must have been the problem."

"What's going on here?" I asked. Kimberly's head moved back and forth between Grayson and Charlotte. Walter quietly arrived and stood standing off to the side.

"She poisoned me," Grayson growled, pointing a finger at Charlotte.

Charlotte laughed merrily. "I didn't poison him. It's a simple herbal concoction my mother taught me, meant to increase male ardor." She grinned at me. I felt my face drain of color. Charlotte had given Grayson some sort of herbal mixture to increase *ardor* before they'd left for the weekend? Why? And... *Oh God*. Had he said he'd almost molested me while I was unconscious? *Um*...

Walter moved forward. "It's hardly my place, sir, but—"

"When has that ever stopped you, Walter?" Grayson glared.

"True," Walter agreed without remorse before going on. "I've found personally that plenty of water throughout the day helps the, uh...effects wear off sooner. However, I do recommend the proper dosage. It's quite...helpful."

Grayson let out a pained sound, looking up at the ceiling. "I'm in hell."

Charlotte stepped forward. "Would you like me to prepare you—?"

"No! I'll never let you prepare me anything again. You're fired! I'm surrounded by crazy people." And then he strode off toward the door, slamming it behind him so hard, a vase on the shelf next to us wobbled and almost fell.

I gasped, my eyes flying to Charlotte. She smiled again as if she hadn't just been sacked.

"He fired you?" I breathed.

Charlotte waved her hand in the air as if it was nothing. "Oh, he's fired me twice a month or so since he was sixteen." She turned back toward the kitchen, calling after Kimberly and me. "Come join me for a cup of coffee, girls."

Kimberly, grinning broadly, led the way. "I love this place!"

Charlotte stood at the counter, a large butcher block in front of her as she rolled dough for some type of baked good. I introduced her to Kimberly, and she poured three cups of coffee as Kimberly and I sat down.

"What were you thinking, Charlotte?" I asked her, trying my best to glare, knowing I could have been the victim of molestation while unconscious due to her actions. Of course, the fact that I felt a tingle between my legs at the picture that popped into my head made it clear the word *victim* might not have been exactly accurate. Also…even despite herbal meddling, I just didn't see Grayson taking advantage of an unconscious woman. Then again, men had blindsided me before. From my experience, they were mostly untrustworthy. Two cases in point: my father and my ex-fiancé.

As for Charlotte, her intentions, though misguided, had been pure. I was sure of it.

Charlotte's eyes twinkled. "It seemed to me you two were avoiding each other. But then you went to dinner. And I was thinking maybe Grayson needed a small push in the right direction. And then if you two were alone all weekend…" She frowned. "But I may have gotten the dosage wrong, and of course, I should have considered his virility…"

I groaned and put my forehead in my hand for a moment before I looked back up at her smiling face. I hardly wanted to think about my husband's virility. "I don't know that he exactly needed a push in that direction," I confided.

Charlotte stopped what she was doing, her eyes twinkling as she set her rolling pin aside. "And you?" she asked.

"I…" I tilted my head. "I'm attracted to him too. I…" I circled one finger around the rim of my coffee mug. "Well, there are moments when I even like him, believe it or not." I shook my head. "But I can't give him what he wants for several reasons." I glanced at Kimberly, and she gave me a sympathetic look. "But the main reason is that *he* would probably have no problem sharing his body with me and then going on as if nothing had happened. But I wouldn't be able to." It had always been the way with me—where my body went, my heart tended to follow. I didn't necessarily like it, but it was true and to lie to myself would be a personal disservice. Grayson Hawthorn could so easily destroy me if I gave him the opportunity. I'd learned that lesson once, and I didn't care to repeat it. This time, I would not give in to my stupid, reckless whims.

Especially not when it came to a highly virile dragon.

Charlotte patted my hand that was lying on the counter, leaving a small smudge of flour on my knuckle. "That's how us women are built, my dear. When we give our bodies, we give our hearts. When men give their bodies, well…" She looked up as if trying to come up with the right words.

"They give their bodies," both Kimberly and I finished in unison, and then the three of us dissolved into laughter. My heart soared with affection for both of them. I had missed having girlfriends around.

"Yes. So that's off the table," I said.

"Well, we'll see," Charlotte replied.

"No evil plotting," I warned. Secretly, though, my heart was warmed to know Charlotte wanted to see a true relationship between Grayson and me. Perhaps, for her, it was mostly because she didn't believe in the fake marriage we'd arranged—making it real would allow her to be happy for Grayson, rather than disappointed for him.

"Oh, no," Charlotte said unconvincingly. "At least not so I get caught."

I laughed softly and took a sip of my coffee. I was tempted to ask Charlotte about some of the things I'd learned about Grayson the other night, especially regarding Vanessa. But one, I didn't feel exactly right talking about those things behind his back, and two, Kimberly was there.

"Will he forgive you?" I asked Charlotte.

"Oh, eventually. This right here," she said, nodding to the dough in her hand, "is for his favorite blueberry scones. He likes them with jam and cream. He'll act angry for a couple days just to preserve his pride, but after a few of these, he really won't be." She held up a finger. "Oh, that reminds me, Kira. I'll need to go to the south field to collect the apricots so ripe they're falling on the ground. Do you want to help me make a couple batches of my apricot jam?"

"Sure. I made strawberry preserves with my grand-mother once," I said, thinking back fondly to that day.

"I love this place," Kimberly said again. "I think you belong here, Kira."

Her words alternately brought me happiness and dread

172

because I was beginning to love a lot of things about this place too.

And as we sat in the warm kitchen, fragrant with the smells of blueberries and coffee, eating oatmeal honey muffins, Charlotte prattling on about her weekend trip, it suddenly hit me: Grayson had said that, for all intents and purposes, he'd grown up with no parents at all. I still didn't understand the exact dynamics of that situation. But he'd been wrong on one account. He'd *had* parents all along. Their names were Walter and Charlotte Popplewell, and they loved him as if he were their own. I wondered if Grayson even realized it.

After a little while, Kimberly told me she had to get going. I walked her outside, and as we stood at her car, she smiled. "This has been such a nice visit. I meant what I said." She looked around at the Hawthorn property. "It feels like you fit here." She studied my face for a second. "But take care of yourself. I couldn't bear to see you hurt again, Kira Kat."

I gave her a brief smile. "I will, I promise."

She looked away for a moment. "I almost hate to tell you this, after seeing how well you're doing here—"

My heart sank. "My dad's been calling you, hasn't he?" I asked, guessing immediately. She always got the same tight look on her face whenever my dad came to her mind.

"He's called several times, even hinting once that if I didn't get you to call him, he'd pull some strings at Andy's job somehow—and I don't think he means to get him a promotion."

"That controlling bastard." I seethed. Kim's husband, Andy, was a police dispatcher, and I supposed it wasn't out of the scope of the impossible that my father had some pull at the San Francisco Police Department, but for my father to even consider that? Was there no limit to the depths he would sink to control me?

Kimberly put a comforting hand on my arm. "Now listen. I didn't tell you that so you'd contact him on our account. Andy is a little bit worried, but frankly, we'd rather collect unemployment than let your father influence our lives. I just thought you should be aware. Who knows what else he's up to. It might be best for you to go to him now, so he doesn't figure out where you are before you're ready and show up here."

I shivered at the thought alone. I agreed though. And I would *not* let this become my friend's problem. "I will. Thanks, Kimberly." *Please let that marriage license come soon.* I just needed to cash that check first…

I hugged her tightly, promising to visit soon and update her frequently, and then I watched her car drive out the gate.

I turned, staring blindly at the nonworking fountain, wondering what it would look like when it was fixed and flowing, wondering how far it was down on Grayson's list of priorities. *Grayson…* He had spent the entire weekend in a state of utter torment thanks to Charlotte, and yet he'd selflessly cared for me, soothing my fever, and making sure I was never alone. Apparently, I'd been wrong about the Dragon, in some ways at least. He wasn't the uncaring beast I'd originally thought. I pondered momentarily how he'd been betrayed by his brother, father, and stepmother. He was just a man—a man who held deep hurts and was trying his best to get by in a situation that, until me, had offered very little hope.

And I thought again about how I knew he'd been wronged not only by his own father but by mine too. Would he understand why I hadn't mentioned that if he knew? I thought about telling him now… Only, our plan hadn't changed. We would still part ways soon enough. What purpose would it serve?

My mind filled with worries, I wandered back into the house and headed toward the office—the room where I'd first officially met Grayson Hawthorn. I sat down at the large desk and started rifling through the pile of new mail Charlotte must have retrieved from the mailbox when she returned this morning, along with the large pile of old, unopened envelopes, separating it all into three piles: what looked like bills, junk, and personal correspondence. There were several unopened letters addressed to Grayson in what looked like a feminine script. I set those aside, but when I came to a postcard with the picture of a bicycle leaning against a tree and turned it over, I noticed the same handwriting and that it was dated very recently. I hesitated only briefly before letting my eyes drift away from the address to the message.

Grayson,

Remember when we were thirteen and I splashed mud all over you with my bike and felt so bad? You told me it was impossible to stay mad at me for long. I'm praying you still have it in your heart to forgive me. I'll never stop trying…

All my love, Vanessa.

Vanessa. *All my love?* She still loved him? She was trying to persuade Grayson to forgive her? For marrying his brother? A strange ache had settled in my chest, making my skin feel prickly. I didn't like it. And I didn't like that I didn't like it. Because none of it was my business.

I started to put the most recent mail aside, deciding I was done with the task, when I came upon a business envelope addressed to me. I sucked in a breath, tearing it open. I let out a small shriek, the prickly feeling dissolving into hopeful excitement when I saw that it was our official marriage license. I tossed the other mail onto the desk and walked quickly to the front door, calling toward Charlotte in the kitchen, "I'm going into town. I'll be back soon."

I heard her singsong, "Okay," before the door swung shut behind me.

I had some money to collect. Quite a lot of money, in fact.

CHAPTER THIRTEEN
Grayson

By three o'clock, I was too exhausted to work for another minute. I returned to the house where the smells of Charlotte's blueberry scones hung sweetly in the air. "You don't play fair," I said, feigning hostility as I entered the kitchen. "I was going to give you the silent treatment for at least another day and a half. Give me one of those."

Charlotte beamed happily, placing a warm scone on a plate with a dollop of clotted cream on top and a spoonful of jam on the side.

"Cheater," I mumbled. "Don't think this means I forgive you," I said after I'd taken a big bite of heaven.

"I do apologize," Charlotte said. "I caused you pain, and I would never have done such a thing on purpose." She studied me for a moment. "I just—"

"You want Kira and I to have a real marriage." I shook my head. "I'm sorry, Charlotte, that's not going to happen. I don't have the time or desire for a wife."

As far as the physical aspect...I had tried. Not that

Charlotte needed to know that—it'd just give her false hope. Kira had said no but I wasn't going to give up on that front. After all, for now at least, we *were* husband and wife—why not reap the temporary benefits? I couldn't stop imagining it. And the more I imagined it, the more I wanted her. But surely two months, perhaps a little less, would be plenty of time to quench that fire. I'd know the feel of her under me, around me, on top of me…and then it would be over. I'd be sated. And I would move on. And so would she.

"I didn't give you that herbal mixture so you'd act on a physical attraction to her, you know," Charlotte said, seeming to read my thoughts. "I hope more for you than that. That was just to get the blood flowing, if you know what I mean." I scowled. Disgusting that we should discuss this. She had practically raised me. But she continued on before I could stop her. "To the body *and* the heart. And as for Kira, she doesn't want a purely physical relationship with you either, you know."

Purely physical? What did that mean? That she wanted more? I paused, not able to help my interest. "How do you know that?"

"Because she's a woman. That's how I know that."

I considered her words. If we enjoyed each other's bodies, would Kira really want more? She barely seemed to *like* me half the time. No, Charlotte was wrong about that. I did know for sure that Kira liked my touch however. Thinking back now, that constant hum of sexual awareness had been there from the very beginning. It had been present the first time my skin touched hers. I just hadn't acknowledged it because I'd been too busy judging her, resenting her, and then being driven to distraction by her outlandish behavior. But I wasn't denying it anymore. I didn't think there was any reason we couldn't keep things on a physical level. For my part, I knew I could enjoy her body without falling for her. I *would*. I was finished denying myself where it came to the mostly exasperating but highly desirable little witch. Now I'd just have to convince her too.

The protectiveness I'd felt toward Kira when I'd found her sick and feverish in her bed had worried me for the first couple hours I'd cared for her. But then, before I'd had time to fully consider it, Charlotte's herbs kicked in, and it had just been all I could do to survive my own body, the effort at self-control making me too exhausted to think. Perhaps in some strange way, the distraction—awful though it'd been— had been partially positive. And maybe the initial concern over Kira's well-being was nothing more than a natural male reaction to want to protect your own wife—even one of nothing more than convenience. How would I know? I'd never had a wife before. Eventually, I expected that would go by the wayside. Just like our marriage.

"Speaking of Kira," I said, "where is the little troublemaker?"

"I don't know. She went tearing out of here several hours ago."

I raised a brow, wondering what had been so important. Before I had the time to ask the question aloud, I heard a vehicle in the driveway. And then a few moments after that, Kira's voice rang out, "Hello?"

"In here, dear," Charlotte called.

I looked over my shoulder as Kira walked hurriedly into the kitchen, setting a large box on the floor with holes in the top. "What's that?" I asked, pointing at the large container.

"A surprise," she said, grinning.

I groaned. What on earth had she come up with now?

"But first," she said, sitting down on the stool next to me, "we're officially married. I brought the marriage license to Mr. Hartmann. Our check will be processed and cut later today. We can pick it up first thing in the morning."

Excitement shot through my body. "Really?"

"Really." She grinned.

I couldn't help myself. I stood and picked her up in a hug, spinning her around as she laughed. "We did it," I said almost unbelievingly, coming to a standstill and setting her on her feet. She smiled up at me, her eyes shining, her smile bright. *And* I earned the dimple.

"I know," she breathed. God, I wanted to kiss her. And the intensity of that want was such that I had to wonder if it was natural or if Charlotte's herbs were still running rampant through my system.

The soft sound of something scraping from inside the box still on the floor behind us interrupted that thought. Kira's grin increased, that bewitching dimple popping out again, as she stepped away from me and moved quickly to whatever was in the box.

"What have you done?" I asked.

She squatted on the floor, opened the box, and lifted out what looked to be a large puppy or a small dog. Soulful dark eyes stared at me warily and bright green ones regarded me excitedly.

"Oh my," Charlotte gasped, hurrying over to Kira. "And who is this?" Charlotte lifted the metal tag at the dog's neck and read: "Sugar Pie?"

Kira nodded proudly.

I gave my head a small shake as I took stock of the dog. "What's…going on with its face?" It looked as if its nose and jaw had been mangled in some way.

Kira pulled the thing, what I could now tell was an older puppy, some kind of mutt, into her chest and covered its ear with her other hand. "Shh," she said. "She can hear you, you know." She gave me a contemptuous frown. "And Sugar Pie is a *she*." She beamed down at the puppy who looked up at her with what looked like barely contained hope. "Aren't you, baby girl? Aren't you, sweet Sugar Pie? Yes you are, you're a *girl*, a good girl. Such a good girl. A sweet, good girl." I grimaced at the sound of the high-pitched baby talk. But apparently the puppy didn't mind it one little bit.

The dog, trembling in an obvious attempt to hold back her rapture at Kira's attentions, licked her face with that strangely deformed mouth. Kira laughed and then covered the puppy's ear again. "I rescued her. Her first owner muzzled her when she was barely weaned. And then he didn't take it off as her face grew. When she was found, she was almost dead and had to have the contraption surgically removed!" Her voice had risen as she spoke, clearly deeply distressed about what had happened to the dog. It was sad. Humans could be really fucking shitty sometimes. But I wasn't sure what any of this had to do with me.

Kira took her hand off the dog's ear and resumed babbling to it in baby talk for a few deeply painful moments.

Charlotte, who was clicking and cooing like a grandma meeting her grandbaby for the first time, scratched the puppy's ears. "Oh, the poor little dear. You don't worry about a thing, Sugar Pie. You're going to fit in just fine around here." In her obvious excitement, the puppy let out a small squeak and then lowered her head as if expecting dire consequences as a result of the small, escaped noise. She looked at us, her eyes raised dismally, her head still lowered.

"Whoa, whoa, around *here*?" I asked. "No. The last

thing I need is an animal running around, getting in my way. I don't have the time for a pet."

"I rescued Sugar Pie for *you*. She's yours. Consider her, um, my wedding gift. And a thank you for your kindness this weekend." She thrust the dog at me, forcing me to take it from her.

I tried to hand it back. "What? No way. No. I don't want a dog. Where's my money?"

Kira crossed her arms and Charlotte tsked. I brought the dog back to my chest and looked down at it, those large, dark eyes trained on me with a mix of fear and hope. It was very ugly. But also, kind of...cute. I felt a strange stirring in the region of my heart as I remembered another pair of trusting brown eyes. *Oh Jesus.* Kira had gone and gotten me a puppy after the story I'd told her about my father. *Irritating little witch. Sweet, compassionate, irritating little witch.*

It had been a kind thought. Still... "Kira, I can't have a dog named Sugar Pie. No man owns a dog named Sugar Pie."

"Oh." She put one finger up on her lips. "Well, that's what I named her, and she seems to be attached to it. Her full name is Sugar Pie Honey Bunches." She was holding back a barely suppressed smile. This amused the little witch.

I considered the animal again and let out a long sigh. Despite her deformity and her unacceptable name, I couldn't bring myself to send her away now that she was in my arms, looking at me with such raw hope. I did have a large property. She could run around—I'd probably never even see her. Although at the very least, she'd need to be trained not to eat the grapes, as they could be dangerous to dogs. I set her on the ground. She stood stock-still, staring at me. "She's still a puppy, and you just got her today. She can learn a new name." I backed up. "Come here, Scout." She tilted that ugly head, sitting down squarely on her butt.

Kira moved back too. "Come here, Sugar Pie," she called. The dog scampered over to her immediately, its overly large paws clicking on the floor. Kira scooped her up and started cooing to her in that same highly irritating baby voice.

"Come here, Sugar Pie," I called experimentally. Kira put her down on the ground and the puppy scampered over to me, squeaking again and then lowering her head in that scared, bashful way. I scooped her up and looked her in her eyes. "First off, you're allowed to talk around here." She regarded me with those expressive eyes as if she understood what I was saying. She licked my cheek tentatively. I looked up at Kira and Charlotte who were both grinning broadly. "Fine, she can stay," I grumbled, clenching my jaw and turning around with my new puppy and heading for the door. What the hell was happening to my life? "I'm going to show her the house and get her used to a new name," I called as I left the kitchen.

Happy feminine laughter followed me up the stairs, a sound I suddenly realized I'd never heard so often in this house…before Kira had come along.

———

The next morning, bright and early, Kira and I headed downtown to pick up the check that had been the catalyst and reason for this whole marriage. Mr. Hartmann handed it over and wished us happiness and good luck, and not ten minutes after we'd entered the building, we were back out on the street, staring at each other as if in shock. I grinned at Kira and said, "Let's go open a bank account."

As we headed to a different bank down the street, we

walked past the one where Kira had first seen me. Kira might have good memories of that particular bank, but I couldn't stomach opening an account at the place that had rejected my loan request—whether their rejection had been justified or not. Still, I thought about the last time I'd been there, how hopeless and low I'd felt. I grabbed Kira's hand and gave it a squeeze. She grinned over at me, her dimple popping out. A lock of her fiery hair fell in front of one eye, and I couldn't help myself. I stopped and walked her backward toward a building and pressed her against the wall, giving her a quick, hard kiss, and then grinning at her surprised expression.

"Get a room," someone walking by mumbled. Kira looked briefly shocked, and I gave her my best devilish grin, raising my eyebrows.

"No," she said resolutely, slipping out from under me. But she glanced back, a teasing smile on her face. My heart flipped in some unfamiliar way and I laughed, walking quickly to catch up. I felt...new. Hopeful. Like the world had just opened up and I wanted to spread my arms wide and welcome it.

An hour later, we had separate accounts, each containing almost half a million dollars. That hopeful feeling was still there, but as we drove back to the vineyard, a nagging shame began pricking at the bubble I'd been floating in. Yes, we'd struck a deal but really? It was her money I was about to spend. "I'm going to pay you back. You know that, right?" I asked, my eyes meeting Kira's.

"If you want," she said, studying my face.

"I do."

Kira was quiet for a minute and then her voice came out softly. "I need to go see my father today."

Her expression was a mixture between sadness and something that looked like dejection. It surprised me—Kira's eyes were normally so filled with vibrancy. It was as if the idea of seeing her father sucked the radiance right from her body. I felt like I should say something, but I had no idea what. "Okay," I mumbled.

She looked at me as if she wanted to ask me something, but instead she just nodded, getting out of my truck when we pulled up in front of the house and calling behind her that she'd see me in a couple days.

I watched her walk away. She'd be gone for a couple days. It should have made me happy. I'd have some peace around here for forty-eight hours at least. I wouldn't have to worry about an insurance risk romping all over my property, causing trouble and mayhem. And if she was out of sight, maybe my blood wouldn't be constantly churning with need.

So why, instead of being glad about her impending departure, did I have this vague feeling of melancholy? I shook off my meandering thoughts and went to my office to put in the orders for supplies and equipment I'd had bookmarked for weeks now. At least that was something to be excited about. Everything was falling into place.

The dog padded into my office and lay down at my feet as I worked at the computer. Forty-five minutes later, when I'd placed all the orders, I stood up and called the ugly mutt from where she still lay under my desk. "Here, Buddy." Nothing. She didn't even lift her head.

I considered her for a moment. She was a girl, so perhaps she just wanted a name more fitting for a female. "Here, Bailey." Not even a muscle twinge. I gritted my teeth. "Here, Sugar Pie," I said under my breath. The dog's ears perked up, and she let out an excited squeak and stood quickly, taking the few steps to where I stood. I pressed my lips together and gave her a bitter glare. She panted up at me, and I swore that crooked mouth was smiling.

"All you women are enjoying this, aren't you?" I asked, turning toward the kitchen as the dog trotted after me.

Charlotte met me in the hall. "Kira's putting her suitcase in her car," she said. "You're not going with her?"

I glanced toward the door. "Why would I go with her?"

"I just thought it would make more sense for both of you to show up to tell her father you're married. Wouldn't that make it more convincing?" Obviously Kira had told Charlotte where she was going and why. *She'd have told you if you'd asked too, Grayson.*

"If she'd wanted me to go with her, she would have asked," I insisted. I turned my attention to the dog. "Come here, Maggie." She sat looking at me. I sighed. "Come on, Sugar Pie." The insufferable animal stood up to trot after me as we walked toward the kitchen. Charlotte laughed. "I'm sure this is very amusing for you," I said, glaring at her.

Charlotte smiled as she began to take items from the refrigerator. "I'm making Kira a sandwich to take on the road. Would you like one?"

"Sure," I said, sitting on a bar stool.

"As for this sweet girl," she said, smiling down at the dog who wagged her tail gleefully at Charlotte, "I imagine the first time Kira called her Sugar Pie, she said it with such adoring love, this dog couldn't easily let it go now. I suspect it was the very first time she had heard a loving tone attached to herself in her short, sad life. That's a very powerful thing, you know."

I met Charlotte's wise eyes, considering her words, thinking about the fact that my wife had brought this dog home for me to try to heal something that had happened a long time ago. By the look of sadness that had been in her eyes earlier, maybe Kira needed something from long ago healed as well. Perhaps we were husband and wife on paper only, but she had shown me undeserved kindness. She hadn't had an ulterior motive; she'd simply done it because she could. *Maybe she deserves the same.* "Wrap both the sandwiches, Charlotte," I said. "I'm going with her."

Charlotte only smiled.

CHAPTER FOURTEEN
Kira

I was setting my suitcase in the trunk of my car when I saw Grayson emerge from the house with what looked like an overnight bag of his own and a small cooler.

I closed the trunk and stood watching him as he approached. "What are you doing?" I asked.

"Coming with you," he replied, opening the trunk and removing my suitcase.

"Coming with me? But—"

He shut my trunk again and turned toward me. "It will look more convincing if we both go to your father. We made this business arrangement together, and we should both be involved in what's necessary to make it work. Consider this me earning part of my share." He was coming with me? My heart gave a small gallop of both happiness and uncertainty. He walked to his truck parked nearby and put my suitcase and his bags behind the front seat.

"Okay," I said, walking him. "But why are you putting my suitcase into your truck?"

"Because I like to drive."

I sighed. *Controlling man.* And here I was traveling to see another one who liked to trample all over me. That uncertainty suddenly ratcheted higher than the momentary happiness I'd felt.

Grayson got behind the wheel and I opened the passenger side door, looking up at him but not climbing in. "You don't have to feel obligated to do this," I said. I wasn't exactly sure if I wanted Grayson to meet my father for the first time when I'd be telling him about our marriage. I could only imagine the frigid disdain he'd show not only me but Grayson as well. And I had to wonder if Grayson's name would be familiar at all. I doubted it—my father only remembered those who could continue to serve his agenda in some way. Plus, what had happened had been quite a few years ago and had transpired in a few brief moments. Still, I'd never pictured Grayson being in the room when I informed my father I'd gotten married without telling him in advance. Things could get ugly, and I didn't want anyone—most especially Grayson Hawthorn—to see it. Especially considering that I was pretty sure my father wouldn't strive to spare Grayson's feelings in any way, shape, or form. God, when had I begun to care so much about the Dragon's feelings anyway? It was really somewhat concerning.

"It's the appropriate way to handle this, Kira. Now, can we go? I don't want to hit any traffic in San Francisco."

"Who will take care of Sugar Pie?" I asked, attempting one final argument.

"Charlotte. Virgil will help out too. The dog seems attached to him already."

Okay then, fine, he could come and see for himself exactly why I would rather marry him than take anything from my father in this life or any other. He would see... well, he would see exactly who I was. And that scared me. *Why?* And then it came to me—I wanted the Dragon to respect me. I didn't want him to see me as the spoiled heiress he'd obviously judged me to be that day in his office when he'd shown me such coldness. I didn't want him to see the grandeur of where I'd grown up and think that was any part of who I was or what I wanted out of life. I had married this man, and yet I'd never intended on letting Grayson Hawthorn into my private life, my private pain. I had set up this arrangement as a business venture. And now, suddenly, I realized, it was turning into more—for me at least. I *cared*. And that scared me.

I swallowed down my turbulent emotions and got in the car. As we drove through the gates, I rolled down the window and inhaled a deep breath of the air, still sweet with the scent of late summer.

"Where are you planning on staying?" Grayson asked once we'd turned onto the freeway.

"A hotel," I answered.

"Not with Kimberly?"

"No. Now that I have the money to stay at a decent hotel, I'd rather not impose on them. Their apartment is so small."

Grayson nodded. "She seems like a good friend."

"She is. She's the best." I smiled, leaning my head back on the headrest. "We grew up together. Her mother came to work for us when we were both five. She's more like a sister, really. My mother had just died"—I bit my lip—"a skiing accident, and well...Kimberly's mother, Rosa Maria, took me under her wing during that time." I smiled, happy to turn my thoughts to anything other than confronting my father with my marriage. "Kimberly's birthday happened to fall a couple days after her mother first started working there, and Rosa Maria threw a very small party for her and invited the children of the other staff members. I was desperate to go and begged my father to take me out to get her a present, but he'd said, 'You won't need to buy her a present because you won't be going. A Dallaire does not belong in such low company.'" I had deepened my voice to mimic my father's masculine tone, and when I looked over at Grayson, he was wearing a small frown. *Well, good, you should get a taste of my father's winning personality now before you're confronted with it in person.*

"As you might imagine," I went on, "I wasn't going to accept *that* for an answer, so I took a necklace my mother had given me with a silver heart on it and had our gardener, George, clip it in half. I put it on a string, snuck into Kimberly's party in their living quarters, gave the makeshift necklace to her, and declared it meant we would be best friends for all eternity." My heart filled with warmth at the memory of how openly and lovingly she'd accepted it, and also that Kimberly still treasured the first token of our friendship.

Grayson was silent as he sucked at his lip, not looking at me. I stared ahead, feeling awkward, and after a few moments, I felt his eyes on the side of my face. "Are you still close to Rosa Maria?"

"No," I said sadly. "My father dismissed her years ago. It was awkward and painful since he'd been having a relationship with her and essentially traded her in for a newer, younger model to serve as both his new housekeeper and new bed partner. Rosa Maria didn't respond to any of my attempts to reach out to her after that." I waved my hand, trying to wave away the subject and the associated hurt that always came from discussing it.

"She blamed you?" Grayson asked, a strange edge to his voice.

"Kimberly says she doesn't, but it's too painful to have any contact that reminds her of what my father did to her. She loved him, I believe. While he…well, he saw her as nothing more than a convenient way to keep his house clean and his bed warm."

"I see," he said, his voice tight. I glanced at him, feeling as if, somehow, he really did see—even more than I was sharing with him.

I gave my head a small shake. "So, what were you and Kimberly talking about before I came downstairs yesterday morning?" I asked, realizing I hadn't had the chance to ask Kimberly before we'd been interrupted by his confrontation with Charlotte over the *herbs*.

He smiled, breaking the somber mood that had existed as I'd discussed the subject of Rosa Maria and my father. The afternoon sun slanted through the window and hit Grayson's face, bringing out the deep, rich brown of his eyes and highlighting the ruggedness of his still-unshaven jaw. I looked away, pressing my fingernails into the fleshy part of my hands. *Ignore the bright scales*, I repeated in my mind. "We were talking about you," he answered, and when I swung my eyes back to his, his smile widened. "She was telling me some interesting stories about the trouble she's had to pull you out of over the years."

I snorted and then sighed dramatically. "That Kimberly is a nice enough girl, but she exaggerates. It's one of her very worst flaws."

Grayson's chuckle was deep and warm. "I don't know.

I'm inclined to think she doesn't," he said, still smiling. "She says you get these ideas in your head…"

"Just fun," I defended. "Not trouble."

"With you, it seems to be a very fine line."

I gave him an irritated look, but it dissolved when I saw that his expression was full of charm and what looked like genuine affection.

"I've made a concerted effort to curtail the follow-through of my 'ideas' since I've been living with you," I insisted.

"Dear God," he groaned. "I shudder to imagine what happens when you don't hold back."

I started to laugh, but then a sign telling us we were headed toward San Francisco—toward my father—whizzed by and my stomach cramped. I sighed, frowning. "Just ask my father," I said, secretly hoping he wouldn't. "He'll tell you what a burden you've taken on when you meet him. I have no doubt." I turned my head to stare out at the scenery going by.

"Hey," Grayson said, and I felt his warm hand grasp mine on the seat next to me. I glanced down at our joined hands and then met his eyes. Our gazes held for a beat, then two, before he looked back to the road again. "This is going to be fine, all right?"

I nodded but feared he was wrong. I could very well be walking into a situation where I would be completely humiliated in front of Grayson. No, this wasn't going to be all right. This was going to be decidedly *un*-all right. And yet, there was really no turning back now.

The soft yellow and vibrant orange of approaching twilight

bathed the Italian Renaissance hilltop mansion in dreamy light. Nestled in the ritzy Pacific Heights neighborhood of San Francisco, it was among the most expensive pieces of real estate in the city, probably in the country. The Dallaire estate. Home sweet home. I cringed inwardly. There had been very little sweet attached to this place for me.

In fact, this house and its memories only served to make me crushingly aware that most of my life I'd lived in the shadow of my father's self-serving expectations, when all I'd ever longed for was to be loved for who I was.

I glanced at Grayson's enigmatic expression as we got out of his truck and parked on the street in front of the massive structure. He turned in a full circle at the top of the sprawling outdoor staircase, admiring the undeniably stunning view of the Golden Gate Bridge, Alcatraz, Angel Island, and all the way to the Marin Headlands. Distantly, I could hear someone hitting tennis balls in the outdoor court behind the house.

Grayson remained silent as I rang the doorbell. I refused to let myself into this house as if I belonged here. A few seconds later, I heard the click of shoes on the marble tile within and the door swung open to reveal a young woman whom I had never met in a maid's uniform. I smiled. "Hello, I'm Kira Dallaire. I believe my father is expecting me." I had texted him on the drive, but he'd never responded, so I had no idea if he was actually expecting me or not.

The pretty young woman smiled and swung the door open, and we stepped inside. "I will go get him," she said in a heavy Spanish accent. "Would you like to wait in the—"

"We'll wait here." I didn't intend on staying long. *I already want to leave.*

The woman nodded and turned away.

"Just give me a moment to talk to my father," I said to Grayson. "And then I'll introduce you." His eyes ran over my face and then he lifted his chin in silent agreement.

Several minutes of standing in the lavish, marble foyer later, I heard footsteps approaching once again—only this time from above—and looked up to see my father's tall figure appear at the top of the stairs. I glanced at Grayson who was leaning casually against a marble pillar a short distance from me.

"Kira," my father said, descending quickly, his eyes trained on mine, his lips thinned in that same disapproving expression I was extremely familiar with. "I'm glad you've finally seen fit to come home." He sounded anything but glad. He didn't even glance at Grayson.

"Come into my study so we can talk," he said, turning abruptly and heading in that direction.

"This is fine right here," I said loudly, stopping him in his tracks. I had no intention of following my father into his study, where he would sit behind his desk like a judge handing down his sentence.

My father turned slowly, his jaw ticking in warning as he walked back to where I stood. That's when he looked at Grayson. "And who are you?" he asked.

I stepped forward. *Here we go.* "This, *Daddy*, is my husband, Grayson Hawthorn."

For the span of three heartbeats, my father didn't utter a sound. A deep red color moved up his neck as he stepped forward. "You can't be serious."

"I am serious. We were married several weeks ago. I'm sorry I didn't invite you, but I know how full your social calendar always is."

The blow took me unaware, the sharp slap echoing

loudly through the open foyer. I gasped, hot pain spreading across my jaw and up to my eye socket. I raised my head in time to see his hand moving toward my face again and braced for the second slap, but it never came. I jerked my eyes open to see Grayson holding my father's wrist, the look on his face filled with murderous dragon rage. "What the *fuck*?" he gritted. He must have moved at the speed of lightning to make it from where he was standing to where he was now preventing my father from hitting me again. I let out a ragged breath.

My father, his own face filled with hot anger, pulled his hand out of Grayson's grasp and trained his eyes back on me as I stumbled backward, away from him. I took a second to collect myself, standing as tall as I could and holding eye contact even though the whole left side of my face was throbbing.

"Thank you," I said, lifting my chin, refusing to let him see how much he'd hurt me. "I'll consider that my wedding gift."

"Only you, Kira." My father shook his head and made a sound of disgust in his throat. "You really are a ridiculous fool, aren't you?" He gestured his chin toward Grayson but didn't look at him. "You've hooked yourself up with a damned fortune hunter, I imagine, and you're too stupid to see it." He did look at Grayson then. "She won't get a dime from me, so you're both out of luck, Grayson Hawthorn." He said his name as if he might be related to Satan, but my heart stuttered, when my father narrowed his eyes as if the name were familiar to him. He shook his head slightly and trained his glare back on me.

"We don't want a dime of your money," Grayson said coldly. "Let's go, Kira." I started to turn when I heard footsteps coming from the direction of the back of the house. I turned my head to see Cooper. My heart stuttered. Cooper was here? This was no coincidence. God, they had planned to ambush me! My stomach dropped as if I'd just jumped from a very high cliff. Cooper hurried toward me, his golden good looks highlighted by the tennis whites he wore.

"Kira," he said, his eyes wandering over me. I cringed and turned my head again, away from him as he brushed his hand down the side of my hair. How had I ever thought I could spend a lifetime with this man? I could barely stomach being in the same room with him now. I sensed Grayson stepping closer and suddenly felt his hand take mine. Cooper looked at Grayson in confusion and then back at me, his eyes questioning. "Kira?" He touched my cheek and then looked sharply at my father. "Did you hit her?" Cooper asked disbelievingly. As if he himself had never struck me. Anger and contempt bubbled up in my throat until I felt like I'd choke on it.

My father pressed his lips together. "She's married, Cooper," he said, his voice mocking and full of condescension. "Congratulate her."

Cooper's eyes widened, suddenly swinging toward Grayson. I'd say he looked hurt if I didn't know better. "Married?" Cooper asked, shock lacing his tone. "What the hell, Kira? Who is he? What's his story?" he finally asked, his eyes stopping on Grayson, although he was clearly talking to me.

Grayson narrowed his eyes, regarding Cooper with a mocking half smile.

"He runs his family business in Napa," I said. "It's where we met." I hoped that would be enough information for both of them.

Cooper's gaze swung toward me. "Where you *met*? What? Two weeks ago?" There was the hint of a growl in his voice.

I straightened my spine. "It's not any of your business, Cooper," I said. "*I'm* no longer any of your business."

"The hell you're not," he said, stepping closer. Grayson moved right next to me in a protective stance, and before I could think, I turned just slightly into him, keeping my eyes on Cooper.

"Did you really think I'd ever want anything to do with you again?" I asked Cooper.

"We could have worked it out, Kira," he said, his voice sounding pained.

I was tempted to laugh. What a performance. He really should have pursued a career in Hollywood rather than the court system. "I assure you, we couldn't have nor will we ever, for reasons far beyond my marriage to Grayson."

For several seconds, we all stood in this tense standoff.

"Stop this nonsense," my father barked.

Cooper took a deep breath, regarding me for a second longer before he said, "We're going to need to figure this out, then." There was a note of resignation in his voice. They'd go into "fix it" mode now—we didn't matter anymore.

My father's overheard words from a year ago suddenly came back to me. *Don't worry, Cooper. I'll send her away until things die down. Just keep focused on the end goal.*

"This is their territory," I said to Grayson. "Let's leave them to it." I knew I sounded bitter. My voice hitched at the end, betraying the deep hurt and anger pummeling my heart.

"Kira—" Cooper started, but I shook my head and pulled at Grayson's hand.

Grayson resisted, letting go of mine. He moved closer to my father.

"You may be her father," he said quietly, his voice deadly calm, "but you will never lay a hand on my wife again. Am I clear?"

My father looked contemptuously at Grayson and then at me. "Have a nice life, *Kira Hawthorn*," he said scathingly.

His words hit me like another slap to my face. *It was what I had wanted, wasn't it? So why did it hurt so badly?* These men were supposed to protect me. But they'd done the opposite. The only one standing up for me now was my temporary husband.

My father turned and strode out of the room. Cooper remained where he was as Grayson and I turned and let ourselves out. Grayson gripped my hand as we descended the outside steps silently. It felt as if his hand in mine was the only thing keeping me standing.

CHAPTER FIFTEEN
Grayson

I dropped Kira's suitcase on the hotel room bed and turned toward her. She still hadn't spoken since we'd left her father's house. I hadn't attempted any conversation either—I'd needed to process what had happened too. I would have driven straight back to Napa, but I knew Kira wanted to visit her drop-in center, and I imagined it was already closed by this point. We'd stop by in the morning after a good night's sleep and some time to shake off what had happened with her father.

She lifted her head and those stunning eyes met mine, large and luminous and filled with pain. Her suffering affected me like a fist to the gut, and I let out a sudden exhale. That was what this beautifully vibrant girl had grown up with? I understood the pain of being a constant disappointment. But how had she retained that free, open spirit in the midst of nothing but coldness and contempt? How had she risen above it? When she'd told me the story about Rosa Maria, I had thought I'd gotten the picture: her father—though clearly a bastard to his staff—had been hard on his daughter, not knowing how to handle a highly spirited little girl. After all, I could relate to being stunned by some of her antics. But I had given the man way too much credit. Far, *far* too much credit.

"You must hate me for involving you in that," she finally said, looking away and worrying her lip. "I'm so sorry."

Hate her? I moved toward her. "No, I'm the one that's sorry." I ran my knuckles softly down her bruised cheek. "If I'd had any idea he was going to hit you, I would have been close enough to stop it."

She shook her head. "I should have taken the time to come up with a better way to break the news to him. He's rarely ever hit me though. I didn't expect that. But I did shock and embarrass him." She let out a deep sigh.

"It's not your fault he hit you, Kira."

She nodded but only looked slightly convinced. "I think I'd just like to take a long, hot bath and get cleaned up. Maybe order dinner in…"

I understood; she was asking to be alone. "Yeah. Of course. I'll go get settled in the other room." Kira nodded and I moved to the door separating her room from the rest of the suite, picking up my overnight bag from the floor where I'd left it. I would have liked to make myself comfortable in the room she was sleeping in, but after what happened with Kira's father and her ex-fiancé, I knew this was not the time to push my physical agenda on her. I felt a new sense of guilt for trying to push anything on her at all—it was suddenly obvious she'd had enough of that for one lifetime.

"Oh, and, Grayson," she said, turning halfway toward me. "Thank you for what you said to my father about me being your wife."

I paused. "You are my wife."

Her lips tipped very slightly. "You know what I mean. You made it sound like I was your *real* wife. It was very convincing."

I frowned but wasn't sure what to say. It was true—she wasn't my wife in any real sense. If she were, I would know what to do right now to clear that haunted look in her eyes. Instead, I only nodded. "I'll see you in the morning."

I went into my room and took a shower, washing the road dust from my body and trying to cleanse the feel of the confrontation with Kira's father from my mind. Everything in me had wanted to punch Frank Dallaire in his face when he'd slapped Kira. But I'd held back. Assaulting someone would only send me back to prison and I wouldn't risk it. In that way, the incident had served to remind me of my shame, brought home my limitations as a man. If I needed to, how would I even fight for my woman now? *My woman.* No, perhaps Kira wasn't my woman in that sense, but the point still held weight.

I tilted my head toward the water and let it run over my face, moving my mind back to Frank Dallaire. I'd never paid a whole lot of attention to San Francisco politics, but I'd perceived him to be a well-liked mayor, tough but fair, a friend to minorities and the middle class. I guess it just went to show what a farce politics could be, full of lies and double-speak. I found it hard to believe a man who treated his beautiful daughter so abominably was much of a real friend to anyone but himself.

And now he was my temporary father-in-law. God, what had I gotten myself involved in? I could only hope Kira was right—he'd put some spin on it for the public if need be and let us both go about our business. Why did I have a bad feeling that wouldn't be the case?

I stepped from the shower, dried off, and then got dressed and went to sit on the balcony for a little while. I wondered what Kira was doing in the other room. I couldn't help but picture her naked body submerged in water, her skin slick and wet, that wild hair falling in disarray from whatever clip she'd used to hold it back. Heat surged in my veins, but at the same time, I wanted to take her in my arms and soothe the hurt and embarrassment I'd seen on her face as I'd left the room. I was surprised and slightly troubled by these feelings, aware of the complications they potentially posed. But sitting there, something powerful gripped me. Yes, I still felt a masculine desire to possess her physically. To kiss her, to taste her, to push inside her. But now it was also combined with that same protectiveness I'd felt a few days before when I'd cared for her.

Stop this. Stop this right now.

But I couldn't help it. I wanted to put that bright light back in her eyes, to comfort her, see that bewitching little dimple. I leaned my head back and let out a groan. I had to rein myself in. None of that was in the agreement. We had started this marriage as a business arrangement and even if we gave in to our attraction to one another, it had to remain on those terms. We were married—our relationship had to be all or nothing. We couldn't wade into the murkiness of something undefined. It wouldn't end well for either of us. Knowing about Rosa Maria and her father, I had a little more understanding about her hesitance to get involved with me. She probably saw a physical relationship between us as little more than what *they'd* had. And in all honesty, it was exactly what I'd proposed. Was that what I really wanted?

Confusion swirled within me. Perhaps I should abandon the idea of satisfying my physical need for her now that I could admit there was more involved than just sexual attraction, now that I could admit I cared about her as a person. But for some reason I always seemed to lose control around her and all my best intentions went out the window. And I still couldn't understand exactly why. What was it about her that unbalanced me so much?

I let out a sigh. Maybe I should stop thinking about my own turmoil and consider that what she really needed right now was a friend. And so, tonight at least, all that other stuff should go by the wayside.

After looking over the room service menu and putting in an order to be delivered to our suite, I knocked on the door to her bedroom. She answered wearing a pair of jeans and a black top, her feet bare and her hair still partially wet. Her face was free of makeup and she looked very beautiful and very young. Of course, she *was* very young, only twenty-two. I didn't think about her age very often, perhaps because sometimes she acted like a naughty child and sometimes she seemed so very wise. And of course, those glimpses of depth and insight had only served to make her more interesting to me. I entered, inhaling the light flowery scent that was hers.

"Hi," she said, eyeing me suspiciously.

"I took the liberty of ordering dinner for us," I said, entering her room though I hadn't been invited. "I know you like Charlotte's beef stroganoff. I'm sure the chef here isn't nearly as good as her, but…" I shrugged.

Kira looked slightly unsure, but then let out a breath, obviously acquiescing. "That sounds good. Thank you. Although I might not be the best company."

She turned and walked back toward the balcony, where she stood looking out over the city. I joined her, leaning my forearms on the metal rail and looking over at her. She looked away, tilting her chin down as if attempting to hide her face from me.

"Hey," I said gently, turning toward her. I used my fingers to nudge her chin toward me. Her eyes were shining with unshed tears. She sucked in a sharp breath, a tiny sob coming up her throat. I pulled her into my arms, tucking her head under my chin. "Shh," I said, "it's okay." My throat felt tight as her body tensed in my arms, like she didn't know how to be held. God, growing up with no mother and a father like that, she probably didn't. I had only slightly more to draw upon but enough to take the lead.

"Kira," I whispered, "relax. Let me hold you, sweetheart." She struggled weakly for a brief moment, but when I tightened my arms around her, she sagged into me and gave way to her tears.

Kira sobbed in my arms, her face buried in my chest for a long while. Finally, her sobs began to abate, and she raised her face to me. The tenderness that pulsed in my chest was unlike anything I'd ever felt before. Again, it concerned me, but I pushed my feelings aside and brushed my thumb across Kira's soft cheek, wiping away the wetness of her tears. I smoothed her hair back from her face. "It's okay," I said. "I'm here. I've got you."

"Said the Dragon to the witch," she said softly, a small twinkle in her still-teary eyes.

"There's my girl," I said.

She smiled softly and pulled away. My arms suddenly felt very empty. Kira sagged down onto one of the balcony chairs and I sat down in the other one, a small round table between us.

"Will you tell me about what happened with you and Cooper?" I asked.

She leaned back in her chair, sighing. For a moment I thought she'd say no, but then after taking a deep breath, she said, "I met Cooper at a charity event hosted by my father. I was home for the summer from my first year at college. My father had taken Cooper under his wing and was grooming him to win his first judgeship." She bit her lip and looked away for a moment. "Although my father's not in politics anymore, he's very involved in the San Francisco court system." Her eyes darted to me for a quick second and I wondered if she was thinking about *my* involvement with the San Francisco court system. Thankfully, though, I'd never come in contact with Frank Dallaire. She was quiet for a few moments. "Anyway, Cooper and I started dating and my father was so damned happy about it." She looked out at the horizon, seeming to be lost in memory. "It was the first time in my life I felt like I was pleasing him. It felt...well, I felt *wanted*. It was a heady feeling. Almost addictive," she mused, shaking her head dejectedly. "I wanted more."

"Was that it?" I asked. "Or did you love Cooper?" I hated the tiny stab of jealousy at the mention of Kira with another man—even one who was mostly in her past.

"Oh, I thought I did, I suppose. He was all polish and country-club manners. My father thought we were a brilliant match and we'd perfectly balance each other. Cooper would finally tame me, and I would offer the Dallaire name to his campaign and his future career as a judge."

"And then?" I asked, a feeling of dread settling in my stomach at the empty look that had come into her eyes.

"We were engaged around Christmas and I, well, I gave him my virginity." She frowned and looked away for what seemed like a long time. My muscles were tensed and I consciously focused on relaxing. "I only tell you that because it relates to the rest of the story."

"Okay."

Kira cleared her throat. "I planned to come home that summer and start wedding planning. Cooper was heavily involved in his first campaign and his team was working out of a hotel downtown." Kira picked at her fingernail for a few seconds before continuing. "I got out of finals early and instead of going straight to the apartment my father kept for me here, I decided to surprise Cooper at the hotel." Her frown deepened. "Cooper had always seemed...displeased with me in bed. He never said it exactly, but he communicated the message clearly enough. I thought maybe if I surprised him, wore something...you get the idea." A blush rose in her cheeks. "Anyway, I went to his room and a member of his campaign opened the door, obviously expecting room service. He tried to stop me from going back to the bedroom, but I wouldn't let him, and I walked in on Cooper with...women."

"Women? Plural?"

Kira nodded. "There was one under him and one behind him using some sort of..." She shook her head and closed her eyes, obviously trying to shake the image from her mind. "God..." She put her face in her hands for a brief moment, taking a deep breath.

"I don't need a full description. I get the gist," I said. *Jesus. What a pig.*

She let out a breath. "There were lines of what looked like cocaine on the coffee table, half-empty liquor bottles everywhere."

"Fuck," I said, moving my hand through my hair, picturing Cooper, the golden boy in his tennis whites this afternoon.

"Cooper…disengaged when he finally noticed me, but he was drunk or drugged or both. I don't know. He started off apologizing, but it deteriorated into him screaming at me about how he didn't want a whore for a wife. He had actual whores for that. I tried to leave, but he pulled me and I fought him. We tumbled to the ground and he hit me, but I got away. Only as I turned to leave, he caught my ankle and I fell on the glass coffee table, breaking two of my ribs, banging up my face even more, and slicing my arm. It had happened so *fast*, but I was a mess. There was blood every-where. Members of Cooper's campaign team who had been in the other room came running. They got me out of there and called a doctor when we arrived at my father's home."

"Kira," I said, my voice raw, my guts churning. I now fully understood why she'd been so insecure about sex. It wasn't just about her father and his dismissal of Rosa Maria. It was even more personal—she'd basically been told her passion in bed was somehow inappropriate and disgusting. *And she'd believed it.* And who could blame her? It'd been her first experience.

Kira looked off into the distance again. "When my father got home and learned what happened"—her face screwed up as if she was going to cry again, but she regrouped with a deep breath—"he told me *I'd* ruined everything. And then he went into recovery mode: contacting the hotel staff, putting out the story that I'd gotten into trouble with drugs and went wild in case anyone else had seen me leaving the room or in case other staff talked about the cleanup. Of course, he wouldn't hear of me calling the engagement off, but I was very final about that."

"He threw you under the bus."

She nodded. "Yes. Cooper's campaign and status was

more important than his own daughter. He suggested a trip to Europe to make it look as if I were in a recovery program and then upon my return, we could turn the story in our favor, making me look like a success. Can you see the headlines now? 'Heiress turns to drugs, ruins life, but thanks to the love and devotion of selfless fiancé, turns life around.' What a perfect love story. Of course, Cooper would look even more like a hero. His current campaign, and all future campaigns, would be even more successful with a story like that attached to him. And me, I'd be the fall girl, but all for a good cause."

"Fuck," I repeated, staring in disbelief. I could hardly wrap my mind around that type of public betrayal. How did she come to terms with it?

She sighed. "Well, as you can imagine, I wasn't going to go along with my father's plan to send me to Europe on a shopping expedition, but I did need to go away. Even returning to college here in California seemed too close. I wanted an ocean between us—very literally. I was devastated and needed to heal both physically and emotionally. I needed time to come up with a life plan. I remembered Khotso's invitation to help with his hospital—an invitation I hadn't been able to accept originally—and cut myself off from my father and Cooper. I took an extra day to have a full STD checkup and then flew to Africa using the very last of the money I had in my bank account."

She paused for a few moments and I watched as her expression turned thoughtful. "When I got there, I felt so empty, so grief-stricken. But see..." Her eyes suddenly brightened, and my heart thumped. *There it is, that light.* "I worked with these women who had lost so much—they were rejected by their villages and their families because of the stigma of something they had no control over. Many of them had lost their babies. They were sick and traumatized and grieving. They had lost so much more than me. And yet…despite their circumstances, they were so *strong*, Grayson, so committed to healing, to hope, to moving forward. They inspired me to find that same courage within myself. People suffer all over the world every day. But people triumph all over the world every day too. And those beautifully brave women helped me reach for triumph as well. And though our situations were very different, I healed along with them."

Reach for triumph. The words echoed in my head. *How though? How is it possible in the midst of so much hurt?* "You make it sound easy." My voice held a scratchy note.

She shook her head. "It's not easy. It takes work and faith and a whole heart full of hope. It takes letting the pain in too. Because what I learned in Africa as I went through the process, is that you can't shut off one emotion without shutting off all your emotions. You have to feel the pain if you're going to feel the joy. It's just the way it works. So no, it's not easy, but it's possible. And now, all I want is for my father to leave me in peace, to allow me to figure out on my own what I'm going to do with the rest of my life."

I understood now. I understood why she'd been willing to go to drastic measures to gain some freedom. I understood why she'd been willing to marry a stranger rather than ask her father for a single dime of his money—money that surely had any number of soul-stripping strings attached. She had chosen to split the money fifty–fifty, as if it was the only bargaining tool she felt she was worth. She had chosen *me*, and I suddenly felt gratitude that far outweighed the financial gain. "And what have you come up with so far?" I asked. *What are your dreams?*

210

"I might go back to college. I might become a pirate and sail the seven seas." She gave me a wry smile, but it dissolved into a sigh. "The point is I have choices. Because of my gram, and because of *you*, I can do practically anything." Our gazes locked and I had the very brief but sharp urge to fall to my knees and swear my everlasting servitude to her. *Relax, Gray.*

"You'd make a really hot pirate," I finally said.

She laughed right as a loud knock sounded at the front door. "Room service," I said with a smile.

There was no table in the suite, so I set up the food on the coffee table in the spacious living room, and we both sat down to eat. The mood seemed to have lightened despite the very heavy topics we'd discussed and despite the fact that Kira had just shared her very personal, painful story. Maybe that's what she'd needed, though. I imagined she hadn't spoken of it much, if at all, given she'd left immediately after it happened and had only returned recently.

"I owe you an apology," I said through a bite of stroganoff that wasn't nearly as good as Charlotte's. "I misjudged you from the moment I met you. I had you completely wrong. I'm sorry for that."

Kira shrugged. "I'm used to it. And I did my own share of misjudging, dragon." She shot me a wink.

"Kira," I said after a minute, "I know we agreed on two months, but you can stay longer if you'd like. I mean if it will help give you time to figure out what your next step is."

She looked at me sideways. "You may come to regret that offer."

I suppressed a smile at her sarcasm. "Probably. You relentlessly try my patience. But even so, I mean it."

She turned toward me and grinned, that witchy little

dimple appearing, and the lust that shot through my body was sharp and sudden.

"I appreciate it. But I think it will be good for me to set up a place of my own."

I didn't want to acknowledge the disappointment I felt at her words. "Will you stay in Napa?" *Please say yes.*

She looked pensive. "I don't know. If we're trying to elevate your social standing in Napa, I'm not sure moving to my own place there makes sense. But I'll stay in California for a little while at least. Until we file for divorce."

I nodded and an awkward silence ensued. *She* was thinking of *my* circumstances in all this? Why did she care at all? I wasn't sure what I felt in that moment and was even less sure I wanted to analyze it. Things were getting more complicated by the moment.

We finished dinner and I placed the dishes outside the door for pickup. When I came back into the suite, I found Kira back in her room, standing at the sliding glass door of the balcony, peering out. I watched her for a few seconds, taking in her relaxed posture, the long waves of her hair falling down her back. Tenderness filled my chest. She was so strong and so beautiful. I walked to stand behind her, moved her hair over one shoulder, and leaned in and kissed the back of her neck. It felt as natural as breathing. She shivered but didn't pull away.

"Kira," I murmured, inhaling her sweet fragrance. I was unsure whether I should be touching her, whether I should be attempting to move our relationship in this direction. Maybe I needed to be protecting her from myself. But for the life of me, I couldn't make myself stop. And when I kissed her neck again and she let out a soft moan, I came undone completely.

I turned her in my arms and brought my hands up to hold her face, being careful not to put pressure on the bruise on her cheek where her father had hit her. I leaned in to kiss her sweet mouth, a deep moan emerging from my throat as I threaded my fingers into the silky waves of her hair, tilting her head so I could plunge my tongue deeper. I wanted to devour her, become part of her fire, her life force.

I walked backward, pulling her with me gently until I hit the bed. Then I turned her so she fell back and I followed her down. I forced myself to slow, taking a long, shuddering breath. Kira stared up at me with half-lidded eyes. God, she was beautiful. "I want you," I said, my voice sounding raw to my own ears.

She blinked, her expression filling with uncertainty. She wanted me too, but she wasn't ready. I swore to myself, a sudden flash of how she'd looked earlier in my arms, her eyes reddened by tears, her bottom lip trembling. I could probably convince her to sleep with me tonight, but that didn't feel right anymore. Not now that I knew her story. When she came to my bed, she had to come willingly. But I could still do something for her. I leaned in and kissed her again. "Let me give you pleasure, Kira. Let me show you how beautiful you are when I make you come." She still looked uncertain, but she didn't tell me to stop, so I took that as a yes and leaned in to kiss her neck. She tipped her head back and let out a small sigh as I licked and nipped at the soft, tender skin of her throat. The taste of her was new and familiar all at once, and I felt my heart beating rapidly in my chest. "You are bewitching. Perfect," I whispered in her ear, rising above her to remove her shirt. She lifted her arms over her head, the look in her eyes less wary than it had been, heat burning away her previous reservation.

I unsnapped her bra and took a moment to gaze down at her naked breasts. My cock pulsed against the restrictive zipper of my jeans, and I moved my hand to her rose-colored nipple. I scraped it gently with the nail of my thumb and she jerked her hips off the bed, moaning. "Gray," she rasped. At the sound of my name on her lips, frantic lust spiked through my body again and I gritted my teeth. I licked my thumb and wet her nipple, stimulating the hard peak until she was letting out sweet little pants. Then I leaned down and sucked the other one into my mouth, swirling my tongue around, biting gently and then laving again. Her hips pressed upward into my swollen erection, and we both moaned.

Kira's fingers threaded into my hair as I kissed down her stomach. I stood to remove her jeans and our gazes tangled, hers bright and luminescent with passion, her eyes fluttering closed after a moment. "Beautiful," I murmured. "So beautiful." My fiery little witch was squirming and moaning and so beautifully vibrant with passion. How would any man alive not find this stunningly erotic? How would any man alive not want to experience this response from the woman he was making love to? From the woman who belonged to him? Looking at her this way felt like inhaling a bright ray of sunlight.

I tossed her jeans and underwear aside and went down on my knees on the floor in front of her and gently dragged her closer to me so my face was directly between her legs. She was bare and so shiny and slick with arousal. I almost growled at the scent of her, pure need roaring through my veins. I was practically shaking with desire for this woman. "Gray." Her voice broke on my name.

She turned her head to the side, muffling a moan into the thick pillow next to her head.

"No, Kira, let me hear you," I begged.

She looked at me, hazy confusion in her eyes, but she pushed the pillow away.

I leaned in and licked her, swirling my tongue around her swollen tissue, the taste of her bursting across my tongue and, impossibly, making me even harder. I was going to orgasm just from pleasuring her. I had never felt this desperate. She keened softly, pressing herself into my face. I sucked and licked and tasted her slick flesh for long moments as she moaned and panted, her sounds of pleasure making me feel wild. Finally I pressed two fingers into her wet entrance and she let out a small scream, her thighs quivering, as her body shook and contracted around my fingers. After she'd stilled, I raised my face and kissed back up her stomach.

Kira let out a contented sigh, taking my face in her hands as I pressed my lips to hers so she could taste her own passion on my mouth and tongue. We kissed slowly for long moments, my erection still throbbing painfully with unspent lust for the beautiful woman in my arms. I gave her one final kiss and then I rolled to the side and pulled her with me before bringing the blankets up over her. "You are beautiful," I repeated, feeling something in my chest that felt startlingly like fear. *Why do my feelings for her scare me so damn much?*

She sighed contentedly again and snuggled into my chest. As I drew lazy circles on her hip, trying to tamp down my still raging arousal and the confusion of my emotions, I recalled how I'd told her she wasn't my type. I almost laughed. Not only was she my type…it was as if she were made for me. I pushed that disturbing thought aside. I couldn't let myself think things like that. It must have hurt her though, hearing those words from a man's mouth—even one she disliked at the time—after her fiancé had made her feel so inadequate. Thoughts of Cooper Stratton, and my own regret, worked to cool the blood in my veins, but only moderately.

Kira's breathing evened and she let out a small, delicate snore. She was asleep. God, if I'd realized being married would be so sexually frustrating, I might have asked for more compensation. She drove me crazy, riled me more than anyone else I knew. Yet she made me laugh, made me smile, impressed the hell out of me. She'd even bought me a damn dog. And now she'd given me even more. She'd given me her trust with her delectable body. Horny? Fuck yes. Satisfied? Absolutely.

I smiled to myself, kissing the top of Kira's sweet-smelling head.

CHAPTER SIXTEEN
Kira

Nerves fluttered in my belly as I knocked softly on Grayson's bedroom door. I'd woken alone in my bed this morning, still nude and wrapped in the hotel sheets. The memory of Grayson's mouth on me had me simultaneously stretching in pleasure like a cat and wanting to duck back under the covers. I felt happy and shy and slightly uncertain. But mostly? Tenderness warmed my heart. He had obviously understood the pain and humiliation Cooper had caused and had sought to remedy some of it. And surprisingly, it had worked. He had made me feel beautiful and desirable. And at a cost to himself. In fact, I was pretty sure he had been left severely frustrated. I felt sort of bad about that, but when he finally answered his door with a smile, I let out a relieved breath, setting my suitcase on the floor and smiling back. He had obviously survived. But he'd left my room. I wondered why he hadn't stayed, why he hadn't tried to satisfy his own arousal. I would have let him. I might have begged him if I hadn't fallen asleep directly afterward, half-drunk with pleasure and the exhaustion of a long, emotional day.

"Morning," he said.

"I expected you to be there this morning," I blurted. *Subtle, Kira.* I relaxed my stance. "I mean, good morning. You…um, left after I fell asleep."

He leaned against the doorframe, his eyes moving over my face for a moment as if trying to read my thoughts. I lowered my lashes to conceal my eyes. "I thought you needed a good night's sleep, and I didn't know if you'd be okay if I stayed. I didn't want to wake you to ask. You'd had a hard day."

"Oh." Well, that was nice. Thoughtful. "Thank you," I said. "For…everything."

A satisfied smile tilted his lips. "You're very welcome," he said. "Ready to get going?"

I nodded, still staring at his mouth—that beautiful, sensual mouth I now knew could bring so much pleasure. When I realized those lips were curving into an even bigger, knowing smile, I ripped my eyes away and looked at the floor. Grayson chuckled softly as he grabbed his bag and my suitcase and we both walked out to the hall.

"You sure you don't mind making a stop at the drop-in center?" I asked, eyeing him sideways as we headed toward the elevator. I loved the way he looked fresh from the shower—dark hair partially wet and tousled, his clean masculine smell meeting my nose. I wasn't sure how what we'd done the night before was going to change anything as far as our relationship went, so I'd wait for a signal from him. Maybe it wouldn't change anything at all. That's what he'd indicated to me when he'd first talked about altering our deal. *Temporary*, I reminded myself. He wants our relationship to be temporary. *Don't get any ideas, Kira.*

"Not at all," he said. "As long as we don't stay too long. I'd like to get back to the vineyard early enough to get some work in today."

"We won't stay long," I reassured him. "Just long enough to say hi and write them a check. I have a few other charities I'd like to write checks to as well, but I can put those in the mail."

Half an hour later we pulled in to the drop-in center's parking lot in the Tenderloin district, one of the most high-crime neighborhoods in San Francisco. But rent here was semi-affordable, unlike most other locations in the city, and there was a high population of people who were homeless.

When Grayson and I entered the building, an old man mumbling to himself pushed past us, and the noise of talking, laughter, and a crying child somewhere in the background filled the air. I recognized the smell: sloppy joes were for lunch.

A woman with short, black, curly hair came rushing toward us, the familiar face I'd missed so much. "Is that you, Kira Dallaire?" She let out a small screech as she drew me into her arms, hugging me to her soft body.

I laughed, squeezing her tight. "Hi, Sharon."

"Girl, I was so upset I wasn't here the other day when you stopped in. Carlos told me you'd been by. It's been far too long." She looked at me with motherly love, sizing me up. "Well, you look good. But how are you? And what happened to your face?" she asked, pressing her fingers gently on my cheek and turning my head so she could see the red mark that still hadn't entirely faded.

I smiled, Sharon's concern a balm to my soul. "I'm good. And that is courtesy of my father, but I'm okay."

Sharon scowled, pressing her lips together. "I'm glad I never voted for that man. In fact, I'd like to kick his ass."

"It's okay. It's taken care of." I looked at Grayson beside me. "Sharon Murphy, this is Grayson Hawthorn." I purposefully didn't offer an explanation of our relationship. Sharon eyed me suspiciously but held her hand out to Grayson and smiled warmly at him. "We can't stay long, Sharon, but I wanted to write a check. I talked to Carlos about the situation with funding."

"A check? Really, Kira? We were prepared to close the doors until the grant comes through."

"Well, now you don't have to."

Sharon blew out a big breath of relief and hugged me again. "You have such a huge heart, sweet girl. Bless you." With tears shimmering in her eyes, Sharon turned to Grayson. "Would you like a tour of our facility? Kira, there are a few kids you know outside. They'd love it if you went and said hi."

I glanced at Grayson, who was looking around the facility I'd spent so much time in. It was so strange to see him there; it felt like two distant worlds colliding. "Do you mind?"

He shook his head. "No, go ahead."

Fifteen minutes later I'd written out the check and was outside playing a game of tag with the kids. I looked up, laughing breathlessly and trying in vain to control the hair wildly flying all around my face, and caught Grayson's eye. A small boy named Matthew tagged me and shrieked with delight and I laughed again, high-fiving him for his stealth moves. Grayson was standing just outside the door, a small smile on his face as he watched our game. I felt momentarily embarrassed that I'd been so involved in child's play and went jogging over to him, calling goodbye to the kids.

"Hey," I said, attempting to catch my breath.

"Hey, yourself. Looked like you were having fun."

I shrugged. "Yeah. They're great kids. Ready to go?"

He nodded. "I can see why you're so supportive of this place. It seems like they do great work."

"They do. Not only do they make meals for the people in the area who are homeless, but they help them apply for services too. Most of the kids here have parents who work and nowhere to go after school. The center helps them with their homework and provides a safe place where they're looked after and also have friends to play with. If not for the center, many of these kids would be targeted by gangs or offered drugs. There's no telling how many lives they improve."

His eyes lingered on me for a moment. "I can see why you're a supporter."

I nodded and his eyes moved to my cheek, a frown appearing, before he looked away. *It still bothers him that I was hurt.*

After saying goodbye to Sharon, we got on the road and headed back home. To my temporary home, I reminded myself. And yet, I was excited at the prospect of returning to my small cottage and seeing Charlotte, Walter, Virgil, and José, and sweet Sugar Pie Honey Bunches. The emotion concerned me slightly too. I was becoming attached to Hawthorn Vineyard, but it wasn't my home. In fact, I'd be leaving there in a matter of weeks. Although Grayson had offered me the option to stay longer, I now knew that would only make things harder. I'd relented and been physical with him, beyond mere kissing, and while I didn't regret it, I knew it would only make our parting difficult for me—even if in some small measure. I'd meant what I said to Charlotte—where my body went, my heart tended to follow, and I suspected that would be the case here. Perhaps it already was. I'd never let Grayson know it, of course, but *I* knew it was the truth.

But...now that the damage was done, was there really

any reason not to enjoy him while I could? At least we'd gone into this honestly. It wasn't going to be a surprise when things ended. Perhaps I'd leave Grayson with my heart slightly bruised. But wasn't a slightly bruised heart worth the electricity we created together? I shivered just remembering the way he'd touched me the night before, the way he'd seemed to know my body so well.

"Cold?" he asked, putting his hand in front of the vent to test the temperature of the air.

"Maybe a little," I said, trying to explain why I'd shivered.

The ride went quickly, with us chatting mostly about mundane topics. I knew for myself I'd had enough heavy with what had happened at my father's house and then telling Grayson my painful story at the hotel.

"Oh," I said when we were about half an hour into the drive, "I forgot to mention your party has a theme."

"My party..." he repeated. "What's the theme?"

"Well, I thought about the first thing I said about your house when you took me on a tour."

He glanced over at me, obviously thinking. "That it was the lair of a dragon?"

"No, I said that about the maze."

His lip quirked. "Ah, right. You'll have to remind me what you said about the house."

"I said it looked like a fairy-tale castle."

"Okay..."

I laughed. "The theme will be a fairy-tale masquerade," I said, clapping my hands together. "Perfect, right? And the date is two weeks away. I circled it on the calendar in the kitchen and in your office."

"Two weeks? Will anyone even show up with such short notice?"

"They'll be even more likely to show up. Planning it with such little notice sends the message we don't care whether they're there or not. They'll be intrigued. The whole town will come." *Hopefully.*

Grayson chuckled. "Okay. I'll save Party Psychology 101 to you."

"Plus, I have limited time to make my mark on your life," I reminded him.

"Oh, you've made your mark, Kira."

I chuckled softly. "I mean a *positive* mark. Something lasting," I mused, thinking about all the ways I hoped my plans for the party would benefit him for the long term.

He glanced at me for several beats and then looked back to the road. A small smile played on his lips, but he didn't comment.

When we arrived back in Napa, it was just after noon. Grayson took our bags out of his truck and started for the house. "I'm going to put these in the foyer. Why don't you come down to the winemaking facility with me and see what you've invested in?" He shot a charming smile over his shoulder, squinting into the sunshine, and my stomach flipped. God, he was gorgeous.

"Okay." I was looking forward to seeing the winemaking facility. I'd lived here for weeks now and had never been invited inside that mysterious building where Grayson seemed to work constantly. I was eager to find out what was inside.

He was back outside a minute later, telling me it appeared Charlotte and Walter were out and they must have taken Sugar Pie with them. I accompanied him down the hill, past the lush-smelling rose bushes and small white flowers that were both sweet and woody. The scents mingled, and I inhaled a deep breath, sighing. "It smells so good right here."

"Roses and hawthorn flowers," he said, but his expression had turned grim. *Why?* "My stepmother planted them years ago when she was pregnant with Shane. Charlotte told her the rose symbolizes balance—the flower is the beauty and the contrasting thorns are a reminder that love can be painful. The hawthorn flowers are obviously for our name. They're the last things she ever planted on the property."

"Oh, why?" I asked, thinking about the rose pin Charlotte had let me borrow on my wedding day.

"Because she was planting the day my mother—the woman my father cheated on her with—showed up to drop me on their doorstep. She never ceased telling me that the fragrance of these flowers reminded her of the worst day of her life: the day she'd discovered she'd been betrayed and that every time she looked at me she'd be reminded of that fact."

My heart froze and then thrummed painfully in my chest. "Oh," I breathed, taking his hand and squeezing it as we walked. "That's… I'm so sorry. How cruel." His father had thrown his puppy in the pool, and his stepmother said things like that to him? It was a wonder he still wanted to live here at all.

I thought back on the small hints he'd dropped about his family. *You must favor your mother,* I'd said. *Yes, to everyone's dismay,* he'd answered. *Oh, Grayson.* Now I understood his bitterness and also his…deep loneliness.

"She actually tried to have them ripped out several times, but they just wouldn't go away. Kind of like me, she'd said." He smiled as if what he'd said was the least bit humorous, as if he were unaffected by the cruelty of those remembered words. It must have wounded him deep inside his heart though. It was impossible that it hadn't.

I squeezed his hand again and moved closer as we

walked, offering the comfort of my presence if he wanted it. The thought of the beautiful man walking next to me being unwanted and unloved by anyone made my heart ache. But at the same time, I couldn't help but feel honored. He was such a private person and usually so reserved. And yet he'd shared a secret pain with me.

"Speaking of witches," I murmured. "Your stepmother sounds like one." *The evil kind.*

"Not to everyone else. My stepmother was involved in so many charities in Napa, I could barely keep track. She was a regular philanthropist. So generous. Truthfully though? I think she was mostly in it for the ladies' luncheons."

I studied his profile, understanding suddenly that initially, he had judged me to be like her. No wonder he'd disliked me immediately. If I met a man that I assumed had qualities similar to my father, I'd feel disdainful of him too. "I guess there are different types of generosity. I'm sorry your stepmother couldn't find the generosity of heart to show more kindness to a little boy who wasn't hers."

Grayson sighed. "It's all in the past, I guess." *Is it, Grayson?*

Hesitantly, not knowing how far he would open up to me, I asked, "Will you tell me about your mother?"

"My mother?" His brows knit together. "Honestly, I don't know much about her other than she was a ballet dancer. She was a member of the New York City Ballet when she met my father. They had a one-night stand. She got pregnant. Because of her pregnancy she was asked to leave the company. She had trouble supporting me, blamed me for the ruin of her career, her body, and decided she couldn't look at me anymore. She dropped me here with my father and left. I never heard from her again."

Geesh, who were all these people? Villains, all of them.

"How terrible and selfish," I said. And then to be dropped here to be the subject of even more blame, bitterness, cruelty, and exclusion. No *wonder* he was so guarded. No wonder he spit fire sometimes.

"We're quite the pair, aren't we?" he asked, a small smile of wry amusement on his lips.

I released a breath. "Yeah, I guess we are." We'd both dealt with our share of villains. "Funny how much we have in common."

"We don't balance each other at all, do we?"

I laughed softly. "Not at all. We're all wrong together."

He moved in front of me and turned around so I was forced to stop in my tracks. He took my face in his hands and smiled down at me. "Not all wrong," he murmured, bringing his lips to mine. His mouth was soft, his kiss slow, but it spread sensation through my entire body just as his kisses always did. He pulled away too quickly, leaving me gazing dizzily up at him, my hands flat on his hard chest. His smile was slow and very cocky, and I couldn't help laugh and roll my eyes.

"Come on, dragon," I said, pulling on his hand. "I'm going to find out what you do in the depths of that dark cave you inhabit so often."

When we opened the door to the stone building at the bottom of the hill, Grayson called out, "José?"

"Back here," I heard José call.

The room we entered was large with overhead skylights that lit the entire area with shafts of sunlight. There were several large machines that stood to either side of the doorway and what looked like huge stainless steel barrels behind those.

Grayson walked over to the nearest machine. "This is

a sorting belt where the grapes go when they first arrive after being picked. They're sorted by hand to remove any undesirable-looking fruit or leaves." He walked along the enormous piece of equipment, past conveyer belts, and finally pointed up to what looked like a small escalator. "That's the destemmer. The stems come out right there"—he pointed to a metal receptacle—"and go back into the vineyard soil." He moved along and I followed him. "This is the second sorting table," he explained, pointing to another table with room for at least eight people to stand at. "It moves the fruit past the workers, and they pick out any final pieces of stem or undesirable fruit by hand." He gave me a look filled with charm and a note of self-mocking. "Here at Hawthorn Vineyard, we believe the quality of the wine comes from the quality of the fruit. We spend as much time as it takes to ensure the fruit is sorted with care and diligence."

I gave him a smile as I raised a brow. "I have no doubt. How many people did Hawthorn Vineyard employ when it was in full running order?"

"A hundred seventy-five."

And Grayson now had a virtual skeleton crew. If I hadn't realized exactly how much he was struggling before, I sure did now.

He showed me the stainless steel fermenters and then walked me into a second large room where there was similar-looking equipment. José looked to be installing something and was focused intently on what he was doing. He gave us a quick nod and then went back to work. Instead of stain-less steel barrels, this room held what looked like very large wooden fermenters at the back of the wall. As he walked me through the area, I listened as Grayson described the varied functions of the equipment, paying attention to his descriptions but also noting the enthusiasm emanating from his entire body. *He loves this.* I wanted to stand back and simply watch him as he moved, his eyes bright with pride and his broad shoulders held high. He seemed to be alive with energy. *This is what you're meant to do.*

"José is installing a new shaker berry sorting machine," he said. "One of the first things I ordered with the generous Dallaire investment."

I laughed softly. "A good investment, it seems." I studied him for a moment. "Your father would be proud of you, Grayson."

Very suddenly, an expression came over his face that made him look like a little boy—shy and vulnerable. He stuck his hands in his jeans pockets and rocked back on his heels. "I think he would have been," he said softly. "Do you want to see where the barrels are stored for aging?"

I smiled and nodded, realizing how very much he was still affected by his father's judgment of him. I understood it more than most, but for some reason, it made me incredibly sad too. He was looking to earn the love he'd never fully received during his father's life now that the man was gone. *An impossible dream.* Grayson took my hand and led me to a door at the back of the room. The air was suddenly cooler and there was barely any light. I followed him down a long cement hallway of sorts. The hallway opened up and there were rows upon piled rows of barrels. The air smelled of damp, pungent wood. I inhaled, drawing the earthy air into my lungs.

"These are burgundy barrels, made with burgundy wood from France," he explained.

"Hmm," I hummed. "How long do you age the wine?"

"This wine has been aging five years. It's almost ready to

be bottled. Which, again, thanks to the Dallaire investment, can now happen." *So it was put in barrels right after his father became ill. One of the last things accomplished here at Hawthorn Vineyard. Until now.*

"You bottle it here?"

"We will," he said, "once my new bottling machine arrives."

"I never knew so much went into the process," I mused, looking around at the barrels.

"I've just shown you how the fruit is processed. Even more goes into the winemaking itself. I'll show you that someday too." *Someday…and yet, my days here were numbered.* Before I could dwell on that, I realized Grayson had moved closer to me. I sucked in a breath, noting the look of intensity on his face. Even in the dim light, I could see the fire in his eyes. I took a step back and pressed my body into the cement wall. He leaned toward me.

"You're so warm," he murmured. He was too. The air in this room was so cool, and his body pressed against mine felt especially warm. He leaned back in and brought his lips to mine and then ran his tongue along the seam of my mouth, and with a groan, I opened for him. He brought his hands up to my face, and I wrapped my arms around his shoulders, holding him so I didn't slide down the wall. Why did his kiss enflame me the way it did and yet relax every muscle in my body at the same time? His kiss was filled with confidence, his body so solid as it pressed into mine. Our tongues danced and tangled, and I tried to hold back the moan that came up my throat, but it was a wasted effort. I pressed against him, moaning again, my heart beating insistently between my legs, my sensitive nipples rubbing deliciously against his hard chest.

I had kissed men before, but suddenly I realized that no, no, I had never been kissed. Not if this was the way a kiss made you feel. I had never ever been kissed like this. Grayson's whole body participated in this kiss.

"You," Grayson said as he broke from my lips, "are so delicious. I can't get enough of you." And then, thank the Lord, he leaned back in and kissed me again, his tongue slipping into my mouth as I ran my hands down his lean, muscled back. He was so beautifully built, so broad and tall, so solid. A thrill shot through me at the intriguing feel of the unfamiliar contours of his masculine body. I wanted to know every part of him, every dip and plane. I could feel the hard press of his erection at my hip, and it sent a jolt of arousal through my blood.

He let out a soft groan and it made me bold as I moved my hand down between us and rubbed it over the bulge at the front of his jeans. He jerked, pressing himself into my hand.

"Kira," he rasped, "I have to stop. God help me, if I don't now, I won't be able to."

I shivered. I felt the same way, almost wanting to beg him *not* to stop, to take me right here against this cold wall or down on the dirt floor. I almost laughed at my own desperate thoughts. But no, José was right outside the door. He could walk back here any minute. When I gave myself to Grayson, I wanted to have lots of time, and I wanted it to be in a bed.

Grayson stepped away from me, and my eyes wandered down to the evidence of his arousal. The front of his jeans looked strained and full. I swallowed, wanting very much to feel it in my hand again.

Yes, I wanted him, I admitted. I wanted him with an aching desperation that both scared and excited me.

I had thought I could resist him, but I had underestimated the power he possessed when he was not only bent on seduction but when he allowed me to glimpse the tender side of his personality. And now, I had no desire to resist.

"We should get back," I said, smoothing my hair as best as possible.

He studied me for several beats before using one finger to move a wayward curl of hair off my cheek. "Stay with me tonight," he whispered. "Come to my bed, Kira."

Fear and want coiled simultaneously in my belly. It would be playing with fire. I knew it would be. And yet...I wanted to. I wanted to know him intimately. I wanted him to make me feel beautiful and desirable like he'd done the night before. I wanted to know the feel of his body as well, what he liked, what made him wild with passion. I might develop feelings for him that would be difficult to get over—in fact, I almost certainly would. I was halfway there now. But I'd manage them. After all, what was life without a few exciting adventures? Wasn't it worth a little heartache to know a touch like Grayson Hawthorn's? One that lit me up from the inside out. What if I never knew one like it again? Shouldn't I snatch this experience up while I had the chance? Even if difficult, I *would* manage my emotions. And I would never *ever* allow myself the foolish hope that becoming physical with my husband would lead to feelings on his part.

"Yes," I said, meeting his eyes.

Happiness filled his expression and he took my hand. We called goodbye to José and then stepped outside into the bright sunshine. We strolled up the hill and when we entered the house a few minutes later, I grabbed my suitcase, which Grayson had placed inside earlier and turned around to return it to my cottage.

"Hey, whoa, where are you going?" he asked.

I turned. "To my cottage."

"You're not staying there anymore. I moved you up to the house."

"You moved me?" I asked, narrowing my eyes. I *liked* my little cottage. I liked having my own space. And if things were going to advance between Grayson and me in…other ways, it was going to be imperative I had a place that was only mine.

"Yes. Part of the reason you were sick is that you were breathing in all that dusty air, taking cold showers—"

"That's ridiculous. I had a virus. You don't get a virus from dusty air or cold showers."

"Maybe. Maybe not. You're still moving into the house."

The nerve of him. "I'm not."

"You are."

We stood in a standoff in the foyer for several moments until Grayson crossed his arms, leaning casually against the wall. "You already agreed to stay in my room tonight."

"Yes, *tonight*, but that doesn't mean I'm moving in with you."

"You are."

"I'm not," I ground out. My ire rose. *Give this dragon an inch, and he tries to take a mile!* The grand staircase caught my eye and I looked at Grayson, an idea coming to me. "I'll race you," I said. "Winner gets his or her way."

He laughed. "*Race* me? Oh, little witch, you don't stand a chance in a race against me. You might as well surrender now."

"I'll never surrender. And I don't mean a foot race. I'll race you down the banister. You take one side, I'll take the other." I'd been dying to slide down that banister since

I'd first seen it. This was the perfect opportunity. I was a banister-sliding expert. If anyone knew grand stairways, it was me. My father's home had three.

Grayson laughed again. "You must be joking."

I raised both brows in answer.

"No, of course you're not joking. This is ridiculous, you do know that, right?" But he began walking toward the staircase. It appeared he wanted what he wanted and was prepared to fight for it. I followed, and when we'd made it to the top, he moved to the right and I moved to the left. I positioned my butt up on the dark polished wood.

"I can't even believe I'm doing this," Grayson muttered, positioning himself on the other rail.

"If you're nervous, I'll give you a head start," I said.

He grinned back devilishly. "No need, witch, let's do this."

I wiggled my butt on the rail, settling into place. "On your mark, get set, go!" I squealed as we both took off, sliding quickly down the smooth wood. I balanced precariously, shrieking when I almost tipped off the side but righted myself before I fell. I heard Grayson's deep laugh next to me but didn't dare look over at him. Gathering speed faster than I thought I would, the end came quickly, and I went flying forward into empty air, unable to land on my feet and instead catching myself on my hands as I hit the hard marble floor. I felt briefly winded and thought I heard the door open and close in front of me but couldn't help breaking into peals of giggles when I heard Grayson's deep laughter from next to me and looked over to see him sprawled on the floor as well. I was pretty sure I'd hit the floor first. *Winner!*

We both lay there for a moment catching our breath, our laughter fading. I glanced up and realized there were four pairs of shoes standing in front of us and when I raised my head, I saw Walter, one brow raised. Next to him, Charlotte gaped at me, and then moved her eyes to gape at Grayson.

I began standing slowly, the laughter fading entirely as I noticed the equally shocked looks on the faces of the tall, handsome blond man and the stunning blond woman standing next to Walter.

The blond man suddenly broke into a big grin and startled chuckling.

"Hi," I breathed, coming to my full height and taking a step forward. I held out my hand. "I'm—"

"Shane," Grayson said, his voice strangely clipped. "Vanessa."

I swung my gaze to him and saw his expression was very suddenly without humor and instead coldly removed. "What in the *hell* are you two doing here?"

CHAPTER SEVENTEEN
Kira

Oh my God. Shane: Grayson's brother. Vanessa: the woman he'd been about to propose to before he'd been sent to prison. Now his *brother's* wife. Here. In the flesh. I pulled in a deep breath and then smoothed my hands down my hips and tried my best to look cool, calm, and collected. Or at least as cool, calm, and collected as a person could look after having just removed herself from a sprawled position on the floor after flying off a banister.

"Is this her?" Shane asked, apparently ignoring Grayson and instead looking at me. I wasn't sure exactly what to make of his question, but the look on his face was decidedly excited, so I smiled and held out my hand again.

"I'm Kira Dallaire," I said.

"Hawthorn now, isn't it?" Shane gave me an open, boyish smile and took my hand in his.

I glanced at Grayson, whose expression was still shuttered. I remembered this version of my husband. It was the one I didn't prefer. "Um, right. Hawthorn. Well, yes." I cleared my throat. "I keep forgetting," I murmured.

"That's understandable. It's still new, right?" Shane said.

"Right…" I whispered. *New and…over soon.*

The tall, striking blond smiled warmly at me and stepped forward, grasping my hand in both of hers once I'd let go of Shane's. God, she really was gorgeous—Grace Kelly's even more beautiful sister.

Shane looked at Grayson. "When Charlotte told us the news, you can imagine our shock. But we hoped it meant—"

"That you'd be welcome in my home?" Grayson asked icily. "You were wrong. You can turn around and leave again."

"Gray!" Charlotte scolded. "They came all this way to see you and to meet Kira."

"You manipulated this, Charlotte," Grayson said, his livid stare resting on her.

"Grayson," I whispered, feeling awkward in the middle of this frigid family reunion. "Maybe I should…"

He swung his eyes to me, pausing momentarily. "I won," he said, and for a minute I had no earthly idea what he was referring to. Then I realized he was talking about our race down the banister. I would have argued with him—*for he certainly had not*—but I thought what he really might mean is that I had no choice but to stay in the house now if we weren't going to raise suspicion with his brother and sister-in-law—his ex-girlfriend, nearly fiancée. *Good Lord.* That was *if* he was going to allow them to stay. And *if* he was going to make it look as if we had a real marriage. My heart was beating a mile a minute and I had this instinct to bolt. Instead, I just nodded.

Walter cleared his throat. "I believe I'll excuse myself." *Can I come with you?*

"I'll just"—I nodded toward my suitcase and Grayson's

236

overnight bag still sitting by the door—"take these upstairs and let you all talk." I felt severely self-conscious and on display as I moved to pick up the bags. The foyer went utterly silent except for the sound of my clacking shoes. My face felt hot as I turned at the foot of the stairs. "So I'll just, then"—I cleared my throat—"see you at dinner." I looked around, but Grayson wasn't looking at me. He was staring at Vanessa with an expression on his face I'd never seen before. He didn't answer, didn't even tear his eyes from Vanessa long enough to acknowledge me. My stomach cramped.

I heard Sugar Pie's nails clicking on the stone floor and she appeared around the corner, halting, her eyes moving between us. She gave a small chuff and dropped her head. "Here, Sugar," I said quietly and she trotted toward me.

"Nice to meet you, Kira," Shane said, giving me a sympathetic look. *Did Grayson still love Vanessa?* Charlotte nodded at me, wringing her hands at her stomach. *Why had she pushed me toward Grayson if that was the case?* Vanessa gave me a small half smile, her eyes darting to Grayson and quickly back to me, her cheeks pink. *She loves him too?* Oh God. It was all too much. I didn't want to be in the middle of this. *You're not, Kira. You're a temporary distraction, nothing more.*

I turned and hurried up the staircase and into the room I'd stayed in when I was sick, Sugar Pie on my heels. I tossed my suitcase and Grayson's bag down and leaned against the closed door long enough to catch my breath.

What was wrong with me? *A few kisses, a few personal revelations, and you thought Grayson was, what? Your friend? Your true husband?* I felt like a total fool. The way he had looked at that woman downstairs was…not how he had *ever* looked at me. She was married to his brother… It wasn't like he

237

could ever have her again. But God, just the fact that he still wanted her hurt. *And I hate it. Hate it.*

I stood up straight. *This situation can still be salvaged.* Thank goodness I hadn't given myself to him completely. Things were fine. I was fine. So we'd shared a few personal moments. Now we'd go back to the original plan, which was a much better idea anyway. How I'd let myself veer so far off track, I had no idea.

There was a sudden knock at the door and I startled, stepping away from it and turning around. I pulled it open to find Vanessa standing before me. "May I come in?" she asked on a shy smile.

I swallowed but returned her smile and gestured for her to enter. "I'm just showering in here," I lied. "The shower in the master bath is broken."

Vanessa sighed. "God, what isn't? It looks so different around here…" She trailed off, the look on her face saying it all—she didn't mean "different" in a positive way.

Sugar Pie came over and sniffed at Vanessa's feet. Vanessa stepped away, beginning to bend down to offer Sugar Pie her hand, but then withdrawing it quickly when she got a good look at the dog's face. "Oh, she's…is she—?"

"Her name is Sugar Pie," I said, scooping her up and depositing her on the chair to the right of the bed and giving her a few pets before walking back to Vanessa.

She took a seat on the vanity bench and crossed her shapely legs. I sat down on the storage trunk at the foot of the large bed. Vanessa was wearing a short, flirty pink skirt and a pale gray, silky tank top that showed off her summer tan. There were several strands of beads knotted between her breasts. She slid her fingers down them in a nervous gesture as she studied me. I was tempted to make a funny face but held myself back.

"I love your outfit," I said. And I did. It was classy but fun and fashionable too.

She smiled broadly. "Thanks. It's one from my own collection. I have a little boutique in San Diego. I'm considering opening one here too, actually. That's part of the goal of this trip—to find a space. My family didn't have a lot of money growing up and dressing fashionably on a small budget became my creative outlet and my passion. That's the focus of my shop—fashion chic for less." She blushed prettily and lowered her eyes. "I'm sorry, I'm babbling." She cleared her throat before raising her eyes to mine and continuing. "Shane and I were so filled with happiness when we heard Gray had gotten married," she said, changing the subject. And she looked sincere.

I wrung my hands in my lap. "Thank you," I finally said. "I mean, I…don't know exactly what happened between Grayson and Shane, but I hope they can find a way to work things out." *God, this was so awkward.* Was I supposed to be pretending Grayson's and my marriage was real? I wished Grayson had taken a moment to talk to me before I had to have a one-on-one with Vanessa Hawthorn. Maybe he'd already told them we were fake, and here I was, stammering along. Vanessa looked like she was struggling too, and I had to wonder how much she still felt for Grayson. Or was she really in love with his brother, her husband? Why had she done what she'd done? I wanted desperately to ask her, but it didn't feel right, and I wasn't even sure I should act as if I knew anything at all.

"I hope we can all work things out too," she said. "Shane and Grayson are in the study talking. Anyway, I really just wanted to take a few more minutes to say hi to you and let you know how happy I am to have a sister."

"Thank you, I appreciate that. And me too." I smiled. "I'm happy to have a sister as well." *Even though I'll be a temporary one.* I twisted the ring on my finger in nervousness as Vanessa stood. Her outfit was perfect and unwrinkled. How had she managed that if they'd been traveling? I really wanted to hate her for many reasons, but she was making it difficult with her kindness and sincerity. I could see why Grayson had loved her.

Her eyes moved down to my ring finger. "May I?" she asked, her brow creasing slightly. I glanced down at my hand and then lifted it as she grasped it in hers and studied the ring Grayson had given me.

She drew in a breath. "An opal. Look!" And she lifted her engagement ring to show me her center stone was an opal as well. "It's my very favorite stone," she explained. "It signifies love and passion." She grinned, her teeth straight and perfectly white. "Well, this proves it, we both love opals. We were meant to be sisters." She moved forward and hugged me quickly, the scent of some light, expensive perfume that was just as lovely as her hitting my nose before she stepped away. "We'll talk more later?"

"Sure." I smiled weakly.

When she left, I sat down on the bed, my eyes narrowed on the ring on my finger. I recalled Diane Fernsby saying she knew Grayson had bought a ring for Vanessa, though he'd never had a chance to propose. I hadn't imagined this ring was an engagement ring because of the unique center stone, but I'd been wrong. "He gave me the ring he'd intended to use to ask *her* to marry him," I whispered disbelievingly. Anger and hurt lanced down my spine and I twisted the ring until it came off.

"Scaly beast," I murmured halfheartedly under my breath. But somehow, calling him a name didn't diminish the hurt. Calling him a name didn't repair the tiny fissure in my heart, the one his blindingly beautiful scales had created. But I'd done this. He wasn't the only one to blame.

After taking a shower and letting the conversation with Vanessa roll off my shoulders as much as possible, I went downstairs in search of Grayson. We were going to have a sit-down and talk about exactly what I was supposed to be doing in this strange, uncomfortable situation.

I called hello, but when I didn't receive an answer, I walked outside to find Shane tinkering with the fountain. He had a small toolbox on the ground next to him and was leaning all the way over the apparatus in the middle of the empty well. "Hey," I said.

He sat up. "Hey there," he said on a smile.

"I was hoping someone would be interested in getting this thing fixed at some point," I told him.

He smiled more broadly. "It seems it just needs a new part. I'll run into town tomorrow and pick it up."

I nodded and there was an awkward silence before we both started laughing softly. I saw so much of Grayson in his smile. He really was a very handsome man—more boyish looking, whereas Grayson was striking, but just as tall and masculine. "Do you know where Grayson is?" I asked.

His smile faded. "He went into town for dinner."

My heart plummeted. Grayson leaving without a word— leaving me to fend for myself in this awkward situation— only confirmed that I mattered very little to him. I noticed that Vanessa was nowhere in sight either. "Did he, um, go to dinner with Vanessa?" I asked. She had said he and Shane were talking. Maybe now they were too.

Shane shook his head. "No. Vanessa drove out to see her parents."

I let out a breath. "Oh. Right." I hadn't even thought about Vanessa growing up here too. My stomach clenched when I thought about all the history these three had together. And that realization made it starkly clear that I didn't fit in at all. And I never would because I was temporary. But it made me feel like an outcast, and God, I'd felt that so often in my life. I just wanted once to belong somewhere.

Shane sat down on the edge of the fountain and inclined his head, silently asking if I'd like to sit too. I walked the few steps and took a seat, turning and facing him. He tilted his head. "Can I ask how much you know about the situation with Vanessa, Gray, and me?"

So we were going to cut right to the chase. "Not much," I answered honestly. "Just that Grayson and Vanessa were… together, and you and Vanessa got married while he was in prison."

He offered a slow nod. "And that, naturally, he feels betrayed by us."

I nodded, my eyes trained on his face, trying to read his expression. If I had to assign any name to the emotion that seemed to cross over his features, I'd pick deep sadness, maybe even grief. "Naturally," I murmured.

"There's more to it than that," he said. "I love my brother, Kira."

I studied him and found that I believed him. His expression was so somber. "Then why?" I asked.

Shane exhaled a deep breath. "I really owe it to Grayson to explain first. I realize we've put you in an awkward situation—and with no warning. I just wanted you to know we've tried everything." He shook his head. "He won't answer letters, won't take phone calls. The only thing we *haven't* done is strap him to a chair with duct tape and force him to listen to us."

I laughed without much humor. "You might want to consider it. I find the Dragon especially stubborn. I don't see him giving in easily."

Shane squinted at me, smiling with amusement. "The Dragon? Is that what you call him?"

"Only when he breathes fire and goes flapping around the house."

"Flapping around the house." Shane's grin broadened. "Charlotte said as much, but I could hardly believe it about my serious, detached brother. Then I saw him sliding down the banister like the child he never was…"

"Oh, that? We were just settling a bet."

Shane squinted at me. "I think you're good for him. And I had hoped he would be more willing to listen to us now that he's found happiness with you."

My face flushed, and I hoped Shane didn't notice. "Well, he didn't kick you out anyway, right? That's a start."

"Yes, that's a start." Shane stood up, offering me his hand. "Charlotte and Walter are having dinner with friends. She put something in the oven and it's just about time to take it out. Join me for dinner?"

I took his hand and stood up. "Sure."

We went inside and he took Charlotte's stuffed chicken out of the oven and I mixed up a small salad. We sat and ate together as Shane told me about the software business he'd started in San Diego. It sounded like he loved it, and it allowed him to work from home as well.

"So you had no interest in making wine?" I asked, taking a bite of salad.

He shook his head. "No interest and no skill. Computer technology has always been my thing. When my father left me a little chunk of money, I used it to start my own firm."

I nodded. "Well, luckily your brother did want to make wine."

Something crossed over his face that I couldn't read, but he quickly covered it with a small smile. "Yes, luckily."

I told him a little bit about myself, skirting around the fact that I was estranged from my father—it would only invite questions that I didn't feel up to answering. Once we'd eaten and cleaned up the kitchen, I told him I was going to head to my room and read since it'd been a long day and I was tired. More truthfully, though, I was nervous he was going to start asking questions about Grayson and me that I wasn't prepared to answer.

After getting ready for bed, I decided to send Grayson a quick text. I had felt like we were building *something* between us, though I refused to try to define it at this point. Surely he was upset and vulnerable right now with the unexpected arrival of his brother and ex-girlfriend. Perhaps he could use a friend. I grabbed my phone and typed in: *Are you okay?—K*

I waited several minutes, but when there was no response, I picked up my book and tried to focus on the story I'd been reading. When Grayson still hadn't responded to my message an hour later, I turned off the light and hugged my pillow, closing my eyes and trying desperately to will myself to sleep despite the early hour.

I came awake with a start, the feel of strong arms lifting me out of bed. I struggled, kicking out with my legs and flailing my arms until the person holding me let out a loud, "oomph," dropping me on the soft bed and coming down next to me. My eyes met Grayson's in the semidarkness, his expression pained as if I'd made contact with something vulnerable.

"What are you doing?" I hissed, coming up on my knees. I could feel my hair a wild mess all around my face and down my back. He rolled to his side and lay looking up at me, his head on my pillow, his eyes dreamy looking.

"You were supposed to be in my bed tonight," he slurred.

"Your bed?" I asked. "You expected me to…" I leaned in, inhaling. "You smell like liquor and cheap perfume." I tried to keep the hurt out of my voice. He was likely too drunk to notice anyway.

Grayson came up on one elbow. "Some blond was all over me at the bar."

"Oh." What was I supposed to say to that? I fisted my hands on the tops of my thighs. His ex shows up so he goes to a bar and lets a stranger grope him? *Why couldn't you have come to me, Grayson?*

"But apparently," he said, running a finger along my bare thigh, "I don't like blonds anymore. I like redheads. Or brunettes. Or the perfect mixture of both. I like *you*." He squinted up at me, his expression suddenly confused. "Why aren't you in my bed?"

I scoffed, turning my head away from him and crossing my arms over my breasts. "You must be kidding. You take off without so much as a word to me, leaving me to contend with your brother and your ex. And then you get drunk and let women grope you in a bar, and you expect me to be conveniently waiting at home in your bed? What do you take me for exactly?" I seethed, anger mixing with the hurt.

Grayson leaned up higher. "I take you for my wife." His smile was filled with intimate warmth despite his inebriated state.

I raised my chin, refusing to let him charm me. He had hurt me. "In name *only*."

"Let's change that. Tonight. Earlier…you were willing." He gave me a boyish smile and my stupid heart stuttered. "Please, Kira, tell me you want me. I just…I want you, I need you." His voice sounded raw. He *needed* me? So I *was* nothing more than a convenience. Nothing more than a way to temporarily slake his physical desires. But I wanted *more* than his lust. I wanted… *No, shh, don't go there.*

My chest filled with sudden panic. "Are you still in love with her?" I blurted.

Grayson's expression hardened immediately, and he pulled himself to his feet, obviously—even in his drunken state—having no question about who I was referring to.

"You're not going to answer me?" I lifted my chin, refusing to look away.

"I don't want to hurt you, Kira. But the situation with Vanessa, my brother, and me isn't any of your business. It has nothing at all to do with you."

If he hadn't wanted to hurt me, he had a funny way of proving it. I would not let him know how his words had caused a pit to open in my heart. I barely wanted to acknowledge it myself. "Please just go," I said, my voice unwavering. "I don't want you. I don't want you at all."

He ran his hand through his hair, seeming to be deliberating something, looking as if I was the one hurting *him*. But then he swayed slightly on his feet, catching himself and letting out a sharp breath. He swore softly, turned and walked out of my room, closing the door softly behind him.

If they weren't staying here, I would leave for the sanctuary of my cottage. I had planned on sleeping *with* Grayson tonight. And now, sleeping in a room in the same house as him felt unbearable.

I collapsed on my pillow, hugging myself and refusing to cry.

If I had thought the dawn of a new day would have the Dragon flapping into my room and begging for forgiveness, I would have been sorely disappointed. In fact, I barely saw him at all over the next few days. Evidently, he had escaped to the winemaking facility, installing new equipment and ensuring everything was in working order. Or at least, that's what I learned from Shane, who seemed nearly as frustrated as I was that Grayson was ignoring all of us. Clearly Grayson didn't even care if our marriage appeared to be a sham.

"I'll just stick around and put myself in his face whenever possible," Shane said. "Eventually I'll wear him down." He gave me a wink, although his expression said he wasn't particularly convinced by his own statement.

I, however, wasn't willing to do the same. In fact, my MO had always been to run from hurtful situations, and that was my instinct now. But I had a party to plan and the clock was ticking on that. What had I been thinking to give myself such a short window in which to do it? I could barely remember now. All the same, invitations had gone out and people were expecting an event, one which my absent husband surely wasn't going to put on. It was up to me, even though, at this particular point, it was difficult to remember why it even mattered at all.

I spent the first part of the week cleaning up Grayson's

office and trying to make some sense out of the financial files. Walter helped me where he could, since he'd been the one keeping the books updated as much as possible, although he didn't know the programs as well as I did.

"Walter," I asked, as he went through the accounts payable with me, "do you think I could see some of the financials going a few years back? I don't want to overstep my bounds, but I want to get a better idea of where things started going downhill for the winery." I thought if I understood why things had crumbled—literally and figuratively—so quickly once Ford Hawthorn had become ill, I would better be able to help manage the vineyard accounts, maybe even offer some advice to Grayson—not that he deserved it. I should probably watch in glee as he failed to fulfill his vow. But I couldn't do that. My heart wasn't in it, and I wanted to see Gram's money go to good use as well.

Walter cleared his throat, and I thought he looked vaguely uncomfortable at my request. "The records weren't well kept back then. Everything was neglected once Mr. Hawthorn became ill."

"But surely there's something? If I could just take a quick look at whatever there is, I think it might help. I don't know how effective I can be now if I don't understand what happened in the past."

Walter was quiet for so long, I didn't know if he'd heard me. But when I looked up, he was staring at me intently. I blinked. I'd never seen a look that was anything other than impassive on Walter's face. "I'll see what I can find," he finally said, turning away.

Well, that was weird. "Thanks, Walter," I mumbled.

But despite his seeming hesitance, later that day, when Walter brought me a number of thumb drives, he looked me pointedly in the eye and said, "These are the accounting records going back five years."

"Okay, great," I said, stepping closer to him to take the backed-up files. "Thanks so much."

I put my hands on them, but he held them as he said, "Like you said, it's easier to help in the present if you understand the past. I hope these are useful."

I frowned. "Me too."

Walter let go of the stack, giving me a nod and walking stiffly away. What had that been about?

I didn't have time to begin going through the discs until I had the current files updated, so I put my effort into that. I also sought out Vanessa in the kitchen and asked if she was willing to help me with the party preparations. We'd already received a handful of RSVPs, enough to make me slightly nervous—people were going to show up; we'd better be ready. And I could use some assistance. I explained the theme to Vanessa and showed the lists I'd made so far.

"Oh my goodness, of course. I'd love to," she said. "What an incredible idea."

"What's an incredible idea?" I heard in a deep dragon timbre from behind me. We both whirled around to watch Grayson as he strode to the refrigerator and took out several bottles of water, Sugar Pie trailing behind him. My gaze raked over Grayson. I hadn't seen him in days and it felt like my eyes had been starved. He was sweaty and gorgeously flushed. I looked away, feeling pained by my reaction to him. In general but also because he was clearly completely unaffected by me now that Vanessa was around.

"Kira's party idea," Vanessa said. "Did she tell you? It's a fairy-tale masquerade—"

"She told me," Grayson said, opening a bottle of water

and taking a long drink. I watched as his throat muscles worked, swallowing the water, and when I looked up at his face, his eyes were zeroed in on me. I looked away again, pretending to concentrate on my list. I felt my cheeks flush with the excitement of his perusal and wanted to kick myself. *How pathetic. He hasn't spoken to you in days and you fall to pieces when he shoots you a glance?*

Vanessa grinned. "My very favorite fairy-tale character is Tinker Bell." She laughed. "Is that silly?"

I smiled at her. "Not at all. As long as you can convince Shane to dress up as Peter Pan."

She laughed again, the sound as musical a sound as I'd ever heard. She'd be the perfect Tinker Bell. She'd be the perfect anything. I looked at her standing there in her long coral-and-white-striped halter dress, her hair sleek, golden, and straight to her shoulders. She *was* perfect. I hated her. No, I didn't. I liked her—I hated that I liked her. She was nice and genuine. Why couldn't she have been a total bitch? "I'll make sure he's a *masculine*-looking Peter. With just enough boyish-ness. Just like him."

"What?" I asked distractedly. I shook my head, forcing myself back to the conversation. "Oh…Shane…Peter Pan, right."

I glanced up at Grayson who was slowly screwing the cap back on the water bottle, his expression hard, a small tick working in his jaw.

Sugar Pie tentatively sniffed Vanessa's feet and Vanessa leaned down, her hand petting her head quickly and then drawing back. "I feel like I'll hurt her every time I go to touch her," she said, her voice filled with sympathy.

"You won't," I said. "She needs love more than anything. It will hurt her more if you hold it back."

Grayson stared at me for a moment and then, without a word, turned and walked out of the kitchen. Sugar followed him, looking back at the doorway and letting out a small moan, then lowering her head and running to catch up to Grayson.

My heart clenched. I looked back at my list to hide my face from Vanessa's probing eyes. *He can't even pretend to like me for appearance's sake? What must Shane and Vanessa think?*

"I'm sorry, Kira," Vanessa said. "Our presence is putting a strain on your marriage. We should go—"

"Not on account of me, no. Shane and Grayson have something to work out. I won't get in the way of that." I'd be gone soon enough, but Shane would always be Grayson's brother. I refused to be the reason Grayson didn't give him a chance to—at the *very* least—explain himself. Whatever physical interest Grayson had in me was long gone. And I could see why. Who could compete with Vanessa? She was beautiful inside and out, and I felt like the witch Grayson called me—ugly, ragged, and excluded. Only able to cast a short-lived spell that quickly wore off. No one ever wanted to be with the witch, after all. Not in the end.

Charlotte came bustling into the kitchen a few minutes later, shooting nervous looks between Vanessa and me. Since Shane and Vanessa had arrived, I hadn't gotten any alone time with Charlotte, but whenever I did see her, she seemed to be wringing her hands and saying prayers under her breath. It didn't give me a lot of confidence this situation would turn out well.

Vanessa, Charlotte, and I went over the lists in detail and split up the tasks. "Now who's going to help me make a butterscotch peanut butter cake? Shane requested it—it's his favorite," Charlotte said delightedly.

"Oh, I'll help," Vanessa said. "I need to learn the recipe so I can bake it for him myself sometimes."

Charlotte grabbed two aprons from the drawer, handing one to Vanessa and offering one to me. "Actually," I said. "The next thing on my list is that I need to go outside and figure out what has to be accomplished there. I think I'll do that now." But really, I realized Charlotte and Vanessa deserved time together. I was only going to be here for a short time, while Vanessa was a true part of this family. At the thought, the sharp ache in my heart seemed almost excessive, but it was there nonetheless. I loved this kitchen—the warmth, the smells, the way comfort was always waiting here both in the form of delicious food and Charlotte's wise advice. I was beginning to love Charlotte too.

Charlotte looked at me with sympathy but nodded, almost sadly. I couldn't be angry with her. She knew about the deal Grayson and I had struck. Vanessa would be here forever, whereas I would be leaving soon. It was more important that Charlotte help build a bridge between Shane, Vanessa, and Grayson than try to push Grayson and me together more permanently. It would be a wasted effort anyway. Perhaps she'd finally realized that.

Feeling alone and melancholy, I wandered outside to look at the facade of the house. I had a crew of gardeners scheduled to work the rest of the week. Getting the grounds looking decent was going to take quite a bit of effort, but it was necessary. The house was going to look so much better once the ivy was cut back. I jotted down the few things I thought could be accomplished to the outside of the house in time and then turned to walk behind it to make some notes about that area. I would love to open up the massive back patio and get the pool cleaned if possible. I imagined twinkle lights strung in the trees, casting a magical, fairy-tale glow...

For a moment I stood there, picturing the scene, my gaze rising to the rows of grapevines beyond. Why did I feel this desperate longing inside? I thought about what Grayson was doing right now, how much I was growing to love this vineyard and the people who lived and worked here. I thought about how I'd imagined Grayson and I were moving in the direction of...*what, Kira?* Love? Is that what I had secretly begun to hope for? An emotion not unlike dread clenched my gut, and I walked a few steps so I could lean against a nearby elm tree, closing my eyes in misery. I had the terrible feeling that, somewhere along the way, I had begun to fall in love with my husband. There was no other explanation for the agony I was feeling at his sudden cold indifference and the possibility that he was still in love with another woman. It *hurt*.

Staring out at the afternoon sun glinting on the grapevines, I admitted, only to myself—only *ever* to myself—that maybe I had even started falling in love with Grayson Hawthorn the first moment I'd laid eyes on him. My knight in shining armor standing in front of that bank, the promise that he would save me, and I, him, flowing through my heart like a secret whisper.

Oh, Kira. Oh no.

This was a disaster.

An epic disaster.

I wanted to run, to flee from these feelings, from these realizations. And I knew that was exactly what I would do just as soon as the party was over. I couldn't stay here knowing I could fall even more head over heels for my husband at any moment. He'd never love me back. I was somewhat sure he would still be agreeable to me sharing his bed, but that was all it would ever be. For him. But for me, it would only result in misery.

My desperate—and somewhat dramatic—thoughts were cut off when I saw a lone figure walking around the perimeter of the hedge maze below me. I squinted, recognizing Shane. Hesitating only briefly, I put the list and pen in the back pocket of my jean shorts and walked down the hill to join him.

"Hey," I said softly. He spun around, obviously startled, letting out a quick breath.

"Hey, Kira."

"Sorry, I didn't mean to sneak up on you."

"You didn't. I was just deep in thought, I guess." He sat down on a stone bench next to him and gestured for me to sit as well. I did, leaning my palms behind me.

I looked at the maze next to us and inclined my head toward it. "It's really incredible. You must have had fun in it as kids."

Shane let out a breath, running his hand through his hair like Grayson sometimes did. "God, no. My father would walk us to the middle once it'd turned dark and have us find our way out. He tortured us with this godforsaken thing."

I felt the blood drain from my face and I turned toward Shane. "Why?" I breathed.

He shrugged, looking suddenly like a little boy. "Who knows why my father did what he did? He had ideas about how to make men out of us. That was one of them. Of course, Grayson got the brunt of it, being the oldest." He paused, looking down at his hands in his lap. "I could hear Grayson out here crying for our dad, trying to find his way out, night after night." Sadness swept over his expression as

254

if he were back there again, hearing his brother call out for help, being unable to do anything about it.

"After searching through Dad's files, Walter found a map of the maze and gave it to Grayson. Of course, I only learned this years later. Grayson must have been seven or eight. Walter told him, 'You study this. Go in during the day and learn every single turn, every nook and cranny, and when your father walks you inside, you'll be the one in control. Make sure your father doesn't find out but know the maze like the back of your hand. Then there will be no fear.' Well, that's just what Gray did." He smiled suddenly, the shadows fleeing from his handsome face, and I couldn't help smiling too. *Walter. God bless, Walter.* Oh, God, now I loved Walter too. This was growing worse—and more wonderful—by the moment.

"Later, when my dad brought me inside," Shane went on, "Grayson snuck in from the back, found me, and led me out without our dad knowing. He'd stay hidden in the maze until we'd gone inside, and then he'd sneak inside too. I never knew the same fear he once did because he rescued me. I only knew those brief moments before he showed up. And, God"—his voice broke slightly, but he cleared his throat—"there's nothing on earth like the feel of someone who loves you grasping your hand in the dark when you're lost and afraid."

I let out a breath, my heart constricting. *That poor little boy.* I didn't know what to say, was at a total loss of words, a lump the size of an orange blocking my throat. No wonder Grayson hated the maze—once upon a time, it had served as a massive torture chamber for him.

"My brother did that for me in a hundred different ways over the years—found me in the dark and grasped my hand," Shane said.

"Then why?" I whispered, blinking back tears.

Shane turned his head to look at me. "Why Vanessa?" he asked.

I nodded. "Please tell me, Shane. I'm trying to understand. I'm just trying to understand and maybe if I do, in some way, I can help." I wanted Grayson to have love. The love of family he'd been denied.

Shane sighed. "Because all my life, I've loved her." He paused, smiling a small, sad smile. "We grew up together, you know, the three of us. Grayson never seemed to notice her the way I did." He squinted off into space for a moment, probably remembering specific events. "But then he asked her out first, and I thought maybe he'd just been hiding his feelings, and so I...stepped back when I would have thrown my hat in the ring, so to speak. I would have bared my heart had it been *anyone* else. But I couldn't. He had always gotten the short end of the stick and had sacrificed for me over and over again, all my life. How could I not do the same for him? And so...I loved her, but I let her go without ever saying a word."

I pressed my lips together, sadness moving through me as I stared out at the blue sky. "But then he went away..."

"Yes," he said softly. "You must think I'm such an awful person."

"No. I'm not your judge," I said softly.

Shane sighed, running his hand through his hair.

I didn't ask him any more on that subject. I knew he wanted to explain the rest to his brother first. But I thought I had a little bit of a better understanding of the situation from both perspectives. I only wondered how Vanessa felt about Grayson now. What a mess. A mess I needed to step back from and let them figure out, especially in light of my own realizations about where my heart lay. I had been right. There was no place for me in this. And maybe Grayson had been right too. Perhaps none of it was really my business at all. Sitting there in the shade of that giant maze, I felt suddenly lonelier than I'd ever felt before. But it was Grayson who'd spent so many lonely years on this property, trying to earn the acceptance of his father and continually failing, and having no mother figure to turn to. I understood his loneliness because I'd lived it.

"He told me about your mother—his stepmother—that she never accepted him," I said softly. "Did you have a good relationship with her?"

Shane blew out a breath. "My relationship with her was fine, although I hated the way she treated Gray. She didn't hate him, but she hated what he represented. She considered her life perfect before Grayson's mother showed up on her doorstep. I hadn't even been born at the time, but I heard her remind him enough over the years. And our father... he wasn't the most nurturing of fathers anyway, even to me, but he treated Grayson especially coldly as a way to send the message to my mother that he recognized his mistake and the result of that error would never be fully accepted. There was no atoning for it in her eyes, though. Not that that was the proper way to do it anyway." Shane suddenly turned his head toward me. "I'm surprised he told you anything about that, actually. I've never known him to talk about it, even to me."

I shrugged. "He said it so matter-of-factly, as if explaining the course of the weather."

Shane's smile was wry. "Trust me, Grayson doesn't express himself a whole lot, but he feels anything but matter-of-fact about his father and stepmother. I was there."

I nodded again, knowing I shouldn't be delving more deeply into Grayson's hidden torment. It'd only make me love him more. What was sexier on a man than great abs and a heart full of hidden torment? They should bottle it and sell it by the truckloads. Or perhaps write a book: *Abs and Hidden Torment: A Man's Guide to Bagging Babes*. I would have laughed if I didn't feel so much like crying.

And it was clearer to me than ever that he'd never love me, even if he could move past his love for Vanessa. He'd built a fortress of ice surrounding his heart. I'd witnessed portions of it melting, but as soon as Shane and Vanessa had shown up, he'd quickly filled in the gaps. I understood the initial necessity, but I'd be a fool if I imagined I'd ever be enough to melt it permanently.

"Hey, don't look so sad. We do have a few good memories here too. Our childhoods weren't all horror and trauma. We also used to steal cookies from Charlotte and frequently annoy Walter by trying to get him to break into a smile."

I laughed despite myself, creasing my brow at the same time. "Did it ever work?"

"Rarely." And yet, despite his comment, he smiled affectionately. He loved Walter too.

"Thank you for sharing what you did with me, Shane. It means a lot that you trust me enough to confide in me."

He studied me for just a second, his face breaking into a smile. Without thinking, I leaned forward and hugged him, picturing the small boy he once was, alone in the dark as his brave older brother took his hand. He laughed, hugging me back. When I pulled away, he started to say, "I'm mostly—"

"You already stole one woman from me. Figure you might as well steal another?"

We both stood quickly as if we'd been caught doing something wrong. "Grayson, we were just—"

"Stay out of this, Kira," he said, his furious gaze focused on Shane.

"Jesus, Gray," Shane said incredulously. "We were just talking."

Grayson stepped forward to Shane, his jaw hard and tight. I sucked in a sharp breath, not knowing if I wanted to cry or start throwing things. "I'm familiar with how *just talking* works," Grayson said, his voice raised but his tone deadly cold, "and it doesn't involve arms and bodies. So tell me, is that it, Shane? One isn't enough? Looking to seduce Kira too?"

"Seduce Kira? What the fuck? God, you really are an idiot when you're jealous. Do you think I would seduce your *wife*, you stupid fool?" he yelled.

Out of my peripheral vision, I saw Vanessa and Charlotte rushing toward us.

Grayson's jaw ticked at the word *jealous*, his eyes lowering to slits as he glared at his brother. "Jealous? You think I find you untrustworthy because I'm *jealous*? Not because you're a lying, betraying bastard? I'm not *jealous*." He moved a step closer. "Jesus. She's not even my real wife. We got married for money," he growled.

I sucked in a breath of air that felt like I was inhaling razor blades, my face flushing with heat. The entire vineyard suddenly went quiet, not even the flutter of a leaf could be heard. I looked around: Shane's and Vanessa's expressions, shocked; Charlotte's expression, pained. Grayson was still glaring at Shane, but when he saw that they were all looking at me, he turned his gaze in my direction, his expression seeming to clear momentarily as he became aware of what he'd just said. "Kira—" he started to say, but I turned around and ran, away from the looks, away from the judgment, away from the shame and searing pain. *Away.*

CHAPTER EIGHTEEN
Grayson

I was a damn bastard. Not in the way my stepmother had often tossed it at me. In the way that meant I was a total ass. *A jealous ass.* Shane had been right. I'd walked up on him and Kira hugging and I'd lost my damn mind. I'd shut myself off completely since Shane and Vanessa had arrived, even ignoring Kira after I'd gone to her room and tried to sleep with her like a drunken fool. I could only blame myself if she went looking for comfort and companionship with Shane. *Shane*, who had always been the easygoing charmer. Shane, who had never disappointed anyone.

I don't want you. I don't want you at all.

No one wants you. No one ever has.

Of *course* she felt comfortable and safe with Shane—who didn't? I felt another spear of jealousy, and I gritted my teeth. The possessiveness I'd felt when I'd seen Kira and Shane embracing had thrown me over the edge. I'd watched them over the past week, seen the way they strolled around the property, talking, even laughing. Something that felt close to despair swelled in my chest. Jesus, I needed to get ahold of myself. What was I jealous of anyway? She'd been willing to come to my bed—even if that was off the table now. What else did I want? Was I upset I'd sabotaged that for myself just like I seemed to sabotage everything good in my life? Or was it really just because Shane had stolen Vanessa from me? I hadn't let myself think too much about it since they'd been here—hadn't wanted to explore any of that. And so I'd simply shut down.

And then even worse, in some idiotic effort to prove I *wasn't* jealous—and perhaps to hurt Kira too, I acknowledged that much—I'd exposed the truth of our marriage in a cruel, heartless way. The deep hurt and humiliation I'd seen in her eyes had sent guilt crashing over me. I'd become yet another man in her life using her as the scapegoat. *Fuck.* And then she'd run.

I turned the other way, heading down another path to find her so I could try to make it right after I'd left Shane, Vanessa, and Charlotte gaping after me. What a fucking mess this was. What a fucking mess *I* was. I felt like everything I'd been holding back all week was swirling inside me, coming to a boiling head.

What in the actual hell had happened to me?

I'd met Kira Dallaire, *that's* what had happened to me.

I spotted her out in the south field, looking as if she was…collecting apricots off the ground. Was she holding them in the bottom of her shirt? For a second, I just stood and watched her as she hopped among the fruit, bending and collecting, bringing a piece of fruit to her nose now and again. What was she up to anyway? I tilted my head, watching the bewildering sight. I'd expected to find her sitting somewhere with her shoulders hunched or perhaps curled in the fetal position under a bush. Maybe I should have known by now only to expect the unexpected when it came to Kira.

Something pulled tight inside me—why did my aggravating wife have to fascinate me even as my guts were churning with too many emotions to name? I began walking toward her, approaching slowly, and by the time I got to the edge of where hundreds of overly ripe apricots littered the ground, she had ten or fifteen pieces of fruit weighing down her blousy shirt.

"Kira," I said as calmly as I could, "what are you doing?"

"Collecting fruit for Charlotte's jam—the jam you love so much, the jam that makes you *happy*. I've been meaning to do it all week, but what with organizing your office and planning a party so it might be easier for you to rejoin Napa society, entertaining your family, *and* trying to figure out how to sidestep certain questions from Shane and Vanessa—which, come to think of it, I'd like to thank you for just blurting out the truth because *that's* one stressor off my plate. I can't tell you how relieved I am not to have to *lie* anymore—"

"Kira," I said, moving closer. "I'm sorry. I didn't think that through."

"Plus," she went on as if she hadn't heard me, "all these apricots lying on the ground? It's such a waste of food! There are people who don't have enough to eat—right here in Napa even. And here's all this fruit almost going to waste. It's unconscionable, really."

"Kira," I repeated, moving closer still.

She whirled toward me, her hair hanging long and wavy down her back, wisps and curls framing her face. Her eyes were bright green and stormy, bringing to mind a tropical

262

tempest about to make landfall. About to wreak havoc. Her cheeks were flushed, and I could see she was so filled with anger she was having trouble catching her breath. The barest glimpse of her flat stomach was visible where her shirt had been drawn up in a makeshift basket, heavy with fruit. My breath caught as I took her in. She was the most beautifully wild thing I had ever seen.

I knew I should be groveling and—God, I knew she deserved as much—but after days and days of keeping Kira at arm's length and seeing her now standing in front of me, all fire and life, I lost the control I'd so carefully held on to this past week.

I strode toward her as her eyes widened, and she dropped the fruit collected in her shirt, soft apricots making wet plopping sounds as they splattered on the ground at her feet. She was mine. The jealousy I'd felt when I'd seen her in Shane's arms flared again as I pulled her to my body. I suddenly realized how desperately I wanted her, how these past days had been like living without light and I felt jealous all over again. I didn't want to feel that way. I'd tried so hard never to feel that way again. Vulnerable. Easily hurt. I wanted her to soothe the wild agony raging inside, to reassure the wounded part of my heart that she thought there was something worthy about me, to tell me that she wanted me too. But I had no idea how to put those feelings into words, didn't know how to ask, especially when I had so much to apologize for. And so I claimed her the only way I knew how. I pulled her to me and pressed my lips to hers.

I had only planned to kiss her once and then let her go, but the taste of her sent a flame licking from low in my belly. I grasped for her, unable to tear my mouth from hers. She fought me for a few brief moments, both of our arms scrabbling around each other as I sought to pull her close and she fought to pull away. But then she let out a small sob and wrapped her arms around my neck, kissing me back with passion. I licked at her tongue, the taste of her soothing the ache inside, bringing me simultaneously a loss of control and the first small taste of peace I'd had for what felt like so very long. Maybe for a lifetime. *Kira, Kira, Kira.*

Before I had time to sink into the kiss, Kira pushed at my chest, stumbling back several steps, her eyes filled with renewed hurt. "Kira," I said, noting the pleading tone in my own voice, "I'm sorry. Please come here. I'm asking nicely."

Her chin went up, and she took several more steps backward. "No."

I hesitated. What did she want? "Meet in the middle?" I nodded toward a spot on the grass between where we stood facing each other.

"No," she spit out.

What did she *want* from me? I stepped toward her again, but she suddenly scooped something off the ground and flung it, the loud splat of a mushy apricot exploding on my forehead to drip down my face. I was momentarily stunned. I reached my hand up and took a finger full of apricot off my forehead and brought my finger down to look at it, disbelievingly. "You defiant, little she-devil," I said, my eyes meeting hers. With one quick movement, I scooped up a soft apricot and hurled it at her. She squeaked as it made contact with the small bit of skin showing at the V-neck of her blouse, breaking apart in a splatter of juice and pulp and sliding down her shirt. Her mouth dropped open and she looked at me as if in shock that I had followed her lead.

"You self-serving, slimy monster," she hissed.

We both started scooping up the fruit and chucking it

at each other in a burst of a hundred emotions I couldn't identify in myself, much less in her. *What is happening?* My blood felt hot in my veins, and it was as if the cold indifference in which I'd wrapped myself recently was melting down my skin. Squishy fruit flew at me again and again, most making contact, sticky wetness matting my hair and dripping down every part of my body.

Our wills clashed as the sweet, pungent smell of apricots scented the air. Kira looked about the same as I imagined I looked—like she'd rolled in a vat of fruit. When she paused for a breath, glaring at me, I lunged for her, both of us rolling onto the soft grass, her body coming to rest under mine. Lust surged through me, sharp and almost painful. I had no idea who initiated *that* kiss, but I thought it might have been her. We licked at each other's mouths wildly, greedily, groaning and grasping. I slid my hand up her shirt, feeling soft, smooth skin, and she bucked beneath me. I felt the strong rhythm of her pulse as I brought my other hand to her throat, rubbing my thumb in circles over it, glorying in the feel of her lifeblood right beneath my fingers. My desire for her burned, scalding my heart. Beautiful, willful, tender, stubborn, compassionate, infuriating little witch.

"Oh, please, Gray," she panted, pulling at my shirt.

"Yes," I managed, rolling my hips against hers. "Tell me you want me, Kira, please say it," I begged.

"I do, I want you. I want you so much."

Relief exploded in my gut, sudden and fierce. Oh God, I was ridiculously and hopelessly enchanted with her. I couldn't wait a second longer. I wanted her so much, every part of her. My cock throbbed eagerly between my thighs. She was going to be mine. I didn't care if we were rolling in the grass—

"Oh my *God*" came a woman's voice from above us.

"What the—?" came another voice.

"For the love of—"

"Well, I've never seen anything—"

We both froze, blinking at each other, fog clearing from Kira's expression as we both looked up. I squinted into the sunshine but could only see the dark outlines of six figures hovering over us. I felt stunned and it took me several long moments to get my bearings and for my blood to cool, Kira pulling away from me as if I were fire and she'd been burned. When I realized she was standing, I pulled myself up too, gelatinous apricot goo sliding down my face and bare arms.

When I was finally able to make out the faces before me, my eyes roamed from Charlotte to Walter, to Shane, Vanessa, a woman with pink hair I didn't recognize, and to a new face, but one I knew immediately. "Harley," I said with surprised wonder.

Harley, as big and rough looking as I remembered him, a big bear of a man covered in tattoos, stepped forward, his eyes raking over Kira and me. "Well, I'll be damned."

"What? How?" My mind grasped to make sense of this situation. I forced myself to pull my focus from Kira long enough to gain some mental footing. "How are you here?" I wiped my sticky hand on my pants but only came away with more sticky fruit pulp.

Harley stared at me for a moment and then burst out laughing, his chuckle deep and warm. "Man, I got out a month ago." He looked me up and down, an expression on his face between disgust and hilarity. "I think I'm more interested in hearing about what's been going on with you though. Looks like things have been...sticky."

Kira suddenly stepped toward us, her face mostly

unrecognizable beneath gobs of apricot innards. "Wait, Harley? *Harley?*" she asked, her voice breathless.

Harley turned toward her, squinting. "Kira?" he asked.

My head moved back and forth between them. "You two know each other?" I asked, my voice filled with the surprise I felt. I could see everyone else in my peripheral vision, their heads swinging back and forth from person to person as well. The only thing missing was popcorn.

"Oh my God!" Kira said excitedly, rushing toward Harley, heedless of the fact that she was about to cover him in the same sticky muck she was covered in. He didn't stop her, though, when she threw herself at him, hugging him tightly. I might have had another moment of jealousy, but the hug was brief and Harley was smiling at Kira with friendly affection. "I can't believe you're here."

"How do you know each other?" I asked again.

"From the drop-in center," she said, not even glancing at me. My head was swimming, not only from this strange blast from my past but from the transition between what had been happening with Kira and me to what was happening now. If the silence of everyone else watching this exchange was any indication, they were shocked too. "How do *you* two know each other?"

"From prison," I said.

"Oh," she breathed, finally looking at me and then focusing back to Harley. "Harley, you served time?"

"Yeah, Kira, I did, I'm sorry to say. Turned out to be one of the best things that could have happened to me actually. Life is good. Although"—he turned back to me—"I'm hoping there might be an employment opportunity here."

"You need a job?" I asked. "Yeah, of course you can have a job. Man, whatever you need."

Harley's beefy face broke into a grin. "I was hoping you'd say that." He turned to the woman with pink hair wearing a skimpy leather skirt and an even skimpier tank top next to him. "By the way, this is Priscilla."

I showed her my sticky hand as explanation as to why I wasn't offering it. She laughed softly and said, "Nice to meet you, Grayson. Harley's told me a lot about you. I can see he might have left out some." She looked between Kira and me, her expression amused.

Charlotte cleared her throat. "Gray, perhaps you and Kira can get yourself cleaned up from…well, from…well, cleaned up, and we can all get acquainted up at the house?" She looked hopeful. I assumed they had all rushed down here thinking Kira and I were in some kind of physical showdown after what had happened near the maze. Maybe that was somewhat accurate.

"That's a good idea," I said. "Kira?" She looked at me, seeming like she couldn't decide *what* she wanted to do.

"Yes, okay," she finally murmured.

I pulled on her sleeve and she halted, looking down at where my hand was touching her. "Kira—"

"Let's just get cleaned up, Grayson," she said quietly, not meeting my eyes, not allowing me to attempt to read her expression.

I nodded, releasing my hold on her. I felt off-kilter too and slightly deflated, like I was coming down off of the adrenaline that had recently shot through my veins as I'd tussled with my wife on an apricot-strewn field. God, what had she done to my life?

We all started for the house, Kira walking ahead, Harley telling me how he'd located me here in Napa and about the small place Priscilla had in Vallejo, a nearby town. "I remembered you were in Napa Valley and I looked you up and knew this had to be the place. Man, I can't believe it's been so long."

I looked at Harley regretfully. "I know I wasn't great about keeping in touch. I'm sorry about that. Once I got here and realized how much work I had cut out for me, I got tunnel vision."

"It's understandable. No apologies. This place, though, wow. I know you said it was beautiful here, but I didn't imagine this," he said, sweeping his hand in the direction of the hills of bright green vineyards in the distance, and in the other direction where the majestic mountain vistas created a breathtaking silhouette.

"It's on the way to being what it once was," I said distractedly, glancing ahead at Kira as we approached the house. She turned back quickly, seeming to consider something before she went inside.

She kissed Harley on his cheek and squeezed his hand. "I'm so glad to see you looking so well," she said, sounding like she was going to cry. I frowned, but she didn't glance my way and didn't wait for Harley to answer. She turned and disappeared inside the house, leaving me to stare at the empty place where she'd just been.

"Grayson," Shane said as he approached me, "after you get cleaned up and get a chance to chat with Harley and Priscilla, we should talk." Vanessa stood behind him, nervously biting her lip. God, that was right. I'd blurted out that Kira and I had a marriage of convenience. And now I needed to explain. Only, how could I begin to do that when I barely understood the situation myself anymore? It had seemed clear-cut once upon a time… *Now*, it was about as sticky and sludgy as I currently was.

"Sure," I mumbled, heading inside. "Charlotte, will you get Harley and Priscilla something to eat and drink? I'll be downstairs shortly."

"Of course," Charlotte said, leading them both toward the kitchen.

I tried the door to the room Kira was staying in, but she had locked it and when I knocked, she didn't answer. She was probably in the shower. I'd shower too, and then come back. I needed to talk to her first and foremost. We had unfinished business. And I wanted to make sure she was okay. I wanted to make sure *we* were okay. I owed her a more heartfelt apology than the one I'd given before practically attacking her in the field.

I showered, balling my sticky clothes into a heap and wrapping them in a towel to take to the laundry room. God, what in the hell had come over us? What *was* that? After dressing in clean jeans and a T-shirt, I walked barefoot to Kira's room and knocked on the door again. When there was still no answer, I tried the doorknob and found it unlocked. Had she already gone downstairs? I peeked inside the room and noticed immediately that her suitcase was gone. Panic swirled in my gut, and I entered the room, calling her name. The closet was open, but there was nothing inside except for a few garment bags that held some of my stepmother's old clothes.

I spotted the note on the dresser as I turned to leave. The ring I'd given to Kira for the sake of our ceremony—the one she'd been wearing ever since our first dinner date— was sitting on top. The light caught the diamonds as I lifted it. *What had I been thinking giving her this ring?* I wasn't sure I wanted to read the note.

Grayson,

I think it's obvious after today we require some space from one another—and you need time to work things out with Shane and Vanessa without me in the way. I'll be at the party next week to perform my final act as your wife, and then I'll be moving out for good.

Kira

P.S. I think this ring belongs to Vanessa, not to me. Not that it ever really did.

A lump rose in my throat, coldness creeping up my spine. That was it? I dropped the note. She said she wanted me and then she left without hearing me out? *Fine.* I turned and descended the stairs, the ice moving swiftly up my spine to fill my chest and surround my heart. I took comfort in the frigid feeling. It was what I knew, what I deserved, and how I would survive the hurt.

Following the voices to the kitchen, I joined Harley, Priscilla, and Charlotte at the table. Charlotte started to cut me a piece of her sour cream coffee cake, but I held up my hand, declining her silent offer.

"Harley was telling me how you saved his life." Charlotte studied me, a look of both tenderness and sadness in her expression.

I ran my hand through my hair. I'd never spoken to anyone about my time in prison. I wasn't necessarily willing to now, but I also couldn't exactly throw Harley out. I owed him so much. He'd been there with me—he'd lived it. "More like he saved mine," I said.

"Nah, that's not the way I remember it," he said, leaning back and lacing his fingers behind his bald head.

"I did one thing just by luck—you had my back for the next five years," I said, something catching in my throat. "If it wasn't for you, I wouldn't have survived that place." And it was true. When we'd first arrived, I'd been in shock, numb with disbelief that I'd been sentenced to a five-year term after my lawyer had assured me I'd get community service at best, six months at worst. I'd been in the yard with Harley—who I didn't even know at the time—when something shiny had caught my eye. Instinctively, I'd pushed him away and it'd given him time to turn and disarm the man who otherwise would have gutted him with the makeshift knife. From that day forward, Harley—who had done several prison stints and understood how the system worked with inside connections—had protected me from any number of horrors I might have experienced had it not been for him.

"Well, you're family then," Charlotte said before she looked away, her eyes bright with what looked like unshed tears.

Harley gave Charlotte a warm smile before he looked back to me. "And now," he said, leaning forward, "to come here and find you married to Kira Dallaire. Life is full of surprises."

I made a small sound of agreement in my throat, deciding not to mention the circumstances of our marriage or the fact that it'd be over soon anyway. Or the fact that she'd just left me.

"Where is she, by the way?" he asked.

"Oh. She, uh, had to go out," I murmured.

Harley was eyeing me in that still-familiar way of his. Harley might look big and mean, but he was about the best judge of people I'd ever known. He'd told me it was necessary growing up on the streets of San Francisco—it was either anticipate a person's next move or become their next victim. "Can I tell you a story about Kira?" he asked.

"Sure," I said warily.

"About six years ago, I was in a real bad place." He paused, glancing at Priscilla and then taking her hand in his. "I couldn't figure out how to get myself sober, had lost everything, alienated all the people who cared about me. I planned to end my life. Got a gun and everything. It was loaded, ready to go."

"Jesus, Harley," I muttered. "I didn't know."

"It's difficult to admit how low I was, how little I valued my life back then. But it's the truth of my story. I went to the drop-in center for what I intended to be my last meal, and that's where I met Kira. She must have been just a teenager at the time."

A teenager. Teenagers weren't typically known for their selflessness. But Kira had been kind, even then...

I focused back in on what Harley was saying. "She served me some food, sat down with me, and we chatted for a while. She had brought this magic kit to entertain the kids and she did a few tricks for me—completely amateur. She was all animated about it though, full of life, you know?" *Yes, I know.* "And it was the first time I remembered smiling for a long time. She told me if I came back the next day, she'd show me how she'd done them. Well, I probably would've been able to figure them out on my own if I even really cared—they weren't complicated. But just the fact that someone asked me to return and seemed to want it enough to try to bribe me with the answers to some silly tricks"—he chuckled softly—"well, I did come back that next day. And then she did something else to spark my interest, and it was the first time I realized I had any interest *left*. She made me laugh and she always made a point to ask exactly when she'd see me again. Those simple things gave me the hope I needed. So I kept showing up, and I guess you could say I got distracted from ending my life. That's the truth."

God, that sounded like Kira—sounded *just* like her. I felt my breath catch and the ice that had started to rebuild around my heart began to melt and slide away. I couldn't decide if I was angry about it or not. She always seemed to do that. Where *was* she?

Harley continued, "I wasn't ready quite yet to turn my life around, made some mistakes, ended up serving time with you. But I'll tell you this, as God is my witness, if it hadn't been for Kira saving my life, I wouldn't have been around to be saved again by you, and then to do what I could to make your time inside a little easier. Funny how it worked out like that, isn't it? Funny how one life can affect another, and then that life affects the one after it and on and on."

"Funny," I breathed. "Random."

Harley winked. "If you're a believer in random." He paused, a smile appearing, "Well, listen, my man, we'll have lots of time to reminisce. But if I'm going to be at my best for work tomorrow morning, I better get home so I can rest up. Plus, Priscilla has to work tonight."

"Oh," Charlotte said. "What do you do, dear?"

"I'm a pole dancer," she said.

"Oh, a dancer! How lovely," Charlotte answered, bringing her hands together as if Priscilla had just told her she was the lead on Broadway.

I cleared my throat and smiled at Harley and Priscilla as I stood up. "I can't tell you how glad I am you looked me up. It's good to see you."

"You too, brother." We shook, bumping fists like we'd always done in prison. Charlotte gave both Harley and Priscilla a hug and walked them to the door. After they'd left, but before anyone had a chance to seek me out, I grabbed my keys and left out the back door, circling around to the front and getting in my truck. I drove toward town—I had a wife to look for and some errands to do.

"Oh, you're back," Charlotte said, holding the laundry bin from my bathroom and two shirts she'd obviously just ironed. I was staring out the window and I barely spared her a glance. I'd been ignoring her too for the past week— mostly for the stunt she'd pulled in luring Shane and Vanessa here under false pretenses and forcing me to contend with their presence.

I'd just gotten home from driving around Napa looking for Kira's car. Harley's story had convinced me to go out searching for her, but maybe she didn't want to be found. She'd said she wanted me but perhaps that was just the heat of the moment. Or she'd meant it in a purely physical sense. Or she'd lied. Or…who cared what? She wasn't here, that was the bottom line.

I don't want you. I don't want you at all.

If you were worth more…

Maybe she'd driven to San Francisco to stay with Kimberly.

"Well, when you're done feeling all sorry for yourself, dinner will be—" Charlotte's words ended abruptly and I looked up. She was standing at the closet door, having just hung up the ironed shirts. She turned toward me sharply. "So this is how you see yourself? The villain? Or wait, perhaps the *victim*. Captain Hook to your brother's Peter Pan? *This* is what you've come up with?" she asked as she held the costume I'd stopped and rented after being unable to find Kira. There was only one description for the look on her face—utter disappointment.

"What would you have me dress as, Charlotte?" I asked. "A prince? It's just a stupid party anyway. It means nothing. And I'm no prince."

"It's a party your wife is throwing for you out of the kindness in her heart."

I glowered at her. "My *wife* is gone. She left me. She's only coming back for the party and then she's leaving again—permanently. Just as we'd planned."

Charlotte looked shocked for a brief moment, but then her knowing eyes roamed over my face as silence settled between us. "But it's not just as you planned, is it? Nothing is as you planned. And that scares you very, very much." Charlotte approached me and reached out her hand. I took it and she squeezed mine between both of her own, the comforting scent of her—baked goods and talcum powder—causing my breathing to calm. "Ah, my boy, you've fallen very hard, haven't you?"

"Fallen?" I took my hand from Charlotte's. "Fallen where?"

"In love of course. With Kira. With your wife."

I swallowed heavily and turned toward the window. "I'm not in love with Kira," I insisted, but the words felt flimsy, as if they didn't hold any weight and might simply float away.

Charlotte sighed. "For the love of all things holy, you're both so stubborn. You two probably deserve no less than to be shackled to each other for life. It's a wonder watching you together hasn't driven me to drink."

I snorted. I was not in love with the little witch. *Was* I? No, I couldn't be—my emotions for her were too turbulent, too out of control, too...*terrifying*. Maybe I was obsessed with her, enchanted, beguiled. But love? No, not love. "She makes me crazy," I said, turning back to Charlotte. "When we're together, we act like out-of-control children half the time." *And the other times like desperate lovers, unable to keep our hands off each other...*

"We should all be children when it comes to love— open and vulnerable." She paused. "I don't know everything there is to know about Kira's past, but I know *you* have good reason to guard your heart. And good reason to want to choose someone who doesn't inspire such passion, such intensity, and such fear because you learned early that love hurts. I suspect Kira's been hurt too. And for those such as yourselves, true love is a scary prospect. True love is the greatest leap of faith there is."

I ran my hand through my hair. This was all too much, and I didn't even know where to start, what to focus on. I was all twisted up inside, angry with Kira one minute, wanting her desperately the next...needing to push her away two seconds after that.

"I think a good place to start," Charlotte said as if reading my mind, "is to talk to your brother and Vanessa. And *listen* to them, not with your hurt but with your heart." She grasped my hand again. "And bear this in mind: love is not always smooth and easy. Love can be piercing. Love means exposing yourself—*all* of yourself, every tender part—to being hurt. Because true love is not only the flower; true love is also the thorns."

I sighed. "Sharp and painful," I confirmed. Why would anyone seek out love anyway?

Charlotte's laughed softly. "Sharp, yes, piercing, yes. But not always painful. It's meant to strip you bare and expose your wounds so they might be healed. Be brave enough not to fight it. Surrender, my boy. Let go. For just once, have the courage to let go." She leaned up on her tiptoes and kissed my cheek, and I bent slightly to let her. Then she smiled warmly and left me where I stood.

Love is not always smooth and easy. Was that why I had chosen Vanessa once upon a time? Because my feelings for her were lukewarm? As soon as I posed the question to myself, I knew in my heart the answer was yes. Shane and I had grown up with Vanessa. She'd always been a friend—beautiful and sweet—and I'd noticed the way Shane had looked at her and the way she'd looked back at him, hoping he'd make a move. Neither one realized the other had feelings for them. But *I knew*, and I asked Vanessa out anyway, knowing Shane would step back for me. My shoulders dropped. Oh God. Why had I done that?

I'd wanted her because I'd felt perfectly in control of my feelings where she was concerned and that sort of calm, that lack of risk, *the absence of thorns*, was something I craved after the deep hurt I'd experienced growing up. After the humiliating grasping for love never returned, the loneliness of being unwanted, I didn't want to grasp anymore. I didn't care to hope any longer. It hurt far too much. And so I chose someone who didn't inspire any of that in me. *Vanessa had been too sweet to say no.* And somewhere inside, I'd felt a certain satisfaction taking something I knew rightfully belonged to Shane. Shame swept through me. I'd given all my life, made sure he never suffered the way I'd had to. I'd thought I deserved to step ahead of him where Vanessa had been concerned. *Jesus.*

He was my brother and I'd betrayed *him*—even if he didn't know it. And I hadn't even thought of her either. Would my tepid feelings have ever been enough for her in the long run? Of course not. I had been wandering into a permanent state of cold detachment, and it was only *Kira* who had been able to beckon me back with her warmth and exuberance. Vanessa and I would have never made each other happy. I'd told myself there was never a need to confide my secrets to her because she knew my family dynamics, but the truth was, I hadn't wanted to. I'd never wanted to share all of myself with her and so I never had. And if I'd loved her, it had only been as a...friend.

She'd told me she wanted to save herself for marriage, and after all the women I'd already been with by the time we started dating, that had seemed right. That I should wait for my wife. Likely, she'd been saving herself for *Shane* more so than marriage, whether she'd realized it at the time or not. But now...thank God I'd never made love to my brother's wife. The things we *had* done suddenly felt incestuous and one hundred percent unappealing. I ran my hand down my face, smoothing out the grimace.

I'd gone to prison and they'd somehow found their way to each other. But truthfully? As far as them being together? All I'd felt was a hollow sense of betrayal. Mostly, I'd grieved for the loss of one of the few people who had always been in my corner: my little brother. Since then, I hadn't allowed myself to feel at all. And it'd been somewhat easy. But then came Kira, who stirred up all my emotions and forced me to acknowledge the needs I kept guarded inside. And her warmth and vitality melted the cold walls I'd built up.

Kira, who never did anything in half measures.

Kira, who had suffered as much or even more than I had.

And suddenly, I felt even smaller because I saw so clearly that, despite the similarities in our stories and despite the fact that she'd been severely wronged, Kira had chosen to face the world with hope and optimism. And selflessness. And me? I had withdrawn, focusing only on my own selfish desires. Unlike my wife, I'd been a coward.

But I longed to be better, to be worthy of her. And I wanted her. God help me, I wanted her body, yes, but I wanted so much more than that too. I wanted her approval, to hear her thoughts, to know her secrets. And I wanted to keep telling her mine.

I sat down heavily on my bed, feeling battered and bruised by all the thoughts and realizations pummeling my mind. *I love my wife.* Beautiful, bewitching Kira who had brought me back to life with her combination of fierce defiance and deep vulnerability.

A small scratching came at my still-cracked-open door and Sugar Pie pushed it fully open with her nose and then trotted over to me. She chuffed softly and instead of lowering that injured head of hers the way she usually did, she placed it on my knee and stared up at me with her soulful eyes. I scratched her ear. "That's a good girl, Sugar Pie," I said, praising her for finding her voice and being brave enough to use it. "Beautiful girl," I said, running my hand over the places where she'd once been hurt.

"When did I fall in love with her?" I asked the dog my wife had gifted me, scratching her other ear. Sugar Pie offered no answer other than a small satisfied whine. When had it happened? The first time she'd called me a dragon? Was it those ridiculous O-named rats? The first time I'd kissed her? Watching her playing with those kids at the drop-in center, her hair flying wildly around her face as she shared her open and loving spirit, even though she had every right to be miserable after her father's cruelty only the night before? When had I fallen in love with her and not even realized it?

I fell back on the bed. *Oh God, I do—I love her.* And I wanted *her* love. I hungered for it. And I was terrified to want like that. I didn't know how to feel the emotions I was suddenly acknowledging, knew even less how to expose them to her rejection.

Surrender, my boy. Let go.

For just once, have the courage to let go.

I let out a staggered breath, not knowing if I was able, not knowing if I could be that brave.

CHAPTER NINETEEN
Kira

The 1902 mansion that had been transformed into a charming bed-and-breakfast was just a short walk from the downtown riverfront. It's where I'd been staying for almost a week as I simultaneously licked my wounds and completed my portion of the list for the upcoming party at Hawthorn Vineyard. I had been in contact with Charlotte via text, and I knew all was going well with the projects both inside and outside the house. Charlotte had offered repeatedly to come visit me, but I declined. I appreciated it, but there was nothing anyone could do for me. And it would only hurt more in the end if I continued to get closer to the people who were Grayson's family...and not mine. I had to start pulling away, lest I be even more devastated in the end than I already knew I would be.

It was telling, I supposed, that Grayson hadn't even texted me once, much less tried to call.

What a mess my latest scheme had become. I had to comfort myself with the knowledge that the end goal had actually been accomplished. I was financially independent, in possession of the freedom I'd sought, and as for Grayson, his vineyard was on the way back to being operational and, hopefully, very successful.

And now here I was, putting the finishing touches on my costume for the party tonight. I'd attend as I'd promised, make sure everything went well, and ensure Grayson and I looked like an upstanding married couple, and then I'd immediately leave town. I couldn't return to the bed-and-breakfast without it looking suspicious. I'd made friends with the owners and they thought I was staying here because of all the work being done at the vineyard. I'd complained the construction dust was stirring up the asthma I didn't actually have.

So…I wouldn't be able to stay in or near Napa after all. If anyone in town found out we *weren't* in fact a happily married couple, they'd feel duped and the whole point of this party—to improve people's perception of Grayson—would be for nothing. I'd ask Grayson if I could spend one last night in my little cottage, and then have Walter give me a ride to collect my car and leave in the morning. My heart sank and I swiped at the tear before it fell down my cheek. I'd cried enough this week. And I didn't have time for tears right now, not to mention that I had spent quite a bit of time on my makeup. And so, I squared my shoulders and slipped on my shoes just as my phone dinged with the text letting me know my ride had arrived.

I took one final look in the mirror, picked up my suitcase, and left my room. I heard staff in the kitchen off to the left of the front entrance preparing dinner, but no one else was around. I'd already paid my bill, and I'd see the owners at the party, since they'd been invited.

The car was waiting in front of the house and the driver looked me over with wide eyes when I descended the stairs. "Wow," he said, "that is quite the costume." He took my suitcase and opened the door, offering me his hand, but his eyes moved over me appreciatively.

"Thank you," I said, climbing inside the car and gathering my long, poufy gown around me and arranging it as best as I could so it didn't swallow me up. This gown was the main reason I wasn't driving myself. I would never fit behind a steering wheel. The dress was a confection of black and deep green satin and tulle, the skirt made larger by three hoops. It was strapless and had a built-in corset that made my waist look tiny. I'd accessorized it with long, black, sheer gloves. Black jewels wound around my neck, and a wide-brimmed, sheer witch's hat completed the look. My hair was left long and made even wilder than it normally was with the help of a curling iron. My eyes were rimmed in black, lipstick bright red, and my mask was black and covered only my eyes, making them look even more catlike.

I had considered a number of costumes, and in the end, this was the only one that felt right. I'd leave Grayson as I had arrived to him: his little witch. No, I thought dejectedly, not his. *Never* his. Despair swirled inside at the knowledge that this would be the last night I'd spend time at Hawthorn Vineyard. Maybe this costume was really just my pathetic way to privately acknowledge my love for him. I wanted him to accept me as I was. All of me. Instead, Grayson wanted my body and nothing more. I would never be enough in his eyes, just as I'd never been enough in my father's eyes, or even in Cooper's. I needed to be enough in my *own* eyes, and for now, that would have to be okay.

The drive seemed to take only moments, and I forced

myself to breathe deeply. Thank goodness I was wearing gloves. I was sure my hands were cold and clammy.

My car pulled to a stop, and when the driver opened the door and I took his hand and stepped out, I sucked in a breath, my heart dipping into my stomach and then rising again.

The fountain was filled with water splashing softly as it cascaded from the top tier down to the shimmering pool below. The pinks and purples of approaching twilight filled the sky and offset the golden lights of the fully lit house. The ivy was trimmed and tended, the window boxes on each balcony filled with lush greenery and white, cascading flowers. The scent of roses and what I now recognized as hawthorn flowers drifted on the breeze rustling the now beautifully landscaped foliage. I turned slowly in a full circle, taking it all in, noticing the twinkle lights that filled the trees leading up the driveway, adding to the magical ambiance. It was gloriously beautiful, captivating—the perfect setting for a fairy tale.

How I wish it were mine.

I took in a deep sustaining breath, pulled my shoulders straight, and nodded once to the driver, who handed me my suitcase and nodded back.

The only vehicles in the driveway were a catering van and two other cars that most likely belonged to the musicians I'd hired, which meant I'd made it in perfect time to greet the first guests. I'd be welcoming them with Grayson by my side. I stumbled as panic threatened to shatter my composure, but collected myself and brought my chin up, whispering a quiet prayer to my gram, asking her to send me strength.

You can do this—one final thing.

I nodded in greeting to the two valets dressed in black

pants, white shirts, and red vests, who stood off to the side, waiting for the first cars to arrive. I rang the doorbell even though I had become accustomed to letting myself in since Grayson and I had gotten married. Walter pulled it open, his eyes widening before they crinkled very slightly at the corners. I blinked. Had I just received my first semi-smile from Walter? I grinned at him as he took my hand in his and bowed his head. "Mrs. Hawthorn."

"Walter..." I said, about to tell him to call me Kira for the hundredth time, when my voice caught in my throat at the sight of the foyer and emptied living room beyond. I set my suitcase down so Walter could store it somewhere, my eyes widening. The wood molding was shined to a high polish, the chandeliers glittered brightly, and the very last vestiges of daylight streamed in through the windows, creating shifting shards of prisms on the walls. Tall vases of roses, lilies, and greenery were on every exposed surface, scenting the rooms with their intoxicating sweetness.

As I wandered into the living room, I saw the small string quartet had set up in one corner, and a fully stocked bar had been installed in the opposite corner. The furniture had been arranged to provide ample seating, but also plenty of room to mingle and even slow dance to the orchestra, should guests desire.

I walked to the window and looked out over the clear, clean aqua water of the swimming pool below, where a small band would begin playing after the cocktail hour concluded. Small, intimate tables dotted the patio, and beautifully positioned votive candles set the whole scene alight with a romantic aura.

I faced the room again and took a moment to stand silently, feeling joy, mingled with sadness, spread through my body. I loved this place deeply. And I was leaving it.

This night was a goodbye. But at least in some ways, it was a beautiful one.

I felt the weight of someone's stare and raised my gaze. Grayson stood across the room. And as that beautifully sensuous mouth curved into a grin, my eyes widened and I sucked in a breath.

His costume. Oh my God. His costume.

My delight was sudden and fierce, and I brought my gloved hands to my mouth, bending forward as I laughed joyously. Elation, hope, happiness, surprise, and sorrow, and a hundred other emotions, blossomed inside. I took a step toward him at the same moment he began to walk to where I stood. Had he done this for me?

He was wearing a black tuxedo. The mask he wore covered only the top half of his face, made to look like iridescent blue, green, and black dragon scales curving around his eyes and the sides of his head. There were small horns at the top, and threads of shimmering red and orange running through it to look like fire.

He was dressed as a dragon.

He paused and turned slightly to show me the wings attached to his back—black with the same blue-green scales and threads of fire. His grin grew as he turned toward me again and we met in the middle of the room, rushing together and stopping suddenly when we were a few inches apart.

We stood gazing at each other for several heartbeats before he said, "Hi, little witch." His voice sounded raw and as I stared into his eyes, seen only through the holes in the mask, I swore I saw longing. "You look beautiful. No... ravishing."

"Hi, dragon," I breathed. He was devilishly gorgeous as he again smiled down at me, and my heart flipped once and then twice inside my chest. "So do you. I can't believe you did this." I grinned. Whatever barriers stood between us, he'd done this for me. To make me smile.

"Oh I did," he assured me. His grin faded as he took one step forward. "I missed you."

"You did?" I whispered, taking one step forward as well.

He took another step closer. "Yes, God yes. Kira, this week... I have so much to tell you. We have so much to talk about. I hope—"

"We do?" I asked, my words colliding with his, hope rising inside me again.

"Yes."

I looked down. "You didn't even call me," I said, trying to keep the hurt from my voice. "I thought—"

"Charlotte tried to find out where you were."

I blinked. *Oh.* "I didn't know she was asking for you. Why didn't you just ask me yourself?"

"I didn't think after... Well, I wanted to *show* you rather than tell you, and so I thought it would be best if I waited for tonight," he said, a throaty edge to his voice. "I needed to look in your eyes. Kira—"

"I—"

"Kira!" I heard singsonged loudly from the doorway. Charlotte came rushing toward us, dressed as a fairy godmother. I laughed happily, turning to her and letting her sweep me into her warm embrace. "Oh, I don't want to crush you. Let me look at you." She turned me one way and then the other. "Perfect, simply perfect."

"You too, Charlotte," I said. "You should wear this all the time. Or...maybe you don't need to. You are a fairy godmother. You've been mine." And I knew she'd always been Grayson's too.

"My darling girl," she said, "you know how much I've come to care for you, right?"

"Yes," I said, hugging her again. And I did. Despite the reasons she'd brought Shane and Vanessa here—and I was suddenly beginning to believe her reasons were deeper than I yet knew—I didn't doubt the purity of her motives or that she cared for me. I felt it in my heart.

Seconds later, Vanessa and Shane came into the room. Vanessa dressed as the most perfect Tinker Bell I'd ever seen and Shane in a tuxedo with a green mask and Peter Pan hat, a sword strapped to his side. I felt heat rise in my cheeks at the thought of the last time I'd seen them, but when they smiled at me, and because Vanessa hugged me warmly, I relaxed, and I felt a measure of relief. I looked over to Grayson, whose expression seemed calm.

As Vanessa and Shane went to get a drink at the bar, I turned to Grayson. There seemed to be a peace in his eyes I'd only caught glimpses of before. "You've made up with them," I said incredulously.

"Yes. There were a lot of apologies to go around. And I explained all about…us. I told you I had a lot to tell you about."

I opened my mouth to speak, wanting very much to hear exactly what he'd told Vanessa and Shane, but the doorbell rang. The string quartet began playing, the crooning melody of "I See the Light" adding to the fairy-tale ambiance, as food staff entered from the kitchen holding delicious-smelling hors d'oeuvres on silver trays.

The next two hours were a whirlwind of greeting and chatting with guests, making sure everyone was comfortable and enjoying themselves, and ensuring the party got off to a seamless start.

The costumes were wonderful, some no more than beautiful masks combined with evening wear, and others entire creations from head to toe.

Once I had a moment to take a break, I took a glass of champagne off a passing tray and stood back to admire all the hard work I'd participated in. Everyone looked like they were having a great time, and if the admiring looks on everyone's faces as they glanced around were any indication, Hawthorn Vineyard had impressed them. Hopefully they'd spread the word in town that Grayson had been welcoming and hospitable and his home was beautifully inviting. This place was not in shambles as the gossip indicated. On the contrary, his home sent the message there was every reason to believe the vineyard itself was on the rise under Grayson's management. Who didn't like a good comeback story? Who wouldn't wish to be part of one? That was my hope, and the point of the party.

I glanced around for Grayson and saw him among a group of guests, one of whom I recognized as Diane Fernsby, and they were laughing and obviously entertained by something he was telling them. He looked up and caught my eye, shooting me a smile. It was the expression in his eyes that made my breath catch though. *That dragonish smile. It will be my undoing.*

My attention was snagged by Harley, dressed as the Beast, and Priscilla dressed as a punked-out version of Beauty. I hugged them both, delighted to see them. Harley had begun working at the vineyard, which was wonderful. Despite his internal and external scars, he was such a good, kind man. I was so glad Grayson had someone like him. I spent a few minutes chatting with them and getting to know Priscilla better, and then moved off to mingle with the other guests.

I greeted Virgil, dressed as Aladdin, and chatted with José and his wife—dressed as the Wolf and Little Red Riding Hood—for a short time before excusing myself to make sure everything was going well outside.

The outdoor patio was awash in the glow of candlelight, guests milling around the pool, the sounds of laughter mingling with a new song the band had just begun to play. I stood for a moment, observing. There hadn't been a moment to talk more with Grayson, and I couldn't wait to get him alone. The night had been a whirlwind so far though, and despite my impatience, I was very satisfied with the way the party was going.

"May I have this dance?"

I whirled around at the feel of a warm body behind mine, the whisper of breath on my bare shoulder. A beautiful dragon was grinning down at me, his hand held up to take my own. "I just realized I haven't danced with my wife yet...or ever, for that matter." I let out a small breathy laugh and took his hand as he led me to the middle of the dance floor. I recognized the song from the movie *Enchanted*, although I couldn't have named it.

"I didn't realize dragons could dance."

He pulled me into his arms and began to lead. Leaning close to my ear, he whispered, "Oh yes. People assume we're cumbersome, but it isn't true. It's a little known fact—dancing with a dragon is like dancing with firelight." And then he spun me around. My heart leapt and I laughed out loud, my hair flying out behind me. He spun me back the other way as he grinned, and as silly as it might have sounded, I felt as if I was glowing. And I knew for sure I loved him. I was in love with my husband. Which might be tragic, but God, I hoped it wasn't.

We slowed then; I was lost in the music and the sway of his body against mine. I wanted to ask him so many things, needed to hear him say the words I thought I saw reflected in his eyes, but I needed to be alone with him. I needed the moment to be just about us. I was still nervous and grappling with how quickly things had changed—I'd been prepared to say goodbye to him tonight, and now...and now there was a whisper of hope, even if I was almost afraid to dream.

The song ended and I stepped away slowly, unable to take my eyes off my husband as he gazed down at me as well, something in his expression I'd never seen before. He reached up, as if to touch my cheek, when we suddenly heard applause. I looked around and saw that we were the only ones on the dance floor and that the guests were clapping as if we'd just performed for them. I laughed, warmth rising in my cheeks as I gave a small curtsy and Grayson bowed, looking just a bit embarrassed too.

A woman approached us, walking with the slightest of limps, a kind smile on her face. "That was lovely," she said, reaching out her hand. I took it in my own. "I'm Virgil's mother, Trudy Potter."

"Oh!" I said. "So nice to meet you. Virgil's become part of the family here. We all love him."

She let out a breath, looking teary as she shook Grayson's hand. "I won't keep you, but I"—she breathed in sharply as if trying not to cry—"just wanted to thank you, Mr. Hawthorn." Her words ended on a whisper.

"You're welcome," Grayson said softly.

She nodded at him and turned, disappearing into the crowd.

"I only gave the man a job," he murmured as though her appreciation had been excessive. But I could tell that to

Trudy Potter, the word *only* didn't begin to encompass it. What Grayson had given her son was a chance.

Suddenly, off to my right, I heard the soft clap of a singular person approaching us and turned, my smile fading as my heart stuttered. Grayson grasped my hand.

"Hello, Kira," my father said.

I eyed him warily, looking around quickly to make sure no one nearby could hear us. He was standing in shadow and apparently no one had recognized him as of yet. Not that it would be peculiar, I supposed, for my father to be at a party I was hosting, but I certainly didn't want him to stay. "What in the hell are you doing here?" I hissed.

"I planned to visit you at your new home. Forgive the intrusion. I had no idea I'd be interrupting a party, but I didn't like the way we ended things in San Francisco. I wanted to learn a little more about the man you married." He suddenly looked to Grayson. "It seems you're more than Kira led me to believe," he said. "Of course any father would be worried about his daughter under these circumstances."

"Can we discuss this somewhere more private?" Grayson asked, stepping forward, his jaw hard, words clipped. "This is hardly the place." He nodded to the people all around sipping champagne, laughing, and beginning to fill the dance floor behind us.

My father narrowed his eyes but nodded once, and Grayson, not letting go of my hand, led the way to his office. When he'd closed the door behind us, his tone was arctic as he said, "Let me give you some advice—things won't turn out well if you ever just drop by our home again."

My father turned to him, his eyes equally as cold. "You'll understand, of course, if I choose not to take *any* advice from a murderer." He spoke through his teeth, his lips barely moving.

Grayson eyed him, no emotion whatsoever in his expression.

"What do you want?" I asked dejectedly. This night had been so full of magic before he'd shown up.

He looked back and forth between the two of us, eyeing our costumes, but obviously choosing not to comment. "You and I haven't always seen eye to eye, Kira. But clearly I don't want my daughter married to a murderer and an ex-con."

"Don't," I responded. "You don't know anything about who he is." Nausea pressed against my stomach, and I brought my hand there as if to hold it back.

"Kira," Grayson said. "You don't need to fight my battles. Let me speak to your father alone, please." His voice was clipped, but he gave me a small, reassuring nod.

"Grayson, you don't know what he's—"

"I think that's a good idea," my father said. The smile he shot in my direction looked as flimsy as his campaign promises.

Grayson made eye contact with me. "I can handle myself, little witch." His voice became tender. "Go back to the party, please."

I let out a frustrated breath, glaring at my father for a moment before meeting Grayson's eyes again. "Fine." I acquiesced, not knowing what else to do. I walked out of the room, grasping my hands in fists to keep the shaking to a minimum.

The moon cast a golden glow from above and feathery fingers of mist encircled my feet from below. I sat on the bench next to the hedge maze, the one I'd sat on with Shane, what seemed so long ago but in reality had only been a week. I removed my gloves and then the pins holding on my hat and sat them both on the bench next to me, using my fingers to lift my hair off my scalp.

The dread I'd felt in Grayson's office had settled into a lonely lump of cold fear. I could barely attempt to categorize all the worries that swirled in my gut at the thought of my father and Grayson conversing alone. Why was my father here, and what could he possibly want? What did he know? It hadn't sounded like he remembered Grayson... even though he'd obviously looked him up. What would he attempt to control now? Once I had hoped so hard to be loved by him. Now, now I just wanted to be free of him.

When I heard footsteps approaching, I stood, turning in time to see Grayson appear around the curve in the path. He'd removed his mask. I let out a breath, feeling a flare of panic.

"What happened?" I asked.

"Your father offered me a whole hell of a lot of money to walk away from you permanently, even more than what your grandmother left in trust."

The lump previously in my throat dropped to my stomach. I exhaled a sharp breath and turned away, wrapping my arms around myself. Well, the good news was he evidently believed our marriage was real. "Is he gone?"

"Yes."

"You should take it," I said, the words emerging on a rush of breath. "The more money...the more you can do with the vineyard. We're divorcing anyway. He doesn't have to know it was already planned." I tried to sound sincere. I only hoped the scratchiness of my voice didn't entirely betray me.

"You're shaking," he said.

"Am I?" I rubbed my hands down my arms. "It's a little chilly, I guess…"

His hands replaced mine, warm and solid on my skin. "Kira," Grayson whispered. "You don't have to worry about him anymore. I'm your husband—it's my job to take care of you now. I don't want his money. I told him that. And I don't want to walk away."

That wild hope soared inside. "You…you don't?" I turned back to him.

He smoothed a piece off my cheek. "No, I don't. I realize it might be difficult to take a man seriously who's dressed in a dragon costume, but…"

I laughed softly. "That's the *reason* I'm taking you seriously."

He smiled. "Good, because I was hoping…well, I was hoping we could give this marriage a real try. I was hoping you'd agree to be mine…for real. My wife, my lover, my friend." Vulnerability was etched in the hopeful set of his features, in those deep, dark eyes, and my heart leapt with joy.

"Make our marriage real?"

"Yes."

I wanted that too—so much. I wanted to stay here, to love him and feel his love in return, and yet there was still so much unresolved between us…

"What about Vanessa?" I asked. I needed to know he'd resolved his feelings for her if I was going to truly put my heart on the line.

He exhaled. "I never loved Vanessa, Kira. Or if I did, it wasn't the right kind of love. I realize that now. Vanessa was meant for Shane. I know because I understand what it feels like when a woman is meant for a man, the way you're meant for me."

"Gray," I murmured, leaning into his hand when he brushed it along my cheek.

"We all talked this week. Vanessa and I were never destined to be married. We were friends. And, Kira? We never…well, we never slept together either. I think it's important that you know that. I…knew. I knew I didn't love her and that she didn't love me. I owed them both apologies."

"Oh, Grayson, I'm so glad." I let out a deep breath, a feeling of peace settling inside.

He smiled then. *Gorgeous dragon.* "I told them about us—told them I was going to try to convince you to give me a chance. It's like a weight has been lifted from all of our shoulders. And I have my brother back."

"That's wonderful."

"Kira, I'm sorry about that stupid ring. I…" He pursed his lips as if choosing his words. "I didn't mean to hurt you. I just didn't think about it, and when I found that ring, I figured it'd do well enough as a prop. I'm sorry that's what it was at the time. If I was choosing jewels for you, I'd choose something entirely different…maybe emeralds for your eyes or rubies for all that fire inside." He gave me a sweet smile. "Nothing as colorless as diamonds or opals. Not for you."

I felt like I was in a dream. But I had spent a week talking myself out of this, so filled with fear of rejection and the instinct to run. "Will this work? We've done this all backward. I'm your *wife*."

He chuckled softly. "Yes, you are. My enchanting wife." His eyes roamed over my face as his expression became serious, filled with need. "Just tell me you want me too, Kira."

My heart quickened. He'd asked me twice before if I wanted him. The first time, in my hurt and confusion, I'd said no. The second time, I'd said yes and then I'd left. But now, I saw what he was really asking. Apart from Charlotte and Walter, who'd filled in as many holes as possible in his life, he'd never felt truly wanted by anyone. He'd been needed by his brother but rejected by the people who should have loved and accepted him but didn't. Yes, I wanted him. I wanted him to know he was worthy of being loved. Was I ready to give him my trust again though? And was he willing to give me his?

"I do, Grayson," I said, bringing my hand to his cheek. "I do want you. We just…in some ways we know so little about each other."

He turned his head and kissed my palm. "I know what I need to know, and the rest we'll learn."

I smiled, my hand dropping. He took it in his, and we began walking along the path toward the front of the maze, the sounds of the party drifting to us on the faint night breeze. "What's your middle name?" he asked.

I laughed. I guess we did have to start somewhere. "Isabelle, after my gram. What's yours?"

"I don't have one."

I turned to him. "No middle name? That's…criminal!"

He laughed. "Apparently it's not."

"It doesn't seem right that someone should have *no* middle name."

He shrugged and smiled, his lips curving up into a soft, vulnerable smile. I felt absurdly furious that no one had bothered to give this man a middle name. After everything he'd told me about his family, it felt like another slight. I huffed out a breath and he shot me an amused glance.

We halted, and he looked up at the night sky. I let my eyes drink him in. Standing there under the stars. I hadn't known he had no middle name. But I knew so many other things about him, moments that I strung together to form a full picture. And I suddenly saw him so clearly, not just his striking looks but *all* of him: his intelligence, his goodness, his loyalty and protective nature, his wit, and his deep sensitivity—the thing he let so few people see. Joy spread through me. *I was his wife.* This beautiful man had chosen me. I wanted to love him, heal him, transform all his dark memories into light. I wanted to be worthy of him, and I longed for him to love me back.

"What made you realize how you felt?" I asked, needing to know but feeling shy.

He smiled, glancing at me as we started walking again. "Charlotte helped me realize. She encouraged me to take a leap of faith—to let go."

Charlotte. Sweet Charlotte. Our fairy godmother. Of course. "Ah. Letting go. It's difficult, but important." And crucial to moving forward. I understood that all too well.

"And you? Did you know before tonight?" he asked.

"I think I've known for quite some time now."

"You have?"

"Yes. Until tonight, I considered it extremely unfortunate."

He chuckled softly. We stopped next to the entrance to the maze and I turned toward him, grasping his hands in mine.

"Here we are," I said softly, nodding my head toward the maze.

"Yes," he said, his eyes flickering away from the maze and back to me. "Here we are."

He moved closer, pulling me into his arms and whispering against my lips. "You bring me peace, little witch, and you put a fire in my blood."

I smiled against his mouth. "But do you trust me?" I asked, placing my palm flat against his jacket, running my hand over his chest, feeling the strong beat of his heart beneath.

"Trust you?" A crease formed between his dark brows.

I ducked under his arm and he spun to face me. "Come find me, Grayson," I said and I ran into the maze.

"Kira," he called, a low edge to his voice, "what are you up to now?"

"Helping you let go of something," I said, turning a corner and then quickly turning another. I heard Grayson behind me, walking slowly as I ran. "If you can find me, I'm yours."

"Kira," he said, and despite the distance, I heard the warning tone. "I know this maze well—there's no hiding from me here."

Ah yes, but I know that.

A thrill fluttered through me as I turned another corner. "Really, dragon?" I called. "We'll see. I'm waiting." I was already hopelessly lost, simultaneously feeling a small thread of fear and sympathy for what Grayson must have felt being alone in here all those years ago, but also the tingle of excitement at the knowledge that he'd find me. The shrubbery was tall and untended, and as I ran by, holding the hoops of my skirt as close to my body as possible, my long dress trailing on the ground behind me, branches seemed to reach out and grab me. The moon and stars and the glow of the house beyond cast the only light.

He didn't say another word, but I heard him walking

with purpose through the weeds and fallen branches straight toward me, as if he'd known where I would run. I turned one more corner and there in what seemed the middle of the maze was an old fountain in ruin and disrepair, a stone bench in front of it. I sat down and waited for Grayson to find me.

The distant strains of music and voices from the party took a back seat in my mind as I listened intently for his footsteps, my pulse quickening, my heart thumping.

"Where are you, little witch?" he asked, much closer now. But it didn't sound as if there was question in his voice. Yes, he knew exactly where I was. He still remembered every turn. My heart rate increased.

He came around the corner at the far end of where I sat, and my breath stuttered in my throat. In the glow of the starlight, I could see his gaze was trained on me. I stood slowly and as he started to approach, I held up my hand, motioning for him to stop so I could come to him. Because here, in this place, he had always done the rescuing.

He watched as I approached, his eyes dark and fathomless.

As I drew nearer to him, it came to me that watching Grayson in front of the bank that day, I *had* fallen in love but only in some romantic, girlish way. I had fallen in love with the idea of him. But here, in the deep, dark of the maze— where he had once been lost and frightened and alone—I reached out my hand, and I fell in love with the man. I fell in love with my husband.

His hand in mine was solid and warm and real. And he grasped me back.

CHAPTER TWENTY
Grayson

The party was winding down as I made the rounds as fast as possible, stopping to chat quickly with those still there and say good night to others leaving. When I spotted Charlotte chatting animatedly with José's family, I greeted them and asked if I could borrow Charlotte for a moment. When she stepped aside, I said, "Charlotte, I'm heading upstairs for the night. Will you encourage the guests to stay and enjoy the music and the food? If they ask, make Kira's and my excuses?" *My wife is waiting for me in our bedroom.*

"Excuses? Are you sure? There's still—*Oh*," she said, understanding coming into her gaze and a smile gracing her lips. "Good night, Gray."

"Good night, Charlotte." I winked at her and strode away. I made it past a few guests who were deeply engaged in conversation and turned the corner to the stairs. I took them two at a time. It might have even been three.

When I opened the door to my bedroom, Kira was sitting at the small writing desk brushing her hair, a towel tucked around her. At the sound of the door locking, she turned and smiled softly at me. The makeup she'd worn earlier had been washed from her face, her hair hung soft and long down her back. She looked so beautiful and just a tad shy as she stood and stepped around the chair to face me.

"No longer a little witch," I murmured, stepping up to her.

She smiled, a quirk of her lips. "On the outside anyway." She reached up to undo the bow tie knotted at my neck. Though she seemed anxious to undress me, I noticed the slight tremor of her hands, and when I went to help her, she laughed self-consciously. "I feel like a new bride." She delivered the words with a hint of humor, but her eyes were wide and vulnerable.

"You are. That's what you are." *My bride.* Suddenly I felt on shaky ground too. The air in the room seemed to close around us, so only she and I existed within it.

My hands dropped, and I let her finish removing my tie. Then she tossed it aside and unbuttoned the top two buttons of my shirt. My breath hitched as she leaned in and kissed my throat, her warm, soft lips feathering along my skin. Her tongue darted out to taste me and then she kissed the spot again, leaning back to undo the rest of my buttons. I watched her, her gaze focused on what she was doing with her hands. *This woman is mine*, I thought, my gaze drinking in the dark shadow her lashes made on her cheeks, the way her lips were slightly parted, the bottom one fuller than the top, the very tiny beauty mark to the side of her right eyebrow, and the exact spot on her cheek where I knew her dimple would appear if she smiled.

"You are so beautiful," I said reverently.

Her eyes met mine, large and full of wonder, as green

303

as grassy, rolling hills in some misty, mythical land that I'd stumbled upon in a dream. My beautiful little witch—there was magic inside her. Sweet secrets and hidden wells of strength. She could transform what had once been dark into light. I'd never again look at that maze and not think about her walking toward me in the moonlight with a look of love on her face as she reached out her hand.

She brought my jacket down my shoulders and let it fall to the floor, and then did the same with my now-unbuttoned shirt, her palms trailing down my bare biceps. "*You* are so beautiful," she said. Her eyes met mine and she loosened the towel wrapped around her and let it drop to the floor. I sucked in a sharp breath at the sight of her naked beauty, so lush and sweetly curved. I took her face in my hands and leaned in to kiss her, a moan coming up my throat. I felt weak with wanting, my cock surging fully to life within the tight confines of my pants. I kicked off my shoes as I sucked at her bottom lip, and brought my hands down to undo my belt and then tossed it aside.

We continued kissing as I unbuttoned my pants and let them, along with my boxers, fall to the floor, kicking them both off and bending momentarily to remove my socks. When I, too, stood naked before her, her eyes roamed down my body, stopping on my swollen erection. Her eyes shot to mine, the flush on her cheeks deepening. "Can I touch you?"

"Yes, God yes," I choked. "I'm yours. Please touch me." I had waited decades to feel her hands on me. Centuries. Eons. *Forever.*

She reached down and took my testicles delicately in her palm, testing their weight. A gust of breath emerged as I forced myself to remain still while she explored my body, both exciting and torturing me. I moaned when she gripped my length and slid her hand from base to tip, where she used her thumb to swirl around the head. God, it felt good. "Kira," I murmured, placing my hand over hers and drawing it away. I wanted this to last.

Her lips parted as she gazed at our linked hands, and I watched her throat move as she swallowed. I brought my thumb to it, wanting to feel every reaction her body had to me. I moved my thumb up and down her neck, slowly for only a moment before I cupped the back of her head and leaned in again to taste her mouth. I shuddered at the feel of her silky smooth skin against my own, relished the feel of her softness melding against my hardness. Giving. Yielding.

I leaned back to look into her face, desperately needing to see what was in her expression—did this mean as much to her as it did to me? Was this new for her too? Different? I didn't know the words to ask, how to pose the questions, and so I looked for answers in her eyes. I became caught in the spell of her gaze before her lashes lowered, and she took my hand to led me to the bed.

When she lay back, I moved over her, keeping my weight on one knee as my other parted her thighs. "Here we are," I murmured, repeating the words she'd said to me at the maze. *Finally. Finally.* As the word echoed in my head, it felt bigger than just the wait I'd endured to make Kira mine. It felt as if it summed up something I'd waited to feel for so very long. All my life.

Finally you're here. With her.

"Yes," she said. "Here we are."

I couldn't stay still another moment. I rolled my hips against hers and we both moaned, her head tipping back into the mattress. Her hands came up to my head and she raked her fingernails over my scalp, causing me to moan in pleasure.

My gaze ran over her beautiful body, and for a moment I almost didn't know where to begin. I knew what brought women pleasure, what brought me pleasure, and what resulted in a mutually fulfilling experience. But with Kira, it all went out the window. I tried to remember what I should do first and where I should move on from there, but it all fled my mind, so all I had to draw upon was instinct. I could only focus on the heaviness of my own arousal and the heat of her soft flesh beneath me. I felt unsure and unskilled, as if Kira were the first woman I'd ever touched.

I've done this before, I reassured myself, but the words felt false. I wasn't sure of anything anymore. I could barely remember my name.

She lifted her head and brought her mouth to mine, and suddenly I felt anchored again. God she tasted good. Everything about her was fresh and sweet and soft, and I felt like I might never get enough. I angled my head so my tongue could fully penetrate her mouth and she made a deep sound of approval, her tongue meeting my own to twist and tangle as her pelvis thrust upward onto my throbbing cock, and her soft breasts pressed against my chest. I grunted at the delicious impact and broke from her mouth, trailing my lips down her throat and licking at her hardened nipples, first one and then the other. I rubbed and bit softly and then soothed with my tongue until she went wild beneath me, gasping and pressing her body into mine. *God I love that*.

"Kira," I moaned. I wanted to worship her. Every secret spot, every sensitive valley, each tender curve. I nudged her gently until she flipped over, mewling softly as I kissed down her spine, inhaling the feminine scent of her skin, breathing her in. I licked the tiny dimples above her buttocks and then feathered my lips over her ass cheeks and down to the backs of her knees and up again. I'd lost all control, surrendered completely to the dictates of my body. The sounds she made had me wild with want, desperate with love for the sweet, sexy woman beneath me.

"Kira," I whispered again. It seemed my entire vocabulary had been reduced to that one word.

She turned over, and I moved my hands down her body, stroking, shaping, molding as she arched up, offering herself to me. I wanted to know her, every part. I leaned down and kissed the inside of one thigh as her hands again raked through my hair. "Please," she gasped as I brought my tongue to her swollen clit and licked around it for several delicious minutes, my body growing even hotter and harder at the gasping sounds of her pleasure. I couldn't take it any longer. I was going to orgasm without even being inside her, and I desperately wanted to cover her body with my own, to sink inside, to pump and thrust into her hot, slippery softness. But I also didn't want it to end. It felt like I'd been waiting all my life for this and now that it was here, I didn't know whether to rush toward it or make it last. "Grayson," she mewled as she pulled at me, making the decision.

I smiled as I settled my weight on top, our eyes meeting as I rolled my pelvis over hers, my cock aching with need.

Kira gripped my shoulders, a look of pure desperation on her face. "Please," she said again, her voice raw.

"Yes" was all I could manage, my mouth returning to hers, our kiss wild as her hands stroked my arms, my back, my chest, seeming to be everywhere. *Yes, yes, yes.* Somewhere in the recesses of my muddled brain, I thought, *What is this? If this is lovemaking, then I've never done it before. If this is lust, then I've only experienced the halfway version of it*. This, *this* was like dancing with lightning—making love with a woman I loved. I pulled back only momentarily to look into her eyes as her hands gripped my shoulders and I entered her slowly. She blinked up at me, her expression the most wonderful mix of desire and impatience.

"Kira," I murmured again, pressing myself inside her. Her body was warm and wet and soft, but so tight I could barely fit myself inside. I gasped out a groan, shaking for control, as I pressed just a little bit farther inside. She lifted toward me as if I were going too slowly for her, and despite my desperate need, a smile tugged at my lips.

My God, she's enchanting.

My God, she's mine.

I entered her a fraction more and Kira let out a small whimper, wrapping her legs around my hips. I pressed deeper, finally sinking all the way inside her on one final thrust. Her eyes fluttered closed, her lips parting as she let out a small sigh. Her gaze met mine again as I started moving, and the intimacy of staring into her eyes while I was joined with her became almost too much to bear. I felt overwhelmed with love, with lust, with emotions I couldn't even identify, all glittering around me, infusing my skin like magic. Her breath was coming faster and faster, her hips meeting mine thrust for thrust, and I struggled to hold back the pleasure that swirled through my abdomen, drawing my balls up tight, prickling my skin.

I vaguely heard myself whisper words to her that were not words but merely emotions put into sound—they were disjointed, raw, and they came from the very deepest part of my heart.

Her hands skated down my back, exploring until they

came to my ass, and she gripped it as I moved inside her.

"Faster," she moaned, and I felt the hairs prickle on my nape at the excitement of that single command. I picked up the pace, thrusting into her harder, my breath coming out in sharp exhales. I had no idea where I ended and she began. When she let out a small gasp and I felt her muscles begin to contract, I leaned back slightly to bear witness to her surrender. I watched with wonder as she came undone, this woman who had once resisted me and still challenged me at every turn, this woman who fascinated me and pushed me to my limits and always kept me guessing. *My wife.*

"Kira," I groaned one final time as I burst apart in a shattering climax, stars shimmering before my eyes as the pleasure peaked. I sagged limply into her, my head resting in the crook of her neck as our breathing slowly, slowly returned to normal. Her hands still ran up and down my back, and I needed her touch, shaken from what we'd just done and the unfamiliar weight of loving a body and a soul.

After a few minutes, I rolled off her and gathered her in my arms, staring blindly up at the ceiling fan above, reeling from having experienced something that made a sad mockery of every sexual encounter I'd ever had before. *Because you never loved them. You love her.*

I felt strangely vulnerable, as if she held all the power. I wasn't sure what to do with these new feelings. Sex had always made me feel like the one in control. And now...

"How do you feel?" she whispered.

"Like your husband," I said instantly, a smile pulling at my lips. "How do you feel?"

She tilted her head up to look at me, the expression on her face happy and satisfied. "Like your wife," she whispered.

I smiled again and pulled her closer.

Kira circled one fingertip around my nipple and I shivered, drawing her closer. She tipped her head back and looked up at me. "Is it always like that?" she asked, a teasing note in her voice.

"No," I answered immediately. I gazed down at her, letting her see the sincerity in my eyes. "I've never experienced anything as wonderful as that. I've never experienced anything as wonderful as *you*."

Happiness flashed in her expression, and she smiled gently. "Will it always be like that with us?"

I studied her vulnerable expression. *Yes*, I thought, *it will always be like that for us*, because Kira was part of it—her joy, her passion, her beautiful spirit. But I thought I knew what she was really asking. She had once been shamed for something that came naturally to her. An uncomfortable feeling of jealousy threatened, and I was unwilling to bring her ex into the room, so I moved my mind away from him and back to her. I smiled and kissed her forehead. "We'll have to find out, won't we?" I turned suddenly and hovered over her, kissing her once, hard, on her mouth as I brought her arms up and pinned her hands above her head. She laughed and then writhed beneath me, the moment turning light and flirtatious.

I kissed her again and then let her go. "We didn't use a condom," I said, my eyes moving over her features to gauge her reaction. I'd only realized afterward that, for the first time ever, I hadn't even thought about it. Somehow, though, I wasn't very concerned. I was worried she might be, although she hadn't mentioned it either.

She hesitated, obviously just considering it now for the first time too. "One time is probably okay. I'll get on birth control so we don't have to think about it."

"Okay," I said, nodding and wondering at my lack of worry. We'd be safe from now on, but we were married. We had a home. I didn't think I was ready for kids, had never even thought about it. But it wouldn't be a tragedy either. I wanted my new wife to myself for a while, but if it did happen, we'd figure it out.

"Need some water?" I asked, rubbing my nose along hers and then kissing the corner of her mouth.

"Yes, please," she said.

I stood and Kira sat up, moving back against the pillows at the headboard. I took a moment to drink her in: her mahogany hair splayed out all around her, her green eyes lazy and half-closed, the expression on her face one of pure satisfaction, her naked beauty fully on display—that beautiful body I'd just been inside. Before I forgot the water and returned to bed to enjoy her again, I turned and headed for the bathroom. When I caught a glimpse of myself in the mirror, I was surprised to see the smile I hadn't even realized I was wearing.

―――――

"Will you tell me about it?" she asked softly, leaning up and kissing my neck. We'd just made love for the second time and were lying against the pillows, Kira's head resting on my chest.

I paused, confused for a second about what she might be talking about. "You mean going to prison?"

She nodded, her lips still on my skin, the scent of her hair drifting up to me and making me feel peaceful and content.

I sighed. I wanted her to know everything about me. I wanted to share things with her I had never shared with anyone, but forcing the words out was difficult and not something I had any practice with.

311

I smoothed my hand down her silken hair, grasping a handful of it. "I had just gotten back from New York, where I had gone to see my mother."

"You went to see your mother?" she asked, surprised.

I nodded. "The trip virtually ended before it had even begun. I've tried to forget about it. I should never have gone. But back then, I…well, I had graduated college, and I thought if she saw me, saw the man I'd become, that she'd, I don't know, fall to her knees and beg me for forgiveness?" I let out a soft chuckle holding little amusement. "I envisioned that very thing, as ridiculous as it sounds." I sighed and she nestled closer. "I flew to New York and looked her up, went to her door with no invitation." I was silent for a moment remembering the hope I'd carried so close to the surface as I'd stood in front of her apartment. "She was married, had a family—two young sons."

"Please tell me she was glad you came to see her," she said softly.

"No. She was so bitter—she told me she had been on the verge of a huge career when I put an end to that. She said it was better that she didn't have to look at me every day and be reminded of all she could have had. Then she asked me to leave. The worst part, though, was the way she looked at her two other boys while I was there. And I realized that it wasn't that she was incapable of love—it was just she was incapable of loving me." I delivered the words as casually as I could, but I felt the slight flush on my own cheekbones. The memory of that moment still burned.

"Gray," she said, a whole world of compassion in her eyes as she reached up and stroked my cheek. I leaned into it. Her touch was a cool balm and it gave me the courage to continue with the story about that awful night.

"Anyway," I went on. "I flew into San Francisco and decided to go to a bar. I needed a drink, or ten."

"You were hurting," she said.

"I…yeah. God, I wish I had just gotten on the road and come home," I said. My voice cracked on the final word. I still carried so much regret. It hurt. Part of me wanted to let it go, but another part thought I deserved to keep it. Because of my choices, a man had lost his life. Kira wrapped her arms around my body and hugged me to her.

"I had been at the bar for about an hour when I ran into Brent Riley, a rich kid I'd known through acquaintances and had gone to some parties with over the years. His family lives in a town about half an hour from here. He was in San Francisco for his bachelor party—there was a whole group of them there. I hung with them for a while. Brent and I had never gotten along though. He was this perfect, upstanding golden boy on the outside, but behind the scenes he was mean and self-serving. I don't want that to sound unfair or like I'm justifying what happened, but that was just truthfully what I knew of him."

"I'm somewhat acquainted with the type," she said.

Right, Cooper. Yeah, her ex fiancé sounded a lot like Brent.

"We were walking outside to the parking lot and he laughs and starts telling me how he had roofied some girl, and that he and the other guys were going to take her back to their hotel and have some fun." Kira grimaced. "He asked if I wanted in on the action and pointed over to a car where a girl was slumped in the back seat." I paused. "I was looking for a fight, Kira. I *welcomed* a reason to fight with him. To fight with anyone, truth be told."

"It was a good reason, Gray," she whispered.

313

"Maybe. Or maybe I should have just called the cops. Instead, I got right in his face and told him what a piece of shit he was. He was the one who pushed me first, but it was all I needed. I didn't show him any mercy. He got a few good hits in, but most of the punches were mine. I enjoyed it. And then he fell..." I paused, closing my eyes as I pictured that terrible moment, the one that had forever changed the course of my life. "The way he landed...I knew right away he was dead. People started scattering, cars drove off, soon the police showed up..."

She looked up at me, her eyes so compassionate and understanding I wanted to fall into them. Maybe I'd find redemption there. "You didn't mean to kill him," she said.

"No. God, no, I never meant to kill him. I just wanted to hurt him, teach him a lesson. But I had all this pent-up anger inside, and instead of him sitting in jail, it was me who was sentenced to prison. I acted as his judge, jury, and as it turned out, his executioner that night."

Kira brought her hand up and ran her thumb over my cheek. And amazingly, that same love was still in her eyes, even after what I'd told her. I exhaled a silent breath.

"Did they ever find the girl who'd been roofied?"

"Yeah. When the police showed up that night, she was already gone. They were able to identify her, but naturally, she didn't remember anything at all, and it was too late to do any drug testing. My defense couldn't use her at trial. Brent's friends denied any knowledge of him slipping narcotics to anyone. Hell, for all I know, he was lying about it to me. But...I don't think so. Even now."

I took a deep breath. "My father wouldn't pay for a lawyer—he left me to hang. I had to use a public defender. The guy was totally incompetent. Even so, he was sure I'd only get minimal time for what happened—six months at most, community service at best. There were all kinds of witnesses that testified we'd both been fighting and that his fall was just a freak accident. And so when the judge came back with five years, I was...I was floored, shocked. It felt like my life was over."

I felt Kira's body tense but she remained still. I let out a deep breath. "I waited for my father to visit me—even just once—but he didn't. And then Shane came to see me to tell me he'd married Vanessa..." The hurt of that moment still affected me, even if the outcome didn't anymore. And then I'd cut Shane off too, taking him off my visitor list. He'd tried. All those years, he'd never stopped writing, trying to visit me, nor had Vanessa.

"It must have been terrible for you. You must have felt so abandoned, so cheated," Kira said.

I nodded. I had felt cheated by the justice system, but I could have handled it a lot better if I'd had some outside support. "I wouldn't have survived if it hadn't been for Harley. And if you didn't know, you had everything to do with that."

Her brow dipped. "How?"

I told her about what Harley had shared with me. She leaned her chin on my chest, a small, serene smile on her lips. "Maybe in some small way I was there with you then," she whispered.

I thought about that, about how actions created reactions and on and on, each link a chain that stretched over time, from one person to another. Yes, then. A small part of her had been there with me. And very suddenly, when I pictured that gray, lonely cell, it seemed just a little brighter in my mind. The result of her transforming magic once again. I gazed down at her, my heart beating swiftly. Her sweet, soft body pressed against mine and amazingly, desire filled me again. But the aching wasn't only between my legs. The aching was in my heart. *You are magic and I love you*. I wanted to profess the words, but they stuck in my throat, that final fear rising to choke down any sound. I felt them, so why wasn't I ready to say them? I leaned down and kissed her, surrendering but not completely. I wasn't brave enough for that. Not just yet.

CHAPTER TWENTY-ONE
Kira

How strange it was to be in love with my husband. Strange but completely wonderful. I found myself walking through Hawthorn Vineyard with a small dreamy smile on my lips more often than not. I moved my things into Grayson's room, and we started over as an actual married couple. I felt as if I was in a constant state of dizziness, not quite able to believe my current circumstances were real.

We said goodbye to Shane and Vanessa, promising them that once the fall harvest was over, we'd come spend some time with them at their beach house in San Diego. How different their departure was from their arrival. I smiled to myself at the thought, giggling at the memory of Grayson and me sprawled on the foyer floor, thinking perhaps we needed a rematch as the Dragon was still under the impression he'd won.

The Dragon. My *dragon.*

I spent the days organizing his office, paying off the large pile of accumulated bills, and making my way through six years of accounting records. It wasn't going to be a quick or easy job. Still, I was determined to understand what had happened to bring on the rapid decline of the vineyard that was now my home and would remain so from here on out. I wouldn't let it fail again.

I waited with eager anticipation for Grayson to get done with his work at the end of each day so we could eat dinner together. And then we'd take long strolls around the vineyard, talking and laughing, sharing secrets and learning about the other as if we were newly dating. For all intents and purposes, that's what we were doing, only for me, with the added element of already being in love. And I dreamed of the day he might fall in love with me too.

But we had time. There was no need to rush.

When the hour was decent enough, or sometimes when it wasn't, we'd retire to our bed where we spent long nights making love. I learned things about Grayson that made him go wild with passion, discovered ways to use my body and my mouth that caused him to let go of some of that control he always seemed to carry. And I allowed him to know me too, more deeply and intimately than anyone had before. With every moan, every masculine gasp of breath, every trembling caress, Grayson reassured me that Cooper had been wrong—I brought joy and satisfaction in bed. Cooper's actions were the result of his own twisted morals or unexplained emptiness or *whatever* but had nothing to do with me.

When we went into town for dinner a couple times, several people who had been at the party approached us to say hello, and Grayson was warm and personable. It was almost as if I was watching the cold demeanor he'd adopted slide off him in large pieces. Of course, there were still those who eyed him cautiously, but that would just take time. I'd put my mind to work coming up with some other ideas, I told him. He just laughed and said he was sure I would.

One morning, a couple weeks after the party, I decided to take Sugar Pie and stroll through the vineyards. All this time and I hadn't walked the rows of the plants I constantly admired as a distant view. The day had a slight chill to it, though the sun was shining brightly—fall was in the air. Soon, this fruit would be harvested and the real work at Hawthorn Vineyard would begin. I inhaled a deep breath of the crisp, earth-scented air tinged with sweet, ripening grapes. Sugar Pie snuffled at the ground, exploring the things interesting to a dog's nose. Grayson had said he was mostly prepared for the upcoming harvest. He had some hiring to do, but other than that, the equipment was all in working order and ready to go.

That couldn't have made me happier—our plan had worked. The vineyard was primed for success where it wouldn't have been without my gram's money. I stared out blindly at the vines of fruit, chewing on my lip. This morning, I was troubled. There was something very worrisome about the accounting files Walter had given me. I didn't want to admit even to myself what I thought I'd figured out, but the more I went over them, the more certain I was becoming. And I didn't know what to do.

"You look deep in thought."

I whirled around, bringing my hand to my mouth and laughing as Grayson swooped me into his arms. "How'd you find me here?" I asked as he pressed his lips to my throat. "I thought I was properly hidden from you."

"You can never hide from me. I'll always sniff you out." Then he placed his nose to my throat and started sniffing around like an overeager dog. *Or dragon*. I squealed, laughing at the feeling of his breath tickling my skin and then pushed him away as he laughed too.

"And here I went to so much trouble to plot and scheme so I might get you alone somewhere hidden and do all sorts of dirty, dragonish things to your body."

I laughed. "Haven't you done enough of that already?"

"Never." He turned and it was then I spotted the basket, which he picked up and brought over to where I was standing. He glanced around, setting his sights on a small grassy area in a warm spot of direct sunlight. Then he opened the basket and removed a large quilt and spread it out. Grayson turned to Sugar Pie, who was sniffing something nearby. "Give us some privacy, Sugar Pie. Go chase a mouse or something." Sugar Pie chuffed, moving on to a grapevine farther down the row, avoiding the fruit as she'd been trained.

"You *have* been plotting," I noted. "What is this about?"

"This," he said, sitting down and tapping a spot next to him, "is about teaching you to recognize the different grapes. Come here."

I joined him, sitting next to him on the quilt.

"If you're going to be the proper wife of a winemaker, you need to know about the variety of grapes we grow so when people ask, you can answer them with knowledge and confidence."

"Ah." I attempted to open the basket, but he snapped it closed, making me laugh.

"Patience, little witch. First, I'll need you to undress."

I raised a brow. "This lesson requires nudity?"

"As all good lessons do. Obviously," he said, the glint of dragonish devilry in his dark eyes. My heart flipped, and my feminine muscles clenched at his blatant masculine beauty. And God, I loved when his dragonish side came out.

"It's a little chilly for nudity, don't you think?"

"I'll keep you warm. Promise."

I laughed softly but obeyed, removing my long-sleeved T-shirt, kicking off my shoes, and unbuttoning the top button on my jeans. I lay back and Grayson held the bottoms and tugged them off. No one had ever studied me quite so intently, and under the bright light of the sun and I was tempted to feel insecure, but by the pure appreciation on his face, I let that go.

"You're so beautiful it hurts," he murmured. He leaned in, feathering his lips down my throat and then whispering in my ear. "I once thought to myself that when I made love to you, I'd always want to do it in the light so I could see every vibrant part of you—this beautiful, richly colored hair." He picked up a strand and let it fall through his fingers. "Emerald eyes…"

"Grayson," I murmured, dragging my fingers through his dark hair as my body relaxed, heated under the blanket of his warmth. He went up on his knees momentarily and removed his T-shirt and then leaned forward to unsnap my bra. It fell to the side, and he brought the straps down my arms, his eyes lingering on my nipples, hardening immediately in the crisp air.

"Just like rose petals," he whispered. And then he came back over me, his tongue slipping into my mouth. I shivered, sparks igniting between my legs. Why couldn't I ever get enough of him? And why did I love that so much?

My hands skated down his spine, his skin like warm velvet. He was so broad, so hard everywhere, so perfectly male. I loved the feel of his weight on top of me, the feel of his shifting muscles beneath my palms causing a delicious stir in my belly. He was so much stronger than me, and yet he treated me so gently. The slow movement of his pelvis on mine set my blood on fire, and I moaned into his mouth. We had made love countless times already, but somehow each time felt new and different. Each time I made delicious discoveries not only about him but about myself as well.

I brought my hand between us and ran my fingers over his stomach muscles, feeling them tense under my touch as he sucked in a breath. He smiled against my mouth, drawing away from me as I let out a small whimper of loss. *Ah, so he's the one in control today.* He leaned back and removed a bunch of grapes from the basket and placed it on the blanket next to us. "This," he said, his voice husky, "is a chardonnay grape." He plucked one from the bunch, sucking it between his lips and biting it in half. I watched, spellbound as he took it between his fingers and brought it to my nipple. I moaned softly, leaning my head back as my eyes fell closed. The feel of the wet fruit, warmed by his mouth, felt delicious against my tender skin. He leaned down and licked the juice left by the grape, kissing each nipple before bringing the piece of grape to my lips.

"The flavor of a chardonnay grape is usually neutral, the flavors brought out by the oak," he said, rubbing it on my mouth. I licked my lips as he watched my tongue, his eyes growing dark and lazy with desire. I saw the pulse in his neck beating rapidly. I took the grape between my teeth and bit down, closing my eyes as the sweetness burst across my tongue. Grayson leaned in again and kissed me, swirling his tongue in my mouth.

"Hmm," he murmured against my ear as he pulled away.

I liked these lessons very much. "How am I doing so far?" I asked.

"Very good. I like the way you pay attention," he teased.

I laughed softly. "You're kind of hard to ignore."

His lips tilted up in a small, satisfied smile and he leaned back and pulled another bunch of bluish-purple grapes from the basket. "Cabernet sauvignon," he said, his voice low. He again took one to his lips and bit it in half, before trailing it down my belly. Then he leaned in to lick the juice, the feel of his hot tongue on the sensitive skin of my stomach causing my pulse to jump frantically. I clutched his head in my hands, gasping out a breath. He lifted his head and for one brief second, our eyes met and held, something unspoken flowing between us.

I love you, I thought. *My heart is yours.* I let my head fall back, too afraid to say the words for fear he wouldn't say them back.

"These grapes make a full-bodied wine," he said, his voice sounding as if he was fighting for control. *Either I will never remember this lesson, or I will remember every word. Every sensation.*

Before I even realized it, Grayson had stood and apparently taken off his shoes because he was now stripping off his jeans. He was back down beside me in only seconds, plucking another grape from a different bunch of deep-purple fruit. He held it in his teeth and hooked his thumbs in my underwear. As I lifted my hips, he pulled them off, tossing them aside. He knelt beside me and ran his index finger between my legs and I moaned, parting for him. He slid the grape over my most sensitive skin as I fought to control my hips from thrusting toward him, wanting more. "Merlot," he purred. "Yields wine with rich berrylike flavors."

I sighed in torment and relief as he licked up the juice. As his tongue swirled and lapped at me, the pleasure was so intense I practically vibrated with it. I squirmed, panting out his name. He suddenly came over me again, my cool skin warmed once more by the cover of his heat. He took himself in his hand and rubbed his swollen head on my entrance as I tilted my hips toward him in open invitation.

"Yes," he breathed, thrusting inside.

My breath caught at the now-familiar feel of him filling me. *Nothing more wonderful. Nothing.* Except, yes, there was.

He began to slowly thrust.

I let out a high-pitched gasp at the sudden, intense pleasure and ran my hands down his back to end at his ass, relishing the hard feel of his working muscles under my palms. We moved together, the pleasure building higher and higher, until there was nowhere else to go except over the edge. I cried out, blissful spasms wracking my body as, distantly, I heard Grayson grunt his own climax, his hips making two last clumsy thrusts as he came, shuddering and then breathing harshly into the crook of my neck.

The world was suddenly still as I floated back to earth, Grayson's ragged breath slowing against my skin. I blinked at the clouds floating lazily above, registering the sounds of birds singing in the surrounding trees, and my husband's heart beating against my own. And it felt as if the world was only filled with beauty.

"What other lessons can I look forward to as a winemaker's wife?" I asked breathlessly as Grayson pulled his body from mine and laughed against my skin.

"Oh, I have lots of teaching to do. That's only the very beginning." He rolled off me and kissed me once more, smiling against my mouth. I shivered slightly in the crisp air, and we sat up and pulled on our clothes.

Grayson took out a thermos of coffee, Charlotte's

cranberry orange muffins, and a plastic container of straw-berries. We ate our picnic breakfast together, laughing and chatting. *If there's happiness greater than this*, I thought, *I can't imagine what it is.*

The next afternoon, the rain came down. It drummed on the window, painting the outside world in misty watercolors. I sat in Grayson's office, staring out at the oak trees and the front gates beyond, the printouts of accounting records spread out on the clean desk before me. I'd organized his office, and now everything had a place, whether it was in a file folder labeled neatly in his bottom desk drawer or in one of the stacked paper trays sitting on top of his desk. As I stood up, Sugar Pie chuffed at my feet and then yawned.

"Stay here, girl," I soothed. "I'll be right back."

I found Charlotte and Walter in the kitchen, sitting next to each other at the large dining table, a cup of tea in front of them both.

"Oh hello, dear. Would you like to join us for a cup? The temperature has certainly dropped today."

"Sure. But I'll get a mug. You stay there," I told Charlotte distractedly when she began to stand. I sat down at the table, holding my cup toward Charlotte as she poured from the pot already on the table. "Thank you," I murmured as I put my hands around the warm mug and let the heat seep into my skin.

"Is everything okay with you and Gray?" she asked, a note of worry in her tone. "It seems like—"

"Yes, everything's fine with us. Better than fine." I smiled but it quickly dropped. "It's something else." I looked back and forth between Charlotte and Walter, not wanting to put into words what I suspected but knowing I had to.

"What is it?" Charlotte asked. She and Walter had seemed to become very still.

"I've been inspecting the old accounting records, and it seems...well, it seems as if Ford Hawthorn purposefully ran this vineyard into the ground. Is that even possible?" I whispered.

Charlotte and Walter glanced at each other, their expressions grim. "You mustn't tell Grayson what you've discovered," Charlotte said. "I'm not generally in favor of withholding the truth, but...he's suffered enough at his father's hands and this...it would destroy him. Maybe someday...I think we'll know when the time is right, but not now. He's only just begun to heal."

I exhaled a large breath. "It's true," I choked out, a shudder running through my body. "Why? Why would he do that?"

"It was his last message to Grayson," Charlotte said, her eyes tearing up. "Walter tried to undo as much as he could, tried to preserve anything possible, but when Ford found out he was sick, and Shane and Jessica said they didn't want anything to do with this vineyard, he realized he could only leave it to Grayson and he set about destroying it. Thankfully he had less time than he thought, but he did enough damage even in the short time he lingered."

I felt ill, nausea roiling in my stomach. "He hated him that much?" My body suddenly felt chilled to the bone, despite the warm tea in my hands. I realized I was squeezing the mug and released my grip.

"He hated *himself*," Charlotte said, and for the first time since I'd known her, I heard heated anger in her voice. "And he channeled that into his relationship with his son. He meant to leave a worthless piece of nothing to Grayson as his final slap across his face. It was cruel and ugly and vindictive and—"

"It's a lie," Grayson's voice came from the doorway.

We all startled, hot tea sloshing onto my hands as my body jerked.

"Grayson," I breathed.

"No," he said, but his voice broke as he sagged against the doorframe.

Charlotte, Walter, and I all stood quickly and rushed to him.

"Gray," Charlotte said, reaching out to grasp his hand, her expression deeply pained.

"Tell me it's a lie, Charlotte," he said, his gaze beseeching her.

Her face registered deep grief, but she lowered her eyes. I could see that she couldn't lie in response to a direct question, not to Grayson. The damage had been done. Grayson turned and walked stiffly out of the room, heading for the stairs.

Charlotte and Walter went to follow him, but I put my hand up. "Let me talk to him," I said. "Please."

They both nodded, Charlotte wringing her hands, looking anguished.

"If you need us, we'll be right here," Walter said.

"I know," I said, putting my hand on his arm and giving him a gentle squeeze.

I climbed the stairs, disbelief still pummeling my heart. How was this possible? As I'd meticulously gone through the records, I'd been deeply suspicious, but I had had a hard time believing it could actually be true. Why would anyone do that to something they'd spent so much of their life on? For spite? Could anyone be that evil? Could anyone hate that much at the end of their time on earth? *That* was the legacy he chose to leave? I couldn't wrap my mind around it. Was it because Grayson had gone to prison, shaming him further? Never doing anything right in his eyes? Confirming that he was the mistake his father saw him as? The one his wife— Grayson's stepmother—had never forgiven him for?

I entered the master bedroom Grayson and I shared and found him standing before the window, staring out at the rain. "Gray," I said tentatively, moving closer. He turned to face me and the look of stark devastation on his face stopped me in my tracks. I sucked in a breath.

"I made a vow to him," he said brokenly. "Because I thought…and all this time…" He moved away from the window, pressing his back against the wall next to it. His legs collapsed beneath him, and he slid down to the floor, burrowing his head in his arms. I let out a small startled cry and rushed forward, dropping onto the carpet with him and wrapping my arms around his shaking body. And as I held him, he did what he had probably needed to do for six long years, or more likely his whole life: he cried.

CHAPTER TWENTY-TWO
Kira

Hawthorn Vineyard was far too quiet. Grayson had stayed in our room for the rest of the day, not returning to work, lying on the bed staring at the wall. I'd come into the room several times, but he hadn't spoken more than a handful of words. I understood that he needed to process what he'd learned. Who wouldn't? He was deeply wounded, anguished, the belief that his father had loved and accepted him in the end now completely obliterated. He'd been living to fulfill a singular vow—a vow based on what he now knew were falsehoods. And the truth that lay beneath was ugly and soul-crushing. I didn't have to wonder if he felt directionless—I'd been there once too. I just wished he'd talk to me. Instead, we went to bed, and for the first time since I'd moved into his room, he didn't reach for me.

I'd woken in the middle of the night to find his side of the bed empty and cold, and alarmed, I'd gotten up and gone in search of my husband, tiptoeing through a dark, silent house, in my nightshirt. "Grayson?" I called softly. No answer. I stood still and listened, finally hearing something very far away that sounded like breaking glass.

I followed the distant noise until I came to the door in the living room that I now knew went down to a wine cellar, although I'd never been inside. It was open just a small crack, a light shining from below. "Grayson?" I called again. When there was still no answer, I opened the door tentatively and descended the narrow, spiral staircase. The sounds grew more distinct, one loud crash startling me and causing me to pause before moving forward.

When I got to the bottom and peeked around the corner, I saw Grayson sitting on the floor, leaning back against a shelf, drinking from a bottle of wine.

He saw me and brought the bottle away from his lips, wiping the back of one hand across his mouth and holding the wine toward me. "Kira, try it. It's a Domaine Lefl... blah blah blah who cares, from France," he slurred, giving me a wry smile. Then he tossed the half-drunk bottle and watched as it shattered on the cement floor amidst several other smashed bottles, their contents pooling together in a now-worthless mixture of wine, glass, and soggy bottle labels. "Oops, sorry, slipped right out of my hand. I'm not usually so accident-prone. Here, let's sample another." He reached behind him and grabbed a different bottle off the shelf and picked up the wine opener sitting next to him on the floor.

I rushed forward, kneeling down next to him. "Grayson," I said, leaning forward and putting one hand on his cheek, "what are you doing?"

He stopped in his efforts to open the bottle, looking blearily up at me. "I'm sampling my father's rare wine collection," he said. "Walter did a good job protecting it from him before he could destroy it himself, but I'm really only doing what he would have done if he'd been given the chance." He paused, hurt skittering over his features before he continued. "Do you know that of all the things I sold in this house, I avoided these because I believed it would disappoint my father? When you came along and I didn't have to part with this"—he waved his arm backward indicating the shelf behind him which still held quite a few bottles—"I was so damned relieved I'd done something else that would have made my father proud." He laughed, a hollow sound filled only with pain.

Ah, so he was bent on taking what justice he could into his own hands. Only, if the look on his face was any indication, it wasn't proving to hold much satisfaction.

"So," I said, scooting closer, "how about we sell the rest of them instead of doing exactly what *he* would have done? How about we make some money off of these prized bottles and buy…a pet monkey and name it after your father? Or…a double-seated bicycle? We'll ride around Napa talking about what an ass your father was. Or…a parrot! We'll teach it to say nasty things repeatedly about Ford Hawthorn." I placed my hand on his knee. "There are better things to do than this. We'll come up with something together."

Grayson touched my naked thigh with one finger and trailed it upward, lifting the material of my nightshirt as he went. "You are so beautiful," he said.

"And you are so drunk."

"In vino veritas," he whispered, repeating the phrase etched above the doorway I had meant to look up. His finger traced the waistband of my underwear. "In wine there is truth." *Ah. So that's what it means.* Grayson paused, his brow furrowing. "Only here, there's no truth. There are only lies and deceptions."

331

"Grayson, no…"

He shook his head, bringing his hand away. "Think about it, though. It really was such a perfectly devious plan—the most impactful way to tell me how much he hated me and how disappointed he was, right up until the very end. The perfect vengeance. If he had had just a little more time, I would have come home to a pile of worthless ashes." He took a loud, shuddery breath. "I thought it was a *gift*, and he meant it as a curse. After everything…I thought he finally… *Jesus*. It hurts so much, Kira," he said, his voice filled with anguish. The look on his face made me feel as if my heart would crack into tiny pieces to lie among the shattered bottles littering the floor.

Oh, Dragon.

"There's so much pain for me here," he said on a broken whisper.

"I know," I said, moving right up against him and taking him in my arms as he leaned his head into my chest. God, I *knew* the pain he was feeling now. I understood it, and I ached for him. "Listen to me, Grayson." I leaned back and took his face in my hands, looking him in the eye. "I know how you're feeling, I do." I'd wrestled with similar emotions as I'd lay on a floor mat in Kenya, staring up at the ceiling, the warm, still air pressing in on me along with hurt and doubt and the ache of betrayal. "Sometimes pain is so great, it feels as if it carves out vital parts of who you are. But love is meant to fill that empty space. If you let it, grief makes more room for love within you. And the love we carry inside makes us strong when nothing else can. Let it make you stronger. Better. You can get there. I know you can." *Let me help you. Let me love you.*

His dark eyes searched mine. "Do you believe that?" he asked.

"I *know* that."

Grayson let out a long, shaky breath, burrowing his head into my chest again. "My Kira…" he murmured, "if only I could believe it too."

"You will. In time. Let *that* be the legacy your father leaves you. *That's* the perfect vengeance."

We sat that way for what seemed like a long time, me holding him until my legs beneath me began to cramp.

Grayson finally looked up at me, running his thumb over my cheekbone. "Would it ruin the moment to tell you I want to take you upstairs and fuck you until I can't see straight?"

I laughed softly. "I'm at your service. But first, let's make some coffee and get you sobered up. You're going to feel like hell tomorrow. And we have a long day of monkey shopping to do."

Grayson let out a laugh that ended on a half groan–half sigh. "Okay," he finally said. "Okay."

"Grayson's not working today?" Charlotte asked, her face etched in deep concern.

"I don't think so. He didn't get out of bed this morning. But he needs to sleep—he drank quite a bit last night." I'd already told Walter about the mess in the cellar and he had cleaned it up, taking inventory of the bottles Grayson hadn't smashed. Maybe the monkey was a little over the top, but I was serious about the parrot.

"Perhaps I should go up and talk to him…" Charlotte said.

"Later, Charlotte. He needs to sleep," I told her gently. "But I'm sure he'd appreciate what you have to say. He seems so"—I chewed on my lip for a moment—"grief-stricken."

"I'm sure that's exactly what he is," she said. She shook her head sadly. "And he can't be happy with me nor with Walter…"

"You withheld the information out of love for him. Inside he knows that. He'll come around."

Charlotte nodded, but her look was doubtful, and her lack of confidence only served to make me more nervous. She seemed so distraught that I gave her a hug. "He's going to be okay," I said. But my tone lacked conviction, even to my own ears. The lost look in his eyes when I'd left the room this morning had sent a chill through my blood. Had he lost all motivation to make this vineyard a success?

I was further troubled by the fact that I was keeping something from him too. In the beginning, it hadn't seemed like information that required sharing. But then everything had happened so quickly…and now, it was a secret between us, and I knew I needed to tell him, but I didn't know how he'd react. He was still on such emotionally unstable ground. How many secrets could he process right now? How much pain could a person handle before they broke?

It's me again, Gram. If you could send me some wisdom… What do I do?

Charlotte pulled me from my worried reverie. "Gray got a call this morning that his bottle labels are ready," she said. "I guess I'll go into town and pick those up for him."

"I'll take care of it. I need to get out for a little bit anyway. I feel like I'm breathing down Grayson's neck. He probably needs a little time to process everything on his own. I don't want to get in the way of that. If he does come down, will you text me?"

"Yes, of course, dear. See you soon."

I drove into town, going straight to the small print shop

where Grayson had ordered labels for the wine about to be bottled. The woman at the front desk brought the box out to me and then ran my bank card, frowning slightly at the machine. "I'm sorry, Mrs. Hawthorn, it says your card is declined."

"What? That can't be right," I said. There was plenty of money in that account. "Will you try it again?" She did, with the same result, looking uncomfortable.

Despite the chill that went down my spine, I shook my head. "My husband probably bought something and didn't tell me. I'll have to stop in at the bank. Men."

She chuckled softly. "It's happened to me before too. Do you want me to try another card?"

I didn't have another card. I dug in my purse, counting out the money I had. Thankfully, I had quite a bit. I'd taken out cash to tip all the vendors at the party several weeks ago, but Grayson had given Walter the cash for that, so I hadn't used what was in my wallet. It was all still there. I counted out the money for the bill and handed it over, thanking her, and leaving the shop with the box of labels.

I placed the box in the trunk, got in my car, and drove straight to the bank. The feeling of panic that had swept through me inside the print shop was now a full-blown case of buzzing nerves. There was absolutely no reason that card should have been declined. My heart pounded in my chest as if it understood something terrible was about to happen. *Oh God, please let this be some strange misunderstanding, a bank error, anything. Please, please…*

I parked, took a moment to take deep, calming breaths, and walked into the bank. Thankfully, it was practically empty, and I approached a teller without having to wait. When I told her why I was there, she looked up my account and frowned at the screen. "I'm sorry, Mrs. Hawthorn. It appears there's been a hold put on your account." *Oh God*.

"A hold?" I squeaked. "Does it give a reason why?"

She shook her head. "No, I'm sorry. You should receive something in the mail if your account is being garnished or if there's another legal reason for the hold."

My heart was beating so rapidly, I had trouble catching my breath. "Are you able to check my husband's account?" I asked. "Just to tell me if there's been a hold placed on his as well?"

"Well…"

"Please," I said. "I don't want any other information. I know it's only in his name. Just if you could…" I drew in a sharp breath, panic overwhelming me for a moment. I brought my hand to my chest. "I'm sorry."

The older woman smiled sympathetically. "Let me just…" She began typing on her computer. "Yes, it appears the same hold has been put on his account as well."

"Thank you," I said, the contents of my stomach coming up my throat. I swallowed heavily. "I appreciate it very much."

I turned to walk away, and she called after me, "I'm sure it will be cleared up, Mrs. Hawthorn."

I turned my head but kept walking. *No, no it wouldn't. Oh God.* "Yes, I'm sure. Thank you."

I walked briskly to my car, my skin cold and prickly, and once I was seated behind the wheel, I pulled my phone out and dialed my father's number.

He answered on the third ring.

"What have you done?"

Pause. "Kira."

"My gram's money," I burst out. "What have you done?"

336

I heard his deep sigh and then he seemed to put his hand over the receiver as he spoke to someone in the background. I thought I heard a door close before he came back. "He's not right for you, Kira. He's a criminal."

"You bastard," I swore. "You *did* do this. Why?" My voice cracked, sorrow and rage overwhelming me. "Do you really hate me that much?" The words sounded familiar. Hadn't I just asked that question about Grayson and his own father? We really were a tragic pair.

"Of course I don't hate you, Kira. I just don't want you making choices for your life that will lead you in the wrong direction."

"It's my life!" I yelled. "I'm a grown woman. You had no right to do this. And now you've put his business in jeopardy too—he has employees who count on him."

"If your husband counts on your money for his success, then he's no man at all." His voice was tight, unrelenting.

"You have no right, no leg to stand on. That money is legally mine. My gram left it to me."

"Yes, perhaps, but I can tie it up in court until you see the logic of my position and the folly of your choices. I'm doing this for your own good, Kira. I'm your father. I can't let you ruin your life."

Tears slid down my cheeks. "You're doing this for *your* own good," I hissed. "You've never given my happiness a moment's consideration. You're doing this because of your own pride—you can't bear to see me do anything that doesn't work into some agenda of your own making. You can't bear the thought that I'm not under your thumb just like everyone else in your world."

He sighed. "Kira—"

"Haven't you done enough to him?" I asked, realizing

there was nothing to lose now if we discussed it. He'd already done what I'd feared most. "I remember, you know. I was there when the judge in his case came to your office. I heard your advice. I heard you tell him to throw the book at Grayson, to make an example of him. And that's just what he did."

"I give a lot of people counsel. There's no law against it. And if that boy got the book thrown at him, it's because it's what he deserved."

He did remember. The quickness of his reply gave him away. He hadn't when we'd gone to him in San Francisco, though, I was sure of it. He'd looked more closely at Grayson at some point after that. I knew it in my gut. Whether it was before or after he'd offered him the bribe money, I didn't know.

My dad had taken part in screwing Grayson and all along—not only had Grayson's crime been an accident, but the reason for the fight had been based on valiant reasons— Grayson had been trying to protect someone. Maybe he'd have gotten some time anyway—after all, his actions had resulted in a man's death, accident or not. But he wouldn't have been put away for five years.

For a moment, the only sound was my harsh breathing as I attempted to swallow the sobs desperate to escape my chest. "That counsel you give affects lives, *Daddy*. Real, live, breathing humans who have hopes and dreams. Like the advice you gave Cooper on how to handle the situation with me. You *crushed* me. Did you know that? You crushed Grayson too. Please, please don't do this. Just put a stop to whatever you've done and let us be happy. Please." I did sob then, a harsh, gasping sound. Just when I'd thought I found happiness. Why? Why was it always snatched away? How many times could I begin again?

"I'm sorry, Kira. This is for your own good, and Cooper's too, yes. But you'll see the wisdom in my vision someday. As for your current husband, I've made him a very generous offer to walk away from you. I suggest he take it if he doesn't want his business to fail."

"And what strings are attached to that?" I spit out.

"Not many. He's receiving a significant amount of money for very little sacrifice. I asked only that he walk away from you permanently and go along with the story that he took advantage of you—a troubled girl with a significant trust fund."

Very little sacrifice. That's what he thinks of me.

My blood turned to ice water, not at the fact that my father would throw me under the bus again but at the realization that he had no qualms about ruining Grayson's life too. *Again.* "He's just beginning to earn back his reputation. And now you're asking him to *lie* and have people look at him like a pariah again? How do you expect him to make a life for himself in a place where people have no respect for him?"

"That's not my problem. With the money I'm offering, he can make a life anywhere."

He sees himself as some sort of hero. His ego is so colossal, he views himself as an agent of justice. He's truly delusional.

"Is that why you married him?" he asked. "Another charity case to you?"

"No. I love him," I said simply and truthfully. There was no reason to try to convince him of anything anymore.

I suddenly felt numb. My father would never leave me alone. I'd spend the remainder of my life being his pawn in some form or another. Staring unseeing out the windshield, I ended the call without another word.

I didn't remember the drive back home. *Home.* Another

sob threatened to choke me as tears slid down my cheeks, one faster than the next. "You're okay," I assured myself. "Everything will be okay. Grayson and I will work this out together. He said he'd take care of me now." *Oh God, but neither one of us has a cent to our name once again.*

I pulled through the gates and immediately noticed a black town car parked in front of the fountain. *Oh God, now what?* As I pulled in behind it, Cooper stepped out of the back seat. My heart stuttered again and then took up a staccato beat. At this rate, I was likely to die of heart failure before this day was over.

I took one last deep breath and stepped out of my car, closing the door with a quiet click. Cooper was already walking toward me. "Kira, what's wrong?" he asked, a look of concern on his face.

I swiped at my eyes. "Do you really not know, Cooper? Or are you in on this too? You and my father—some sort of sick duo," I suggested flatly.

He took a deep breath, his brow creasing. "Yes, I know what he did. I'm sorry. But I have to agree with his desire to get you out of here." He waved his arm behind him at Grayson's home. "He's a *murderer*, Kira," he said harshly. "You're probably not even safe."

"I'm about a million times safer with him than I ever was with you." My voice rose in volume as I spit the words at him. But suddenly another wave of defeat crashed over me. Fighting with Cooper wasn't going to solve this situation. I changed my tactic. "Cooper," I said, moving closer to him, my voice shaking slightly, "I know what you did was…"—I shook my head, searching for words that would persuade him, rather than anger him—"because of the drugs and alcohol. I know that wasn't the real you."

He seemed to consider that explanation momentarily and then nodded. "It wasn't, Kira." *Liar.* "It wasn't me. I was out of control. But no one can know that. It would ruin me." *But you were perfectly fine with ruining* me.

I shook my head briskly. "I don't want to expose you. I'll never reveal what happened between us. I'll take the fall. It's okay. I'll do whatever you ask of me. Just please, convince my father to take the hold off my gram's money. Convince him to leave us in peace. Will it really hurt you to come up with a new plan, one that doesn't involve me? Please, Cooper, if you ever loved me at all, please let me be happy."

Cooper worried his lip, appearing to contemplate my words. Hope leapt in my chest, and I moved a few steps closer. "You don't know everything he does, everything he's capable of. I know you're better than him, Coop. Don't align yourself with my father any more than you already have."

"What he does?" Cooper asked, moving a lock of hair away from my face. I glanced at the house, hoping against hope Grayson wasn't looking out the window. No, he was most likely still sleeping, still processing. I didn't want him to walk into the middle of this. I needed to convince Cooper to help me. Help *us.*

"He manipulates people for his own schemes. He even used Grayson. He's already hurt him, used him so terribly."

"Used me how?" came the cold hard voice next to me. I sucked in a ragged breath, my heart leaping. I hadn't seen Grayson because our cars had concealed him as he'd approached and I'd been so focused on Cooper. I hadn't expected he'd be working today, but he must have been, at least for a short time. That's the direction from which he'd come.

"Grayson," I breathed, stepping away from Cooper.

Sugar Pie came from behind Grayson, looking straight at Cooper and letting out a singular snarl, followed by two barks. My eyes widened. It was the first time Sugar Pie—to my knowledge—had ever barked in her life.

"I think you should leave," Grayson said. "My dog doesn't like you."

Cooper smirked. "I'm sure she's about as good a judge of character as you are."

"She doesn't lie," Grayson answered, his expression tight, his voice frigid. "She's a dog, not a politician. Get off my property."

"I was just leaving." He turned his attention to me. "You know my position, Kira. I'm as concerned about you as your father is. We're here to help you. If you need me, please call. I'll be here in a heartbeat."

Grayson stepped forward. "I can assure you my *wife* will not need anything from you—either now or in the future."

Cooper stared at Grayson for a tense moment, my own breath suspended, and then he wisely backed down, turning and striding to his vehicle. I let out a harsh exhale.

Neither Grayson nor I said a word as Cooper got in his car and his driver pulled away, around the fountain, and out the front gates.

"What in the hell was that about? Were you crying?" Grayson asked, moving toward me, a look on his face that was a cross between anger, concern, and wariness.

"I… Yes." I let out another shaky breath. "We need to talk, Grayson." I shook my head, my arms hanging loosely at my sides. "Can we go inside?"

He studied my face for a moment, the wariness suddenly taking center stage. Oh God, I was going to hurt him, and he was already so hurt. Dread made my shoulders curl forward.

He led me toward the house as I tried my best to ignore my shaking legs and follow him into his office. I wondered at the choice, but perhaps he led me there simply because it was the nearest room to the front door. "Do you want to sit?" I asked.

"I'd rather stand," he answered tersely. He was suddenly acting so businesslike with me. I shivered, wrapping my arms around my body. "What's going on, Kira?" His posture and the watchful look on his face reminded me of a man expecting a blow.

"The money's been frozen," I whispered, my face crumbling.

His expression registered first confusion and then shock. "What? How?"

I took in a deep lungful of air. "My father… I don't even know the details. He's done something, made claims, tied it up somehow until they can be investigated."

"Okay, well, whatever claims he's made, they're baseless. That money's yours via the terms."

"I know," I said, my voice breaking. "But he can tie it up so long we're forced to start selling things just to survive. He can. He will."

Grayson swore harshly, running his hand through his hair.

"I'm so sorry. I underestimated him. I didn't think…"

Grayson stared somewhere beyond me, his expression an unreadable mask, quiet for so long, I wondered if he'd speak again at all. "Why was Cooper here and what were you talking about? You mentioned your father using me," he finally said, bringing his gaze back to me. "What did you mean by that?"

"Cooper…he was just, I don't know, pretending to be

concerned about me. I don't want anything to do with Cooper." I moved toward Grayson, putting my hands on his biceps and looking up into his face, using my eyes to plead with him. "Please try to understand what I tell you next. Please understand why I'm only telling you now. At first I didn't think it was necessary…and then the more time that passed…"

Grayson had grown stone still. "Spit it out, Kira. Now."

I turned away from him. "I told you how I interned for my father. I was frequently at his office. I'd overhear things…" I dropped my arms, turning back to Grayson who was listening intently. I shook my head, trying to find the right words. "My father, he's always had this idea that if he has influence with the local judges, he has the ultimate power." In that respect, he wasn't wrong. Truth didn't matter; facts didn't matter if you had the people who made the final decisions in your pocket. "He grooms them if he can, as in the case of Cooper. He curries favors, makes deals… He's done it for years." *Power, it all comes back to power.*

"What does this have to do with me?"

My eyes moved over the hard lines of Grayson's expression. "One night we were at his office after hours. I was finishing up a few projects as I waited for him. Judge Wentworth, the judge in your case"—I glanced at him, but his expression didn't change—"came in to consult with my father on a few cases, one of which was yours."

"Go on," he said, a muscle ticking in his clenched jaw.

I expelled a long breath. "I was delivering a file and I only overheard enough…enough to understand. It was an election year, see, and my father advised him to throw the book at you—give you the ultimate sentence to send a message that he wasn't only tough on crimes committed by the poor and minorities, but that he also delivered harsh

344

sentences to rich white criminals as well. It's all a game—a game of perceptions and manipulating 'facts.' The players don't matter, the individual *lives* don't matter—anything can be twisted if you come at it from the right angle. You were a pawn. It's the reason you didn't get community service or a minimum sentence like your lawyer believed you would. Because of my father, you went away for five years. And I...I never forgot your name. That day at the bank, I heard it and I remembered."

I finally braved a glance at Grayson's face, looking for understanding, but although his skin had paled, his expression held nothing except cold impassivity. "And then you decided to use me too. It was all one big setup."

I furrowed my brow. "What? No, that's not...Running into you at that bank was like fate and I—"

"You expect me to believe that now? Using me is exactly what you did." He laughed then, an ugly sound full of disdain. "What a perfect way to get back at your own father. Talk about the perfect vengeance. Marry the man he helped put in prison—no wonder he was so livid. Jesus, you're just like him, scheming, using people."

I was suffocating, the room growing dark at the edges around me, as if I had tunnel vision. *Scheme? Use people?* No, I didn't do that...did I? I admitted I did often come up with plans and ideas, but they weren't used to hurt people... Suddenly I was sick and confused. I put my hand on the edge of his desk, steadying myself. Did I? Is that what I did? Had I done that to Grayson?

I shook my head in denial, but Grayson was watching me closely and a minute flicker in his expression made me believe he saw the doubt in my eyes. "I didn't use you, Grayson. I wanted to try to make it right. I thought—"

"Make it *right*?" he yelled, startling me. "How have you made *anything* right?" He laughed again, running his hand through his hair and grabbing a handful before bringing his hand down again. "Was that the plan all along? Use me to get the money and then take it back somehow? Holy fucking God. You're *all* liars. And look where you've left me—penniless, shackled to a schemer, and now having to contend with your father *again*, the man who once ruined my fucking life!" His face had gone from pale to flushed, and his voice shook as he yelled.

"Grayson," I said, holding out my hand and moving closer, "of course I didn't plan it. You're seeing this all wrong. After what your father did, I can understand you thinking everyone is against you, but you're looking at this through the eyes of someone who's just been hurt very badly. Please, if we come together—you and I—we can think of something that will—"

"Come up with something? Still conniving, Kira? Just stop. I can't take anymore. It's making me sick. You make me sick. I'm just sick of it all—the manipulations, the lies, the half-truths." He stepped back away from me, the look on his face full of disgust.

I dropped my hand. "You're making this out to be something it's not. Please, just take some time to think about it. I'm not like my father. I'm not like *your* father." My voice ended on a whisper and I could hear the confusion in my own voice.

"This has nothing to do with my father," he spit out. "This has to do with *you* and the fact that I'll never trust you again."

I shook my head, denying what was happening, denying the cold distance in his expression. "I know it must seem like

346

you can't believe in anything anymore. But you can believe in me."

"I thought I could."

A single tear slid down my cheek. "Grayson, I'm your wife. What we have together—"

"I can get down at the corner bar any day of the week," he said icily.

I put my arms around myself again, trying desperately not to believe his vile words. "I know you don't mean that. I didn't mean to hurt you. I love you," I croaked brokenly.

He leaned his head back and laughed, causing me to wince with deep hurt. "Love? *Love?* You know what *love* has gotten me in my life?" He picked up a paperweight off his desk and threw it hard at the window. The glass shattered as it hit, flying straight through and landing somewhere on the ground outside. I let out a little yelp. He turned to me, his hands fisted at his sides. "You don't *love* me. I was bought and paid for, nothing more. I played the part and now our business arrangement is over. Get out," he said. "Get out of my house."

"Get out?" I asked. "I'm your wife. I live here. This is my home—"

"Not anymore. I'm calling your father this afternoon and taking him up on his offer. At least the rest of the people who work at this vineyard won't have to suffer because I married you. Get out!" he yelled, his expression furious.

I let out one singular sob and then I turned toward the door and flung it open. I raced past Sugar Pie, who whined mournfully, following along behind me. Sobbing openly now, I ran to the master bedroom and stuffed clothes and toiletries in my suitcase. I was sure I was leaving a few things behind but was too distraught and grief-stricken to do a thorough search.

Hadn't I done this before? Stuffed clothes in a suitcase to make a hasty escape? Only that time someone was pursuing me. This time…this time I was being tossed out.

By my husband.

By the man I love with all my heart.

And maybe it's what I deserve.

I bent down and looked Sugar Pie in the eyes, rubbing my hands over her wounded head, attempting to control my harsh breathing. "There's my beautiful girl," I said. "You take care of everyone here, okay? And know I love you and that you're a good girl, such a good girl." I stood up before I collapsed in more tears and made my way down the stairs.

When I got to the front of the house, I paused to look in the open door of the office. Grayson was standing behind his desk, leaning over, his hands flat on the surface in front of him. I almost stepped toward him, but he looked up, his face hard and remote as he stared at me wordlessly.

I backed up, then turned and ran through the front door, out to my car, where I tossed my suitcase in the back seat and got behind the wheel. Another sob shuddered from my chest as I again struggled to catch my breath. It felt like the world had collapsed all around me.

Grayson was standing at the window now watching me leave, just as he had that very first day.

I started the engine and pulled around the bubbling fountain, past my little cottage and the oak tree I'd once climbed, out through the gates, speeding away from Hawthorn Vineyard. Speeding away from the only home where I'd ever felt I belonged.

CHAPTER TWENTY-THREE
Grayson

Misery. It was the only emotion I seemed capable of feeling. Everything I thought I knew—everything that gave me reason for moving forward—had come crashing down around me. They were all liars. Liars, cheats, users, manipulators. I couldn't count on anyone, least of all myself.

My home now felt more like that small prison cell I'd lived in for five long, lonely years—dark and bleak. I prowled through the rooms at night, drinking when I couldn't sleep, and then drawing the blackout shades and sleeping the day away. Work no longer held the welcome distraction it once had. What was the point in bringing this vineyard back to life? So I could live in the place my father had wished to use as a tool to punish me, reminding me how worthless I was? Seeing it thrive held no satisfaction anymore. It was only one giant, painful reminder of how much that man had hated me and how I'd pathetically never given up hope that he'd come to love me one day, blindly grasping on to the belief he'd left this vineyard to me out of that love. I saw my father everywhere here, and now, instead of bringing me pride in my own accomplishment, it brought only shame and bitterness. If he hated me, I could very well hate him in return. It became my new vow.

The words I'd heard my father swear in the midst of a fight with my stepmother came back to me now. *Goddammit, Jessica, it was a fucking mistake. If I could take it back, I would. I* was that mistake. Well, I'd made one too. Trusting him was the most desperately foolish thing I'd ever done. Trusting anyone at all was foolish and stupid. I wouldn't make the same error twice. *Never again.*

I had Walter sell the last few bottles from my father's wine collection. I'd gathered what little strength I had left to meet with José, Harley, and Virgil so I could let them go. I couldn't pay them anymore. I used the money from the wine sales to pay them up until the end of the month. Their shocked and saddened expressions only made me despise myself more.

And then I told Walter and Charlotte they were dismissed too. I'd fired Charlotte often enough over the years, but I could see in her eyes she knew this time I was very serious. Eventually I'd have to sell the vineyard just to survive, to start over, but I couldn't call forth the strength just yet.

Charlotte and Walter both tried to talk to me, but I didn't want to listen to either of them. Even *they* had lied to me—the two people I thought I could trust with my very soul. They'd let me believe my father had loved me in the end, and it had only been a cruel, vicious withholding of truth. They'd watched as I made a ridiculous idiot of myself and it *hurt.*

And Kira... My heart stuttered in my chest. The very worst of all. I'd given over the whole of my heart to her—every last part—and all along, she had been lying to me too. What else was she lying about? What other things would she have me believe, hope for desperately, only to find out I'd been made the fool yet again? I squeezed my eyes shut as I thought back to that moment in my office when she'd told me she'd been lying to me from the beginning. It had felt like a knife plunging into my heart. The only thought going through my mind had been, *Not you, anyone else, but please not you too.*

I threw my wineglass against the fireplace in the living room, enjoying the sharp shattering sound of the glass. I braced my hands against it and then lay my forehead on the cool stone. Even still, weeks after she'd left, just the thought of Kira's name brought a gut-deep, heartsick yearning and a throbbing emptiness.

She had told me she had nothing but disgust for Cooper Stratton. And then I'd seen her talking to him, standing close with her hands on his chest, trying to convince him of something. *Coop* she'd called him. I had recognized the guilty expression when I'd surprised them. Little lying manipulator.

Never again. Never again would I care whether or not someone loved me. I let ice harden over the part of myself that could still be hurt, hating that there was anything left at all. I knew how to do this. I had lived a frost-covered life for years, and I could do it again.

I needed to go to the courthouse and file for divorce, but frankly, I had no idea where Kira was to have her served, and I didn't much want to leave the house anyway. I wasn't going to take her father's money and give him the satisfaction of having me under his thumb. No one was going to control me again, especially that bastard.

Finally, exhausted from the simple act of thinking, I fell onto the couch, not wanting to go to my bed tonight—not when it only brought memories of her. *The scent of her.* And yet I fell into sleep with the sound of her name on my lips.

———

It was a gray, dreary day in downtown Napa, made drearier by the fact that I had just pawned the ring I'd given Kira on our wedding day for some much-needed cash. I felt shamed and embarrassed. This was what I'd been reduced to—*again.* I had originally bought the ring for Vanessa, and yet handing it across the counter to the pawn shop owner had brought a sharp ache to my chest, not because of whom I had originally bought it for but for whom I had ended up giving it to.

I was driving through town on my way back to the vineyard when I spotted Kira's car. I drew in a sharp breath, shock causing me to jerk the wheel. *Kira was in Napa?* Had she been here all along? Where would she have been staying? She had any number of choices in San Francisco, but here? My heart started drumming rapidly. I pulled my truck to the side of the road and hopped out. There were a couple boutiques on this block and a restaurant. I looked through the front windows of the two shops but didn't see her. *What are you doing, Grayson? What exactly do you think you're going to say to her anyway?* I had no idea and yet some sort of excited anticipation made my gut clench. *She was here.* I'd been devastated when she'd told me about her father, acted so harshly, but maybe…maybe if I just talked to her, maybe she'd help me understand. I didn't give myself time to reconsider; I just acted.

The restaurant didn't have a window, so I pulled the door open and walked inside to see if I could spot her, hope blooming in my heart. I saw her immediately, walking toward me.

Cooper Stratton was next to her, his hand possessively on her arm and she was smiling up at him.

The room felt as if it tilted under me and all I saw was red. She'd told me she didn't want anything to do with Cooper. She'd lied. It appeared she was back with him. *Just like that. I was right about her.* That's when she spotted me. A flicker of surprise, followed by a look of something I couldn't identify flashed across her face. Wide-eyed, she looked at Cooper and then back to me.

I was gripped by overwhelming rage. My body closed the space between us before I'd even decided to move. "You didn't waste any time, did you?" I gritted out. "Was this your plan all along? Marry me, get the money, somehow take it back, and then…*him*?" She had not only lied to me about her father's involvement in my life, she'd lied to me about Cooper too. If she truly hated him the way she'd made me believe, she would never give him three minutes of her time, much less be *lunching* with him. *Little fucking liar. Beautiful little liar.* Agony ripped at my soul.

Kira took a step back, but not before I caught a whiff of her delicate scent. Sharp longing overwhelmed me, making me want to roar with anguish. *She's not yours. She never really was. She'll never be again.*

I don't want you.

I don't want you.

I don't want you.

I don't want you.

I don't want you at all.

"Grayson, please, you have no idea what you're talking about," she said, her voice soft as she glanced around.

"Oh, I think I have every idea what I'm talking about." I moved in again and leaned toward her ear, saying softly, "Tell me, Kira, have you opted to be one of his many whores or a trophy wife who turns a blind eye? If it's the latter, you do realize you'll have to divorce me first, right?"

I felt Kira startle at my words and draw in a sudden breath. Then Cooper was next to me, saying, "What the hell are you doing here?" and before he could try to get in the middle of Kira and me, I turned. My rage and pain—everything I had lost—bubbled to the surface, swirling in my chest in a tsunami of pain. I grabbed his shirt and walked him backward to the wall and slammed him into it. Kira screamed and I heard several people gasp loudly from the floor of the restaurant next to the lobby where we were having our showdown.

Cooper's expression was pale, his eyes filled with fear as I pressed him against the wall. I expelled a loud whoosh of breath and let go of him. He almost fell forward but caught himself as I stepped away. Dread crashed through me as quickly as the anger had. *Oh God, what am I doing?* I glared into Cooper's face which was simultaneously expressing rage and some type of barely tempered glee. He pointed his finger at me. "You're going back to prison, you fucking loser." He adjusted his shoulders and laughed, then turned to who I thought was probably the manager of the restaurant—standing there with a look of shock on his face—and said, "Get the names and numbers of everyone who witnessed that. My lawyer will be calling for it later." Then he looked at Kira with satisfaction. "Let's go."

Tears were streaming down Kira's face. "Let me talk to him for a minute," she said to Cooper, her voice cracking.

Cooper frowned. "I can't leave you alone with him. He's obviously dangerous."

354

I stepped toward him again, and Kira quickly moved in front of me, placing her hand on my chest. "We're in public," she said. "We're fine. He's my husband, Cooper."

"For now." Copper narrowed his eyes and looked back and forth between us for a moment and then nodded. "I have to get on the road anyway. I'll pick you up tonight." He leaned in and kissed her on her cheek, his beady eyes on me as he did it. More rage kicked up in my gut. I was tempted to hit him—what did it matter now? Instead, I stood there clenching my jaw over and over again, attempting to regain control of my emotions. Cooper pointed to me. "You'll be hearing from my lawyer."

I simply stared at him. I wouldn't give him the satisfaction of a reaction.

He walked briskly out the door without turning back, my eyes finally moving to Kira. Her face was ashen, her eyes wide. She obviously hadn't expected to see me while she was with her new/ex-boyfriend.

"Gray," she whispered. She took a step toward me and I whirled around, stalking out the door of the restaurant. There was nothing more to say to her. My heart felt like it was breaking open in my chest. I hadn't realized it could break any more than it already had.

"Grayson!" I heard her call behind me. I stopped, turning and then walking straight back to where she was standing on the sidewalk. There was a small alley right next to her, and I grabbed her wrist and pulled her into it, pressing her up against the brick wall. She let out a small gasp. "What are you doing?"

"Trying to remember what I ever saw in you." I put my mouth against hers, licking the seam of her lips. She mewled softly and opened for me, though her body was still tense against my own. I dipped my tongue into her mouth and then quickly withdrew, forcing a blank expression onto my face. "No, not nearly as good as I remember."

Her eyes widened and she blinked at me, confused. I leaned in and ran my lips down her throat. Her body stiffened and I pulled away. "Nope, nothing." Her lips turned down, and tears glistened in her eyes. I shook off the uncomfortable feeling of guilt trying to take hold. *She's a liar*, I reminded myself.

"You know what I think? I think I must have been desperate, and you were...what's the word? *Convenient.* Since you've been gone, I've decided I like more of a variety of women than marriage vows dictate."

She flinched, tears flowing down her cheeks freely now, and although shame swirled in my gut, I showed no reaction. *I won't.* If she was going to jump straight into Cooper's bed, then I could at least leave with a small modicum of pride. As we stood staring at each other, that small chin came up. Even now, she was going to rally. *Damn her straight to hell!*

I wanted to break her like she had broken me.

I would not be the one to slink away in wounded hurt like I'd done so often before. Not this time.

And yet, even still, I wanted to fall to my knees and beg and plead with her to make it all okay somehow—to wrap her arms around me and tell me it was all a terrible nightmare. And I *hated* myself for it.

I hated myself for hoping.

That old familiar feeling of grasping for the love of someone who would never give it to me made a shudder run through my body. She stood there looking pale and stricken and *heartbreakingly beautiful* and she had no right! She had taken everything from me—even more than I ever realized I had to lose.

The torturous vision of Kira tangled in bedsheets with Cooper came unbidden to my mind, and I swallowed down the bile in my throat.

"I liked what we had while it lasted. It turned out you came at a very high price, however." I ran one finger down her smooth cheek and she stared up at me, unmoving. "My name, my vineyard, my freedom as it will most likely turn out…" *My heart, my soul.*

A tear hit my finger, and I pulled it back as if I'd been burned by acid, turning away from her and stepping out of the dim alleyway onto the bright sidewalk. I heard the soft sound of her sobs, but she didn't call after me, and I didn't look back. I left my heart in that alleyway. I wouldn't ever need it again.

I drove home full of icy pain, my skin prickly with more misery than I'd ever felt in my life. When I got there, I went straight to the liquor cabinet and brought out a bottle of aged scotch. Wine wasn't going to be strong enough today.

As I tossed back the first shot, I looked out the window at the vineyards beyond. Right before Kira had left, I'd measured the sugar, the acid, the tannins, and determined when the grapes would be perfectly ready to harvest. They were ready now. But I didn't have the funds to hire anyone to help. I raised my glass to the vines in a mock toast. "You did your part beautifully. Sorry I failed you too." In a very short time, the fruit would be rotting on the vine, a complete waste—the perfect metaphor for my entire life.

I poured another shot and let it burn down my throat. All of it was lost. There was no hope, no hope left at all.

CHAPTER TWENTY-FOUR
Grayson

The world shifted into focus as I groaned, grabbing my head to stop the incessant pounding. I was in the living room, sprawled across the couch, the bottle of empty scotch lying on my stomach, along with the shot glass I'd been drinking from. I didn't bother to move them before sitting up, and they rolled off me onto the floor, not breaking, just landing on the area rug in a soft thud.

I stumbled to my feet and rubbed at the back of my neck, trying to massage the kink out. Outside, the sun was just rising, the sky awash in shades of gold. I blinked and froze. It looked like there were…dozens of workers in the grapevines, harvesting fruit. I squinted, scratching absently at my stomach, trying to understand what I was seeing.

"I figure you'll need these," I heard behind me and turned to find Charlotte setting down two tablets I assumed were pain relievers and a glass of water on the table next to the couch. "Not that the way you're feeling isn't exactly as you deserve. I'd like to smack you upside the head myself, but I won't. Seems you've been doing enough of that by yourself."

"What in the hell is going on outside?" I demanded, ignoring her other remarks.

"The grapes aren't going to harvest themselves," she said.

I took a deep breath. "What I mean is, who hired those people? You know very well I can't pay them."

"Harley called in some favors and he, Virgil, and José pooled the money you paid them up to the end of the month. They'll split it among the men who agreed to work for you this week."

They did what? Why? What a useless waste of money. "Harvesting grapes takes longer than that."

"Yes, well, this will be a start, and if you can get the wine in barrels into bottles, you can start selling it. There's a second crew coming in the evening to help with that."

I turned toward Charlotte, grimacing at the sudden, sharp ache in my skull. "Why? Why would they do that?"

"I suppose because they believe in you."

"Believe in me?" I let out a bark of laughter that only served to hurt my head. "What good is that going to do them when it comes time to feed their families? Speaking of which, why are you still here?"

Charlotte only pursed her lips. "Perhaps you'd like to get showered and go down and join them."

I snorted. "No. A second bottle of scotch and I have plans for the day."

I told myself I didn't care about the disapproving look she shot me before she left the room. She had lied to me as well. The only reason I didn't kick her out of my house was because this had been her home longer than it'd been mine. But she'd be forced to leave soon enough—once I could no longer afford baking ingredients. Or once I got arrested for assaulting Cooper Stratton. I groaned, running my hands through my hair, the mess of my life coming back into blinding focus.

"Charlotte," I called. She halted at the wide archway that separated the living room from the foyer, looking back at me. "Have the police been by? Or called?"

"No," she said, and turned and walked toward the kitchen. I wondered why she wasn't curious about why I'd asked that question. Perhaps she just couldn't take on one more issue right now. *Join the club.*

I downed the two pills Charlotte left and then went upstairs and showered, letting the hot spray soothe my sore muscles. After I dressed, I went into the guest bedroom across the hall to look out at the grapevines beyond. The equipment and the men were still there. *Fools!* It was all a waste of time.

I flopped down on my bed, staring up at the ceiling fan, the one I'd stared at in wonder so many nights after Kira and I had made love. *Stop. Don't think of her—not right now.* Was she waking up with Cooper this morning? Were they having breakfast in bed? My own torturous thoughts propelled me off the bed and I went in hunt of that second bottle of scotch. I'd drink so much I'd pickle my brain and kill all the cells that held memories of her.

Charlotte was in the living room, folding the blanket I'd half slept under the night before. I glanced out the window again and muttered, "They're all wasting their time. I despise this place. Even if I had a way to make it successful, I wouldn't bother now. I'd rather tear it apart like my father did. There are only lies and bad memories here." Perhaps I was starting to understand the old bastard now.

"If that's what you believe, then I guess it's true."

I narrowed my eyes. "I do believe it. I know it."

"Okay."

I pressed my lips together, angry that Charlotte could still aggravate me with only a few words.

Apparently, she wasn't done. "Walter's out there too, you know," she said as I bent to the liquor cabinet. "I just hope his back doesn't give out. And his arthritis makes him slow. And of course, he has trouble seeing well now too." She sighed. "I do hope he's plucking the right grapes…"

I halted, rolling my eyes. "Walter's the picture of health."

She looked at me as though she hadn't noticed I was there. "Oh, sorry. I didn't mean to disturb you. You go right back to brooding and drinking yourself into oblivion."

I glared at her. "Don't you think I have good reason to brood and drink?" My God, my life had recently been decimated—again. A little sympathy wouldn't be out of line.

"Oh yes. Good reason, indeed," Charlotte agreed. "But if you take a break from that, maybe give the men a little wave now and again. I'm certain a thumbs-up from the window will be encouraging too. I'm sure it will boost their spirits as they do hard manual labor for less than minimum wage in the hot sun all day."

"Jesus. You're something, you know that?"

She looked briefly satisfied.

"And it's not even that hot anyway," I muttered sullenly. I was fully aware she was attempting to guilt-trip me. I sighed, my gaze sliding to the window again. The truth was, though, that maybe a day of hard labor would be a better way to clear my mind than alcohol. And at least it wouldn't leave me feeling as if there were a ten-ton boulder sitting on my head.

"If it means not listening to you a second longer, I'll go

out there and work my fingers to the bone," I grumbled, attempting to salvage some pride if possible.

Charlotte shrugged, but I saw her lips curve up into a smile before she turned away.

Damn her.

———————

When I came in that evening, dirty and sweat soaked, every muscle in my body ached. Apparently, Harley had contacted every ex-con he knew in the northern hemisphere and they were all working at my vineyard. I didn't know if it would amount to anything, but the sick feeling I'd had in my stomach when I thought of the fruit I'd cared for so carefully rotting and dropping to the ground had abated. At the very least, it would be in barrels, and I'd be able to start bottling the wine. And when I sold this vineyard, I'd get a higher price if it was a working winery and not one that was back on its way to ruin. I'd divorce Kira, make a little money off the sale of Hawthorn Vineyard, and go somewhere and do… *something*. But what? What did I know apart from winemaking? Not much. The business degree I'd earned long ago in college was a waste now. Plus, few people wanted to hire a convicted felon. Misery threatened. The thoughts that had taken a back seat in my mind as I'd worked all day were back again to torture me.

I took a quick shower and started to head downstairs, pausing in front of the room Kira had stayed in before she'd moved into what I still thought of as *our* room. Pain squeezed my heart as I looked around the empty space. I opened the closet, but she hadn't left anything behind. But when I pulled the top drawer of the dresser open, I discovered two forgotten nightshirts. Shamefully, I brought them to my nose and inhaled, breathing in the lingering scent of her, sweet and delicate. I held back the tormented groan that rose in my throat and placed them back where they'd been. That's when I spotted what looked like a small ring box. I picked it up and opened it slowly, inhaling a deep gulp of air when I saw a platinum men's wedding band. I pulled it from the dark blue velvet and held it up to the light.

My Dragon. My Love.

The words inscribed inside the ring felt like a blow to my already aching heart. I stood there for what felt like a long time, confusion swirling through me. Finally, I put the ring back in the box and placed it in the drawer and headed downstairs to greet Harley, Virgil, and José, who Charlotte had asked to stay for dinner. They were just arriving, all looking dirty, tired, but somehow happy. Guilt piled on top of my heartache. Despite all their work, in the end, I wouldn't be able to offer them much. They'd have to find a job somewhere else.

I fist-bumped Harley as I thanked him again.

"Man, you didn't think I'd stop looking out for you just because we're on the outside now, did you?" He smiled, massaging his brown, beefy arms. I was sure he was as sore as me, maybe more. He'd been working since sunrise.

"I don't deserve it, Harley," I said, rubbing the back of my neck.

"Maybe, maybe not. That's not for me to judge. I only know who my friends are, and I help my friends. I owe you my life. I owe Kira my life too. Anything either of you ask, and I'm all in. No questions."

Sudden emotion welled up and I swallowed it down. All I could offer was a nod.

"My woman feels the same too. You got me? Priscilla's one *hell* of a woman." He grinned.

Virgil lumbered in, interrupting us. "Hey, Virgil," I said. Sugar Pie was behind him.

"Hi, Mr. Hawthorn, sir." He smiled happily. "Picking grapes, making wine!"

I smiled back. "Thank you, Virgil." I reached up and squeezed his shoulder. "You're a good man."

"José," I greeted when he, too, came through the door. "Let's eat."

As we headed toward the kitchen, Walter was coming down the stairs. He didn't look well, and the fact that he'd worked all day for me caused a wave of guilt. Christ, he was twice my age. I frowned as he grabbed for the railing, bringing one hand to his chest. "Walter?" I asked, alarm spiking.

He made a choking sound and pitched forward. I lunged for him, breaking his fall with my body. I heard Charlotte cry out behind me and struggled to sit upright with Walter's weight on top of me.

"Turn him over," I heard Harley instruct and Walter's weight was quickly lifted off me.

Everything seemed to slow, voices coming from underwater, the sound of my heart thumping loudly in my ears. I heard José on the phone with 911 as I kneeled over Walter. He was gasping for air, his hand still over his heart. "Help's coming," I croaked, my chest filled with fear.

Charlotte was crying silently as she rubbed his hair. He seemed to be trying to say something, first to her and then to me, but no words were emerging, only gasps and grunts for air. Finally, he reached for my hand, squeezing it tightly in his as he choked out, "Like…my…own son."

My heart squeezed so tightly in my chest that I gasped for air myself.

"Don't talk," Charlotte said. "And don't you dare leave me. Don't you dare, you stubborn old goat."

Walter let out one final gasp and collapsed, only to lie still and silent. Panic prickled my skin. My breath came out in sharp exhales. I heard one word being repeated again and again. "*No, no, no.*" I finally realized it was my own terrified voice pleading the word like a desperate prayer.

––––––––––

The hospital room was dim and silent, the early glow of dawn filtering through the blinds, the steady beat of Walter's heart being sung by the heart monitor next to where he lay. I sat hunched over in a chair next to his bed, my elbows on my knees, my head in my hands. Charlotte had gone home several hours ago to rest and feed Sugar Pie. She'd wanted to spend the night, but there wasn't an extra bed anywhere in the hospital and it wasn't likely Walter would wake during the night, even though he was now stable. So I'd volunteered to stay, telling her my back was younger, and I'd call her if he woke before she arrived in the morning.

I brought one hand to the back of my neck and massaged the tight muscles.

"I hope you don't mind me saying that you look like hell, sir."

My head snapped up at Walter's voice, and I released a breath. *You're awake. Oh, thank God.* "When has what I minded ever made a bit of difference to you, Walter?" I asked, attempting to conceal the grin that wanted to break free.

"Never," he admitted.

I stood up and poured him a glass of water from the pitcher on the table next to his bed and helped him hold the cup as he took several long drinks. I sat back down on the chair and pulled it a bit closer to him as I reached for my phone. I needed to call Charlotte and tell her he was awake. "It's just like you to pull dramatics like you did last night. I'll let Charlotte know—"

"Wait just a few minutes," Walter said, his voice serious as he held his hand up. I paused and then put my phone away. "I didn't go to all that dramatic trouble to have you walk out of here without hearing me out."

I gave him a small, wry smile but nodded. "Okay. Fine then."

For a moment, Walter didn't say anything. When he finally spoke, his voice was quiet but steady. "When I was lying at the bottom of the stairs, you know what I kept thinking?" I shook my head. "I kept thinking, please don't let me leave this world without telling that boy how I feel about him."

"Walter," I said, running my hand through my hair, emotion rising in my chest. I'd never discussed feelings with Walter. I wasn't sure if I knew how.

"We had a son," he said, clearing his throat as his voice broke subtly on the word *son*.

I tilted my head. "What? You never said—"

"No, it's difficult for us to speak of Henry. We lost him when he was just a baby. Charlotte, she…grieved terribly, as did I."

"I'm sorry, Walter," I said hoarsely. I'd seen that sadness in his eyes before today. I'd seen that face every time my father had dished out his punishments—most of them cold and all of them hurtful. All this time, Walter had cared so deeply about how I'd been treated, and I'd never known of his and Charlotte's loss.

"We couldn't have more children after that. Being there, in the home where we'd had him, became unbearable. And so"—he took a deep breath—"we decided to come here, to America, to begin a new life. We started working for your family and we found a bit of happiness again. And then, one day, a knock came at the door and there you were. Despite the way Ford and Jessica Hawthorn reacted, to Charlotte and me, *to us*, you were our *gift*, and you have been every day since. Not a single moment has gone by when we haven't been proud of you. I want you to know that."

"Walter—" My voice broke.

"We couldn't always intervene, because we feared your father would send us away and we'd be no good to you at all, but we did all we could to let you know…that you weren't alone—not then and not now. Not ever. We only withheld the true motive of your father's bequest because we love you and tried to bear that terrible burden for you as long as we could. We didn't do it out of dishonesty. We did it out of love. I hope you can come to understand and forgive."

I sat back in the chair, allowing his words to flow through my heart. Of course I'd always known—Walter and Charlotte were more my parents than my actual father and stepmother had ever been. But…what if Walter and Charlotte were wrong, and *he* wasn't? "What if he was right about me, Walter?" I choked, voicing my deepest, darkest fear.

"Your father?"

"Yes," I whispered harshly. "All of them." What if I was nothing but a mistake? Unlovable. A throwaway.

"Is that what you think? That Charlotte and I were wrong about you, but Ford Hawthorn was right? Your mother? Jessica?"

"I…"I pictured Walter in his old-fashioned black swimsuit

367

teaching me to swim, saw him leading me through the maze as we counted steps and learned turns, saw Charlotte wringing her hands when she knew I was hurting, thought about all the wise advice she'd imparted to me through the years, all the love she'd readily given.

"Perhaps," Walter said, "you're also asking because you wonder which category your wife belongs in."

Walter had always known everything before I ever told him. I don't know why I thought this situation would be any different. "I...yes. I just, I don't know if I can trust her."

He regarded me for several moments. "Well," he sighed, "I suppose you never actually have to find out if you never truly take the risk. I suppose the better plan might be to haunt the halls of Hawthorn Vineyard like a ghost, clanking around in chains of your own making and scaring little children at the windows."

I let out a small laugh that ended on a sigh.

"Do you know why I call you *sir*? Why I've always called you *sir*?" he asked.

I shook my head.

"As a reminder that you're worthy of respect, and you always have been."

"Thank you, Walter," I said, choked with gratitude for his presence in my life.

"What does your heart tell you?"

I looked down, thinking about the ring I'd found in the drawer. *My Dragon. My Love.* I didn't know what to believe anymore. *I love you*, she'd said, and yet I'd thrown her out. Despair and doubt swirled in my gut. I'd spewed ugly words as she'd cried. I'd called her a conniving schemer, made accusations that didn't even seem rational anymore, not given her any chance to explain more fully than she had. And yet, if I was willing to believe her, that seeing me in the bank that day was really just a stroke of fate, could I really blame her for not coming into my office initially and telling me her father had been responsible for my overly harsh sentence? Hadn't I started out mistrusting her too? Hadn't we both decided our relationship would only be temporary? And if I truly listened to my heart as Walter was suggesting, didn't it tell me it would be *just* like Kira to see sharing money with me as a way to make up for the injustice her father had done in my case? As if *that* had been her fault at all.

Oh Jesus. What I knew to be the truth flowed through my veins like hot molten shame, eating away at my insides. I'd been a mess that day, willing to believe everyone I trusted had or would eventually betray me. Seeing her with Cooper and then hearing her confession had been the confirmation of that fear. In some sick sense, I'd *wanted* to believe the worst of her. Kira was like a brightly shining light, and I had been living in cold darkness for so very, very long. She'd teased me about having a lair, but in some sense, she was right. It felt as if my soul had been peeking out, desperate to feel the warmth of her love and yet so afraid of the agony of withdrawing back into darkness again when she inevitably left and took the sunshine with her. So instead, at the first doubt, I'd turned away from her before she could turn away from me. I'd been unwilling to believe she loved me, even when she'd said it and even though she'd demonstrated her love for me again and again. Yes, I *had* been ridiculously irrational…cold and cruel, sinking so low as to use her deepest insecurities against her. She was a beautiful, tender, twenty-two-year-old girl, and I'd watched as her spirit had broken right in front of me—that bright light I loved so much had grown dim before my eyes.

Torment spiked through me. I'd thrown her out without a cent to her name. God, for all I knew, my wife had been sleeping in her damn car. No wonder she'd gone to Cooper. What other choice would she have had? I'd always had Walter and Charlotte to call family. Kira…Kira didn't have anyone. Shame and self-hatred gripped me with an intensity that almost left me breathless.

When the time had actually come for me to make a choice, to trust her or to push her away, I had pushed her away.

Surrender, my boy.

Only, in the end, I hadn't been able to. Not fully. I'd kept one foot in my internal lair, craving the safety of that familiar space, one that was cold and lonely, but one that offered protection as well. I had failed her. I had failed *myself*.

And then a realization came to me that did steal my breath. She could very well be carrying my child. We'd made love twice with no protection whatsoever. "I pushed her away," I whispered miserably. "I said cruel, heartless things to her. Even if I… She'll never forgive me. I don't even know if I can forgive myself. There's no hope."

Walter, the man who had acted as my hero again and again, regarded me silently for several moments before he closed his tired-looking eyes. I went to stand, to leave the room so he could sleep, when his voice came from behind me: "I believe, sir, that where there is love, there is always hope."

I got home later that afternoon, the men Harley had rounded up still hard at work in the vineyards. I went down and greeted them all, intending to update Harley on Walter's prognosis, which was good. He'd need a stent put in, but his doctor assured us the surgery was straightforward, and that Walter would most likely be home in just a few days. But when I asked about Harley, one of the guys told me he'd shown up for a short while and then left saying he'd be around later in the day.

I went back to the house to shower and join them at the winemaking facility, where José was overseeing the equipment usage. I was bone weary, but there was no way I was going to leave the men out there to work without me. I could sleep later. And maybe, while I was working, something would come to me regarding a way to win my wife back. Because Lord knew, I had no idea what to do right now other than falling to my knees and begging for her forgiveness.

After showering, I went down to the kitchen and started brewing a pot of coffee. I flicked on the television while I waited and froze when I saw Cooper Stratton's face on the screen. Grabbing the remote off the counter, I fumbled with it as I attempted to turn up the volume. The newscaster was midsentence once I'd finally succeeded.

"…seems this shocking video was shot by a call girl who taped Judge Cooper Stratton in a hotel room at the Palace Hotel during a black-tie charity dinner held two nights ago. The hidden camera caught an allegedly intoxicated Judge Stratton bragging about accepting bribes, manipulating case outcomes, and other highly corrupt activities. An investigation has just begun and details are still emerging in this case, but Judge Stratton also boasted of his alliance with former San Francisco Mayor Frank Dallaire several times in the video, claims that Mr. Dallaire is vehemently denying at this time. Some might recall Cooper Stratton's former engagement to Mayor Dallaire's daughter, Kira Dallaire, an engagement that ended in a scandal of its own."

Shock ratcheted through my system and I braced my hands on the counter in front of me to hold myself up. The newscaster continued, "This story highlights the public's deep concern about corruption in politics. As voters and citizens, we'd all like to believe those in positions of power don't trade influence, but this case seems to be bringing those suspicions to the forefront of today's political discussion. Let's show that video one more time."

The video started from the viewpoint of someone straddling Cooper Stratton who was outfitted in a tuxedo and stretched out on a bed. He was laughing as he discussed precisely what the newscaster had said. My whole body tensed, fierce anger and stark disbelief clenching my gut as I listened to him brag about the way in which he'd casually ruined lives, first as a prosecutor and now as a judge. No wonder Frank Dallaire had been so willing to protect him when Kira had caught him with prostitutes. He'd been doing dirty work for him for *years*. And she hadn't had any clue. I swallowed, focusing back in on the video. The girl wearing the camera giggled and spurred him on, stroking his ego by telling him how much his power turned her on. When she leaned forward slightly to undo his bow tie, I caught a glimpse of the ends of her hair swinging forward. It was pink.

I shook my head back and forth. It couldn't be. I squinted my eyes as the person wearing the video camera excused herself to use the restroom and then the grainy picture cut to her walking briskly through what looked like a black-tie gala. There was laughter, chatter, and dishes clattering in the background, and as I moved even closer to the television, I saw a guest off to the side wearing a tux, and it was only in profile, but it looked suspiciously like Harley. And…holy *fuck*, I recognized someone else in the crowd. She was just in profile as well, but I knew without a shadow of a doubt that it was my stepmother, Jessica Hawthorn. What the *hell* was going on?

"Charlotte!" I yelled, remembering suddenly she was at the hospital. "Holy fuck." José didn't answer his phone and so I rushed down to the winemaking facility, where I quickly informed him I'd be back as soon as possible.

"Got it under control, boss," he called in return. I was already halfway out the door. I ran to the house and threw a few things in a bag and got in my truck, driving out through the gate. *Jesus Christ.* How had this happened? My mind was racing a million miles a minute. *Kira.* Kira was behind this. I wanted to shake her and then crush her to me and never let go. The little witch had cooked this up. I knew she had. *Sweet, little, beautiful witch.* She could have placed herself in danger. Was that why she'd been with Cooper here in Napa? I'd treated her so cruelly that day. She'd done this to help me, to help *us,* just as Harley and Priscilla had—I knew it in my gut and I *trusted*. I let out a gasping breath, stepping into the sunlight of full surrender.

But I still needed answers. Questions pounded in my brain, one after the other. And I knew where I needed to go to get them.

As I drove, visions of Kira ran through my mind: turning to me in our bed, the morning light hitting her face as her sleepy, green eyes opened, her lips turning up in a soft smile as she reached for me. I saw her holding Sugar Pie in her arms. *She needs love more than anything,* she'd told Vanessa. *It will hurt her more if you hold it back.* I squeezed my

373

eyes shut momentarily, and an intense ache filled my chest. I saw her jumping from that tree, standing on the tractor in a ballerina pose, sliding down the banister, a look of unabashed joy on her face. And yes, she'd most definitely won that day.

I saw her walking toward me in the maze, reaching out her hand. That night, under the moonlight, she had saved me. And when it came time, I hadn't been strong enough to save her back. I let out a deep exhale, the visions flowing through my mind, through my heart. I pictured her kneeling in front of me on the floor of the wine cellar, a look of tenderness and love on her face. *If you let it, grief makes more room for love within you. And the love we carry inside makes us strong when nothing else can.* That's exactly what she'd done. She'd taken all those empty spaces inside her and filled them with love. And when the worst had happened, I had been too stupid, afraid, and filled with self-doubt to allow her to teach me how to do that too.

But I vowed to do that now because she was everything to me—my dreams, my weakness, and the person who made me want to be strong.

I had fallen desperately in love with an enchanting little witch, a radiant girl with emerald eyes and a wild mane of hair as untamed as she was. She owned my heart and my soul—I would be hers until I drew my final breath. And I was ready now. I was ready to surrender my all, every last bit, come what may. I just hoped I wasn't too late.

Please don't let me be too late.

The woman who answered the door was wearing a housekeeping uniform. She led me into the formal living room and told me she'd see if Jessica was available. I nodded grimly, choosing not to sit on the pristine white sofa.

A few minutes later, my stepmother came gliding into the room, as perfectly coiffed as I remembered her, every piece of dark blond hair in place. "Grayson," she greeted, standing awkwardly by the door. After a short pause, she moved toward the bar on the far wall. "Would you like a cocktail? It's five o'clock somewhere, right? My, but corruption in politics is quite the talk of the town, isn't it?" Well, at least she'd wasted no time. There it was: the confirmation she'd been a part of whatever had happened with Cooper Stratton.

"You were there," I said, also cutting right to the chase.

She poured herself a glass of wine, turned, and held it up to me in question. I shook my head. She swallowed one large sip before answering. "Yes, I was there. Who did you think paid the twenty-five-hundred-dollar-a-plate cost?"

I eyed her warily. "You paid for Harley and Priscilla?"

She took another sip of wine. "And myself. I decided it was a good cause. So you really didn't know about it?"

"No."

"Your wife came to me last week. Apparently, this Cooper fellow was involved in something causing you strife. She said she knew his weakness and she planned to have pictures taken to blackmail him and, therefore, her father."

I let out a loud whoosh of air. *Kira.* I was going to kiss her senseless and then I was going to strangle her. She wasn't back with Cooper—she'd been setting him up. She'd been planning on blackmailing him by taking lewd photos. Of all the crazy, harebrained schemes!

"From what I can see, they got more than they bargained for. Even Washington is all aflutter over this. Crooked government is the talk of every town in America today. As it should be."

I let that sink in. "So, the plan was only to take pictures?"

Jessica shrugged. "Unless they didn't mention it to me. She just asked if I'd fund it."

"And why did you?" I asked, thinking of all the times she'd said cruel things to me, all the times she'd watched as my father punished me simply for existing.

She turned away and looked out her window, sipping on the wine. "I've had time to consider things since Ford's been gone." She turned toward me, placing the wineglass on a side table. "I...could have done better when it came to you. I was bitter and hurt and..." She waved her hand around. "Well, I'm sure you're not interested in hearing my excuses, and frankly, I'm not that interested in giving them. But when I was asked to help, I figured I owed you that much at least. Your wife, she obviously loves you very much, Grayson, and I'm glad about that."

I was stunned. As I gawked at her silently, she moved toward a small writing desk in the corner and took something out of the top drawer. "I was going to send this to you, but since you're here..." She held it out to me and I took it from her, looking down to see she'd given me a check written out for three hundred fifty thousand dollars.

"What is this?" I demanded, holding it back out to her.

"It's part of your father's estate. Hopefully that covers at least some of the damage he did to the vineyard before he died." *She knew. She knew what he'd done.*

"What if I don't want his money?"

"Then you'd be a misguided fool just like he was. Take it and make a life for yourself, Grayson, wherever that may be. Take it and be happy."

"I—"

"Are the roses and hawthorn flowers still blooming?" she asked.

"I... What? Yes."

She nodded, something moving across her expression that looked like sadness, or perhaps regret. She stepped toward the door. "Good, I'm glad to hear that," she said. "I assume you can show yourself out?"

"Yes," I said, confusion and surprise and hope and a hundred other emotions I couldn't identify in that moment making my chest feel tight. I folded the check and put it in my wallet, and then let myself out of my stepmother's home.

I was reeling. Only Kira could soften a heart like Jessica's. *Only Kira.* God, only her.

I had a wife to find and some groveling to do. I was going to grovel so hard they might need to find a new word for it.

CHAPTER TWENTY-FIVE
Kira

"That, right there, is the definition of pitiful," Kimberly said, peeking out the window next to me.

The rain drummed against the glass pane of Sharon's apartment, where I'd been staying for the past couple weeks. The man sitting on the stoop below—the man who was currently my husband—was soaked to the bone, his dark hair plastered to his skull. And he was wearing dragon wings.

"Are you going to take pity on him or what?" Kimberly asked, turning to me, her arms crossed. Knowing Sharon was at the drop-in center and I was alone, Kimberly had rushed over here after Grayson had shown up at her apartment begging her to tell him where I was. She'd caved, but I wasn't so sure I could. Grayson had spent twenty minutes pounding at the front door, calling for me. When it had begun to rain, I was sure he'd leave, but instead he'd sat down and taken up residence on the steps.

I shook my head. "I can't, Kimberly. I'll take one look at him and crumble, and the things he said to me…the things he may have done…I *can't* crumble." Grayson knew my Achilles' heel and had targeted it in the most cutting way possible. *You know what I think? I think I must have been desperate, and you were…what's the word? Convenient. Since you've been gone, I've decided I like more of a variety of women than marriage vows dictate.* I felt a sharp, painful pinch in the vicinity of my heart as his words came back to me. I moved away from the window so I wouldn't have to look at him out there. "Plus, the things *I* did. I plotted and schemed and—"

"Yes, you came up with the mother of Very Bad Ideas, and you're just lucky you didn't tell me about it in advance because I would have tied you up rather than let you go through with it. But also, Kira, you may very well have exposed two of the most corrupt political figures in recent history—ones who would have eventually ruined more lives. I'm proud of you."

I let out a long sigh. "Priscilla did all the potentially dangerous work. But anyway, Grayson won't necessarily see it the way you do."

"Well, along with the rest of America, he already knows about what happened, and he figured out it was *your* plan. And he's still sitting out there like a pathetic wet…bird or something."

"Dragon," I corrected bleakly. "And he may just really want to strangle me. What did he say to you exactly when he came to your apartment?"

"Things you need to hear," she said gently.

Things that had obviously swayed her enough to give him the address where I was staying. I felt my resolve give way just a fraction. Yes, I could at least *listen* to him, which was more than he'd given me.

A relationship isn't a competition. If it is, no one wins.

Kimberly and I both froze when we heard scrabbling of some sort on the side of Sharon's duplex. I sucked in a breath, my eyes widening. Suddenly, the creaking groan of an old window sliding up filled the silence.

"Someone's breaking in," Kimberly whispered. "My phone's downstairs." We both ran out into the hallway and let out small screams when we glanced in the open doorway of the room at the end of the hall and saw someone pulling himself through the window. He was caught on the frame by...wings. I stopped midstride, letting out a loud whoosh of relieved air.

"Grayson," I breathed, moving to stand in the large doorway. So no robber or serial killer. I only felt mildly better.

"What the—?" Kimberly asked loudly, from right behind me just as he hurled his body through the window, landing on the floor in a loud, wet thud. He groaned, rubbing his arm as he came up on his knees.

He caught sight of me standing motionless, gawking at him, and he lurched to his feet. "Kira," he rasped, a puddle forming under his feet. The flare of yearning in his dark eyes made my stomach clench.

"What are you *doing?*" I asked, my eyes raking over him. His grayish-blue T-shirt was plastered to his chest, showing each muscular dip and groove, and his jeans clung to his strong thighs. I swallowed. He looked so incredibly beautiful standing there, even drenched as he was, wet wings hanging limply behind him.

Grayson ran his hand through his hair, slicking it back away from his forehead. He caught something at his chest and I turned my head, realizing Kimberly had tossed him a towel. "I'll just...be downstairs," she said. I nodded, pressing my lips together and looking back to Grayson to find him running the towel over his head. He slipped the wings off, rubbed the towel on his shirt, and then ran it over his legs, finally bending to mop up the puddle beneath him. My eyes followed each movement.

When he came up to his full height again, we stared at each other across the room for several tense moments. Finally, he said softly, "As I was sitting out there in the rain, I thought to myself, what would Kira do right now? She would do *something*. She would come up with a plan. It wouldn't be like her just to sit here and wait for things to play out as they may. She wouldn't let life simply pass her by. She would gather all her courage, and she would *try*, even if it seemed all hope was lost. And I thought about how much I want to be as brave as you."

Oh. I shifted on my feet, fighting not to crumble immediately. "And so you scaled the side of the building and broke into Sharon's house?"

He shrugged, giving me a lopsided smile. "Breaking and entering was the best thing I could come up with at the time." He cleared his throat. "It's actually plan B though. See, initially my plan wasn't so good. I was going to lecture you on the dangers of what you'd done and make some suggestions about your...impulsive ideas. So"—he reached in his pocket and pulled out a wet, folded piece of paper—"I made a list of pros and cons." I let out a small half laugh–half snort, and he shot me a hopeful glance as he carefully unfolded the paper, taking care not to rip it. "I wrote about your spirit, your compassion, and your kindness. But I also wrote about all the ways you make me crazy and bring me to the very edge of sanity." He turned the note upside down and right side up again. "But then I couldn't remember what were pros and what were cons, because they all come together to make you and I wouldn't want to change a single thing."

"Oh," I breathed, hanging on by a thread to the no-crumble pledge. "Well," I said, crossing my arms over my chest, "well, it…it worked, I suppose, plan B, that is. So it wasn't the worst of plans as far as plans go." I shifted my eyes away from him. "But what exactly is it you were trying to accomplish? Now that you're in front of me, what do you want, Grayson?" I cleared my throat, knowing the way my voice cracked on his name gave away my shaky emotions and the underlying hope I was trying so hard to deny.

"I want to tell you what I should have told you that day in my office if I'd been brave enough then, if I'd been *strong* enough then. I want to tell you that I trust you, and that I love you, and that I don't want to live my life without you. And I'm hoping you'll forgive me for pushing you away, for saying such cruel things to you, for lying, and I hope…I hope you can help me forgive myself. I'm sorry, I'm so very sorry." His voice was a raw ache and my heart leapt in my chest.

I tried to sort through all he'd just said, my mind grasping onto three in particular. "You…love me?" I asked, hope almost rendering me breathless.

I took a step toward him, but he held his hand up, halting me in my tracks. I blinked at him. And then tears sprung to my eyes when understanding dawned. *He wants to come to me.* He did so, halting just a few steps from where I stood.

A tremulous smile broke free.

"Yes," he said, "I love you so much I feel like an empty shell without you."

I bit my trembling lip. "And those things you said about wanting a variety of women…" My voice trailed off, the brutal pain of that moment coming back to me and stealing the words.

"No," he rasped. "God, no. I said those things to hurt you like I thought you were hurting me." He closed his eyes, a look of shame passing over his handsome features. "I have been and always will be faithful to you—body and also heart and soul. I made a vow and I intend to live by it."

I smiled on a small, gasping breath, attempting to hold back a sob, suddenly weak with relief. "I've been faithful to you too. That day in Napa, I was only with Cooper because it was part of the plan, and he thought I still lived there. I had to find out what functions he'd be at. After that, I made excuses. I never went anywhere with him that night or any other."

He squeezed his eyes shut for a moment. "I'm so sorry I ever doubted you."

"It looked bad, I know. I would have explained, but—"

"I was awful. Beyond awful."

I put my fingers to his lips, sniffling as I gazed at his face. "You were hurting."

He nodded, his expression pained and guilt-ridden. "Hurting…but awful. I want to be better, Kira, like you said. I want to be strong enough to fill those empty spaces with love. I have a lot of it surrounding me, and I've been so busy focusing on the ones who didn't love me that I forgot to notice the ones who always have. The ones who do."

Oh, Grayson. This was a good start, but there was still more to address. "I thought for sure you'd serve me with divorce papers. You didn't take my father's deal?"

He shook his head. "No, I didn't. I'd rather starve."

"Well, that's a convenient attitude because we both still might." Whether separate or together. "I don't know how

383

long it will take to get the hold taken off my gram's money, or even if my father will still pursue that. He might—"

"Turns out, Jessica Hawthorn was interested in investing in the family vineyard."

I tilted my head, looking at him with confusion. "She did?" I'd only met with her so briefly. She'd agreed to give me the money to fund my plan, but she had been terse and dismissive.

"Yeah." He smiled and there was a note of wonder in it. "And," he continued, "I want you to know that I came to all the conclusions about my feelings for you and all the ways I've acted like a complete jackass *before* I found out what you did for me, for *us*." He paused. "Outrageous and potentially dangerous as it was" he didn't seem to be able to help adding.

I swallowed, my smile fading. "I schemed and plotted…" I looked up into his eyes. "I *had* to, Grayson. I didn't know if you'd truly take my father's deal or not, but if you did, he would have ruined your name and all the progress you'd made in fixing your reputation, and if you didn't, you'd be penniless. And it was all my fault. I had to fix it. I *had* to try." Tears sprung to my eyes.

He stepped toward me, a tender smile appearing on his face. "I know, little witch. And we have a lot to talk about on that subject. But first I want you to know that I was wrong when I said you were anything at all like your father or mine. You do plot, it's true." He smiled and ran a finger over my cheekbone. "But your ideas are filled with love and a joy for life, just like you. Nothing bad could come from you, Kira, because there's nothing bad inside you."

Relief and happiness shimmered through me unheeded. I shook my head. "I won't plot anymore," I insisted. "I mean…unless it's something very, very important." I shifted my eyes to the side. "Or, well, unless—"

His soft chuckle halted my words, his gaze filled with gentle amusement. "Okay," he said quietly. "I love you, Kira. I'll never stop saying it. I'm ready to brave the thorns. I'll plunge myself on them for you."

"That sounds painful," I breathed.

He laughed. "I'm hoping it was a metaphor. Charlotte," he said in explanation.

Ah. Yes, Charlotte. She'd been calling and checking on me every day, and although I hadn't confided my most recent Very Bad Idea until it was over and the thumb drive had been sent to the news, she'd kept me going with her wise advice and words of comfort, and most of all offering her grandmotherly love. "The rose," I said. "I got that one too."

His lips tipped up in a boyish smile as he brushed a lock of hair away from my face. His expression became sadly contemplative. "I wish I had been truly ready to live by her advice. We might have avoided these past few weeks."

Emotion overwhelmed me and a tear rolled down my cheek. Grayson used his thumb to swipe it away. I caught the glint of silver and looked more closely at his hand as it fell away. "You found the ring?"

"Yes," he said. "And if it's still mine to keep, I'll never take it off."

I allowed myself to crumble then, happily. "Yes, it's yours," I whispered. "I'm sorry. I'm so sorry for keeping the secret about my father and your case from you. I never meant to hurt you. I love you too. I never stopped. I never will."

Relief passed over his features before he asked hoarsely, "Can I hold you now?"

I nodded vigorously, stepping into his embrace. He smiled against my forehead, rubbing his rough jaw on my skin. "Come home with me, Kira," he whispered. "Come back home. Please. Let me prove that I can be the husband you deserve."

I nodded against his chest, breathing in the achingly delicious scent of fresh rain and my husband. *My husband who loves me and wants me to come home with him.* The misery and grief and fear of the past weeks suddenly overwhelmed me and I gasped out a sob, burrowing my head more firmly against him.

His arms came around me, and he nuzzled his cheek against the top of my head. "Please don't cry, Kira," he whispered. "I don't ever want to be the cause of your tears again."

I nodded, grasping his shirt and looking up into his expression, raw with love and tenderness.

He took my face in his hands, bending to kiss my mouth. I kissed him back hungrily, glorying in the taste of him, the feel of his lips on mine. I'd missed him so much. He leaned away, kissing the tears as they ran down my cheeks, his breath hot on my skin. Raising my mouth to his, I kissed him again and again, tasting the salty essence of my heartache on his lips, rejoicing in the way our kisses made it sweet again. Both of us were breathless as my tears finally abated.

When he pulled his mouth from mine, his eyes moved over my face as he whispered, "You could be pregnant."

I blinked and then shook my head. "I'm not," I said, recalling the day a week ago when my period had come. I'd been partially relieved but mostly disappointed, and I told Grayson so. "I thought even if you didn't want me anymore, at least I'd have a small part of you forever."

"Kira," he said hoarsely, pulling me to him again and hugging me tightly.

I looked up, my eyes meeting his. "Take me home," I said.

After I'd walked a grinning Kimberly to her car and hugged her goodbye, Grayson and I packed my suitcase and got into his truck, heading home. *Home.* At the thought of the word, my heart leapt with joy.

I'd pick up my car another day. For now, I couldn't bear to be apart from my husband even for an hour.

We spent the car ride updating each other on everything that had happened since we'd parted.

Grayson listened to me explain the plan Harley, Priscilla, and I had all come up with, his hands gripping the steering wheel tightly. "I don't know whether to kill all three of you or to build a shrine to your courage," he gritted out.

"I personally like the shrine idea. I mean, if you're taking votes." I shot him a smile.

His eyes caught mine and he smiled back and then laughed softly. "That damn dimple may have just saved you."

I laughed, flashing it at him again.

"I think Harley deserves a promotion," he said. "He's obviously gifted at task juggling. Not only was he helping you, but he organized a whole crew of men to come work at the vineyard even though I couldn't pay them at the time."

"I know." I smiled. "Charlotte told me."

He glanced at me and raised an eyebrow. "So I was the only one left out of the loop? Apparently, everyone knew everything going on except for me."

I put my hand on his arm. "Never again," I said. "From now on, all my plots will involve you."

"You're not supposed to plot anymore," he reminded me.

I bit my lip. "Oh, right…"

He tipped his head back and laughed.

As we drove through the gates of Hawthorn Vineyard, Grayson grabbed my hand and squeezed it.

We pulled up to the house and Charlotte came outside, clasping her hands to her chest in delight. We both got out and she descended the stairs, taking me in her arms and hugging me so tightly I laughed, struggling to breathe.

"How's Walter?" I asked. The last update I'd received had been very promising, but I would be slightly worried until I saw him walking through the door.

"He's wonderful! He comes home tomorrow." And then she hugged me again. Feelings of gratitude and contentment flowed through me. I was home. *At last*, my heart whispered. *At last.*

Harley, Virgil, José, and several men I didn't know came walking toward the house, apparently just finished with work for the day. They were laughing and joking and called out greetings when they got close. Sugar Pie came running up behind them, chuffing excitedly, and for a moment, time slowed as I grinned around at them: *my family.* A group of misfits and underdogs who, together, had brought a failing vineyard back to life and turned the table on two very powerful, corrupt men.

"Hey, Harley," Grayson called out. "Call your woman. She needs to join us. I have about a thousand toasts to make to her."

Harley grinned. "Will do, my man."

We decided not to watch the news that night. The world would wait. After we had all enjoyed a family dinner full of boisterous laughing and talking and many, many cheers all around, Grayson and I retired to our bedroom. He made love to me first fiercely and quickly, and then again, slowly and sweetly, relief flowing through me at being filled by him again. As I lay in his arms afterward, I felt limp with happiness and love.

"Kira," he murmured, turning to me, "I want you to know that I've made a new vow—one I intend to live by for the rest of my life."

"What?" I whispered, sensing the importance of the words he was about to say.

He tipped my face up to his. "We're married, and there will be times when we disagree or fight or even question the other. There will be times when loving you brings up every fear inside me. But my vow is this: no matter what happens, I will never leave the room until we've worked through it." His eyes moved over my face, his expression gentle and vulnerable. "And by that, I mean I won't draw away inside myself either. I'll stay present until we've solved the issue between us, no matter how long it takes. I don't want you ever to worry that I'll push you away again. I *vow* that to you with my whole heart."

I felt a deep ache of tenderness as I gazed up at him. "I vow the same."

He smiled gently. "And sometimes we'll meet halfway, but other times, I'll come to you. And I'll try my very best to put my pride aside so I know when I need to be the one to do that."

"Me too," I whispered, tears flooding my eyes. He leaned forward and kissed my eyelids, causing the tears to flow down my cheeks. He kissed my tears away and then pulled me closer against him, nuzzling his face into my hair.

And these vows, made in private whispers in the dim light of the moon streaming through our bedroom window, felt sacred and real, for these vows were based on truth and love.

EPILOGUE
Grayson

Eight Years Later

"What exactly are you doing, little sprite?" I asked, staring down at the seven-year-old girl crawling through the grass. Her head popped up, cascades of auburn hair falling down her back, deep brown eyes blinking up at me.

"I'm pretending to be a caterpillar," she answered.

"Ah," I said, holding back the smile that tugged at my lips. "Yesterday you were a daisy, and today you're a caterpillar."

She came up on her knees, putting her hands on her small hips. "Grandpa Walter says you can't truly understand someone else unless you see the world through their eyes."

"Does he now?" That sounded just like Walter, the man who had taught me everything I knew about being a good father. "Well, I don't know if he was referring to daisies and caterpillars."

"But they're my favorite!" she insisted. "I want to understand them most of all!"

I chuckled. "And what have you discovered so far?"

"Well, daisies look up at the sky all day and watch it change. They must think the world is a very pretty place. Caterpillars just look at the ground." She frowned. "Caterpillars must be very disappointed with the world."

I laughed, picking her up in my arms and smiling into her serious little face. "You know what I see? A pretty little girl with a very compassionate heart. Now, where's your little sister? I have something to tell the both of you."

"She's playing dress-up in the cottage. Daddy, did you put another baby inside Mommy?"

My eyes widened and I paused. "How did you know that?"

"You had that same look on your face when you told me you'd put Celia in mommy's tummy."

"What look is that exactly?"

She scratched her arm, her expression contemplative. "I don't know. Kind of like how Sugar Pie looks when she catches a stick."

I laughed out loud, picturing the mostly proud but slightly shocked look on Sugar Pie's face when she accomplished something she found amazing. "Well, you're right. And guess what? It's another sister."

"Another sister?" Her face broke out in a grin, showcasing her missing tooth, and the endearing dimple she'd inherited from her mother. "That's a lot of girls, Daddy."

I grinned. "Yup." Happiness flowed through my heart. It didn't seem that life could hold any more joy than it did right now, and yet somehow, every day it grew just a little bit more. All because of a girl who once bravely walked into my office and proposed marriage. All because I'd finally had the courage to surrender to my sweet, little witch, and in return, she'd given me a houseful of spirited girls who climbed trees, pretended to be caterpillars, sassed me back on occasion, put me in my place *very* regularly, reminded me often I was definitely *not* the ruler in my own home, and generally drove me to distraction.

I set Isabelle down, and we entered the small cottage where, once upon a time, a very beautiful witch had lived, and found four-year-old Celia outfitted as a princess, sipping tea at the miniature table in the front room. Several years ago, we'd had the cottage cleaned, updated, and turned into a playhouse for our girls.

"We're going to have another sister!" Belle shouted.

Celia's plastic cup stopped halfway to her mouth and her eyes grew wide. "Another sister," she said, jumping to her feet. She wobbled toward me on plastic heels and threw herself into my arms as I bent to catch her. "Thank you, Daddy. I wished for a little sister."

I smiled into her beautiful, heart-shaped face, her green eyes bright with happiness and the slight bit of mischief they always held. "It's my job you know, to make all your wishes come true."

Her expression turned thoughtful as she twirled a lock of her dark hair. "Can I have a pony then?"

I used my index finger to bop her on her nose. "And," I qualified, "not to spoil you rotten."

"Hmm," she grumped, but I could see the wheels turning behind her eyes. She was already plotting a way to get that pony.

I laughed and the three of us went up to the main house, where Charlotte was in the kitchen. I took a deep inhale, the air fragrant with a sweet, lemony scent.

"Grammy Charlotte," Celia called. "We're having a baby sister!"

Charlotte laughed and caught Celia in her arms as Isabelle hugged Charlotte's waist. "I know, my loves; I heard the wonderful news. Should we celebrate with a lemon bar, fresh from the oven?"

"Or maybe two?" Celia tilted her head and smiled prettily.

I suppressed a smile. "Watch that one."

Charlotte grinned as I kissed her on her cheek. "Have you seen Kira?" I asked.

"I think she went out back," she said, setting Celia down. "You go find her. I've got these two." She smiled happily, and I left knowing how overjoyed and thankful she felt with a houseful of little girls to spoil and coddle and love. *And* bake treats for.

I winked at her and went in search of my wife, having an idea where she might be. As I walked down the hill, I looked out over the grapevines beyond, my chest swelling with pride. Eight years ago, we'd brought this vineyard back from the brink of ruin with the money Jessica had given me, lots of hard work, and plenty of loyal friends. Since then, we'd grown more successful every year, even winning several awards for the wines produced. Hawthorn Vineyard was thriving, and I was especially proud of the fact that we now employed almost two hundred people, many of whom were previously imprisoned, just looking for a second chance, hoping that someone would believe in them. And I was a fan of second chances. I'd received even more than that and it was my turn to pay it forward.

Harley, now my director of operations, had inspired that idea. And a few other businesses in Napa had even followed suit when word got out about how loyal and hardworking our employees were.

Kira's gram's money had eventually been unlocked, long before the trial was over that put Cooper Stratton behind bars for a whole laundry list of crimes. Frank Dallaire had never been proven guilty of participating in anything illegal, but as he knew better than anyone, in politics, perception is everything. No one wanted to be linked to the suspicion that surrounded his name. He disappeared from the political landscape and, as far as we knew, was no longer involved in government at all. Nor was he involved in our life.

Thankfully though, we weren't lacking for family, including Shane and Vanessa. They now had two boys who visited often and always left looking slightly stunned after our girls ran roughshod over them, playing tricks, forcing them to play dress-up and participate in slightly naughty escapades.

"I thought I'd find you here," I said, turning the last corner of the well-tended maze. I smiled as I joined Kira on the bench in front of the splashing fountain, where she sat with her hand on her tiny baby bump. The emeralds from her wedding ring flashed in the sun, reminding me of the day I'd slipped it on her finger as we'd renewed our vows in a small sunlit ceremony under the apricot tree in our vineyard. I'd wanted to give her a *real* wedding day, one filled with love, joy, and family—and that's what I'd done.

My wife smiled, shooting me the dimple and causing my heart to flip. "It's my favorite place, the heart of your lair. I always know you'll find me here, dragon."

I chuckled softly and gathered her to me, lifting her onto my lap. She wrapped her arms around my neck and put her forehead against mine. "Another girl," she sighed happily.

I nuzzled her neck. "Hmm," I murmured. "Another woman to keep me under her thumb. It's almost like you planned it this way."

Kira laughed. "No, not planned it, just dreamed it. Dreamed of this life you've given me." She took my face in her hands and kissed my lips. "Thank you," she whispered against my mouth.

Gratitude and love overwhelmed me, and I brought my wife even closer, hugging her to my body and inhaling her sweet scent. And in that moment, I knew I would never again believe life didn't hold miracles. With her love, my beautiful, little witch had transformed a place once filled with loneliness and pain into a home filled with joy and dreams. Marriage wasn't always easy. She was tempestuous, and it was my instinct to withdraw or breathe fire when I was hurt. But we'd kept our vow to never leave the room before working out our differences and it'd led to a trust and closeness that I'd never even imagined I'd find. I owed everything to the woman in my arms.

As we held each other, the age-old phrase whispered through the trees, the roses, and the grapevines beyond: in vino veritas. In wine there is truth.

But the greater knowledge that now lived in the peaceful silence of my heart was: in *love* there is truth.

And the truth that love had taught me was you can only be strong once you are brave enough to break, and that pain makes more room for love within. I was grateful for it all because that was the beautiful balance of life.

Want more Mia Sheridan? Read on for
a sneak peek of *BECOMING CALDER*.

"I have taken away the mist from your eyes, that
before now was there, so that you may well recognize the god and the mortal."

—Homer, *The Iliad*

I was assaulted by the smell of exhaust and rancid garbage as
I stepped off the bus. My stomach rolled, and I moved left
to avoid having to walk too closely to the overflowing waste
cans a couple feet in front of me.

The half-eaten hamburger sitting on top of the pile
caught my eye, and my instincts almost made me grab it
and shove it in my mouth, but I clenched my fists and kept
walking. I was so hungry, painfully hungry, but I wasn't at
the point where I would eat garbage—at least not just yet.

I opened the doors to the station and looked around
the dim interior at the signs for the ticket window. I'd need
directions to get where I was headed.

At least everything's labeled in the outside world. As I recalled
those words, I felt a strong rush of grief. I straightened my
spine and moved inside.

I spotted the ticket counter and started making my way
through the people milling around, waiting for the next bus.
I briefly made eye contact with a young man in sagging pants

and an overly large sweatshirt. His eyes widened slightly and he jogged over and started walking beside me.

"Hey, baby, you look lost. Can I help?"

I shook my head, taking in the strange smell wafting off him—something slightly bitter and herbal. I glanced at his face quickly and noticed that, up close, his eyes were red-rimmed and heavy-lidded. From my peripheral vision, I saw him look at me and move his head up and down, taking in my form.

I increased my pace. I knew I looked desperate. I *was* desperate. Scared, lost, grief-stricken, unspeakable anguish sitting just beneath the surface of my skin. I *did* need help. I wasn't worldly—this I knew clearly. But I wasn't naive enough to believe the man walking next to me was the helpful sort.

"You ain't got no luggage, baby? What's up with that? You got a place to stay?" He reached over and moved my hair out of my face, and I flinched back from his touch. I continued walking, even faster now. Fear raced through my veins, my empty stomach rolling with nausea.

"Damn, hair like spun gold. Face like an angel. You look like a princess. Anyone ever tell you that?"

A small half laugh, half sob bubbled up my throat, and I wheezed in a harsh breath to keep it from escaping. My heartbeat ratcheted up a notch as the man started steering himself into me so I was forced to move left in order to not collide with him. I glanced to the side and saw he was attempting to steer me into a dim corridor that looked like it led to a maintenance closet of some sort. I looked around wildly for someone who might help, somewhere I could run, when the man's hand clamped down on my arm. I looked up into his narrowed eyes, his jaw now hard and set.

He leaned in and whispered to me, "Listen up, princess. A girl like you has a whole lot to offer. And I'm a businessman. You wanna hear about my business, princess?"

I shook my head vigorously again, weighing my options for escape. I could scream. Surely there was at least one decent person in the vicinity who would help me. I could try to fight him, but as weak and tired as I was, he would overpower me quickly. That's when I felt the sting of something sharp press into me through my light jacket and the thin cotton of my T-shirt. *Oh God, there's a knife to my side.* I looked down at his hand holding the small silver blade against my body and then back up into his eyes, now shining with something that looked like determination mixed with excitement.

"You come with me, princess, and I'll have no need to use this on you. You'll like my offer, I promise. It involves all kinds of money for you. You like money, princess? Who doesn't like money, right?"

"Take your hands off her, Eli," said a deep voice behind us. I swiveled my head at the same time Eli did and took in the sight of a huge man standing casually, hands hanging at his sides, a seemingly bored expression on his face. My eyes widened as I took in all the designs and colors swirling up the left side of his neck, stopping just under his jaw, and his muscular arms, covered with the same intricate art.

"This ain't your business, Paul," Eli spat out.

"The hell it isn't. When I see a cockroach, I crush it under my boot. Cockroaches offend me. You're a cockroach, Eli. Let her go, or I'll crush you right here in the bus station for all the other cockroaches to see." Paul kept his eyes trained on us, but Eli's head moved to the right and I followed his gaze to a group of men dressed similarly to Eli who were sitting casually on a bench at the front of the station, looking our way and snickering.

Eli turned back to Paul, and I felt his hold on me loosen slightly. He let out a disgusted sound and pushed me roughly toward Paul. "Got too many bitches on the payroll as it is. Take her." Then he turned and walked in the direction we'd come from.

Paul's hand clamped down on my wrist, and I let out a startled noise as he turned and pulled me behind him, tugging me back toward the entrance. I pulled against him, but he was built like a bear and my attempts didn't even slow him down. "Please," I said, "please, let me go." There was hysteria in my voice.

We exited through the door and the once-again bright outside world caused me to squint my eyes. Paul let go of my wrist and turned toward me. "You a runaway?"

I backed up until I felt the wall of the bus station against my heels. "A runaway?" I repeated.

Paul studied me for a minute. "Yeah, you on the run? Someone looking for you?"

I shook my head slowly, his question causing some of the barely contained anguish to seep through my pores. "No. No one's looking for me. Please, I just want to get out of here."

"What's your name?" he asked, a gentle quality in his voice now.

I blinked up at him. "Eden," I whispered.

Paul narrowed his eyes. "Where you headed, Eden?"

I stared up at him, seeing that despite his gruff exterior, there was concern in his eyes. I let out a ragged breath. "Grant and Rothford Company."

"Grant and Rothford Company? The jewelry store?"

I nodded. "Yes. Can you tell me how to get there?"

"That's only about ten blocks from here. I'll tell you how to get there, but then, you don't come back here, you hear me? This is not the place for a young girl who's alone. I think you get that, right?"

I bit my lip and nodded. "I won't come back here." If all went as planned, I'd be sleeping in a hotel room tonight. I'd have food in my belly, and it would finally be safe to cry.

Paul pointed his finger down the block. "Walk in that direction until you get to Main Street, make a right, and go about six blocks down. You'll see it on your right."

I let out a breath. "Thank you, Paul. Thank you so much. And thank you for saving me from the cockroach." I mustered up a very small smile and then turned and began to walk in the direction he'd pointed me.

As I started to turn the corner, Paul called my name and I stopped and turned, looking at him questioningly. "There are more boot stompers than cockroaches in this world."

I considered him for a minute, tilting my head. "The problem, Paul," I said softly, meeting his eyes, "is that cockroaches can survive the end of the world."

Paul gave me a small, confused smile right before I turned and walked away.

When I looked up the street and spotted the sign I'd been looking for, my cold hand automatically reached into my jeans pocket and wrapped around the heavy gold locket within—the one that had the name of Grant and Rothford Company on the back—the only thing of value I had to my name. I completed the rest of the block sluggishly, hunger, cold, and fatigue overwhelming me.

I pushed the door open and was greeted by the comforting warmth of the heated store. For a second I just stood there and breathed, relieved at both having found my destination and at the warmth seeping into my chilled skin. I headed toward the sales counter. But as I passed a display shelf to my right, I caught sight of a glass jewelry box with pressed flowers between the panes creating the illusion they were floating over the velvet interior. I halted, looking more closely, my eyes widening and tears immediately blurring my vision, as I instinctively reached toward it. They were morning glories. I should know, I had fifty-two of them, carefully pressed and preserved in a plastic bag in the inside pocket of my jacket. The locket, the flowers, and a small, round pebble were the only things I had grabbed before escaping. They were the only reminders I had of him. I'd left everything else I had ever known behind. A lump formed in my throat and grief swept over me, so intense, I thought it might knock me down. I reached out to touch the glass, one finger tracing the deep blue petals of the flower I was so well acquainted with. But my body was worn-down, tired, hungry, and my hand jerked ungracefully and knocked into a crystal vase sitting on the shelf next to the jewelry box. As if in slow motion, it wobbled and fell despite my unsuccessful attempt to grab it. It crashed to the floor and shattered at my feet. I sucked in a loud gasp and jerked my head up as a woman came rushing toward me, saying, "Oh no! Not the Waterford!" She brought her hands to her cheeks and pursed her lips as she stopped in front of the pile of shattered glass.

"I'm so sorry," I gasped. "It was just an accident."

The woman huffed out a breath. She was well-manicured beauty: stylish in a dark gray suit, hair swept up gracefully, and her face stunning, with perfectly applied makeup. I shrunk before her. I knew what I looked like. I was wearing clothes stolen off a clothesline from someone who was obviously quite a bit larger than me. I hadn't bathed for three days and my hair hung loose and lank around my face and down my back to just above my backside—far too long to be stylish. The woman looked me up and down.

"Well, accident or not, this will need to be paid for."

My shoulders sagged. "I don't have any money," I whispered, glancing around as my cheeks heated and the few customers roaming the shop looked away uncomfortably. I was almost surprised to find I still had a little pride left.

I brought the gold locket out of my pocket. "I was hoping to sell this—and maybe get some information about it too," I said, imploring the woman to help me. *Please help me. I'm so scared. I'm in so much pain. I've been broken in so many ways.*

She put her hands on her hips and looked from the locket to my face and back at the locket again. She took it from my cupped hand and held it up to the light. Then she looked back at me. "Well, lucky for you, this is gold. This will probably take care of the cost of the vase." She kept looking at it, turning it over in her manicured hands. "There's no way to give you any information about it though—no engraving or personalization." She looked over her shoulder at a man who had just finished dealing with a customer and was coming out from behind the counter. She pointed to the crystal on the floor and said, "Phillip, will you have this cleaned up while I take care of this…girl?"

"Of course," Phillip said, eyeing me curiously.

I followed the woman to the counter. "Wait here while I weigh this. You don't have the chain that goes with it?"

I shook my head. "No, just the locket."

I stood at the counter, my hands resting on the glass in front of me. When I noticed they were shaking visibly, I pulled them back and rubbed them together, attempting to still my body with mind over matter. My heart thumped hollowly in my chest. Fear and hopelessness rose up my throat, making it difficult to swallow.

I looked behind me, where the woman had entered a door to the back of the shop, and saw her talking to an older man through the glass. He furrowed his brow as he looked up at me and nodded his head, his eyes lingering for a moment before he looked down at what he held in his hand. The woman turned and walked back through the door and behind the counter to where I stood. "We can give you twelve hundred dollars for the locket, which is a little bit under what the vase cost, but we're willing to give a discount on that so the matter is resolved."

Vomit rose up my throat. "Please, I need that money," I said, raising my voice. "It's all I have."

"I'm really very sorry, but there's nothing I can do. The vase has to be paid for. We can't just eat that cost. We run a business here."

"Please!" I said again, louder this time, bringing my hands down on the counter with a loud slap. The woman startled and pursed her lips, leaning in toward me so that I leaned back.

"Do I need to call the police, miss?" she asked in a harsh whisper, barely moving her mouth.

Dread raced through my veins and I swayed slightly before pulling myself upright. I shook my head vigorously. "No," I squeaked out. I took a deep breath, "Please, I just...I don't have any money and that locket..."

I sucked in another breath, refusing to cry in front of

this woman, in front of all the customers who were pretending to mill around but were really listening to the exchange between us. "That locket is all I have. I need the money for it to find somewhere to sleep tonight. Please," I ended pathetically.

Something I thought might be sympathy flashed in the woman's eyes, but she leaned back, crossed her arms over her chest, and said, "I'm sorry, there isn't anything I can do. There's a homeless shelter over on Elm Street. The fourteen hundred block. I've passed by it several times. Now I'm going to have to ask you to leave our store."

I hung my head, too sick, tired, and heartbroken to put up a fight. How had I managed to squander my one chance for money and possible safety? Now I very literally had nothing of value to my name. Nothing at all, in fact, except the stolen clothes on my back and the pressed flowers and small pebble in my pocket. I turned and walked out of the store as if in a daze, thoroughly depleted of every ounce of hope.

I wandered down the city streets for a while, hours maybe, I wasn't even sure how long. I grew weaker; my steps grew slower. I saw a bench up ahead and stopped and sunk down onto it, pulling my arms around myself. The night was settling in around me now, and the air was even chillier, my jacket too lightweight to keep me warm.

Where do you find your strength, Morning Glory? he'd asked me.

From you, I'd said, smiling and pulling him close.

But now he wasn't here. Where would I find my strength now?

I looked up at the corner street sign to my right. *Elm Street*. I let out a heavy breath. Did I have it in me to go just

405

a little bit more? Yes, I thought I might—for a warm bed and a meal—even if it was in a homeless shelter. I'd make it through tonight and then I'd come up with some sort of plan. Maybe someone at the shelter could tell me where to find a job…*something.*

I stood up and walked to Elm Street, and after determining I needed to head right to get to the fourteen hundred block, I set off. My teeth chattered and I pulled my arms around myself again as I walked, tucking my head down against the wind.

A line was formed up ahead, and I craned my neck to see if it was the shelter, standing on my tiptoes to see around all the people.

"You looking for a place to sleep?" an older man at the end of the line in a long, dirty jacket with a head of wild white hair, asked.

I nodded, my teeth chattering harder.

"This place is only for men," he said. "But a pretty girl like you could probably make some good cash in the alleyway back there." He inclined his head backward and then leered at me and cackled.

So there it was again—sex. Evidently I did have something of value. I'd like to say I didn't consider it for a brief few seconds. I was so hungry, desperately hungry, and so cold. The list of things I wouldn't do to stop the pain of my empty stomach and the cold that had made its way down to my bones was growing shorter and shorter.

I mustered the very last shred of my pride and turned away.

He's waiting for me, by a spring, under the warm sunshine. *I'll wait for you. But I hope I'm waiting a long time.*

I got about a block before the tears started to slip down

my cheeks. Panic surged inside me. *Oh no, oh no. You can't cry. If you cry, you'll lose control.* That thought brought the terror of my situation front and center. I needed someone. *Anyone.* There were plenty of people walking by, but I didn't belong to any of them and none of them belonged to me. They didn't see me. They didn't care. With neediness came overwhelming grief. I sat down on some steps, put my head on my knees, and I cried.

"Miss?" I jerked my head up and looked through tear-blurred vision at an older man in a suit. I sucked back my tears as much as possible, swiped wetness from my eyes, and attempted a deep, shaky breath, trying to compose myself.

"I own Grant and Rothford Company," he said quietly, looking uncomfortable.

Then it clicked. He had been the man behind the glass door whom the saleswoman had spoken with. *The owner.* Oh no, had he decided I owed more money for the vase? Would he call the police now? I couldn't go to the police. I couldn't.

I stood up too quickly. I managed two steps before the world tilted and fell away.

Acknowledgments

As always, I had a lot of help writing this book.

Huge love and thanks to my storyline editor, Angela Smith, for helping me hone the plot and for believing in this story—even more than me at times. Thank you for being there from the first word to the last.

Immense gratitude to my developmental and line editor, Marion Archer. You are so talented and always full of such brilliant advice. The enthusiasm and diligence you put into this project is appreciated beyond measure.

Thank you to Karen Lawson, who always makes me feel like the final product I'm putting out into the world is carefully and lovingly polished. That is such a gift to me.

To my extremely valued beta readers who read *Grayson's Vow* first and provided such incredibly helpful comments and suggestions: Cat Bracht, Natasha Gentile, Michelle Finkle, and Elena Eckmeyer (who gave my dragon and witch extra TLC by reading through my manuscript twice, and loved my dragon despite his fire-breathing and loved my witch for poking at him until he melted).

Huge appreciation for my location beta, Kimberly Thompson, who made sure all my Napa references were accurate.

Thank you to my wonderful agent, Kimberly Brower, who held my hand through this process in many, many ways. Thank you for always having my back in every endeavor. You are uncommonly generous with your time and care and never fail to make me feel as if I'm your only client. (And I have a feeling we all say that). AIADW forever!

To you, the reader, I wouldn't have the privilege of doing what I do without you and I never ever take that for granted. Unending love and thanks!

To all the blogs who review and recommend my books—so very grateful for you all.

And an updated thank you to Bloom Books for giving this story new life.

To my husband: I hardly know how to express my thanks to you for all your help and support with this story...the extensive plot talk—in cars, restaurants, bed, while brushing teeth—my endless questions, endless doubts, and the endless amount of time I spent in my own head trying to craft these characters. The vow I made to you has led to more joy than I ever dared to dream.

Steamy, addictive and emotional ...

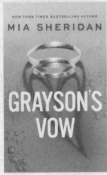

Available now from

PIATKUS